Truth and Fury

Book Two of the Abredea Series

C.H. Lyn

Horizon Publishing

Contents

FOR THE ONES NOT IN CONTROL.

PANGAEA
CAPITAL
TORNIM
MENDAX
DOLOR
CALIDA
ALTHEA

 Grey-Stars:
Government

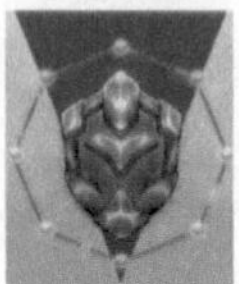 Black-Stars:
Military

 Blue-Stars:
Doctors & Research

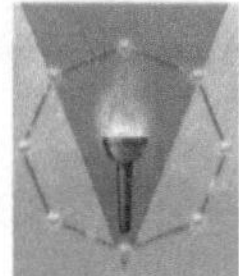 Red-Stars:
Emergency Personnel

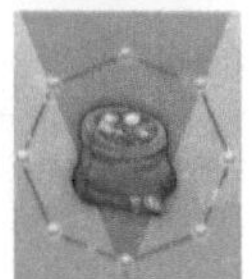 Purple-Stars:
Merchants

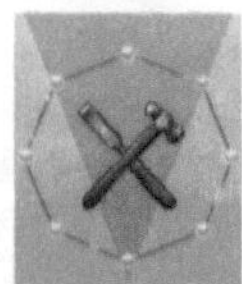 Green-Stars:
Skilled Craftsmen

 Orange-Stars:
City Laborers

 White-Stars:
Undesirables

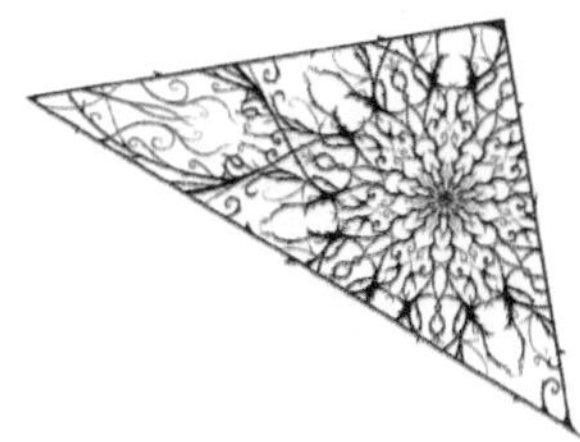

Chapter One

Research Facility Dolor

The far window of Wolfe's office looked out over a series of open-topped exam rooms. The tinted glass allowed her a view of most of the experiments running at any given time. She paced along the window now, her gaze catching on the occasional burst of flame, spark of electricity, or plume of frost.

These children were powerful. Far too powerful for their little bodies and less capable minds. Wolfe clicked her immaculate fingernails against each other. Across the large office, the metal door slid open. In the shadowed darkness of the room, a figure stepped in and slunk to the corner behind Wolfe's mahogany desk.

Wolfe gave no notice of the movement beyond a brief wave of her hand. She inhaled through her sharp nose, a river of frustration coursing through her. If that man didn't hurry up...

Her hands clenched to fists just as a tinkling bell rang from her desk. She straightened and strode across the thin carpet, wheeling around the desk and clicking a button embedded in the wood.

A holo-screen lifted from the desk; the image of the Black-Star captain who worked directly under her flickered for a moment as he moved in and out of frame. The bandage around his bald head was bloodstained and in need of changing. Twin dagger-shaped tattoos curled down his cheeks to the edge of his jaw.

"Report." Wolfe leaned against the desk, heart hammering against her ribs.

"I'm sorry, ma'am."

Her lip curled as heat filled her gut.

Steel went on: "There is no sign of the girl, or her friends, in the camp. My men have scoured the surrounding woods and fields, but—"

"What of the footage?" Wolfe demanded. If he were there in the room with her, she'd pour enough *suggestion* on him to break his mind. His shame at failing her would know no end. "Your men have been tailing her for months. Surely you know where they're headed?"

"No, ma'am." Steel ran a leather-gloved hand across his face. The skin under his eyes was heavy with dark bags. As he stepped away from the camera for a moment, another bandage across his shoulder became visible. He returned quickly. "We do know they met up with others. Looks like your secondary squad didn't manage to capture all the children from the sewers."

Wolfe snarled. "Rich of you to judge, Captain Steel," she spat. "Given your inability to keep track of *one* girl."

He flushed. His head bowed in acknowledgement as a muttered apology rumbled from his lips.

"Speak no more of it," Wolfe said, raising a hand to cut him off. She sucked in a breath and thought hard. "If those children are with Juliana, they are your responsibility now. Get some frosted Reds into the camp, collect your men, and *find her*. I expect frequent updates."

A second wave of tinkling bells filled the office, the sound higher and harsher than the first call. Wolfe's gut clenched with fear that she quickly masked from showing on her face. Behind her, the figure in the corner sucked in a breath.

"Do not fail me, Steel," Wolfe murmured through gritted teeth. Her Black-Star captain gave a sharp nod and was mid-bow when she shut off the call.

The tinkling sounded again. The high pitch, along with the words glowing across the holo-screen, announced who it was without Wolfe needing to answer.

She sank into her chair, smoothed down her hair, and sat as straight as her back would allow. Then, with a glance toward the corner and a swallow, she accepted the call.

"Chancellor, to what do I owe this honor?"

"Cousin." Chancellor Jackie Collette smiled from the screen. Her teeth were naturally sharp, the canines standing out each time she spoke. Her hair, which should have been as grey as Wolfe's, was dyed dark brown. Still, no amount of color could hide the wrinkles at the edges of her eyes or the permanent crease along the ridge of her nose from a lifetime of scowling.

A chill ran through Wolfe as Collette leaned back in her own office chair. The windows behind her desk showed a picturesque scene of the sea. Capital City sat along the coast, plentiful in beaches, cliffs, and fresh seafood. Wolfe had been raised in that place. She loathed it.

"We have a Council meeting coming up," Collette said. "You will be in attendance?"

The question was pretense. Wolfe was on the Council, and therefore was required to attend every meeting.

"Absolutely, Chancellor."

"Good, good…"

Collette went quiet for a moment, and Wolfe clenched her hand under the desk to keep her emotions from showing on her face. The Chancellor of Pangaea, and her cousin, did not call via holo-screen for something as mundane as this. Something else was coming.

"You will have the opportunity," Collette finally said, "to present your latest findings at the meeting." She tilted her head, not quite casually. "The Council is eager to learn of your progress."

Wolfe's bland mask faltered. She blinked and let out a little breath. "Chancellor, we've only had the newest batch of subjects for a week. Surely the Council doesn't expect—"

"There are members on the Council who question your efficiency, Minerva. There are some who wonder if your efforts are too time consuming. We've had reports of stirrings yet again, people speaking out against the caste system, recruiters spotted in lower districts."

Wolfe's eyes widened.

"Nothing I'm worried about." Collette waved a nonchalant hand. "But the Council has been newly motivated to desire the might you promised. You've had a long time to complete your assignment." Her palm pressed into the wood of her desk, eyes narrowing as she leaned forward. "One wonders if you aren't wasting time and resources on your little experiment."

The figure in the corner behind Wolfe shifted and Collette's gaze moved. Her lips curled into a cruel grin.

"Tell me, Minerva, has the girl's power emerged yet?"

It was like standing under a waterfall. The cold running down her back, the pressure pounding across her shoulders. An image flashed through Wolfe's mind. Juliana standing before one of her unimportant White-Star friends, blue light emanating from her fingertips as she healed the girl's lip. Steel had sent it that morning. A victory, quickly soured by the discovery that Juliana and her friends—one of whom was also an Alter—had disappeared.

Wolfe forced the image away, keeping her face passive. "Not yet, Chancellor. But I am certain we will have progress soon."

Collette leaned back in her chair. "Perhaps you were wrong, Minerva. Perhaps the girl didn't inherit the power."

Wolfe cleared her throat. "I have confidence in my hypothesis. And I believe allowing the gift to present itself naturally will result in her being stronger than anything we've seen before."

"She'd better be." Collette looked away for a moment. Someone in the room spoke to her, something about her next appointment.

Wolfe waited, sweat making her hands damp and clammy.

Collette turned back to her. "As I was saying, you're responsible for the loss of the last healer we encountered."

Behind Wolfe, the shadow made a small sound, like the whine of a muzzled dog.

Collette continued. "If the girl doesn't reveal her ability soon, you will step in and bring her to Dolor."

"I *will* complete my mission, Chancellor. I *will* get the power you seek." Wolfe nodded.

Collette's lip curled with derision. "Any fool with a gun can have power over life, Minerva. I want power over death. And since you squandered our last opportunity for that power... I expect you to be more careful with it this time."

Wolfe bit back the mix of fear and anger stirring in her gut. "Yes, Chancellor. I understand."

"See you in a week."

Collette ended the call.

Wolfe sat rigid and still for a long moment. Then, with no warning, she let out a shriek of rage. She rose, slamming her hand onto the desktop. With a rush of blinding fury, feeling helpless and unappreciated, she ripped the holo-screen from its weak hinges and threw it to the floor. The carpet wasn't soft enough to rescue the fragile glass and the thing shattered into pieces.

Wolfe's heels crunched across the glass as she strode toward the door. Without turning back she snapped, "Get that cleaned up." Then she went to find her head of research.

If Collette wanted power, she'd get her power. No matter the cost.

Chapter Two

The Lake Near Abredea

S unrise was slow to greet them. The western trees were so tall, it was mid-morning before beams of light touched their camp.

Juliana was up at dawn. She'd fallen into the routine with May. The two had spent the last few months on May's front porch, drinking tea and watching the sun rise.

A pang of longing, of grief, struck Juliana as she finished rolling up her blanket and tucked it beside her bag. She took in the others, sleeping soundly. Taz snored, sprawled limbs taking up more space than anyone else. Juliana's mouth twitched into a brief grin.

She turned east, the distant mountain tips painted with golden light. She'd dreamed of mountains again last night. They couldn't be these; the ones in her dream were a dozen times larger, towering giants capped with snow. She couldn't get their image out of her mind.

The lake stretched, a hundred or so feet from her, all the way to the base of the rocky, pine covered mountains. Dew soaked through the cuffs of her pants as she strode to the water's edge. Gentle ripples lapped against a collection of pebbles in an array of colors. She knelt, finding a pale blue one, nearly a perfect circle. She rubbed her thumb across the surface.

Juliana hesitated. She glanced back at the cluster of sleeping bodies, then walked along the water until she found a small boulder to sit on.

She inhaled, gaze fixed on the reflection of the sunlight on the water. Lines of gold, far in the distance, both blinding and hypnotizing at once. On the exhale, she closed her eyes.

It took hardly any time to find the core of her power within. It warmed her chest; thrummed against her heart and ribs in a whirling sphere of electric blue light. Pieces arched away, less like sparks of lighting and more like tendrils of water. She reached out, brushing against one of the tendrils. The sphere spun faster, seemingly excited by her attention.

She was new to it, this power within her. "How long have you been here?" she asked softly, her voice barely a murmur in the still morning.

Memories hit her. Moments in Abredea when her anger had surged, when her fear or better judgment had been encompassed by rage and indignation. The Orange-Star questioning her intelligence, Steel calling her simple, Daisy's father and everything he'd done... she recognized it now, that anger had been the flickering core of her power. At least, part of it.

Her life in Tornim, the city she'd lived in until being Coded a White-Star on her twentieth birthday, had been easy. It had been simple and privileged. It hadn't pushed her to find this piece of her being.

She opened her eyes, finding her physical hand outstretched. She lowered it.

"Yeh shouldn' wander too far."

Juliana nearly fell off her rock.

"Nacra, Anthony. We need to put a bell around your neck or something," she grumbled, unable to hide her smile.

Anthony chuckled and reached out a hand. The same one she'd fallen asleep holding last night. Her cheeks flushed, but she took it and let him pull her to her feet.

"You're up early," she said.

Anthony shrugged. "Never liked sleepin' while the sun is up. Feels like a waste."

She nodded. They stood in silence for a few moments. The world continued to wake up. Ripples across the surface of the water announced breakfast for little fish finding insects. A whoosh sounded behind them. As they turned, a hawk flew out from the forest, the sun lighting up its red-tipped feathers as it dove toward the lake. It barely skimmed the water, arcing into the air with a fish gripped in its talons.

"This feels crazy," Juliana murmured.

Anthony glanced at her. "What part?"

She snorted. "All of it. Being out here, knowing we can't go back, helping them." She gestured to the cluster of children near the tree line. "How *are* we going to help them, Anthony? We don't even know where they're going."

He shrugged again, then noticed her frown and turned to face her. "It is crazy. When yeh said yeh wanted tah go with 'em, I thought yeh'd lost it."

Juliana grimaced.

He held up a hand. "But I get it. I wanna help too. We will. When they wake up, we'll do that thing yeh like... make a plan." He smirked, and she lightly shoved his shoulder. "I'm serious. We'll figure out where tah go. I'm sure one of yeh city folk know what we're lookin' for."

"And when we get there?" Juliana's stomach knotted with nerves. "They said Black-Stars took their family. We're probably going to have to fight to get them back."

The smile slid from Anthony's face as his skin went pale. He looked at his hands, and then reached up and seemed to wipe something unseen from his neck and chin. He swallowed. "I don't like the idea of it. Of killin' again." His features twisted in an expression so pained and grief-filled, it broke Juliana's heart.

She took his hand, pulling it away from his face. "What you did saved us. That Black-Star had a gun. He'd have murdered us all. I know how they think, the people from the city. Most of them are terrified of the idea of something different." She glanced back to their friends, now lumpy forms rising from the ground, stoking the fire, and digging through packs for food.

Anthony's hand trembled in hers. "I'm terrified of doing it again, Jules. I wasn' me when I was the wolf. I don' know how tah control it."

Juliana swallowed down her unease, the uncertainty in her gut. Instead, she cocked her head and raised an eyebrow. "That boy, Cho, he helped you?"

Anthony nodded.

"I'm sure he can help again, give you pointers like M... like May gave me."

Anthony met her eye as she nearly choked on the name. The grief in his gaze matched her own. It felt like a minute and a lifetime since she'd learned of Steel killing the old woman who had taken her in when she'd been sent to Abredea. It had only happened yesterday.

Juliana briefly wondered if anyone had found her body yet. She winced and shook the thought from her head.

"Yeah." Anthony squeezed her hand. "Maybe he can."

Juliana returned the pressure of his squeeze and then, on an act of impulse driven by a fresh wave of loneliness, pain, and longing, she stepped toward him, looped an arm around his middle, and pulled him into a hug.

He hesitated for the briefest of seconds before releasing her hand, wrapping both arms around her, and nestling his chin into the crook of her neck. His breath against her ear was steady. A constant. She pressed into his chest and stayed for a long moment. Eventually, they broke apart and, without a word, headed back to the group.

Cho slept peacefully for the first time since the raid on Haven. He was one of the last to wake, the headache he'd been living with for days had eased. It was as though he'd reset.

"Thought you were going to sleep all day," Jane grumbled as she plunked down onto the grass beside him and offered him a stale breakfast sandwich.

Around them, the children from Haven were enjoying the morning. Tommy kept touching the grass, running his fingers across the soft strands, and then digging them into the dirt with amazement in his eyes. Luna leaned against a tree trunk beside Nova. The two of them watched as the White-Star from the camp, Juliana, knelt and took a moment to heal Nova's ankle.

The other girl from the camp, Daisy, chatted with Claire by the burning embers of their fire. A wave of relief crashed over Cho at Claire's smile, her rosy cheeks. He glanced back to the healer; he'd need to thank her. The medicine they'd been giving Claire hadn't helped the way he hoped it would. It turned out there was a shard of metal embedded in her arm; they hadn't seen it. If Juliana hadn't offered to help...

Jane cleared her throat and shook the sandwich in front of his face.

He took it, squinting up at the clear blue sky. The sun hadn't quite reached the edge of the trees; their group was still in shadows. "It can't be that late."

"It's not." She shrugged. "But we have a long way to go."

Cho nodded, chewing. He'd been thinking about their map the night before, about the places Carthik had marked for them. The possible locations of their missing family.

Only one looked close enough to walk to. The others would require transportation.

"We're going to need a vehicle," Jason said from the trees behind them.

Cho jerked around, his heart racing. Jason chuckled and sauntered out of the forest, tucking something thin into his back pocket.

"Just checking our surroundings. No need to worry."

Cho rolled his eyes, a flash of frustration heating his gut. Jason crossed to his bag, snatched the map from a side pocket, and returned to sit beside Cho, leaning in so their legs touched as he spread the map out before them.

"This one is close." Jane pointed to a red dot on the map, a few days walk from Tornim.

Cho nodded, his spine tingling. Jason's mental wards were back in place, as strong as ever. Cho caught the occasional burst of emotion from the new people and Claire, but everyone else had their minds walled off.

Why was his stomach fluttering then? He shifted, putting an inch of space between them.

Jason reached an arm over Cho's knee and touched the other two red points on the map. "These are way too far. But I wasn't thinking about getting there, I was thinking about leaving."

Cho nodded. "We'll have a much larger group when we get them out."

"Exactly."

"How many?" Anthony, the man who could turn into a wolf, dropped a dripping wet sack of freshly caught fish onto the ground beside the fire and knelt as well. He glanced at Jason before meeting Cho's eye. "How many of yeh were taken?"

"Two dozen," Cho said. He steeled himself, briefly shoring up the wall in his mind at Anthony's presence.

The man had just lost someone, his grandmother, and the pain of it oozed from him like blood from an open wound.

"A big vehicle then." Juliana joined the conversation.

Behind her, Nova and Luna had stood and were prancing through the grass on Nova's newly fixed ankle. Each bounding step took them higher into the air until they were skipping along in ten-foot arcs.

"A transport truck." Juliana put a hand on Anthony's shoulder and crouched next to him. She twisted her head, angling to get a better look at the map. "Something with seating in the back for the little ones. Anyone who's injured."

Cho winced at her presence as well. A multitude of emotions came from her: grief, excitement, a rush of something soft as she looked at Anthony.

Cho closed his eyes, inhaling through his nose and breathing out through his lips. His power was enclosed, a brick wall surrounding the spinning saffron light. There used to be a case for it. A chest he'd spent over a year building to give himself an extra level of defense.

The chest had fractured, exploded within the walls of his mind when he'd thought his brother had been killed. He'd thought everyone in Haven, apart from the little group that had escaped, had been murdered when Black-Stars raided their home. Instead, they'd been taken to a secret research facility called Dolor.

Jason was nodding along to Juliana's words. "Do you know where we can get one? The fields are—"

"Off limits," Anthony interrupted.

Jason met his gaze with a raised eyebrow and clicked his tongue. "I was going to say, not an option."

Anthony cocked his head with half a grin. "Good."

Cho braced, but Anthony only felt relieved. Even still, the cracks in his walls were leaking yellow light, his power clawing toward the loose emotions of those around him.

"*Do* you know a place to get one?" Jane directed her question toward Juliana, her usual scornful look in place.

Juliana frowned but pulled the paper map closer and traced the red dots with her finger. "Here."

Jane's eyes widened as a brief flash of surprise crossed her face. Her sneer was back in place by the time Juliana met her eye with a raised brow.

Cho leaned in to look, wincing against the fresh push of emotion coming from Juliana and Anthony. Southwest of Tornim, and the lake and the mountains, was a smaller body of water. The cities were marked with circles, somewhat matching their spoke-shaped districts. This was marked with a star.

"What is it?" Anthony asked.

"Mendax," Juliana muttered. A wrinkle furrowed the space between her eyebrows. "This is close. Well, close enough."

"How long do you think it'll take to get there?" Cho said.

"A few days, maybe a week if we have to stop often." Juliana glanced at Tommy as she said it.

He and Taz had found an ant hill and were watching the tiny creatures scurry about.

"That's a long time," Jane growled.

"Unless you want to try getting back into Tornim and stealing a transport there, this is the only option that isn't even further away." Juliana's gaze was steady, but something of a warning flashed in her eyes.

"There will be vehicles here?" Jason asked.

Juliana looked at him. She blinked and moved her gaze to each of them in turn. "Do none of you know what Mendax is?"

Cho shook his head. The others from Haven followed suit, except Luna and Nova. The twins had finished prancing through the grass and moved to stand behind Juliana with wide eyes.

"You've been there?" Luna said.

Juliana glanced over her shoulder. "We went a few times when I was younger."

"We were supposed to go." Nova swallowed and squeezed her sister's hand. "But our parents had us shipped away before the trip."

Cho grimaced, fury heating his cheeks. His own emotion was strong enough, but his power also reached for the anger spiking in Juliana at the statement.

After a few seconds of staring at the twins, Juliana faced him again. "Mendax is a lake, built and maintained as a get-away for the Blues, Blacks, and Greys. It isn't like the cities. There aren't walls. The whole thing is open, serviced by the lower castes, and designed to be a recreational space."

There was a long pause.

"What does any of that mean?" Anthony demanded, amused exasperation in his voice.

"It means," she said with a sigh and a glance around the group, "we shouldn't have much trouble finding a transport to steal."

Anthony followed Cho as the younger man went to rinse his hands and face in the clear waters of the lake.

They'd formed a plan, ate some breakfast, and were preparing to leave. Cho had stuck to the edges of their group once the planning was done. He'd barely said a word as everyone gathered their things. When Daisy mentioned wishing they could go past Abredea to make sure Naya had gotten the food they'd left behind, he'd stalked away.

"Hey."

Cho jerked around, splashing water across his shirt. He cursed.

"Sorry." Anthony reached out a hand to help him up, but Cho didn't take it. He tried again. "Juliana says I need a bell 'round my neck or somethin'. I've got quiet feet."

Cho nodded, his lips tight as he stood and took a half-step backward. "It's fine. I was hoping to get a moment alone."

"Ahh." The heat of frustration crawled across the back of Anthony's neck. Juliana had been similarly stand-off-ish when she'd first arrived in Abredea, but that had made more sense given her circumstance. Anthony and his friends were helping Cho. They were going with him and the others to save their family.

Anthony stepped back with a shrug and turned to go.

"I'm sorry."

Anthony swung back around with an eyebrow raised.

Cho gritted his teeth. "I'm sorry. I have trouble being around you all, and you don't know why and that's not entirely fair."

A frown creased Anthony's brow. He cocked his head, and Cho went on.

"My power..." He fidgeted with the edge of his shirt. "I can feel people's emotions."

Anthony's eyes went wide, and warmth rose in his cheeks as he realized what that meant.

"See, that?" Cho put his hand up and took another step back. "I can feel that. I'm trying really hard not to, but I can."

Anthony stepped back as well, wrapping his head around this new information.

"You all just lost someone," Cho continued, "and I can feel all the pain and grief the four of you are sharing. It's... it's a lot. Especially after what we went through." He gestured a limp arm toward their group. "I know it's not your fault, but that's why I'm keeping my distance."

Anthony bit his tongue. His thoughts turned to May and—try as he might to stop it—a fresh wave of grief slammed against his chest. Cho winced, and this time, Anthony understood why.

"What can we do?" he asked, taking another step back. "How can we make this easier for yeh?"

Cho hesitated, studying Anthony's face. When he spoke, his voice was soft. "Elaine, one of our people who was taken, taught us all meditation. She showed us how to form barriers in our minds. Ways to keep ourselves safe. Keep our gifts in check. I could show you some of the techniques."

Anthony nodded with a grin. "That's what I came tah talk to yeh about anyway. I was hopin' yeh'd be able tah help me not lose control again."

"We can start now, if that's all right." Cho stepped up beside Anthony and the two walked together back toward the group. "Claire is new; she needs to get some practice as well."

"If it'll help yeh not feel everythin' we're feelin'..." Anthony thought of Juliana and heat crept up the back of his neck. "I think everyone'll be up for it."

Chapter Three

The Lake Near Abredea

Everyone was up for it. Even Taz and Daisy, who had yet to find out if they even had powers to control. The only people with reservations were Jason and Jane. Jane pulled Cho aside when he asked everyone to gather together and take a comfortable seat on the ground.

"We don't have time for this," she growled. "We need to get to the others. Get to Dolor."

Cho nodded, meeting her hard gaze with a steady one. His anxiety about their family was there, a constant presence in his gut and his head. But they had a plan. They had allies. They were moving in a direction that would lead them to Ichi, Elaine, Samaira, and the others.

"These people need defenses, Jane." He glanced at their two groups. Taz and Tommy still sat together. Luna and Nova had joined them, watching with interest as Taz made a small pebble appear and disappear in his hand like magic.

Tommy laughed, snatched the rock, held it in his open palm, and made it vanish.

Taz's jaw dropped.

The younger children burst into laughter as Taz exclaimed his amazement, asked to see it again, and told Tommy how impressed he was.

Cho looked back in time to see Jane holding back a smile at her brother's puffed-up chest and bright red cheeks. "We won't make it far if I keep feeling everything they're feeling. I need to keep working on my own defenses. And, I don't know about you, but I'd like them to have *some* control of their powers before we get to Dolor and face off with a bunch of Black-Stars."

Jane recovered her frown and gave him a dry look. "I hate it when you're right."

"You hate it when anyone is right."

"Yep."

He chuckled and followed her as she went to sit by her brother. A rush of nerves hit him as the group went quiet, watching him expectantly.

Cho cleared his throat. "Uh, so meditation is important because it helps you keep a handle on your power. It also..." His palms were damp, the eyes of the new people boring into him. At the back of the group, Jason caught his gaze with a cocky grin and pulled a ball of flames to his palm. He tossed the fire back and forth between his hands. Cho fought the urge to roll his eyes and instead looked at Juliana and Anthony. "It also helps you build a barrier in your mind. A defense against people with powers like mine, or my brother's."

"Ichi reads minds," Luna explained as Taz started to open his mouth.

"Woah," came a low murmur from Daisy.

"Anyway," Cho went on, "you don't want me to feel every one of your emotions, and *I* don't want to feel any of your emotions. So, let's get to work."

It was a slow process. The Haven children did well, especially considering how long it had been since they'd done a practice. Claire and Nova were the only ones who struggled to keep their attention on the session.

Claire kept falling asleep and jerking awake when her head slumped. Nova seemed to need a hand on her sister at all times, which made the twins have trouble focusing on their own minds.

Taz struggled the most. His busy fingers moved constantly. His knee bounced until Jane put a forceful hand on it and gave him a scorching glare. Eventually he settled enough for Cho to feel a difference in the level of emotion pouring from him. A minuscule difference, but it was progress.

Juliana and Anthony, sitting on opposite sides of the cluster of children, did rather well. Perhaps because they'd both already experienced their powers and understood the need for control.

Cho walked everyone through a set of steady breaths. Then he described how to find one's power, the central spot in the mind that needed to be protected or reined in. He shared, somewhat begrudgingly, his own method for reining in the saffron light that was his ability to absorb other people's emotions.

After a while he perched himself on a tree trunk at the front of the group and gave them all time to practice on their own. He needed to get in some meditation as well.

He closed his eyes, sucked in a breath, and poured his effort and energy into crafting a crude box. He'd fill in the lines, add details, and strengthen it later. For now, simply having the structure there would remind him to continue working on it and would help him focus when he needed to tighten the grip on his power.

"Ohh." The murmur broke his concentration. Though, perhaps it was the emotion that came with the sound. A rush of excitement, a flood of joy.

Cho looked out. Daisy's eyes were wide, her mouth open and a look of awe on her face.

"Hey." Jane's sharp voice opened the eyes of the rest of the group. She glared at Daisy from a few feet away. "What the nacra are you doing?"

"I don't..." Daisy's smile faltered. She glanced up at Cho, then to her friends. "I'm sorry if I was too loud."

"You weren't." Juliana stood, hands by her sides as her nostrils flared. She stared at Jane. "What is your problem?"

Jane stood as well, not as tall as Juliana but with plenty of haughtiness to make up for it. At her feet, Tommy tugged on her pant leg. She put out a hand and he stopped, but his eyes were wide as he watched his sister.

"Your friend is using her power on us," Jane snapped. "That's my problem."

There was a pause. Her words hung in the air for a moment before Taz bolted to his feet.

"You have power too?" he yelped, hurrying to Daisy and pulling her to her feet. "Why didn't you tell us?"

"I don't know what she's talking about," Daisy said in an unsteady voice. Her gaze darted between Juliana, Jane, and Cho. "I..."

Cho stepped forward, hands up in a placating gesture. "Let's all take a breath. Jane, what did you feel?"

"Her." Jane pointed at Daisy.

Cho sighed as Juliana stalked forward. He stepped between the two of them. "What specifically makes you think she was using an ability?"

Jane growled but took in his expression and forced herself to inhale and exhale before responding. "I felt happy."

Juliana scoffed.

Jane's lip curled. "Giddy, Cho. Excited. Bubbly." She turned toward Juliana with a scathing glare. "I don't do bubbly."

"Clearly." Juliana crossed her arms and behind her Taz snorted.

"Daisy," Cho said, "what did *you* feel while you were meditating?" He clenched and unclenched his hands a few times to distract from the anger and defensiveness flowing from Juliana. The thin wards she'd managed during meditation had crumbled the moment Jane had snapped at Daisy.

"I, uh..." Daisy swallowed. Her fingers tugged at the edge of her floral vest. "I found what you were talking about. The core. The center. I found a light like you said."

Cho nodded, a soft smile crossing his face. Daisy radiated apprehension, but underneath was glowing pride. Excitement. Joy.

"You didn't know."

She shook her head, a smile crossing her lips again. "I had no idea. What does it..." Daisy glanced at Jane. "What am I doing exactly?"

Jane scowled, but Daisy's lack of understanding softened the piercing of her dark eyes. "You're sharing your emotions." Her gaze darted to Cho. "The opposite of him, I think. Instead of reading them, feeling them, you're making other people feel them."

The rush then, of anxiety and worry caused Cho to take a physical step back. He bolstered his mental shields and looked at Daisy, trying not to grimace.

Juliana's eyes widened at his expression. She looped her fingers around Daisy's arm and pulled her back. The distance helped.

"Thank you," Cho murmured. He met Daisy's eye. "I'm sorry, my power makes this..."

"A lot," Juliana filled in.

He nodded. Yet again he tried to think of what Ichi would do, tried to channel his brother's kind wisdom. "This is a good thing."

Jane rolled her eyes, but before Cho could tell her to back off, Jason swept forward.

"Blah, blah, blah. Great, you teach the newbies how to keep their shit together. Meantime," he grinned at Jane, "you ready to test out your skills with a real fighter?"

Heat rose in Cho's chest, and he clenched his teeth. Still, he reluctantly admitted to himself that having the children from Haven follow Jason toward the lake certainly eased the tension in the others.

A few seconds later Tommy screeched with delight as Luna and Nova manipulated a ball of fire into the clear water, causing a fountain of steam to erupt.

"Right," Cho said with an exhale. "Let's see if we can get a clearer look at your ability, and work on some control."

Daisy nodded, her fingers clenched tight around Juliana's hand. The apprehension in her face shifted to excitement.

"Ohh." Anthony moved closer to the girls, a gleam in his eye. "I see wha' she meant. There's somethin'... like excitement, movin' through me. It ain't about my frosted power, I know that."

Cho cleared his throat. "Why don't we all sit again, and the rest of you can work on your wards. I'll see if I can help Daisy find the source of her power and figure out a good way to keep it contained."

They settled in. Juliana and Anthony sat side-by-side, their knees an inch apart as they closed their eyes and concentrated. Taz meandered away, shuffling to the Haven kids and joining them in cheering on Claire as she formed a walk-way of ice across the lake.

Cho watched him go long enough to see Jason look over, then scowled and turned to Daisy. "All right. Let's start with finding something for you to put your power in."

Daisy glanced around, confusion etched on her face.

Cho let out a kind laugh. "Not what I mean. In your mind there is a core of power."

She nodded.

"Well, mine is in a box, walled off until I want to use it. Let's get you forming something like that. It will keep your power in check until you're ready for it."

"That would be... yeah." Her hazel eyes lit with relief, and Cho had to throw a wall of energy between them. In his mind, in that part of him where he could see his saffron power locked up, he also saw tendrils of vibrant pink light caress the wall like a gentle wave.

He gritted his teeth but... relief wouldn't be the worst thing to feel. He reached out his hand, and Daisy took it. With a sigh, Cho relaxed his defenses, cracked the lid on his chest, and let loose a few flickers of yellow.

They soared, sucked in the pink, and became a shimmering swirl of peach colored light.

Daisy gasped.

It was different than what he usually felt. Different than the onslaught he suffered when he was forced to feel other people's emotions as his own. His power tangled with hers but was distinctly his. The choice he made to feel her relief was just that, a choice.

For some reason it seemed to make all the difference in the world.

"Do you see that?" Daisy whispered, awe in her voice.

He opened his eyes, but hers were closed. A small smile crossed his lips. "Pink? With the yellow?"

"Yeah," she breathed.

He shut his eyes again, watching the colors dance through his mind. The pink shifted, taking on a tinge of bright blue for a few seconds as the feeling of Daisy's awe entwined with his power. It shifted back to the pink, almost like that was its resting state. Its natural form.

"All right," Cho murmured. He concentrated, sifting his power away from hers. The effort was simpler than it had ever been before. The saffron of his gift parted from the pink without grasping tendrils sticking to it, without it trying to absorb her emotion.

"Oh," Daisy said. "You've gone away."

"You can feel it?" Cho asked, his eyes still closed. The pink lingered, spreading from Daisy still.

"Yes, it's like... it's like I was sharing something. But you pulled away."

"I did." Cho shook his head, unnerved and excited by how new this was. Even with Ichi, able to walk around his mind when he wanted, Cho had never been able to interact with him in this way. It had always been a conversation, a meeting along the lines of Ichi's power. This was sharing.

"I want to try having you put it away." Cho squeezed Daisy's fingers, hoping it was a comforting gesture. "Not because I think you shouldn't use it—"

"For practice," Daisy finished for him.

He nodded, though the movement was lost as they both still had their eyes closed.

"Try to picture a place in your mind. A location you know by heart. You can imagine one if nothing comes to you."

"I've got one."

Cho squinted one eye open, peering at her dazzling smile for a few seconds. "That was fast."

"The square in Abredea. Before they shut off the fountain, before Anthony..." She paused for a split second. "It was one of my favorite places."

"Great." Cho focused back on the connection between them. "Now you need a box, or a chest. Something you can store your power in until you want to use it."

This time there was a long pause. A distinct moment of hesitation before, "Would a book work?"

"A book?"

"Yeah," another pause, "here, like this."

The pink in Cho's mind's eye grew. It engulfed the space around his being and when it melted away, he was standing in a deserted town square a few yards from Daisy.

"Nacra," he breathed. "How did you do that?"

Daisy, the Daisy before him in his mind, opened her mouth, but the sound came out in the real world. It was an odd disjoint. A slight delay. Cho gaped, wide-eyed.

"Is this not..." Daisy's expression wilted. "Is this not normal?"

"I've never seen anything like this before," Cho said. "Normal isn't really a word I'd use to describe any of us but this... How am I in your head?"

Daisy's brow furrowed and an intense, overpowering feeling of confusion and uncertainty slammed into him.

He staggered back and their hands broke apart.

Cho doubled over, opening his eyes in the real world, and nearly retched with the spinning unease of it all. It was like he'd been thrown back into himself.

Daisy stood before him wringing her hands. "I'm sorry."

He held up a hand, sucking down deep breaths for a moment. Then he straightened. "That was," he panted, "incredible. I've never... you've got some real power."

Daisy flushed.

Cho shook his head, his body still catching up to his mind. Physically, he hadn't felt that roiling stomach ache he associated with confusion. His heartbeat hadn't quickened with nerves. Yet mentally he'd experienced it all.

It was a trick he'd been trying to perfect with his own power for years. To be able to read other's emotions in his mind, without his physical body reacting to things like grief, gut-wrenching fear, blood-boiling anger.

"Could we take a little walk?" Cho asked, glancing at Juliana and Anthony. The two were still meditating, the rise and fall of their chests in sync.

Daisy nodded and followed him through the grass.

Chapter Four

Dolor

Samaira strode forward in fuming silence. A pair of Black-Stars walked a few paces ahead of her, another two held her arms as they marched her down the hallway.

She'd reached a new section of Dolor this time. One more piece to add to her growing map. The vastness of the complex frustrated her. Yet she and Ichi were slowly mapping it out, using a series of half-assed escape attempts to get a little further each time. They'd managed to collect quite a bit of information about the facility in between the experiments, and unfortunately, had become quite familiar with the Black-Stars of Dolor.

One of the men in front of her, Colby, came to a halt. Samaira contemplated doing nothing, but the rage within wouldn't let her be still.

She kicked the back of his leg. Colby fell to one knee with a shout of pain. Samaira reached into her mind and grasped her power. A rush of heat trickled down her arms, warming her fingertips. She wrenched her right arm out of Jackson's grip.

Something cold pressed against the back of her neck and she froze. The squad captain, Lawrence, stood behind her holding a thin metal rod to her skin.

She'd been on the wrong side of these shock-sticks often enough to hesitate.

"Don't move," Lawrence's deep, smooth voice warned. He stood a head taller than Samaira, his black gemstones barely visible against his dark skin.

The ball of fire was already in her hand. The Black-Stars were ready to pounce, but just as she had experience with their weapons, they'd suffered lessons from her as well.

Jackson stood so close... it would only take a flick of her wrist.

Samaira grimaced and jerked her arm. Flames flew into Jackson's pale face.

The rod activated, electricity buzzed, and her knees buckled. Pain paralyzed her, spasms of shock coursing through her body even after Lawrence lifted the metal from her skin.

She sucked in shuddering breaths, hot anger, pain, and vicious satisfaction brought a snarling smile to her face. Her muscles twitched. She stayed on the ground, waiting for her body to relax.

Jackson howled in pain, writhing on the ground as angry red blisters spotted his face. His bushy eyebrows were gone. A few seconds of screeching later, his friends helped get him to his feet.

Samaira tried to stand as well, but one of the Black-Stars put a hand on her shoulder and shoved her down.

"Nacra bitch!" Jackson spat. His voice was high and pained, hands tenderly poking at his burnt face.

Samaira bared her teeth, and silently promised to bring him that pain a hundred times more before she escaped.

"Get to the medical center, Jackson," Lawrence said in his low voice.

Jackson turned to his captain. It was hard to tell if the ruddy red of his face was because of the scorched skin or if it accompanied the furious incredulity in his gaze.

"We'll take care of this one for you." Colby clapped a hand on Jackson's back. He and the other Black-Star exchanged a look and a dark chuckle.

Jackson glared at Lawrence, spat at Samaira again, and left, jogging toward the infirmary with his hand still hovering over his charred face.

The captain watched in silence as the other two guards stood over Samaira. She eyed them both with a wicked grin. Scorching, hopefully scarring, a Black-Star's face was well worth the punishment coming.

They hauled her to standing and shoved her against the wall.

Colby sank a fist into her gut. She grunted, bending at the waist just as another blow knocked her to the side.

She tasted blood, cheek stinging from the impact of his worn, calloused hand. Another slam from Colby hit her shoulder blade. She fell to the ground, arms raised to cover her head as they kicked her in the stomach.

"Enough," Lawrence's voice echoed down the stark corridor.

From the ground, Samaira coughed and spat a mouthful of blood onto the white tile. She put a hand to the wall and forced herself to her feet. Pain radiated through her body.

She relished it. The physical hurt distracted her from the rest.

"We haven't paid her back for Jackson's face." Colby's mutinous voice was as deep as his captain's, but jagged and rough. His friend nodded fervently, hands balled into fists at his side.

Samaira's bruised side disagreed. Jackson would be patched up in the medical section. A salve, some gauze, and he'd be back to work in a few days. Samaira would be left to heal from their beating in the cramped cage she'd been living in for the past week and a half.

"This one is due in exam room three." Lawrence's tone gave little room for argument, but Colby snarled, looking like he wouldn't back down.

Lawrence took a step forward, lowering his voice. "She is watching the experiments today. I won't have this one be late on my watch."

A furrow creased Samaira's brow. She licked the blood from her lips, storing away that little tidbit of information to share with Ichi later.

The other two Black-Stars grumbled but reluctantly took hold of Samaira's arms and dragged her forward, eventually turning into a room on the right. The Black-Stars strapped her into the large metal chair and clamped her arms firmly in place, palms down.

"I'm going to check on Jackson," the captain said. "Don't touch her unless the Blue-Star tells you to."

The men raised a single fist in salute. When the door closed, Colby's friend gave Samaira one last backhand across the face.

She bit back a grunt of pain and chewed on her tongue rather than further provoke them. The next few hours would be painful enough without her adding to their anger.

The men moved away, taking positions on either side of the door, and talked in low voices. Samaira picked up a few sentences here and there, but nothing about the complex, or the "*she*" Lawrence had mentioned.

Exam room three wasn't large, but it was familiar. Samaira sat in the center with the door behind her and a table to the left covered with odd instruments. She only recognized a few of them from her previous testing. She'd been in this particular room half a dozen times since the experiments had started.

The wall in front of her consisted of a large, tinted mirror. Samaira glowered at her reflection. A collection of small cuts and bruises, from her other escape attempts, marred her dark skin. Grime, a coat of sweat and dirt and blood from the last week left her with an unshakeable filthy feeling. A new bruise was forming on her cheek, a fresh cut sliced through her upper and lower lip on the left side of her face.

None of that was the reason she looked away. None of it was behind the burning in her chest and the trembling of her hands every time she saw her own features.

The door clicked open, and a petite blonde woman skipped into the room. Her blue lab coat was large on her frame. Long, slender fingers clutched a glass tablet. Two shining blue gemstones stood out on either side of her mousey face.

Samaira didn't recognize this one. Her usual torturer was Keith, the Blue-Star in charge of research at the complex.

The woman glanced at the Black-Stars with an apologetic smile. "Sorry I'm late. I'm not used to the corridors yet. I'm Abilene; just transferred here." Her gaze turned to Samaira, and the smile slipped a little at her furious expression.

Abilene swallowed, taking in the cuts and bruises on Samaira's face. Her pale grey eyes widened at the restraints on both her arms.

Samaira scowled. The anticipation of pain and the fury burning in her gut knotted her muscles. She flexed her fingers.

Abilene cleared her throat nervously. "All right," she said in a peppy voice, glancing down at her tablet. "Subject 1129, let's begin, shall we?"

She started by checking Samaira's vitals. The metal chair tilted back and straightened, stretching Samaira uncomfortably, but allowing Abilene to measure her height. A small screen on the side read her weight. Abilene ran a sensor across her forehead and noted her temperature along-side the other information on the glass tablet.

Samaira sat in jaw-clenched silence for this; she'd been pulled for experimentation every day since they'd arrived.

She closed her eyes for a few seconds when Abilene finished the standard protocol. This was where the pain began.

"All right," Abilene muttered, staring at her tablet. "Now we need to take a look at your powers." She smiled sweetly at Colby, and the Black-Stars moved forward. "Please release one of her arms."

They did as she asked, glaring at Samaira as they removed the restraint and flipped her hand so it was palm up. Even then, the two of them kept pressure on her forearm, pinning her in place.

"Please produce a small ball of flame, let's say three inches in diameter?" Abilene spoke with her face in her notes, not looking at Samaira.

"That's not gonna happen," Samaira growled through a tight grimace.

Abilene's gaze met hers briefly over the top of the tablet before looking back down. "You really must do what I ask. That's why these men are here."

Samaira's voice shook with fury. "No."

"Really, now." The Blue-Star rolled her eyes, barely glancing up from the tablet. "I can't measure your ability without some cooperation."

Blistering anger, the same Samaira had felt every morning since she'd woken up in a cage, since she'd lost her brother, since the monsters here had ripped a gemstone from Elaine's temple, roared through her veins.

"I will never use my power at the whim of someone like *you*," she spat. A bloody bit of mucus landed a few inches short of the Blue-Star's shoe.

At the outburst, Colby pulled the shock-stick from his belt and put it to Samaira's neck.

Abilene, who'd blinked, startled, when Samaira spoke, took half a step back as Colby pressed the button.

Pain shot through Samaira once again. Her muscles jerked uncontrollably as electricity spiked. She fought the spasms but couldn't hold back a yelp as Colby continued to hold the metal to her skin.

The other Black-Star lost his grip on Samaira's arm. She took advantage of the moment, forcing her mind to concentrate through the splintering pain. Heat raced down her arm, and she shot three balls of fire into the air.

A scream pierced the room, and Colby tossed the rod to the floor. He and the other Black-Star jumped forward to pin Samaira's arm back to the chair. Samaira let them, her energy all but spent.

She slumped in the chair, limp body shaking, breath coming in short, ragged bursts. A long moment passed before she was able to raise her head. Two large scorch marks peeled away the paint on the wall to her left. A black burn melted a palm-sized hole into the tint on the glass window in front of her.

A shadow passed by on the other side of the window. A spectator. Through her exhaustion, a spark of rage blossomed at the front of Samaira's mind. Someone was back there to watch her suffering.

A whimper broke through her perception. She glanced in the direction of the sound and nearly snorted. Abilene was pressed against the wall clutching the glass tablet to her chest with a sickly green coloring to her cheeks.

Samaira grinned and licked her lips. This Blue-Star really was new. If that little display frightened her, Samaira could—would—really terrify her when she got the chance.

Another moment passed, and Abilene regained some of her calm. She turned to the Black-Stars and spoke in a slightly quavering voice.

"If you could please give us a moment and wait outside."

Colby and the other Black-Star exchanged a look. Samaira raised her eyebrows, confused, but said nothing as the two men turned to Abilene.

"I don't think that's a good idea," Colby said, his gravelly voice cold and a bit condescending.

The Blue-Star's nose twitched as she frowned. "I have some blood tests to run, and they don't require an armed escort."

Colby scoffed, his sneer in place as he gestured toward Samaira. "These freaks don't listen. She won't do what you want without," his sneer turned vicious, a glint lighting in his eye that sent a shiver down Samaira's spine, "encouragement from us." He gestured to himself and his friend.

There was a pause, then Abilene straightened, her pointed jaw jutting out as she looked up at the Black-Stars. She spoke in a clipped tone, the emphasis on her consonants sharpening the words. "She is restrained. You have just sent enough electricity through her system that most of my tests will likely result in incorrect data. I do not need your assistance to do my job." She inhaled. "Please wait outside." Abilene finished the sentence with a slight incline of her head, a deferential movement that reminded the room which caste was higher out in the real world.

The men grumbled but left, closing the door behind them as they went.

Abilene crossed the room to the medical instruments. Samaira narrowed her eyes.

"That wasn't very smart," she growled.

"Hmm." Abilene glanced at the scorch marks on the walls. "I don't think you'll hurt me." She shifted a few small vials closer to the side of the table and inspected a needle.

"Let me out of these," Samaira jerked at her restraints, her anger not diminished by Abilene's return to calm, "and we'll see."

Abilene ignored the statement. She went to Samaira and wiped the inside of her elbow with a damp cloth. Samaira winced at the cold, pursing her lips as heat rose in her cheeks. Abilene took the needle from the table and pressed it into her arm.

The gentleness of the movements and the softness of the touch surprised Samaira. Every moment since the children from Haven arrived in Dolor had been hard, every interaction cruel and painful. This felt different, like this Blue-Star was trying to make it not hurt.

"Why don't you just do what we ask?" Abilene murmured, almost to herself. "They won't hurt you if you do what we say. We're only trying to help you."

She walked away, crossing the room to put a vial of blood in a chilled cabinet.

Samaira stared, disbelief and fury racing across her face. The words seemed to echo in her mind. *Help.* As though kidnapping, torture, and murder were help. As though she should be grateful for everything that had happened.

Abilene turned back and froze, her grey eyes locked on Samaira's dark ones.

"Help us?" Samaira whispered, her lips barely parted and trembling. "Those men out there... those Black-Star nacras..." She shuddered, voice rising as her fury mounted. "They killed my brother. Murdered him. We lost seven, five were *children*, when they raided our home. Stole us away."

She blinked back the tears, letting her anger burn them away before they had a chance to fall. "My brother..." Her tone dropped again, soft and deadly. She spoke through gritted teeth, pain etched across her face. "Your men came into my home and murdered my family in cold blood. I will *never* use my power—my gift—for you *child killers.*"

Abilene took a step back. Horror and disbelief chased each other across her eyes, her lips parted.

Samaira looked down at her clenched fists; the flesh of her wrists was rubbed raw from the restraints. Tears burned in her eyes.

"That's not... I didn't..." Abilene stuttered.

Samaira ignored her. Ignored the click of her tongue, her pacing to the door and wrenching it open. She barely heard Abilene's quiet demands to the Black-Stars. The pain of losing Jason had so fully entangled around Samaira's heart, she didn't think she'd pull free from it anytime soon.

A moment later Colby's rough hands were pulling Samaira from the chair. He and the other Black-Star walked her to the door, strong grips on her upper arms.

Abilene watched them go, her gaze dark.

Samaira gritted her teeth. "My brother," she growled, "innocent children... and you expect us to just do what you say." Tears came, unbidden, and dripped down her bruised face.

Abilene opened her mouth, but the Black-Stars hauled Samaira through the door and marched her back to the room of cages.

They stopped outside the barred door. With a quick glance in both directions they each sank a fist into her gut.

She doubled over, the air knocked from her lungs. The Black-Stars unlatched the door, dragged her into the room, and shoved her into one of the larger cages already holding two small children.

The room went dark as they shut the door. Samaira's eyes adjusted slowly. The window in the corner of the room provided no light. Night must have fallen outside, or at least sunset was close. The window faced east—they lost the light faster than the rest of the complex.

Her testing should have taken longer.

Samaira tried to make out the shapes of her friends in the dark. Elaine sat in the corner of her cage, rocking back and forth, clutching the hands of the girls on either side of her.

Fresh tears formed in Samaira's eyes. This all would have been different, more manageable, if they had Elaine. Really had her, not just her body. But she'd been just about catatonic since Keith—the Blue-Star in charge of Dolor—had used a machine to pry one of the gemstones from her temples.

It had done something to Elaine's mind. Something not even Ichi could fix. He'd tried to go in with his power, but the jumbled mess he found was not something he wanted to attempt to heal while they were still in this place.

Speaking of which, Ichi met Samaira's gaze across the room. The dim light between them was created by Jacob's glowing blue skin. The boy leaned up against the wall of his cage, huddled together with Sky to stave off the cold.

Samaira needed to fill Ichi in. Needed to discuss the new developments she'd discovered while sprinting down the stark white halls of Dolor, pounding footsteps of furious Black-Stars behind her. They'd been adding slowly to the map over the past week. They had to be close. The complex couldn't be much larger than what they'd already seen. Still, Samaira had yet to see any exits leading to the outside.

She clenched her jaw at Ichi's intense look. Her friend tilted his head, an unspoken question in his gaze.

She shook her head and looked away. They'd talk later.

The confrontation with Abilene had brought thoughts of Jason to the front of her mind. The words she'd spoken were worse than her reflection, worse than seeing her brother's eyes each time she caught sight of her own face.

He was dead. The knowledge pierced like knives in her heart.

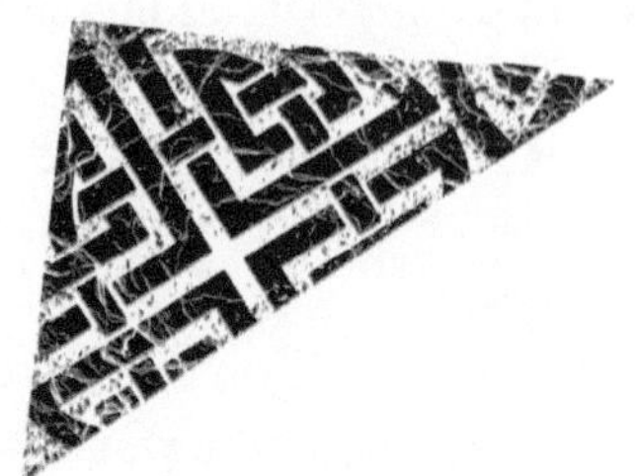

Chapter Five

Tornim - 30 Years Ago

"Are you sure? Twins always get placed together?" The nervous tremor in Brenna's voice filled the kitchen. She bit her pinky nail, tarnishing the bright blue polish glittering against her pale skin.

"Not always," her father grunted from the head of the table, his gaze fixed on his news tablet.

"But..." her sister Marissa said, aiming a kick at her father's leg under the table. "It's more likely than not we'll be in the same caste, right, Mother?"

"Hmm." Their mother took a sip of her orange juice and set it down. The liquid swished around the clear crystal, and a drop spilled onto the table. The Orange-Star standing in the corner of the room swept forward and wiped it up before returning to his spot.

"Hmm?" Marissa glared at their mother.

"Yes dear, 'hmm.' With Brenna's test scores so much lower than yours... well, I wouldn't be surprised if she becomes a Red or Purple."

Brenna swallowed. Her eyebrows furrowed together with worry. Her gaze darted across at her sister. Marissa had scored 102% on their last exam. Brenna barely scraped by with 72%.

"Mom!" Marissa snapped, frustration in her voice.

"It's all right." Brenna flashed Marissa a quick smile. "She's right. But, Mom, I did do all that bonus work to cover my test score. And that's the only one I've done poorly on in a while."

Their mother looked up, meeting Brenna's eye for the first time that morning.

"I know. And perhaps if you spent less time with your friends and more time studying, we wouldn't be having this discussion. But it is too late to worry about it now. You can't get those bad decisions back before your Star Appointment."

Marissa grunted and stood up. She shoved her hand-carved mahogany chair back so hard her father looked up.

"Marissa. Those were expensive."

The tall, beautiful blonde rolled her eyes and looked across at Brenna.

"Let's go."

Brenna hesitated, but an urging look from her sister brought her to her feet.

"Where are you two going?" their mother demanded. "Your appointment isn't for three more hours. I was planning on Josh driving you." She snapped her fingers at the Orange-Star, and he rushed to her side.

"We don't need—" Marissa put up a hand, a pained look on her face.

"Nonsense. We live in direct visual range of the Grey-Stars. Until that wall is finished you will behave as a Blue-Star should. He will at least drive you to Grigoria."

"Fine," Marissa snapped. "Let's go, Josh. You can take us all the way to the Star Office if it will shut Mother up."

"Marissa!"

"Bye." Marissa grabbed Brenna's arm and pulled her from the room.

"Bye, Mom!" Brenna called back into the kitchen. The room responded with silence.

"Ugh." Marissa linked Brenna's arm with hers and led the way to the foyer. "Please ignore them, B. You know how she gets." She looked back at Josh and said in a cruel yet accurate impression of their mother's lofty tone, "Do bring the car around, Josh."

"I know." Brenna leaned against Marissa. The nerves pressing into her didn't seem to bother her sister. She chewed a nail on her free hand. "But she's right, if I spent more time studying..."

"Enough." Marissa slapped her hand away and grabbed their coats from the ornate hook next to the doorway. "This is a good day." She sighed and opened the door.

Sun brightened the chilly air. Brenna shivered and tugged her coat on, pulling the soft collar to her cheeks.

"Today," her sister sang as she pranced out the door. "We finally get to leave this house."

Brenna couldn't stop the grin as Marissa spun in the crisp winter sunlight. Josh sat patiently in the family hydro-car parked in front of the manor.

"Picture it." Marissa took Brenna's hand again and dragged her to the car. "You and me, a tiny little apartment near Grigoria. We'll visit the match-makers tomorrow and get them started on the hunt." She said 'the hunt' with dangerous enthusiasm, causing Brenna to raise an eyebrow. "Starting tomorrow, B... No Mom."

Brenna laughed at the intensity of her sister's voice. The nerves fluttering in her stomach slowed to a gentle pulse.

"No State dinners."

Brenna grinned at her sister as Josh pulled them away from the curb. She joined in the listing. "No forced clothing choices."

"No reading Father's essays."

"No visiting Aunt Renay."

They both burst out laughing.

"How long does Mother have you working today?" Brenna leaned forward, flashing Josh a grin.

Marissa's face fell, and she leaned back against the seat, folding her arms with a soft sigh.

The older man glanced at her in the rear-view mirror with a warm smile. Grey hair poked up from the edges of his balding head. His orange gemstones glistened on his temples. Laugh lines and worry wrinkles pressed into his skin. He'd been working for their family since before Brenna could remember.

"Well, she has that elaborate party planned for the two of you, so past three at least."

"What about your granddaughter?" Concern sneaked through Brenna's voice.

"She's staying with her father tonight."

"Oh good." Brenna smiled. "Why don't you drop us off at the entrance to Grigoria? Mother doesn't need to know you didn't take us all the way over. Go say hello to your family before you head back to the manor."

Josh smiled. "You're a wonderful girl, Brenna. Thank you."

They drove through the gate to Grigoria and past the massive concrete wall that surrounded the Outer Market. Josh pulled to the side, and the girls got out.

They walked arm in arm, huddled together against the cold.

"You shouldn't, you know." Marissa gave Brenna a side-long glance.

"What?" Brenna asked, hesitation in her voice.

"Talk to Josh so much. Be so nice. Mother gets mad at you for talking to lower classes in the shops; if she finds out you're so friendly with Josh... or any of the others."

Brenna's breath caught, and she stared at her sister.

"I'm not stupid, B. I know where you go after school. Your little group of mixed friends... You can't keep spending time with them, not after today."

Brenna frowned but nodded. She bit the nail on her middle finger.

Marissa sighed. "Come on, let's go have some fun before our appointment."

They made their way past the large, ornate gate that closed Agora off from the rest of the city at night. The girls passed several friends and classmates as they headed to their favorite restaurant. Brenna grew more and more comfortable the farther they were from home. Marissa however, became shy and quiet as more people stopped to say hello.

It had always been that way. Marissa excelled in school and dealing with their parents. Brenna was the one who made friends. She was the one who could enter a room and immediately find someone to talk to. They made an excellent team.

"Delicious," Brenna mumbled, her mouth full of the fresh bread she had just dipped into her soup.

Marissa grinned and delicately wiped her mouth with a napkin.

Light poured from chandeliers hung on the ceiling. A fountain of sparkling water dripped down the wall behind their table. Their waitress, a young Purple-Star with matching temporary butterfly face tattoos, knew Brenna and brought the twins a free dessert.

"Hey." Brenna leaned around Marissa, gazing intently at a figure in the corner. "Isn't that the guy from your chem class? Henry?"

Marissa jerked her head around and then faced forward and hunched over her plate.

"Yes. So?" she said in a rushed voice.

Brenna chuckled and rolled her eyes. "Have you spoken to him at all outside of class?" she asked incredulously.

"No. There's no point. I couldn't spend time with him before today anyway. And I'm pretty sure his Coding isn't for a few months. Besides, we're meeting with the match-makers tomorrow. I don't *need* to talk to him."

"Technically you don't need to talk to anyone. But it's nice to have friends."

"I don't need friends." Marissa grinned. "I have you."

They both laughed, finished their food, and walked the rest of the way to the Star Office.

They sat in the packed waiting room. A row of windows ran along the right side of the room, one for each gemstone color. Images flashed on the walls, advertisements for match-makers, apartments, and job consultants for each caste.

Brenna nibbled on her pointer-finger nail. Marissa bounced her leg up and down over and over. Finally, after an hour of waiting, a Blue-Star attendant came to take them to the tests.

Brenna squeezed her sister tight before they entered the separate testing areas.

"It's going to be all right," Marissa whispered in her ear.

They exchanged nervous, excited grins and walked through the separate doorways. Brenna offered up a kind smile to her Orange-Star attendant.

"Long day? It looked pretty busy back there."

The short brunette grinned at her. "Winter is always busy."

They chatted together as Brenna went through the different tests. She scored surprisingly high on the standard, only getting six of the questions wrong. The aptitude test presented more of a challenge, but after a close look at each question, she felt she did acceptably well.

And then she was there, getting a small hug from the Orange-Star, and walking down the sterile, white hallway. The door opened for her. A large metallic chair sat in the center of the room.

A giddy rush went through her. A few more minutes, and she'd be free of her parents, ready to start her adult life.

Cold restraints snapped in place around her wrists and ankles once she sat. Another restraint clasped across her chest. The Coding attendant smiled at her before he ducked into the observation room. A whirring purr sounded above her. An oddly shaped contraption lowered from the ceiling, coming to rest just above her head. Her peripheral vision showed thin needles lowering into place and plunging into her gemstones.

Several moments passed. Her blood raced; sweat beaded at her hairline and dripped down her face. Finally, the machine shut off and rose back into the ceiling. The attendant came out, fear in his wide eyes.

Brenna frowned.

He put a finger to his ear and said, "Get security in here."

Brenna's heartbeat quickened. She jerked at the restraints. "What's going on?"

The man glared at her, hatred replacing the fear. "You're a Moon."

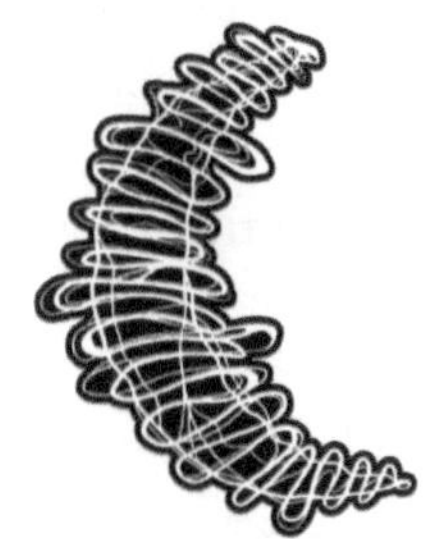

Chapter Six

The Wilds of Pangaea

"It was incredible," Daisy gushed, her eyes alight, bubbling over with excitement. "Like I was able to pull him into my head. Show him my power and…" She flushed. "I almost knocked him over a few times."

Juliana grinned. She wasn't sure if the rush of joy she felt was because she was happy her friend was happy, or because her friend was happy and had the ability to make her feel it.

The whole situation was a bit confusing and painted a vivid picture of how difficult it must be for Cho when he couldn't distinguish between his emotions and others'.

"I need details," Juliana said. "What does that mean?"

Daisy laughed, her cheeks growing even redder. "Each time I had a negative emotion," she waved her hand, as though dismissing the presence of negativity, "it sort of threw him out of my head, and we had to start over."

Juliana snorted.

The two women walked together at the end of the group. Anthony led the way, his silent feet carrying him through the forest, across sections of bare fields and grass and over rolling hills. He'd mapped out a route, a way to avoid the thickest sections of trees, the rocky mountains, and the roads, to get them to Mendax as quickly as possible.

Travel wasn't as difficult as Juliana anticipated. Taz, Jason, and Jane took turns carrying Tommy on their shoulders. Luna and Nova, who she thought would lag behind with their long skirts and small limbs, practiced their power whenever their legs got tired, floating along in the center of their group while Taz gaped in unwavering awe.

Even Claire, who was the youngest besides Tommy, and too big to be carried the whole way, made no utterance of complaint as they walked for hours at a time.

A day had passed since they left the lake. They'd spent the night in a clearing, huddled against the cold until Jason had poured a little power into their fire, letting the flames rise several feet into the air, emanating warmth through the group.

Hope seemed to be on the rise. The trek to Mendax was a long one, but they were making good time. There had been no sign of Black-Stars since their escape from Abredea. Likely because they were sticking so dedicatedly to the wild.

The Haven children were on their way to their family. The anticipation and the excitement was infectious. Cho and Daisy had spent nearly every moment of their stops, either for rest or meals, training Daisy to control her gift.

"It's hard," she said to Juliana as they strode through thigh-high blades of golden grass. "I don't want everyone around me feeling what I feel, but it takes balance to make sure I'm only locking away the power, not also my emotions."

Juliana nodded, sort of understanding. "You put it in a book?"

Daisy grinned. "Yeah. I thought that was a fitting place."

"Absolutely." Juliana chuckled.

"What about you?" Daisy gave her a side-long glance. "You and Anthony have been meditating together a lot."

Heat rose in Juliana's cheeks.

"Where are you storing your gift?"

Juliana stumbled over a large stone. She caught herself before falling and glanced at her friend. She hadn't told Daisy about the kiss yet, the one she and Anthony had shared in Abredea after they'd found out the truth from May. The truth about Alters, their power, the secret rebellion fought decades ago, and Anthony's relation to the woman.

It had been nonstop since then. A rush of violence, fear, grief... no time to breathe, no time to think about the burn of his lips on hers, to think about when she might feel them again.

The two of them had been so set on gaining a handle of their powers they hadn't even discussed what they'd do when they reached Mendax or Dolor, let alone how they felt about the kiss or each other or...

"Um." Juliana dragged her mind from the warmth of Anthony's skin and focused on Daisy's question. "Oh, in the locket my parents gave me. The one the Red-Stars took when I was..." She swallowed, the memory of the Red-Star at the wall between Tornim and Abredea ripping the necklace from her throat and laughing when she demanded it back overwhelmed her for a moment.

"When you were Coded?" Daisy asked gently.

Juliana nodded. "I don't really know why." She shrugged one shoulder. "I only had it for a few hours, but it reminds me of them."

Daisy rubbed her hand up and down Juliana's arm for a moment. "I get it. The book I'm using is one of my mom's favorites. I think details like that are probably important."

"Yeah," Juliana murmured, her thoughts once again dancing away from the conversation as she wondered if her parents had been informed of her escape, if

Black-Stars had showed up at their home, maybe searching for her. Searching for clues as to where she could have gone.

Then again, Anthony was the one they'd really want. He was the one Steel would be after with that crazed rage in his gaze.

She shuddered and changed the subject. "Has Taz talked to you about all this?" She gestured to the trundling group of people walking ahead of them.

Jane was holding Tommy's hand, letting him swing her arm back and forth with bounding exuberance. Claire and Jason chatted in low voices, Jason pausing every now and then to show her a movement of his fingers or wrist as different shaped bursts of flames appeared and quickly vanished into the air. Between the mini-lessons, the man fiddled with a thin strip of metal, always tucking it away before she got the chance to ask what it was.

"A bit," Daisy said, glancing ahead to where Taz's gangly arms swung as he strode along-side Anthony. "Did he say anything to you?"

Juliana sighed. "He seems a bit left out. Not having any power yet."

"Yet? So you think he'll get one?"

Juliana shrugged. "I don't know. But it would make sense. He's only sixteen, and Cho said most people wouldn't show any Alter ability until their mid-twenties. Maybe he's just going to have to wait a while."

"Ahh yes," Daisy said. "Taz is the most patient of us all. I'm sure he'll be fine with waiting."

At that, Juliana snorted again, looped her arm through Daisy's, and jogged them forward so they could walk with their friends.

They'd walked a truly impressive distance. Cho felt it in his legs, his feet, the ache of his back each morning as he rose from the ground and wished Samaira was there to show him the multitude of stretches that would have helped his neck. He only remembered a few of her favorites.

They were making remarkable time. If Juliana's plan worked—and he had no reason to think it wouldn't, especially after some of the stories Taz had been telling them—they'd be at the first possible Dolor location within a week. Longer than he wanted, shorter than it could have been.

They just had to hope the closest mark on the map was the correct one.

The group had stopped for the night, settling under an outcropping of trees on an otherwise empty plain of grass that stretched for miles. Anthony had jogged beyond their line of sight, over a series of rolling hills in the distance, and returned to tell them the road wasn't far. They were staying on course.

A multitude of concerns continued to flood Cho, but after several days traveling with the others, he was relieved to find they were all his own. Juliana and Anthony had mastered shielding their minds quickly. Daisy's power was so like his own, it was easy enough to help her keep control of both it and the mental wards he'd taught her to construct. Only Taz still struggled, but the boy was so energetic and kind that Cho found himself walking next to him on occasion, letting his saffron light suck in the exuberance and excitement when he himself was feeling low.

It was a new use of his power. One he wasn't sure Ichi would approve of. It was something to ponder *after* they rescued everyone.

Jason wandered over just as Cho took a bite of a particularly stale pastry. The food from the truck was running low. Even supplemented by Anthony's hunting, there was no denying they were a large group, and they went through food quickly. Cho's current anxiety—how to feed everyone when they found their family—was amplified by the meager meal they'd all shared for dinner.

"Did the pastry say something insulting?" Jason smirked, plunking down beside Cho and eyeing his snack. "You've got a great wrinkle right here." He pointed to his forehead, just between his eyebrows. "And you look pissed."

Cho frowned. "I'm thinking, Jason."

Jason nodded, his grin not lessening as Cho glared at him. "What problem are you trying to solve now?"

Cho blinked, his frown slackening with confusion. "I'm..." He glanced at Jason, wondering if his question had been genuine, or his usual ploy at conversation only to turn around and make a joke. "I'm trying to figure out how we are going to feed everyone when we find Ichi and the others."

To his surprise, Jason nodded again, stroking a hand down the side of his sharp jaw. "I've been thinking about that too. We're running out already, just us. Maybe we can steal some stuff from Mendax with the truck."

"Yeah," Cho said slowly. "I was kind of thinking that too. It's lucky we have Claire and Anthony, or we'd be out of water by now too."

They both glanced over at Claire. The girl stood at the edge of fire, her tongue peeking out between her teeth as she concentrated. The air around them grew stale and dry as crystals of ice formed under her palms and fell into the little tin balanced on a rock near the flames. She couldn't make much, but it was enough to keep them hydrated when the stream that their path loosely followed curved away for stretches at a time. They weren't on the road itself, but neither did they want to get too far from it.

Anthony came up beside her to stoke the flames.

"He seems... capable," Jason said, a slight tension in his voice.

Cho nodded. "They all do. I was surprised they got a handle on their minds so quickly."

Jason leaned in, lowering his voice a little. "So, they aren't giving you trouble anymore? You seemed..." He faltered, then his usual snide grin slid into place. "Your expression at the lake was constantly constipated."

Cho exhaled, the old familiar frustration rising in his chest. One minute. Jason had managed a serious conversation for exactly one minute. Cho answered without addressing the stupid joke. "Yeah, they've done well. Taz still has trouble but," a smile flickered across his lips, "he's too relaxed for it to be an issue."

Jason followed Cho's gaze across the circle their group had made around the fire. Taz was in his usual spot beside Tommy. The two had spent each night of the trek practicing a handful of magic tricks. Taz's were actual tricks, and Tommy's were actual magic. It had gotten to the point where Luna, Nova, and Claire had them putting on little shows during their lunch stops, laughing and cheering at each successful act.

"Well," Jason muttered. "I'm glad you like walking next to him. You deserve to feel relaxed."

"What?" Cho was sure he'd heard that wrong, but Jason was already moving. He stood and strode over to sit with Anthony and Juliana as they talked about plans for Mendax with Jane.

Cho shook his head, sighing away a frustrated heat rising in him. He had things to say to Jason. Words he needed to utter but couldn't seem to get out. He blamed the flame thrower. No conversation lasted more than a few minutes, and each of them included at least one insult. How was he supposed to thank Jason when he was being told he looked constipated?

He needed to though, and before they reached Mendax. Before they hit a point where something could go wrong. He swallowed as the reason for his anxiety shifted away from food and toward the uncertainty of what lay ahead.

He rose and followed Jason toward Juliana and Anthony. The healer had taken what seemed to be a natural role as leader of their group. Anthony led the way, but Juliana was the one to plan their stops, make sure everyone had a proportionate amount of food, and was making all the plans for their heist.

She was the only one among them who had actually been to Mendax, so it made sense. Cho tried to look at it from that angle. She should be in charge because she had the most experience with where they were going. He tried to shut out the part of him that was disproportionately grateful he didn't have the pressure of taking care of everyone solely on him anymore.

He caught sight of the twins, Luna and Nova, balancing Taz in the air as he stifled gleeful giggles before he plunked down with a soft thud. The girls had taken on a lot since Haven fell. Their fear was still fresh in his mind. Their desperate terror at the thought of losing each other, but also their worry about him. About how he'd stack up compared to Ichi.

Cho shook his head again. That wasn't fair. All of them had doubted his capabilities, even Jane, when they'd been starving in the abandoned warehouse.

He pivoted, turning away from the planning session, and stalked a few yards away from the circle to sit in the grass by himself for a moment.

"Hey," a soft voice said from behind him.

Cho sighed, plastered a smile on his face, and turned to look at Daisy.

She winced. "You want to be alone, don't you?"

He shrugged. "It's fine."

She settled next to him. They sat together in silence. Cho was consumed with his own thoughts.

"I haven't been outside this much at night before," Daisy murmured.

He glanced at her. She was staring out, the fire to their backs illuminating the red in her hair. Her gaze seemed fixed on the horizon and, when he followed it, he noted the dusting of stars beginning to light the sky.

"Me neither," he said. "I haven't been outside this much since before my power started. We didn't get much of a chance to leave Haven, and going at night was especially dangerous."

Daisy nodded. "Juliana told me about the curfews."

He chuckled. "She was raised a Blue-Star, her curfews weren't quite what the rest of us dealt with."

"What do you mean?"

"Well," Cho glanced at the group behind them, "my parents are Green-Stars. We had to be back in our district by nine unless there was an urgent job. Sometimes my dad would be out the entire night to get something finished."

"We had that a few times in Abredea." Daisy plucked a strand of grass beside her and began twisting and knotting it in various designs. She'd done it before, just about every time they found a quiet spot to practice control of her gift. The movement of her fingers was entrancing. "An emergency, or something, they never really said why. But the field hands would have to work 12-hour shifts on rotation for days at a time, even going through the night."

They fell into silence again. Cho didn't have anything to say to that, though bringing up his family had turned his thoughts to Ichi. Worry, the need to move faster, to get there already, dug sharp claws into his gut.

"Are you doing better?" Daisy asked.

"What?"

Daisy gestured back toward the fire. "Now that we have more of a grip on our minds, our emotions. Have you been able to build up that wall you keep talking about?"

The corner of Cho's mouth twitched. "Yeah, thanks. I, uh…" he hesitated, "I think having your friends sort of in charge has helped more than anything. I don't…" He wrung his hands. "I never wanted to be the leader. And," he added with a slight growl in his voice, "it's nice having adults around who are more level-headed than Jason."

Daisy snorted. "Are you talking about Juliana and Anthony?"

Cho nodded.

Her giggle echoed through the night. "Those two are both the most emotional hot-heads I've ever met."

Cho gaped.

"But," she amended, her hand held up as her giggles faded, "I will say they do a good job of balancing each other out. Juliana gets… when she gets mad she loses that rational side. And Anthony," Daisy rolled her eyes, "has been a troublemaker since we were kids. He's mellowed out, but…" Her smile faltered, her expression growing serious. "I mean, you saw him in the clearing when Jules was hurt. He's always gone too far to protect us."

She swallowed and gave a little shake of her head. "I think we're best when we're all together. The four of us. Taz and I don't… we aren't maybe as strong as those two." Her mouth twitched to the side in a brief grimace. "My power certainly isn't as useful. But we even out their tempers."

Cho sat with that for a moment. When he looked at her again, he wasn't surprised to find her finishing a long chain of braided strands of grass.

"I think you're underestimating your power," Cho said. "You can take people into your mind. You can make them feel what you're feeling. And," he added, remembering something he'd wanted to talk to her about after their last meditating session, "I think with some practice you can make them feel memories of emotion."

"What do you mean?"

"Well." Cho shifted towards her, excitement bubbling in him at the realization he'd had earlier that day. "At the moment you have to feel what you want others to feel, right? So if you want someone happy you have to be happy."

She nodded.

"I think, if you can find a way to store and recall emotions you've had in the past, you'll be able to use them without having to feel them yourself."

There was a pause as she thought over his words, the tiniest of furrows in her smooth brow.

"I could..." She chewed on her bottom lip for a moment. "I could put a memory on a page, for example, and when I want someone to feel the way I felt during that memory..."

"You'd pull from that page when you use your power," Cho filled in. "Yeah, I think it could work that way. With practice," he added with a half-chuckle.

Daisy nodded, her expression still distant. "I want to... I'll work on that tonight if you're all right with trying it tomorrow?"

"Sure." Cho sighed. "I should go help with the planning."

Daisy gave another nod. "I'll be here," she said absently, staring out at the stars.

Chapter Seven

Near Mendax

The day before they reached Mendax Anthony transformed.

As it had only happened once before, and Juliana had been unconscious at the time, she'd expressed an interest in seeing it.

Anthony barely wanted to *become* the wolf again, let alone allow others to be near him when it happened.

But Cho had taken him aside after their morning meditation.

"I think you should practice."

"I am," Anthony said, gesturing to the patch of flattened grass where he'd spent the last half hour cross-legged, growing the wall of trees that kept his mind closed off from others. It was a strange thing to attempt. Finding a way to keep someone out of his head, and to keep his own emotions from leaving his mind, was no easy feat. He'd opted away from the brick wall idea Cho had offered up on that first day. Trees grew thick, strong. They'd kept him safe his whole life.

His power... that was another matter. He hadn't told anyone how much trouble he was having controlling the wolf. There was no orb of light in his head like the way Juliana described. No fountain of power that Daisy talked about. In Anthony's head it was a literal wolf, stalking the deepest recesses of his mind and latching onto memories of danger, fear, and fury.

He almost thought it was trying to learn. As though his power was attempting to pinpoint when it would be necessary again.

"Your defenses are great," Cho said with a nod. "But I'm talking about your power. We'll be at Mendax by tonight. If we have to fight? If... when we get to Dolor, if we have to get past Black-Stars—"

Anthony shook his head, his jaw tight. He glanced over to their little group. Juliana was tossing dirt onto the embers of their fire, her head thrown back in a laugh at something Taz had said.

He took a step away and Cho followed. "Las' time I killed someone, Cho. I wasn't... I didn't even know who I was. What if that were tah happen again? What if I hurt someone?"

Cho nodded, the understanding on his face a source of frustration to Anthony. "I get it. But that was different. That was a reaction to Juliana getting hurt. If no one is in danger, you'll probably have an easier time controlling the wolf."

"*Probably*," Antony snorted, scowling.

"Well then," Cho said briskly. "Think of it this way: if you don't learn how to control it now, what's going to happen if someone gets hurt again while we're in the middle of a situation? What happens if Taz or Daisy or Juliana gets attacked and instead of helping, you go wolf and attack one of us?"

The heat that had been rising in Anthony's chest chilled at Cho's words. He glanced at the others, his jaw tight.

The past few days hadn't been easy. Keeping everyone fed, keeping them close enough to the road that they didn't lose their way, but far enough that they avoided Black-Star patrols, was a tricky thing.

But in the time they'd had together he'd grown to like these city kids. Jason was funny and surprisingly good at teaching. How long had Anthony tried to get Daisy to learn how to throw a punch? Years. And Jason had gotten her swinging within a day.

The twins were fun too. They stuck close to each other, but they seemed fond of Daisy. The three of them had showered the whole group with flowery necklaces just that morning, eliciting smiles from almost everyone, a shout of glee from Tommy, and a grimace from Jane—who still put hers on after Luna gave her a warning look.

Tommy. Anthony looked to the youngest of the group. He was so small, so much like Jimmy that it hurt to see the way he grinned up at Taz as the two of them walked together.

Anthony missed his aunt and cousin so much, sometimes it was a physical pain. That was part of how he knew he'd done well with his wards. Cho wasn't wincing with longing and worry as Anthony wondered if they'd found May yet.

They must have. It had been days. May and Steel would both have been discovered. What were the Black-Stars doing without their captain? A small shudder ran up his back at the memory of fur sprouting up and down his arms. He'd barely held it together in the moments when Steel attacked.

Anthony shook his head with a sigh. "Yer right, and I'm mad about it. But I'll practice. Just, not with everyone around. I don't wanna hurt anyone."

Cho nodded. "You should have someone with you though, in case you need help coming back again."

They decided that person would be Juliana. Well, she decided, but Anthony couldn't think of a reason that it shouldn't be her.

The rest of them packed up and Anthony pointed the way southwest. There was a set of cliffs uncomfortably close to the road that would have forced the group to be visible to travelers. Instead of maintaining their path, they opted to veer around the cliffs and hopefully avoid anyone looking for them along the road.

Juliana and Anthony would catch up once he'd finished practicing his wolf form.

Cho and Jane took the lead with Jason at the rear to keep an eye on everyone, and Juliana and Anthony were left alone for the first time since they'd left Abredea.

Juliana watched the others go, and Anthony watched her. When their friends had disappeared around a bend, she turned to him.

"So, how are we doing this?" Her voice was crisp, her light jacket pulled tight against the chilly morning air. It had grown colder as they headed south.

Anthony recalled wanting to get them warmer clothes when they reached Mendax. Assuming the place had need for such things. He didn't know much about the city, and even less about this fancy vacation resort for the top three castes, but he knew they lived in luxury. Maybe that included stuff to control the temperature.

Not dealing with cold mornings certainly sounded like an upper star thing to do.

"I, uh," Anthony fumbled, distracted by how red her cheeks were. He grimaced. "I suppose I turn into a monster now, don' I?"

Juliana stared at him for a moment. Then she snorted. "That feels dramatic."

He narrowed his eyes. "I killed someone last time, Jules." The words came out tight, as though pinched in his throat before he uttered them.

Her amused expression dropped, and she took a step toward him.

Trees surrounded them; not the towering pines and oaks of the forest but smaller ones. Black bark peeled away from white trunks. Delicate leaves fell in little shimmers of fall color against the morning light.

Juliana reached out a hand. He didn't move, the horror from that day pulling his mind down into dark and bloody thoughts.

Her icy fingers skimming his arm were enough to snap him out of it.

"Frost, Jules," he yelped.

She pulled her hand back from where she'd touched his arm. "Sorry, I was..." she flushed.

"No," Anthony sighed, rubbing a hand across his forehead, hard. "I'm sorry, yer hands are cold, is all. And I'm feelin' a little..."

"Jumpy?" she asked with a small smile.

He nodded.

"Odd," her voice held a laugh behind the words, "I seem to recall you thinking my hands were warm compared to—"

The laughter died in her throat, and Anthony's chest constricted at the same time that Juliana's face fell.

Silence hovered around them for a moment. Wind rustled the leaves in the trees. Anthony stood in the wave of grief that crashed over him each time May was mentioned. Taz did it often, bringing up her little habits, things he missed. Daisy less frequently, though she'd checked on him at least once a day to see if he was all right. But he and Juliana hadn't had much chance to talk about his grandmother's death since they'd left Abredea.

He supposed one of them could have brought it up in the evenings, when they were done eating and the group was sharing stories, or coming up with ideas for Dolor, or demonstrating their powers. They could have found time during the quiet hours they spent walking each day.

He didn't know why he couldn't be the one to bring up his grandmother. All he knew was that each time he thought about her being gone, something that felt like a vice closed around his chest and compressed until he was sure he wouldn't be able to breathe.

This time though, with Juliana standing and staring at her hands with so much hurt in her eyes...

He moved toward her and wrapped her slender fingers in his. "I was lyin'."

She blinked; the grief replaced with confusion. "What?"

"I was lyin' when I said yer hands were warmer than May's at stitchin' me up."

"Why—"

"Guess." The side of his mouth pulled up in the half-smile he'd inherited from his grandmother.

Her flush went all the way to the roots of her hair.

Anthony took another step, close enough now that their interwoven hands were pressed to his torso.

Juliana's eyes flashed with an uncertainty he wasn't used to seeing on her face. Her hands tightened in his, but she didn't pull away. "Is now the time for this?" Her voice was barely a whisper.

"I've wanted tah kiss yeh since the last time it happened," he said. "There's been..." He met her bright blue gaze, hoping his words meant what he wanted them to. "So much has happened, and we've been around the others every step."

Juliana shook her head with a smirk. "You didn't want to kiss me in front of everyone?"

He rolled his eyes and pulled one of his hands away, trailing his fingers up and down her arm. His gaze was fixed on the collection of freckles spotted across her cheeks. They'd grown in number, being under the sun all day.

He didn't know what to say to her question. How to explain that he didn't care who saw, but that each time he'd tried to find a moment to pull her away, they'd been approached by someone who needed help with the fire, or wanted to show him something, or had to talk plans for Mendax and Dolor.

He didn't know how to tell her that each time he thought of her lips pressed against his, he also thought of the moments leading up to that kiss. The revelations that had shifted his entire reality.

He opened his mouth but the glint in her eye caused him to pause.

"I'm teasing, Anthony." She glanced at his fingers, flattened her palm on his chest, and moved her hand up to the curve of his shoulder.

A river of heat cascaded down his spine. Raw desire pooled in his gut and his breath caught as her fingers circled his neck.

She held his gaze, the light smile growing serious again. "I understand. We haven't had time." She exhaled through parted lips, her breath smelling of peppermint from the last of the little candies they'd brought from the stolen truck.

Juliana leaned closer, her chest pressed to his as her fingers brushed through the hairs at the base of his neck. "We barely have time now," she murmured.

Anthony dipped his head a fraction of an inch, and she turned her lips to meet his.

It was electric at first. A shock of longing and excitement that rushed through him, through both of them. Juliana raised her other hand, locking her fingers around his neck as his arms slid around her waist.

Her lips weren't smooth after days on the road. They were chapped, almost as rough as his scruffy jawline, but he couldn't have cared less. Her tongue ran across the inner edge of his top lip, and he tightened his grip, wanting to pull her closer, wanting their two bodies to be in the same space, wanting the rest of the world to melt away.

And it did. As the electricity and heat were replaced by a steady warmth, it felt as though there was nothing but them and the trees and the sun breaking through the branches above. When their lips broke apart, Juliana leaned into him, nestling her face in the curve of his neck. The steady in and out of her breath did what days in the wild had somehow failed to do and eased the tension in his muscles, the ache in his neck.

They stood for a long while, probably longer than was smart given that they'd need to catch up with the others. Holding her though... When she finally pulled away, it was hard to let go.

"Ready?" Juliana asked. Her attempt at a brisk, business-like voice was ruined by the hoarseness of her throat and the thrumming heat still buzzing across her lips. She took a drink from the water bottle in her pack, and planted her hands on her waist.

He sighed. "Yeah."

"Any idea how to start?" Juliana asked.

"I'm gonna try how yeh described it. It'll be hard though, findin' the wolf."

Her brow furrowed. "Finding?

He nodded. "It's not like yeh talk about with yers, or like Cho talks about. There's no box or chest or anythin' containin' it." He shifted, squeezing his bicep as his body tensed. "I feel it sometimes, like it's runnin' through my thoughts."

"Your power is..." Juliana puzzled for a moment, thinking of the glowing locket she could picture instantly in her mind: the blue light, the curving J, initialed on the front. It had taken most of the last few days to get the locket to close all the way, and it had felt odd when it did, like she was locking away part of herself. At the same time, when Taz had burned himself preparing dinner the other night, she had healed him on purpose. It hadn't been pulled out of her body in a way she couldn't control.

"Loose," Anthony filled in, his jaw tight. "Yeah."

She met his eye and caught a flash of panic there. Her heart clenched. She reached out and squeezed his fingers before he pulled away.

"Give me a few minutes?" He stepped back and sank onto the long grass, crossing his legs and closing his eyes.

Juliana nodded. She backed away, giving him room to think, to find the wolf apparently running rampant through his mind. A shudder ran up her spine. She recalled the first time she'd used her healing power, how it had spread—unbidden—from her fingers and drained her until she collapsed.

Anthony's had been different. Uncontrolled, not a danger to him, but a danger to everyone else.

She leaned against one of the trees scattered around them, holding her hand before her and surveying her long fingers. She reached inward, releasing the latch on the locket in her mind and pulling a pinch of blue light out.

A smile crossed her lips as tendrils of blue swirled around her hand. With a flick, the light shifted, moving away and then coming back when she called it. There was nothing to heal, no scrapes or bruises to lessen, but her power was there just the same. It was nice knowing she could call on it when she wanted.

She wished she'd known about it before, when Jimmy and Naya had gotten sick. Juliana's gaze slid to Anthony, still cross-legged, lips barely moving as he murmured silently to himself.

They'd talked about his aunt and cousin a few times since leaving. Juliana had expressed her regret over not getting to say goodbye. They both, along with Daisy and Taz, shared a worry about what would become of Anthony's family without him there to make sure they had enough to eat.

They had friends though, Juliana reassured herself. The light at her fingertips dimmed with her worry. She looked northeast, back toward the mountains and Abredea and Tornim. They'd go back, someday. Wouldn't they?

This was all... this was beyond the scope of anything she'd imagined in her life as a Blue-Star. Leaving Abredea, rescuing the other children from Haven, going against the Grey-Stars, all made it feel like seeing her parents again was no longer impossible.

None of them had talked about what would come after they found Dolor. Nacra, they'd barely discussed the frightening reality of what they might face to get the children out. But they couldn't go back to their lives. Juliana knew it logically, and felt it, like a thrumming pressure in her chest. A tug, pulling her somewhere else, away from everything she and her friends had ever known.

She was still dreaming of the mountains. Looking at the map with Jane and the others had revitalized her desire to find them. As she leaned against the rough bark of the tree, letting the wind chill her cheeks, she could picture them in her mind's eye as though she'd grown up at their base.

The thrumming in her chest intensified.

A few yards away, Anthony growled.

Anthony's eyes were shut so tight, he saw stars. His nerves had disappeared for a moment, banished by the feel of Juliana's lips on his.

Now they were back with full force.

Mediating was one thing. He's been doing it his whole life, without knowing what it was called. He hadn't put up the walls—hadn't known to—but walking through the woods, hunting, sitting at the edge of the creek and staring into the water as every thought and worry slipped away in a brief respite, that was pretty close.

Mediating was one thing. Finding the wolf inside and trying to shift into it on purpose, that was another.

He inhaled, relaxing his eyelids, and delved into his own mind. The place he'd created, a clearing ringed by towering trees, brought a sense of comfort. It wasn't an exact replica of the places he'd been in the real world. He'd grown it, borrowed the best things from his favorite spots and made something new. Sunlight—how there was sunlight in his mind he didn't know—streamed down through the opening in the trees. The grass was soft beneath him as he sat cross-legged, mirroring his physical body, and tried to concentrate.

Juliana stirred. Her footsteps moved away, giving him space. He wished she'd gone with the others. The thought of becoming a murderous beast in front of her caused an uncomfortable clench in his gut.

He gave a quick shake of his head. Heat, his own frustration with himself, rose up the back of his neck. The sky above darkened with his thoughts. The idea of losing control, killing again... his stomach rolled with nausea as clouds rolled above.

May's words, some of her last before she died, echoed through his mind.

Sometimes saving the people you love means killing. Those deaths will stay with you. You have to decide if you can live with it.

He had decided, hadn't he? When Steel had burst into the room and shot May. When Anthony had attacked him and dealt a fatal blow to his skull, hadn't that been a choice? Not the savage, mindless attack that had happened in the forest.

Then again, the man he'd killed as a wolf had been armed, had already hurt Juliana, and was moving to hurt the others. The memory stirred Anthony's emotions. A swirling mix of anger, relief, confusion, and fear blew through the forest in his mind like a raging storm.

And there... stepping through the dense trees that made up the wall protecting his mind from others, wind whipping at its fur, eyes glinting and dark...

Anthony swallowed at the size of the beast that had plagued his dreams for the last several nights. The creature would not be caged and, while Anthony knew he should have been trying to contain it during their meditations, he could admit to himself that he was terrified of what might happen if he tried and failed.

It approached him now, in the vast clearing in his mind. The sky, already a stormy grey, crackled with lightning. Its footsteps were silent on the soft grass. Its head tilted to the right as it gazed upon him with wide black eyes—so similar to his own it startled him out of his fright for a moment.

Anthony had seen wolves before. Only twice, when he was young and with his uncle. They'd been distant, barely visible, but significantly smaller.

The dark thing before him, only a few yards away now, was as big as Anthony. Its paws were massive, leaving imprints in the ground as it stalked closer. Stalked? Maybe the wrong word. The wolf was alert, curiosity rather than malice or hunger in its gaze. Still, it seemed to tower over him as it approached.

Anthony shifted and the creature froze. Anthony rose slowly from his seated position until he was crouched on one knee, his head now level with the wolf's.

It remained still after he stopped moving, surveying him. Anthony was suddenly hit with the feeling he'd had many times in his life when May had turned her calculating gaze upon him. More of her final moments came back to him, the pride in her eyes when she'd spoken of his power.

I wish I could have seen you transform. It's a special gift.

He straightened, jaw coming up just a little, and gave the wolf the same crooked smile he'd inherited from his grandmother. Then, fingers trembling slightly as he swallowed down his fear, he reached out.

"I think we're gonna have tah work together," he murmured.

The wolf padded another step forward. It sniffed the air, ears perking up.

Anthony inhaled as well and was hit with the familiar smells he'd come to associate with Juliana. They'd changed on the road; no longer primarily the scents of plain soap and strawberries. Now there were hints of sweat, smoke from their nightly fires, grass where she'd been laying or sitting.

The wolf whined and Anthony's halfcocked grin widened. "If yeh wanna keep her safe, keep all of 'em safe, we're gonna *have* tah work together."

A moment passed as Anthony and the wolf stared into each other's eyes. Something connected during those breaths of time. An understanding. An agreement.

The wolf took another step, lowered its head, and leaned into Anthony's palm.

His physical body reacted. He felt it, even as he kept himself rooted in the clearing. Fur rippled along his arms, his legs, his neck. The temperature of his body changed, warmed. The unnerving, terrifying disjointing of his limbs and cracking of his bones echoed through his mind. The loose shorts he'd changed into ripped apart. Still, he kept his awareness focused as his fingers morphed into claws.

A shudder wracked his body, ending with his tail swishing through the air.

Anthony sucked in a breath through clenched teeth. "Let's give it a try then, aye?"

Before him, the wolf let out a low, rumbling growl.

Anthony opened his eyes in the real world and immediately recoiled. His vision was wrong, different, confusing. He breathed, and the inhale brought enough information to fully distract him from the odd shapes and colors. His ears twitched. Something moved. The fur on his back rose up in a ripple, that same low growl emanating from his throat.

"Hey."

He whirled. Paws gripping the loose dirt and long grass, twisting his long body to find the danger, or the prey.

Anthony hesitated. A nagging pull at the back of his mind brought forth a wince. The shape before him was crisp and clear in his vision and, as he focused, it developed meaning.

A pale hand stretched toward him, palm out, slender fingers steady. Behind the hand, a figure. Tall, strong, intelligent eyes that stared at him, calculating. He recognized her face at the same moment her scent registered.

Lightning blue eyes met his black ones. Her full eyebrows rose. A few seconds passed and then he, like the wolf in his mind, padded forward and pressed the side of his head against her palm.

Her lips split into a wide smile. "You did it."

Anthony recognized the words as not quite a question, but her voice had enough uncertainty still in it that he nuzzled her hand in reassurance.

It was strange, being the wolf. So different this time. It felt natural, as it had before, but now he seemed to have as much control of himself as his power–his wolf–did. Perhaps not as much as he'd have liked, but enough that he was able to channel information into the wild part of his mind.

Still, he wasn't entirely himself, and a flash of worry brought out a whimper as he wondered what might happen if they were faced with a threat while his wolf was still so dominant.

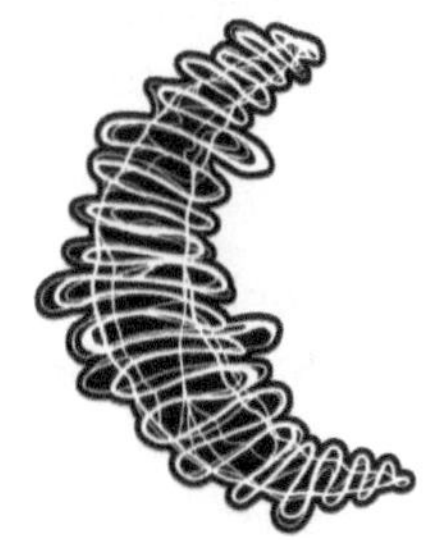

Chapter Eight

Near Mendax

They followed the trail the others had left in the tall grass. Juliana walked, carrying her bag as well as Anthony's. He padded along-side her, still a wolf. They'd spent some time in the trees, waiting to see how Anthony's wolf would react to working together. It was going well—at least, Juliana assumed it was because Anthony hadn't attacked her, tried to run off, or turned back into himself. There had been a rather hilarious moment when a rabbit had hopped by a few dozen yards away and Anthony had frozen, his long nose sniffing toward the prey. Then Juliana had snorted, and the sound seemed to snap him away from a potential hunt.

Juliana's fingers drifted absently through the fur at the scruff of his neck. The coarse black hairs weren't exactly soft, but he was so warm. And massive this close up.

Juliana's schooling in Tornim hadn't focused on wild animals, but she'd learned plenty in her primary years. She knew what wolves looked like, as well as the large sand-colored cats that prowled the rolling hills near the larger mountain ranges. She knew how big these predators were supposed to be.

It made sense for Anthony's wolf form to be on the larger side. He wasn't a small man. His density didn't look to have changed. Instead, he was a 170-pound beast whose head came up to the middle of her torso.

She grinned as they left the cluster of beautiful trees and made their way down a steep slope towards an outcropping of large boulders. She hoped they'd return to Abredea before Jimmy got too big; she wanted to see him shrieking with laughter while on Anthony's back as they raced through the grass.

A thin column of smoke rose up between the tall grey stones below them. Daisy and the others had likely stopped for lunch, waiting for her and Anthony to arrive before they continued for the day. If all went according to plan, they'd arrive at the outskirts of Mendax that night, finalize the plan, and hopefully have a vehicle by the next morning.

The Haven children were losing patience with getting to Dolor, Jane especially.

"Close now," Juliana said, glancing down at Anthony's wolf form. "Do you want to change back here, get some pants on before we meet up with them?"

She barely contained her smile at this. Her cheeks had been hot enough when Anthony had removed his shirt before settling down to meditate, and they were flushing once again.

He let out a throaty growl, and she chuckled.

The growl shifted and Juliana took half a step back. Anthony looked at her, his black eyes alert and wide. His head cocked, ears twitching to catch a sound behind them.

Juliana's brow furrowed, unease growing in her gut. "What is it?"

He jerked his head back the way they'd come with a whine, then turned his gaze toward their friends. His hackles rose, another growl escaping through his powerful jaws.

Juliana shifted the bags and broke into a run. Anthony couldn't speak, but the fear in his eyes told her enough.

Something was coming.

She'd made it a few feet when the wolf sprinted past, aiming for the rocky outcropping.

Sound hit not ten seconds later. A steady whump, whump, whump that reminded Juliana of the helos that occasionally flew over the Black- and Grey-Star districts in Tornim.

She was too far. Anxiety clutched tight to her chest. She shouted anyway, in a high, desperate pitch.

"Daisy, hide!"

The words echoed through the rocky structures, and Juliana heard a response just as she swung around a boulder several times her height and nearly ran into her friend.

"Juliana, what—" Daisy jerked back as Juliana skidded to a stop just in front of her.

Juliana panted, one hand on her knees, the other gesturing to the sky. Before her, the children had risen from their lunch in a panic. Anthony was still a wolf, using his back legs to kick dirt over the fire. The smell of cooking meat hung in the air, the smoke still rising in a small twist of grey, giving away their location.

Not that it mattered anymore.

Juliana dropped her bags, eyes wide as the helo crested the hill she and Anthony had just run down.

One of the twins screamed. Jane grabbed Tommy and raced into the rocks. Claire was close behind her.

"What do we do?" Daisy looked from Juliana to Cho, panic sharpening her voice.

Cho had gone pale, fear etched in the worry lines on his forehead.

Juliana glanced around. They had seconds before the helo arrived. Time seemed to slow.

Anthony had given up on the fire and stood in front of Taz, growling as he stared up at the approaching threat. Luna and Nova were frozen, staring up at the helo in horror.

The whump, whump, whump of the top propeller muffled all other sounds. The wind whipped at them as the helo roared overhead.

It was a small thing. Not designed to transport many. Part of Juliana hoped it would continue on; maybe the Black-Stars on board didn't see the smoke, somehow missed the group of people they flew over, or maybe they had a Grey-Star headed to an important meeting.

The hope was foolish, but that didn't stop it existing. Juliana's heart sank as the helo listed, angled around, and came back toward them.

"Jules." Daisy sucked in a breath. Beside her Cho stood frozen, his body trembling as a tear rolled down his cheek.

Juliana's hands clenched into fists. "Jason," she snapped.

The flame thrower looked at her, fire already hovering above each palm.

Juliana's lip curled as the helo bore down on them. "Take it down."

Jason brought his hands together, the flames becoming one and growing larger than his head. He planted his back foot, pulled back for a split second, then lunged forward and unleashed a torrent of fire.

"Everybody get down," Juliana screeched. She grabbed Daisy, pulling her to the ground and shielding them both with her body.

Fire hit metal with a shuddering, blasting shriek. Juliana looked away, leaning her face into Daisy's tangled braid as sparks, shrapnel, and smoke rained down on them.

The helo fell. It howled through the air and hit the ground near enough that the impact reverberated through Juliana's body. She held tight to Daisy, waiting for the last of the slow whump, whump, whumps to cease.

Anthony was in a full sprint before the thing stopped rolling. The scent of scorched metal and smoke stung his over-sensitive nostrils, but he—and the wolf within—knew it wasn't over.

The crackle of flames engulfed his ears. Wreckage lay before him. His instincts said to run away, get back from the fire. His fur offered no outlet for the discomfort. He flinched back as someone opened the door to the interior section of the craft, and a wave of heat burst forth.

A body stumbled out, wearing the uniform both Anthony and his power recognized as a Black-Star on duty. High ranking with a full helmet, heavy plasma gun, and reinforced but light armor.

The Black-Star stumbled a few feet towards Anthony and ripped the helmet from his head. Coughs wracked his body. He didn't seem to have registered the enormous black wolf standing a few yards from him.

A hand went to his belt, closed around a device, and brought it to his lips.

Anthony tensed.

"Captain," the Black-Star choked out before another round of hacking coughs. He was barely past the billowing clouds of black now gushing from the ruined metal. "We found her, coordinates, 38.99 by—"

Anthony leapt. His eyes burned as he passed through a column of smoke, but his aim was true. The device fell. The man let out a pained grunt as the wolf's powerful front legs slammed into his chest.

He went down hard, surprise and fear etched on his face.

Permanently etched.

The hunter's instincts faded into the background as Anthony realized the man wasn't moving. The wolf's head cocked to the side. Anthony took a step back, his paws leaving the Black-Star armor and settling onto the hot ground.

The wet ground.

It took a moment of examination. The wolf clamored still, raging against this threat that had tried to hurt them. Anthony kept it clamped down, searching the body with his sharpened vision.

"Landed on shrapnel," a voice said behind him.

Anthony whirled, hackles rising until he recognized the tattoo on Jason's forearm. His gaze flicked up to the man's face. Jason's eyes were on the Black-Star.

"There." He pointed.

Anthony, still baring his fangs, looked at the body again. Protruding from the Black-Star's chest was a sharp scrap of metal. Blood coated it, darkening the metal and making it difficult to see against the black uniform.

Anthony backed away, horror once again overriding his power.

"Hey." Jason's deep voice, clear and commanding, caught Anthony's attention. "Let's get back to the others."

Anthony glanced at the dead man. Worry that another may have gotten away flashed through his mind. He jerked his shaggy head at the body before looking again at Jason.

"There was another, round the other side. The crash killed him. Doesn't look like they had more than two in this thing."

Anthony bobbed his head in a nod, and the two backed away from the still smoking wreckage.

Cho broke from his crippling fear a few seconds before the helo slammed into the ground. Metal shattered, sparks flew, and the twins—a few yards closer to the wreckage—screamed.

He darted toward them, worry flooding him.

Jane had scurried into the rocks with Tommy and Claire. Juliana rose from the ground a few yards away, Daisy stirring beneath her. Anthony—in the form of a black wolf—had sprinted toward the burning helo with Jason on his tail. But Luna and Nova...

He reached them just as Luna fell. Her pale pink dress blossomed with dark splotches.

Nova caught her sister, crumpling under her weight, and the two of them hit the ground hard. Cho knelt, simultaneously shoring up his mental defenses and shoving his worry to the back of his mind. His power licked at the walls. It strained against his wards, but they held strong.

"Luna," Cho murmured, his voice strained. Multiple splotches of red grew across her front. He put a hand behind her head.

Taz skidded to a stop beside the girls, his eyes wide. "Wha' can I do?"

Nova shook with barely controlled sobs, her arms wrapped around her sister's shoulders.

"Juliana," Cho shouted; panic laced his voice. The blood wasn't stopping. Color drained from Luna's face. He turned, ready to shout again, but Juliana was there.

Her knees hit the ground, her face nearly as pale as Luna's as she took in the girl's wounds.

"Nacra," she muttered, her voice tight. "Taz, May's vials. Ones for blood loss. Quick."

The boy jerked away, rushing to the bags and digging through them frantically.

Juliana sucked in a breath and blew it out through pursed lips. Blue light emanated from her hands, tendrils of mist-like power swirling around her fingertips as she hovered her palms over Luna's torso. "Hold her still."

Nova's hands tightened around Luna's shoulders, and Cho rested her head on Nova's lap so he could hold down her legs.

"Hurry," Nova moaned, fear carving lines into her young face.

"Shh," Juliana snapped. Her eyes were squeezed closed, mouth twisted in concentration.

Cho kept a tight grip on his emotions. Nova's walls were down again, and his power clawed at the edges of his mind, trying to consume her fear. But then the fear shifted, diminished slightly.

Before them, Juliana's blue light drifted down. It soaked through the stained cloth, the mix of blood and light giving Luna's dress a dark purple hue for a brief moment. Juliana rose up onto her knees, hands shaking as her power grew brighter, stronger.

Luna's body jerked. She thrashed and flailed, still unconscious. Cho struggled with her legs for a few short seconds before a second pair of hands pressed down as well.

Jane had rejoined them. Her pinched gaze met his, regret flashing across her face before she pulled up her usual mask of scorn. Between the two of them and Nova, Luna's movements eased.

Taz rushed back to them. He squeezed in beside Jane and unstopped a vial of liquid the color of watered-down coffee.

"One or t... t..." Taz didn't look at Juliana as he spoke. He and Nova tilted Luna's head back, and Nova gently opened Luna's mouth.

Juliana didn't answer. Her eyes were still closed, breaths coming heavy. Sweat beaded across her forehead and upper lip.

"Two," Cho answered. He caught Taz's uncertain gaze and gave a steady nod.

Taz and Nova handled giving Luna the medicine, and Cho's attention returned to Juliana. Her arms shook as she held them over Luna's slim frame. She growled, frustration rolling off her in waves.

A shock of electricity roiled through Luna's limbs, sending a tingling through Cho's hands.

Juliana opened her eyes. Cho nearly lost his grip. Her blue eyes glowed with electric white light.

Fragments of metal rose through the rips in Luna's dress. They dripped with blood and only hovered in the air for a split second before clattering down onto Luna's torso. A few fell to the ground. The grass around her, dry and golden, shriveled and browned.

Shining motes of light marked the places Luna had been struck. Juliana grunted again, sounding pained this time as the blue tendrils continued to flow from her fingers. Her skin paled even more, and she swayed on her knees.

Luna gasped. Her eyes flew open, and it was only Cho, Jane, and Nova holding her down that stopped her from jerking upright. Cho put a hand up, his gaze meeting her wild, fearful one.

"It's all right. Wait."

The girl sucked down terrified breaths, glancing between him and Juliana, whose hands were still above her.

Another few seconds passed in tense silence. Then Juliana's eyes went dark. Her hands dropped to her sides, and she slumped back onto the ground. Daisy, who had been watching from a few feet away with her arms wrapped around Claire and Tommy, hurried forward and cradled her friend.

Cho and Jane released Luna. Cho sat back, breathing heavy as the weight of fear and panic was abruptly lifted from the edges of his mind. Jane returned to her brother's side. Her hand closed around his, relief playing across her face.

Tears streaked down Nova's face. She cradled Luna to her chest, murmuring in her ear. Color had returned to Luna's cheeks, though her skin was still paler than usual. Her dress was a torn mess. The skin beneath was fresh and pink, stained with blood but no longer marred with gashes.

Cho swallowed a lump in the back of his throat. He unclenched his sweaty palms, only then realizing how tight his muscles were. He eased a deep breath in and out before looking at the others.

Juliana's body twitched with random shivers, her skin sickly white, eyes half-closed.

"Daisy," Cho's voice was hesitant, "is she..."

"She'll be all right," Daisy said firmly. The worry in her eyes didn't quite match the tone. "Water?"

He nodded, rising from the blood-soaked grass, and hurried toward his discarded pack.

Taz was already at their things. He fumbled through his bag, worry aging his features. "I've got f... f... foo..." He let out a snarl of frustration and waved away the words. He pulled a bundle of their remaining food and rushed over to Daisy and Juliana.

Cho followed with the water.

Juliana was sitting on her own by the time Jason and Anthony returned. Anthony was bare-chested and bare-footed, wearing a pair of torn pants Cho recognized as Jason's. He'd rolled the cuffs to make up for the difference in their height.

Anthony's eyes widened at the sight of Juliana leaning against one of the boulders, her face still pale as she sipped on the water. Without a glance at the rest of them he rushed to her side. "Jules, are yeh—what happened?" he demanded, turning to look at Daisy and Taz.

Her friends were still beside her, keeping a close eye. Daisy opened her mouth to respond, but Juliana spoke first, her gaze flicking between Jason and Anthony.

"Are we safe?"

Cho's gut clenched at the weakness of her voice, and he looked at Luna. How close had she been to death for Juliana to be so weak? The healer had fixed a handful of injuries since they'd met, but this one had nearly drained her.

Jason nodded. "There were two Black-Stars in the helo. They're both dead."

Juliana's head dipped in a shallow nod. "We can't stay long."

The others circled slowly. Jane and Tommy moved beside Taz, Claire stood beside Daisy, wringing her hands as ice formed and fell from her fingers, and the twins inched a few feet away from the mess of dead grass and bloody mud. Cho stayed close to Juliana, trying to not notice the intensity with which Anthony was looking at her.

"Was it luck?" Cho glanced at Jason, swallowing down the rush of relief he felt at finding no injuries on the man. "Were they flying by, headed the same direction? Or are they after us?"

Jason shook his head, his brow furrowed.

"They're after us."

All eyes turned to Anthony. He was still looking at Juliana, one hand gently rested on the back of her neck, the other on her forearm. She gave him a weak side smile and a nod to continue.

"One was alive when I got there. He was on a com." Anthony's expression darkened. "Jules," there was a hesitancy, a waver in his usually steady voice, "he talked to a captain. Said they found 'her.'"

Juliana's eyes widened a fraction and, though they'd both kept their walls up, Cho felt the fresh wave of anxiety roll past her mental wards and push against his. He winced.

Jason stepped forward. "What do you mean?"

Anthony gritted his teeth, moving his hand from Juliana's neck and interlacing his fingers between hers instead. "When Steel killed May, he asked about Jules. He wanted her for somethin'. For a Grey-Star."

Cho glanced at Jason, suspicion rising in him. A Grey-Star was behind the capture of their family. It seemed like too much of a coincidence for it to be a different person.

"They're looking for you," Jason said. It wasn't an accusation, or a question. It was a statement of fact.

"Sounds like it," Juliana muttered with a grimace. She took a sip of her water and swished it around before swallowing.

Cho exhaled. "We need to move. The sooner we have a vehicle, the better."

The others made sounds of agreement, but Taz piped up.

"Do they know where we are? Tha' thing," he gestured to the still smoldering helo, "will m... mo... will there be others?"

"I heard one givin' coordinates," Anthony said, catching Jason's eye for a moment.

Cho's stomach cramped with worry.

"But I don't know how much information he was able tah get out before..." Anthony pursed his lips. "It sounded like they didn't give their position before Jason hit. Or they wouldn't be givin' it again, would they?"

Juliana nodded, her gaze darting to Cho. "I'm sure that helo had a tracker, but maybe they thought it was damaged in the crash. We should get going. Stick with the plan to get to Mendax."

She wasn't quite asking, but she wasn't giving him an order either. Behind him, Jane uttered an audible grumble.

Cho bit the inside of his lip. He was more than happy to let Juliana take the lead; she'd already proven herself capable of keeping her head. He'd frozen at the sight of the helo. Terror had clasped a fist around his heart and images of the raid on Haven had slammed through his mind.

His hesitation stretched. Jane stepped forward, giving him a sharp glare as she looked down at Juliana.

"I don't think you should be making decisions for the rest of us. If you hadn't told Jason to destroy that thing," she gestured to the helo as well, "Luna wouldn't have gotten hurt."

A low rumble of disapproval rippled through Anthony and—to Cho's surprise—Jason. Across from them, Daisy's soft expression hardened, her eyes narrowed at Jane.

Juliana, however, flashed Jane a knowing grin. With a grunt of effort, she rose from the ground, using the rock behind her and Anthony's hand to steady her movements.

"That might be true." Juliana's chin rose as she straightened and gave Jane her full attention.

Jane jerked her head in a nod, as though Juliana's words had proved her right.

"It's probably not," Juliana continued, her grin settling into a sneer. "Those things aren't just for transport, Jane. They're for scouting and they have weapons. Plasma guns, but larger." She stepped forward, releasing the boulder as she approached Jane. "We're lucky they didn't start shooting the second they saw us. We'll be lucky if there aren't more of them heading here now."

Jane's fierce fixed scowl fractured for a split second. She regained her composure quickly. "We've handled Black-Stars before. They might have landed. Two would have been easy enough."

Juliana shook her head, and seemed to regret it as her knuckles went white around Anthony's hand. "We've been *walking*. Tornim isn't far. It wouldn't take long for them to call reinforcements. You want to try fighting a full squad of armed Black-Stars?"

Jane opened her mouth, a furious retort building in her expression.

A whimpered "no" interrupted whatever she'd be about to say. Tommy hurried to her side, his wide eyes staring up at her as tears spilled down his cheeks.

Jane's fury broke. Her tense shoulders loosened, and she turned from Juliana without a word, ushering her brother toward the bags.

Cho nodded. "Avoiding a fight of any kind will be best. Especially if we want to get to Dolor as quickly as possible."

"We'll have enough of a fight when we get there," Anthony growled.

"Can you move?" Jason directed the question to Juliana, who nodded.

"I can carry Luna," Taz offered.

Nova, her cheeks stained with the salt from her tears, gave him a grateful smile as he went to the twins. Luna refused the offer; the combination of Juliana's healing and the vials Taz had given her seemed to renew her strength. Still, she leaned on Taz as they walked.

"All right then," Cho said with a heavy sigh. "Let's get to Mendax."

The road split not far from their location. It was a crossroads where one branch continued west toward Mendax and eventually the Capital. A sharp cut south led to the main Mavi River bridge, and another meandered southeast, somewhat parallel to the river and passing a few smaller cities along the Pangaea border.

They put more distance between themselves and the road, taking a western path along gentle cliffs. Occasional thumps of helos sounded in the distance, but Anthony heard them with plenty of time to spare. Tommy's invisibility ensured that even when they couldn't find cover, they remained hidden from Black-Star eyes.

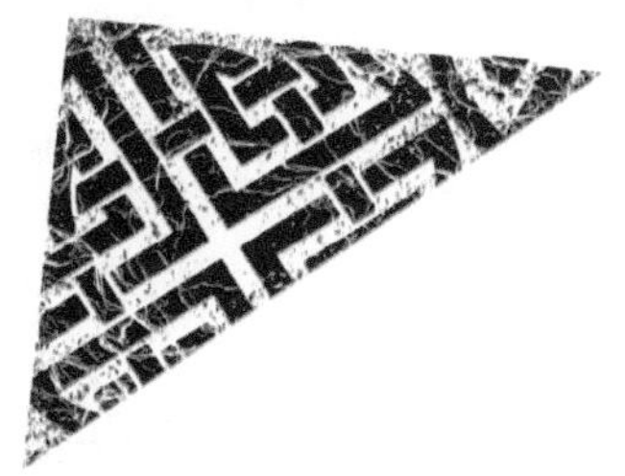

Chapter Nine

Somewhere in Pangaea - 30 Years Ago

The last week had gone by in an insane, headache inducing blur. Brenna rocked a little in the shuttle chair, her heart pounding as nausea rose and fell in waves in her stomach.

The carrier was large, a handful of other men and women around her age sat along the edges. Lift-off had made her bend over, head between her legs, and take shuddering breaths between clenched teeth.

She didn't like flying. That much had been made clear in the past several days.

Leaving the Star Office had been the worst moment of her life, followed by one terrifying experience after another: being shoved into a vehicle, driven away from Tornim, rapid questions and no answers, more vehicles, a helo, strange rooms, and dark gemstones. When she and the others, a dozen twenty-year-olds from across Pangaea who had been grouped in a remote facility, finally got an answer from one of the Black-Stars, it wasn't an answer to any of their desperate questions. It was that they were about to reach their destination.

Her gut lurched. The shuttle was landing.

Theo, a man to her left, glanced over with a half-hopeful, half-nervous smile. He was from Althea, another city the size of Tornim, and had been coded a White-Star a few days before Brenna. That was the one thing each of them, crammed together back here, had in common. They'd all become White-Stars within a few weeks of each other.

Some had been in that holding facility for nearly a month.

Brenna returned Theo's smile, her own mostly nerves. The shuttle hit the ground smoothly enough, but Brenna's knuckles were white as she clenched the straps holding her to the seat.

Two Black-Stars emerged from the cab, stalking down the center aisle without a glance at the White-Stars. A long moment passed as they spoke into comm devices at the far end of the shuttle. Then the door lowered.

Gasps sounded from those closest to the opening. Brenna blinked against the harsh, bright sunlight. When her eyes adjusted, she gasped as well.

The White-Stars followed the Blacks out of the shuttle and down a sloping sidewalk until it turned to blue-grey gravel.

Brenna had seen her share of beautiful places. Her family liked to visit Mendax during the warmer months, and the Blue-Star district in Tormin had recently undergone a redesign. They'd widened the streets and re-planted many of the parks.

This was different; the tension in her fellow White-Stars diminished as they walked. Green grass spread on either side of them as far as the eye could see. Clusters of tall, shade-giving trees dotted the landscape of gently rolling hills.

Ahead of them was a short, gently-swirled iron fence. The gravel path continued through a gate and led up to a structure out of an old story book. Brick—not often used these days—towered at least five stories. Wide windows were thrown open, letting in the fresh, lightly lavender smelling breeze.

Stone steps led up to a massive wooden double-door. A tall woman stood there watching them. Brenna's heartbeat raced as they grew near enough to see the grey gemstones on the woman's temples.

She swallowed hard. The building reminded her of the research school Marissa had applied for, and a painful flash of longing struck her. What would her sister say about all this? She'd probably have gotten answers long before now. She was always better at that kind of thing.

The White-Stars were led to the front of the stone steps and assembled in ordered lines facing the Grey-Star.

Brenna stared up at her in awe. Like a soft drizzle of rain, a new kind of warmth enveloped her. Her rapid pulse slowed, anxiety easing. She wiped sweaty palms on the off-white uniform each of them had been given.

The Grey-Star was tall. She'd twisted her dark brown hair along the sides of her head, bringing it back into a loose bun. Her clothes were crisp and clean, an ivory pantsuit with lavender accents. Her nails matched the pale purple color of her jacket trim.

Low murmurs rippled through the White-Stars, but Brenna was absorbed, her attention locked on the woman as a kind smile curved her thin lips.

"Ladies and gentlemen." The Grey-Star stepped to the edge of the stairs, heels clicking on the stone. "Welcome to Allegi. I know this must be strange, to be coded as White-Stars and not sent to the camps." Her grin widened. "This is because you are not regular White-Stars. You are special. Each of you has a rare genetic signature, something we believe can help Pangaea."

Another rumble of murmurs went through the group, and Brenna hushed the people next to her. A jarring sense of pride rose in her at the Grey-Star's words. Pride and something close to contempt as she imagined her parents' faces upon finding out the results of her Coding. What would they say if they could see her now? If they could hear this woman's words?

The Grey-Star lifted her hands, a subtle call for quiet that brought silence to the front of the building. Only the gentle rustle of leaves in the trees interrupted them now.

"This is all very new," she said. "To you and to us as well. This," she gestured to the wide wooden doors, "is the first facility of its kind. And you, the first participants of this new and exciting study. I trust we will all do our best for Pangaea and our people."

A few of the White-Stars nodded, pride on their faces as well. Brenna took half a step forward, ready to do her part.

"I am Ms. Wolfe." The woman's head inclined in a slight bow. "And I will be leading us down this path to a brighter future. Please, come in."

Brenna's rooms were smaller than she'd expected. Not that she was complaining; they were comfortable and larger than the apartments she and Marissa had been looking at in Tornim. She had a bedroom, bed in the corner, and a neat, wooden desk across from the ornately barred window. The bathroom was large enough for a tub, as deep as the one back home with an array of soaps and lotions along the top shelf.

She caught her reflection in the mirror and couldn't stop the grin from consuming her face. There was a brightness in her eyes, a rosy flush to her cheeks, a purpose behind her straightened shoulders and lifted chin.

The White-Star rooms were together in the east wing of the facility. There were rows of six along each side of the corridor. During a quick, excited conversation they decided the rest of the facility must be research rooms and labs.

"And the others," Theo broke in. "There will be more of us if it's genetic. And Ms. Wolfe and the Black-Stars need their rooms as well."

"What caste did you come from?" Brenna asked. "I wonder if there's some kind of pattern."

"Blue," Theo said. "You?"

"Same." Brenna grinned.

Their excitement at having found a common thread was slightly lessened upon learning that the rest of their group was from a variety of castes. The dozen of them chatted in the hall, and when their curiosity built to a peak, and no one had come to collect them for dinner, they ventured deeper into the facility.

"Are you nervous?" Brenna said, falling back to join Theo walking behind the others. He hadn't latched onto the group as quickly as she had.

He shook his head, his brown corkscrew curls swaying even after he'd stopped. "Not nervous as much as suspicious."

Brenna's eyes widened, and she slowed her pace even more. The other White-Stars let out a string of laughter as they turned a distant corner. The hallways were wide, the hardwood protected by intricately designed carpets. Orbs were affixed to the walls at even intervals, providing light in those areas deeper in the facility with no windows.

"What do you mean? Why?"

Theo matched her speed, putting a caramel-colored hand on her arm. "Why code us as White-Stars? Why not let us remain in our caste while we help the Greys?"

Brenna raised and dropped a shoulder. She hadn't thought of that. Then again, the castes were less important to her than they'd been to most people she'd known. Her sister would have asked the same.

"This facility seems rather secretive," she said. "Perhaps what we're doing here needs to be kept quiet."

Theo pursed his lips and raised an eyebrow. "And that doesn't concern you?"

Brenna chuckled. "All sorts of things are kept secret until they're ready for the general population." She nodded, chewing on a thumbnail. "That's probably it. They don't want our families asking questions so they Coded us as White-Stars. Everyone we know thinks we're in the camps."

Theo gave her an incredulous squint. "How does that not scare you?"

Brenna shrugged and gestured around them. "I'd rather be here than at the camp. Wouldn't you?"

He uttered a grunt of agreement. "I'll still feel better when we find out what's going on."

"Me too." She gave his shoulder a comforting pat and led the way as the two of them hurried to catch up with the others.

It didn't take long for the group to run into a set of Black-Stars walking the halls. After what Theo had said, Brenna half expected them to be furious, but they chuckled at the newly coded White-Stars and instead of returning them to their quarters, walked them to the mess hall.

Ms. Wolfe sat at the front of the room, in the center of a long table with a collection of Black and Blue-Stars on either side. Hope surged in Brenna's heart at the sight of multiple castes sitting as equals.

The rest of the room was split into circular and rectangular tables. Benches and wooden chairs surrounded them, giving space for many times the current number of occupants.

"Told you there'll be more of us," Theo muttered out the side of his mouth as they walked in.

"Yay!" Brenna gave him a side-long grin, watching his expression sink into bemusement. "More friends!"

She laughed as he rolled his eyes, and the two of them joined their group at one of the larger tables in the center of the room.

Ms. Wolfe didn't give any sort of speech or announcement before they ate. The food came out, delivered by Black-Stars who laid out massive trays and handed out plates before joining the others at the dais.

"No lower castes so far." Theo pulled a tray of cheesy potatoes close and piled them onto his plate.

Brenna shrugged. "Not necessarily a bad thing. Maybe they don't want to drive further separation."

"Oh no," Theo groaned. He eyed her for a second before jokingly leaning away. "You're not a caste-hater, are you?"

She gaped at him. He leaned back in with a laugh and nudged her shoulder. "I'm joking."

Brenna offered up a weak smile, but his words rang through her ears—in her father's voice. How often had her parents accused her of being a caste-hater? A 'revolutionary' as they scornfully referred to it.

She swallowed, less hungry now even though her plate smelled delicious. A glance across the table, where her sister would have been if they'd been at the dining table back home, sent another pang of longing through her. It was like missing a piece of her.

"Hey." Theo's expression softened, and he lightly touched her forearm. "I really was joking. I didn't mean to—"

Brenna shook her head, her dirty-blonde hair falling across her eyes. She brushed it away. "It's fine. Just something..." She quieted.

Theo watched her for another minute. When the heat of his gaze made her cheeks grow warm, she stabbed a chunk of chicken and turned her focus to the conversation playing around the table. The feeling of his eyes on her left after another moment.

When she glanced at him, he was listening intently to his neighbor's hypotheses about their purpose here.

The rest of the evening passed with no news. Brenna and Theo stayed up later than the rest, talking about their lives as Blue-Stars, and the ones they left behind after the Coding. Though they'd been raised in the same caste, his city sounded so different from hers.

At ten on the dot, the lights in the hallway dimmed to a low yellow glow. Brenna whispered good night, darted across to her room, and closed the door.

Thoughts whirled in her mind. Hope and worry chased each other, making her stomach question the decision to have that second piece of pie. Still, the excitement of the day, after such a stressful week, let her fall into a peaceful slumber only a few minutes after her head hit the fluffy pillow.

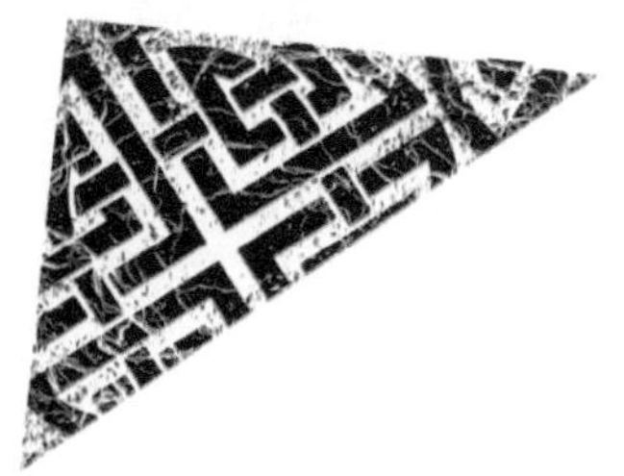

Chapter Ten

Allegi - 30 Years Ago

"Try again," Ms. Wolfe said.

Brenna swallowed, clenched her hands into fists, and concentrated. She was supposed to do *something* to the glass on the table in front of her. What and how were both mysteries at the moment.

A few seconds of intense staring went by before Brenna sighed. "I don't understand what I'm trying to do, Ms. Wolfe."

The familiar feeling of failure heated her blood. This was like every exam she'd taken throughout her life. She'd walked in confidently, prepared to do her part for Pangaea, and now she looked like an idiot.

A flash of annoyance crossed Ms. Wolfe's face before she smoothed her features and crossed to Brenna's side. She rested a hand on the girl's shoulder.

"Let's talk a bit."

Brenna nodded, biting back tears. "I promise I'm trying."

The Grey-Star smiled down at her. "I know. I'm not disappointed with you, Brenna. Much of this is guesswork. It could be that your power doesn't behave the same way as others."

Brenna's gut twisted, the hairs on her arms standing on end. *Power.*

It had been explained over breakfast that morning. An unfortunate decision as the shock had led to many open mouths filled with half-chewed eggs. One of the women in their group had nearly choked.

The real reason they were at this facility. The reason they'd been brought to Allegi: they all had power.

Ms. Wolfe took Brenna's arm and walked the two of them out of the exam room. They strode together down the hallways toward the front door.

"We Grey-Stars have power too, you know." Wolfe murmured, giving Brenna's arm a light squeeze.

Brenna's blue eyes went wide, and she shook her head. "I didn't."

Wolfe nodded. "Indeed. Nothing as impressive as what some of your peers can do, but we are able to calm people, bring them a sense of peace. It's part of what keeps Pangaea such a harmonious place."

"I hadn't noticed... that is," Brenna stammered, trying to find a way to ask if Wolfe had used this power on them.

"No." Wolfe shook her head with a chuckle. "That's part of your genetic signature, Brenna. You and your friends are unaffected by our gifts."

"Oh." Her heart sank a fraction. The idea of being given a sense of calm, even an artificial one, sounded lovely.

The two of them stepped through the wide open doorway and down the stone steps to the gravel path. Rocks crunched under their feet. It was another beautiful day. The chill of winter hadn't yet settled here as it had in Tornim.

They stopped a ways into the gardens.

"Beyond the genetic difference," Wolfe released Brenna's arm and wrung her hands together, a furrow in her brow, "there is a problem among the Grey-Stars. One that..." She sighed, staring up at the branches of a tree above them. Golden and russet leaves fluttered in the breeze. "One that many in the Capital wish to remain a secret. But I think I can trust you, Brenna."

Wolfe faced her, those grey eyes piercing and, somehow, vulnerable. Brenna nodded, her jaw tight as emotion welled within her.

The older woman licked her lips and carried on. "Grey-Stars are facing extinction."

Brenna sucked in a breath, horror sending a chill down her spine.

"Many of our number are infertile. Unable to have children and continue the Grey-Star population. Worse still, each new generation has fewer and fewer who carry our gift."

Brenna's mind worked rapidly. This was much more Marissa's area of expertise. Especially when she finished her years of graduate training. "What can I do?"

Wolfe's worried expression broke into a warm smile. "I had a feeling you'd ask that. Part of why you're all here is to learn more about your genetics, your powers. Another part is to see if there is a connection between these abilities and the gift the Grey-Stars have. If there is, we may be able to extract some piece of the puzzle, some answer to why my kind is losing our power."

Brenna nodded. She chewed at her ring fingernail, thoughts flitting about in an unorganized manner. "I'm sure we'll find it, Ms. Wolfe. We'll find the connection and help the Grey-Stars. Theo has already found his power, and so have a handful of the others. It shouldn't take long for the rest of us."

The relief on Ms. Wolfe's face brought a fresh wave of pride into Brenna's chest.

"Thank you, dear. I know it's a lot to put on your shoulders. But I appreciate everything you've said. And I appreciate your discretion."

"Of course," Brenna said. "This conversation stays between us, but I will do what I can to help."

The others discovered their abilities over the next several weeks. Theo's ability to create orbs of light and manipulate them on currents of air was quickly out done by Dexi's power over shadow and darkness, Tonya's over fire, and Gloria's over plant life.

Allegi grew and thrived. More like them came, one or two every month or so. And still Brenna hadn't found her gift.

She and Theo sat on a bench under one of the massive, now skeletal trees in the gardens. They'd bundled up in sweaters, scarves, hats, and gloves to keep out the winter chill that had settled across the facility. Snow blanketed the world around them. It might have been an uncomfortable thing, but it added to the picturesque beauty of the massive building and surrounding grounds.

"It'll show up," Theo reassured her. "Tonya only figured out her fire thing a couple of days ago. It's slow going, but it'll come."

Brenna couldn't bite at her nails with the thick purple gloves keeping her hands warm, so she chewed at the end of her hair instead. "It's taking too long, Theo. I can't do anything useful. I can't help."

"What are you talking about?" He raised an incredulous eyebrow. "You're at Ms. Wolfe's side almost constantly. Without you helping take notes, guiding people through the experiments, and keeping everyone calm when someone finds something new..." He shook his head. "We'd be a wreck. You were the one who stopped Drolva from flooding half the east corridor last week."

Brenna huffed out a chuckle. It was true; she'd been able to fulfill many of the duties that would normally fall to a Blue-Star. Ms. Wolfe had confided in her only yesterday that she hadn't received the funding she'd asked for to get more Blue-Stars working on the research side of things.

Still... the pit in Brenna's stomach grew deeper with each day that went by without any power presenting itself. How much longer would Ms. Wolfe wait to send her back to Tornim if she proved useless?

"I wasn't sent here to be a Blue-Star," she murmured, pointing to the glistening white gemstone on her temple. "I was sent to do the same as the rest of you, develop my power and help Ms. Wolfe with the research."

Theo's forehead wrinkled. "You're putting so much of this on yourself, Brenna. We are all here to develop our gifts, but it *will* take time. It's all right to—"

But whatever it was all right to do was lost as a scream pierced the air.

Brenna jerked to her feet scanning the grounds for the source. Figures moved in the distance, near the gravel drive. She broke into a run, kicking up the powdery snow and hearing the crunch of Theo's feet behind her.

Another scream, shouts for help. Multiple voices overlapped each other in their frenzy.

Brenna reached the group of White-Stars and blanched at the metallic smell of blood in the air. Drolva lay on the ground, red staining the snow around her. Tonya knelt at her side. A newer White-Star, Logan, rushed toward the stone steps.

"I'm getting help," he shouted back at them, fear thick in his voice.

"What happened?" Brenna demanded gently as she knelt on the crunchy snow.

Behind her, Theo arrived and swore at the sight. Drolva's side was open. Her White-Star uniform had been slit, along with her skin, leaving a massive gushing wound.

"Pressure." Brenna ripped off her gloves and pulled the scarf from around her neck. "She's losing too much blood."

On the ground, Drolva's sunken eyes widened as terror split her features. "Brenna," she gasped.

"Shh," Brenna murmured. "You'll be all right. Hold still."

Tonya met her eye across Drolva's body, tears already glistening on her dark skin. Blood continued to pour. It soaked through the scarf, staining Brenna's shaking fingers.

Theo knelt as well, carefully resting Drolva's head on his bundled scarf to get her off the frigid ground. "What happened?" he asked Tonya.

She shook her head, her voice trembling. "She was practicing with ice. Making blades and cutting through the trees." She gestured to the thick trunk of scarred wood a few yards away. "Logan walked by and deflected a shard. It was an accident." Sobs broke the last sentence.

A vice-like grip tightened around Brenna's heart. Drolva had gone so pale. Her already light skin seemed almost translucent in the bright winter sunlight.

Brenna pulled away the scarf. The wound hadn't changed. The slice was too sharp, too clean.

Time seemed to slow.

The others' voices faded into the background of Brenna's awareness. Warmth blossomed in her chest. So foreign and out of place it struck her with a wash of confusion. She frowned, focused on the heat, and gasped as it spread. A tingling sensation rose to her neck, slid down her shoulders, and eased through her arms to her fingertips.

Before her eyes, a soft blue light emerged from her hands.

"Brenna?" Theo breathed.

She shook her head, barely hearing him, needing to concentrate. As the light drifted in the air, a little globule of soft glowing power, roaring pride surged through her.

Finally.

The light moved of its own accord, drifting down and settling onto the open wound. The bleeding slowed. Brenna frowned, the wound was still there, still gaping. She gritted her teeth and called upon that warmth again.

The heat shuddered within her. It felt weak. It *couldn't* be weak; not after she'd waited so long for it.

Another orb grew from her hands, smaller this time, and floated down. As the light caressed Drolva's skin, the wound itself eased together, skin binding with skin. A moment later, a thick gnarled scab covered what might have been a fatal wound without Brenna's intervention.

She leaned back on her heels gasping for breath. Her vision blurred, and her head swam. Warm hands gripped her shoulders.

"Brenna? Are you all right?" Theo's voice came through a long tunnel, but she heard it and smiled.

She licked her lips, pulling the last dregs of energy to the forefront of her being. A smile curled across her face. She stared at her hands, the faint blue light fading from her skin.

"I'm wonderful," she murmured.

Rising wouldn't happen in that moment, not with how drained she felt. But soon enough she'd stand and go to Ms. Wolfe. She'd sign up for the next round of experiments.

Drolva would live. They'd get her the right medicine to supplement her blood loss, and Brenna would recommend building an outdoor practice arena to avoid problems like this in the future.

For now, she leaned against Theo's solid frame, taking slow deep breaths and basking in the knowledge that Ms. Wolfe had been right.

She was special.

Chapter Eleven

Dolor

Samaira woke to muffled sounds of crying and muttering. She rose, every inch of her body stiff from the beating the day before and the cramped cage she'd slept in. She rolled her shoulders, stretching her neck with a low groan and calling her power to heat the muscles in her back for a few minutes.

Grey light splintered the minuscule patch of sky visible through the window. Sunrise. A new day of torture and experimentation.

She was alone in her cage, but the one beside her held three smaller children from Haven. They were the source of the crying.

"Hey," Samaira murmured, reaching her fingers through the metal grates toward them.

Jacob, the little boy with glowing blue skin, hiccupped, tear streaks glistening on his cheeks. He sat with Kim and Sky, both a little older, both also crying.

Sky had been away from growing things for so long she looked like a plant left in the sun with no water. Shriveled and dry, her lips were peeling, her hands chapped and cracking. Samaira made a mental note to attempt to find something green the next time she ran. She'd seen a few potted plants in the farthest parts of Dolor—near the rooms the Blue-Stars kept.

Kim's tears were silent. The grief on her face matched Samaira's heart. Her dark eyes met Samaira's, and she pointed a shaking finger toward the middle row of cages.

Elaine was just visible in the morning light. She sat facing the window, her gaze distant, rocking back and forth. It was her nearly silent murmuring that had woken the children and caused their tears.

"*Stop, stop, stop, stop.*"

"Hey," Samaira said again, drawing the children's eyes away from Elaine with her low voice. "It'll be all right. You know Ichi and I are working on getting us out. When we're away from here, when we're safe, Elaine will come back to us."

"How do you know?" Kim's voice shook.

Little sparks of near-white electricity danced across her bantu knots. They'd grown disheveled without upkeep. Normally Elaine would block off a few hours during the week to do the younger childrens' hair while Ichi read to them.

Samaira ran a hand over her own short hair. She'd cropped it to match Jason's just before everything had happened. Part of her wished she'd kept it long—if only so her reflection didn't look so much like him.

"What if she's never..." Kim broke off, tears pouring from her eyes.

"She'll come back." Samaira's voice held none of her own fear or uncertainty. "We will get out of here, and she'll be all right. We all will."

Pinpricks of hope returned to the children's eyes, and Samaira forced her lips into a smile.

Movement pulled her attention. Ichi stared at her from a cage a few yards away. His eyes were hooded and dark, miserable beyond anything she'd seen in over a decade of friendship.

He'd managed to steal a sheet of paper after his last experiment. It flew through his fingers as he folded, creased, and created a small crane. His gaze stayed on Samaira, only flicking away when Elaine's murmurs ceased.

She laid down, curled into a ball with her back to them. Beside Samaira, the children had snuggled together, their eyes drifting closed as well.

Terror was exhausting.

Samaira gave it a few moments, watching Ichi until she heard the steady in and out of Kim's breaths.

When she was moderately sure the others were back asleep she flicked her fingers and brought forth a tiny ball of flame.

"What is it?" Her whisper carried to him, but it didn't need to. His presence was at the edges of her mental wards. She cracked them just enough to let him read her thoughts.

What's the matter, Ichi?

"Everything," he breathed. His gaze darted again to his lover, his partner, his best friend, sleeping on the floor of a cage. "I'm sick of this. Sick of lying to everyone."

Stop. Samaira shot the word so loudly through her mind that Ichi flinched. *Don't do that. Not now. You can't give up hope.*

He snorted, his usually kind expression twisted into something dark. "Look at her, Samaira. Look at us. It's been two weeks. We're not—"

Samaira's audible growl interrupted his words. *Don't you dare finish that sentence.* Fury raged through her mind. He had to feel it, had to know how close she was to giving up. If he gave up... if she was truly alone...

Ichi dragged a hand over his face, tears glimmering in his eyes. He glanced again toward Elaine, curled into the corner of the cage with her eyes closed. It seemed sleep was the only time she was at peace.

You're our leader, Ichi. After everything we've been through... Samaira's lips trembled, the fire in her hand growing without her say. She curled her fingers into a fist, snuffing it out. *Don't go down that path. I can't do this alone.*

He didn't respond right away, but when he met her gaze again, the steel was returning to his. They sat for several long moments before he mumbled, "I'm sorry. You're right."

Samaira nodded and tapped a finger to her temple, inviting him to continue reading her thoughts. *Frost right I am. Now, if you're done feeling sorry for yourself, we should get working on the map. I made decent progress yesterday. Got pretty far before they caught me.*

"Lawrence again?"

Samaira nodded. *Yeah, three of his squad.* A wicked smile curled her lips. *I gave Jackson something to think about though.*

Ichi tilted his head with a raised eyebrow.

She brought forth the memory of Jackson's face, burned to a crisp.

Ichi winced, then chuckled. "All right, show me what you saw."

Samaira did so, showing him her route from the day before as she talked over what they'd found so far.

Dolor is definitely circular. And we were right, the whole thing shares one roof, like they built a dome over everything. Even if we got out of this building, we'd have to pass all the experimentation rooms and the living quarters and Wolfe's office. From what I can tell, we are about as far away from the front door as we can be. Unless we find a door to the outside on this end, it's going to be nacra difficult to get out of here.

"We'll find a way. At least we know this room is against the outer wall."

Samaira nodded. The small window in the corner had brightened from grey to gold.

The children stirred. A set of Black-Stars brought in breakfast—a pitiful helping of mushy grains and small cups of water. Samaira met Ichi's eye as the Black-Stars strode past her without leaving any food.

Her friend's renewed spirit invigorated her desire for escape. She'd be one of the first pulled for experiments, and she'd get further today. The Black-Stars were wary, but slow and unwilling to fire plasma bolts in the facility. All she needed was a second to get past them. All she needed was to find an exit.

All she needed was to get them out of Dolor.

They took Jacob first, pulling his little blue fingers from where he grasped the edges of the cage in terror. Samaira didn't look away. Her enraged gaze met every Black-Star who dared to look at her, silently promising more pain than they could imagine.

More children came and went during the morning. Sky actually returned looking better than when they'd taken her.

"They let me grow some flowers," she murmured, guilt flashing across her face as she looked at Elaine.

"Good." Ichi nodded. "We can't let them teach us to fear our gifts. If you have a chance to grow things, do it. Do what keeps you safe."

Heat roared in Samaira's chest, but she bit her lip to keep quiet. His words weren't for her, they were for the small ones. When Sky looked her way, Samaira met her wide, concerned expression with a tight smile.

She'd expected to be taken earlier in the day, but it wasn't until the usual break for lunch that Lawrence stalked down the line of cages and wrenched hers open.

"How's Jackson?" Samaira said with a sneer. "Grow his eyebrows back yet?"

The Black-Star captain pursed his lips and surprised her with an exasperated look. He surprised her further with his response. "Not yet, but he's already started peeling."

He gave a light shove to the middle of her back, but not before she caught the corner of his lip twitch.

She stumbled forward, out the door, and into a waiting cluster of the usual Black-Star guards. A woman had replaced Jackson. Her red hair was up in a high ponytail, tanned skin covered in freckles. Samaira wondered for a moment if she'd get the chance to burn off that pretty hair.

The thought was chased away by focus as they bound her hands, turned, and marched her down the hallway.

Lawrence kept a grip on her upper arm this time. That, combined with the tightness of the ropes and the Black-Stars surrounding her, deterred her plan to make a break for where she suspected the front door might be. Instead, she gritted her teeth and tried to catch a glimpse into any rooms she hadn't already explored.

They made a left and reached the first row of exam rooms. Samaira moved to return to the room she'd been in the prior evening, but Lawrence squeezed her arm painfully and steered her straight.

Her gut clenched as they passed the last exam room of the section.

"No experiments today?" she growled, not willing to let them hear her trepidation.

"Not yet," Lawrence replied, his deep voice steady.

Her pulse quickened. "Where are we going?"

The Black-Stars around her chuckled. A familiar flash of fear cut through her, and she twisted harder against her bonds. It was pointless; the thick black bands had been tightened enough to numb the tips of her fingers.

They walked for several minutes. Tension heightened, like electricity in the air, as they went past the farthest point Samaira had reached during one of her half-assed escape attempts.

She shunted the fear in her gut to the side as she tried to take in every detail. They rounded a sharp turn, and Samaira hesitated. Natural light poured in from a window running along the ceiling. She stared at the roof. It curved, the window reaching down until it disappeared behind a wall.

She'd been right about the dome-like structure, and she'd almost reached the front of the complex.

Lawrence's grip on her arm had loosened during the walk. Samaira didn't know why they'd brought her here, but she'd make the most of it.

She feigned a fall, slipping from Lawrence's hand. The woman to her side reached out. Samaira came up fast, her elbow cracking hard into the Black-Star's face. Blood speckled the ground. Samaira was already on the move, darting between the injured woman and the man who had been leading the way.

She ran, bare feet slapping against the tile floor. She made for the window. The front of the complex. If she could get outside, get a look at the area, their chances of surviving an escape would be much higher.

Samaira rounded a corner and skidded to a stop.

Light flooded her eyes; green shone from the other side of the massive glass doors and windows. A field of grass, trees, sunlight glinting off the top of a pond caught her gaze, for the briefest of moments.

Six Black-Stars stood in the vast lobby-like space. Caleb, his friends, even a couple of people she didn't recognize, blocked the doors and the hall across the way.

Samaira spun around and came face to face with Lawrence and the guards who had marched her this far.

"What is this?" Samaira demanded through clenched teeth. Her gaze darted away, searching for something to cut her bonds before the inevitable happened.

Lawrence raised and dropped a broad shoulder. "They've grown tired of your trouble making. They're going to teach you a lesson in acceptance."

Samaira's expression twisted into a furious sneer. "Acceptance?"

"Accepting your place here." Colby took a step forward.

Samaira spat on the clean tile floor at his feet.

Anger glinted in Colby's dark eyes, and Lawrence moved between them, putting a hand on the other man's chest to stop him from taking another step.

"Remember what we talked about. Don't take it too far."

Colby snarled at Lawrence. "We won't kill her. That's all I can promise."

Samaira took half a step back as Lawrence nodded, and bumped into the woman whose nose she'd probably broken. A move she was beginning to regret.

The captain turned and strode past Samaira, back down the hallway.

"You're really going to leave me here with them?" Samaira couldn't help the tremor in her voice this time.

Lawrence stopped and turned to meet her gaze. "You've been asking for this since day one." He turned to Colby. "Stick to the blind spots, and get her to the infirmary before my shift in surveillance is over." He glanced at a glinting black orb on the far wall, then back to Samaira. Lawrence met her gaze, cocked his head, then turned and walked away.

Samaira's chest rose and fell in heavy breaths. Her mouth had gone dry, fear threatening to overtake her mind. She shoved it away.

Colby and the other Black-Stars advanced. The woman behind her gave a push, and Samaira was forced to stumble forward. The guards before her flexed, clenching their fists and sporting snide, malicious grins.

Samaira looked down at her hands, the palms pressed together by the bindings, far too tight to let her use her fire.

"*Nacra.*"

Chapter Twelve

Dolor

I t could have been worse, Samaira supposed, as the Blue-Star above her bed smoothed a cool lotion across the left side of her face.

She was bruised and broken; blood crusted down her face from splits in her skin, a gash marred her forearm, and the bone was probably bruised from the blows she'd blocked. Her ribs were cracked, evident from the pain she felt with each breath.

Still, she was alive. Breathing. And in bad enough shape that when Lawrence had seen her, he'd demanded she go to the med clinic and get patched up before they took her to any exam room.

Colby had agreed, chuckled, and said he could use some numbing cream for his knuckles.

She'd passed out as they hoisted her off the floor, coming in and out of consciousness each time she was jostled too much on the walk. She'd seen it all now, the entire outer hallway that circled Dolor. The glass windows from the front had shifted to solid concrete after they'd left the lobby.

Once she was able to walk on her own and they shoved her back in a cage, she'd feed the information to Ichi, and their plans would finally start to come together.

In the meantime, she was able to get a glimpse of the place she'd sent a handful of Black-Stars. The walls were beige, the beds in rows of six against the two longest walls. The place was nearly deserted. A curtain blocked off the farthest bed, where Samaira assumed Jackson was still recovering from his burns.

The nameless Blue-Star turned away as the cream on her face eased the bruising. Vision returned as her swollen eye shrank to its normal size.

Where was this kind of medicine when she was a child, charring her hands with powers she couldn't control? Where was it when her father had gotten sick? When her mother had been hit by that patrol car?

A fury she'd long buried, hidden by all the other reasons for her rage, bubbled to the surface.

"Well, I imagine you'll behave a bit better now?" A grating, smug voice coming from the door broke through her thoughts.

Samaira gritted her teeth and regretted it immediately as the ache in her jaw became a piercing pain. She swallowed, meeting Keith's pale blue eyes, but said nothing.

He strode down the center aisle and stood at the foot of her bed, hands in his coat pockets, chin jutted up with the same cocky expression he'd had when he taunted Ichi. She knew he ran the experiments, was the head of the Blue-Star research team, but she hadn't had direct contact with the man since he'd pried Elaine's gemstone from her temple.

He chuckled. "It shouldn't be so difficult for you to follow the simple instructions we give you. And yet..." He chuckled again with a condescending shake of his head.

Samaira flexed her arms, the pain a pleasant distraction as she pictured burning him slowly, little by little until his skin flaked off into a thousand pieces.

"Excuse me." A familiar mousy voice interrupted her fantasy.

The door to the clinic was pushed open, and Abilene's blonde head poked through.

"Abilene." Keith's face split into a warm smile as he turned to look at her. "Come on in. Did you need something?"

She walked forward with small steps, eyes wide as she took in Samaira on the bed.

Samaira's nostrils flared at the fear in the woman's eyes. What could terrify her so? In this moment, when Samaira's uninjured arm was tied so tight to the rail of the bed she could barely open her fingers? Her face so crusted with blood she felt it flake off each time her lips moved?

Still, the petite blonde crossed to Keith's side with trepidation in her movements. She cleared her throat, glancing between the man and Samaira.

"I, uh, well, this seems silly now." Her uncomfortable chuckle sent another roiling surge of rage through Samaira.

The Blue-Star who worked the med room moved back to Samaira's side with strips of thick gauze and another jar of a different kind of liquid. Her frizzy brown hair was swept back into a scarf, her movements brisk and harsh as she pulled Samaira's arm toward her.

Samaira hadn't been expecting it, her sharp gaze on the two at the end of the bed, and a yelp of pain escaped her before she could stop it.

"What's silly?" Keith asked with a grin, ignoring the sound as though Samaira wasn't there. His eyes were on Abilene.

Samaira lost track of the conversation. The Blue-Star at her side was drenching a cloth in the foul, sterile smelling liquid. Her gut tightened with anticipation. The woman pressed the cloth against the bloody gash on her arm.

Samaira let out her pain in a long, low hiss between clenched teeth. This was a different kind of burn. It was like those moments when Elaine had cleaned her cuts as a child, multiplied a hundred times and combined with the animosity clear in the Blue-Star's eyes.

"I'll take care of that."

The words were distant, and Samaira closed her eyes for a few long seconds in an attempt to get rid of the tunnel vision that had come with the pain.

More conversation. Voices talking, saying things she didn't care to hear. Keith made some objection, his tone whiny, like a petulant child not getting his way.

Samaira lost the thread of it all in her efforts to control her breathing, control the pain, the fear, and the anger. It wasn't until someone touched her again that she opened her eyes with a flinch.

Abilene had taken the place of the frizzy haired Blue-Star, perched on the rolling stool beside Samaira's bed with the cloth in her hand and gauze on the table beside her.

Keith still stood at the end of the bed, his arms crossed over his chest and a sour expression on his face. The other Blue-Star had gone, likely through the swinging door into a set of offices.

"This is beneath you, Abilene." Keith's lip curled. "I brought you here for research, not to play medic."

Abilene's laugh was tight. "I appreciate that. But since I'm not going to be able to study my subject for a few days, I may as well get firsthand knowledge of her healing abilities."

Samaira inhaled through her nose, swallowing the sharp pain in her chest. She exhaled, pushing down the anger those words brought forth.

"Ahh, smart," Keith said. He unfolded his arms and gave a nod. "I'll see you at dinner then?"

Abilene's fingers, pressing the cloth to Samaira's arm, trembled. Her voice did not. "I look forward to it."

He smiled down at her, curled his lip with derision at Samaira, and left.

"What did you say to them this time?" Abilene murmured.

Samaira almost didn't hear it; she was staring at the door where Keith had disappeared, promising herself once again that someday soon she'd burn him beyond recognition.

"What?" The question hurt. Her jaw was still tight and swollen.

"To Colby and the other Black-Stars. Or were you running again?"

Samaira swallowed, blinking away her disbelief and fury. "You think they needed an excuse for this?"

Abilene glanced down the room toward the blocked off bed. "You hurt Jackson."

Samaira's mouth twitched into a sneer. "Not badly enough."

The Blue-Star fell silent. She worked quickly, but again with a tender touch that confused Samaira. The injury on her arm lost its swelling. A spray of foam numbed the cut, easing the pain as Abilene wrapped gauze tightly around her forearm.

"Why then?" she asked.

Samaira looked at her this time, met her pale blue eyes with hooded dark ones. Abilene's delicate hand was still on her arm, resting on the gauze.

"Why what?"

"Why did they do this?" Abilene gestured toward Samaira's face. "What provoked them?"

Samaira's eyes narrowed. "What part of child killers don't you understand? Those nacras don't have any qualms about murdering us..." She let out a hollow chuckle. "This is nothing. A lesson at best and entertainment at worst."

"I didn't..."

Samaira blinked at the tone, the sorrow in Abilene's voice.

"I didn't know about what happened to your family." Her expression twisted, lips pursed, brow furrowed. She opened her mouth, then closed it again and moved on to Samaira's face.

Her soft, warm fingers dotted the scrapes with more foam and taped them closed. Samaira was tempted to say more, but her jaw hurt, and her heart hurt. And, as much as she hated it, the feel of Abilene's care was pleasant.

What had Ichi told Sky? To grow things if she wanted to, even if it was for these nacras? To do what she must to survive.

Samaira wouldn't let the hard shell around her crack—she couldn't if they were to escape. But closing her eyes as Abilene touched the slice on her eyebrow wasn't letting her guard down, it was letting herself heal.

She'd need to be strong for what came next. Lawrence had given her everything she needed by letting them beat her half to death. The only section of Dolor with limited surveillance, the full circle of the complex, and how to get there from a handful of different locations she was already familiar with.

They'd escape soon. Before the Blue-Stars tried what they'd done to Elaine on someone else.

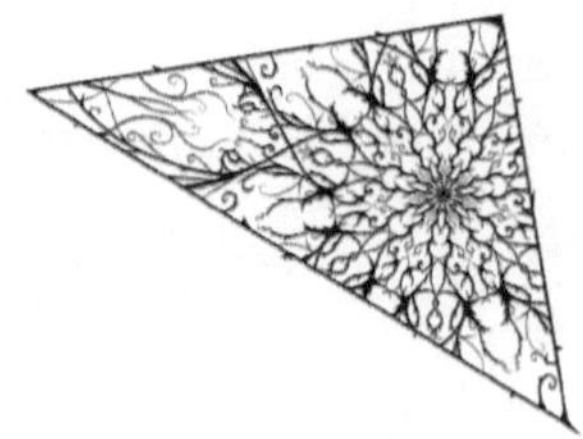

Chapter Thirteen

Dolor

Fury vibrated through Wolfe, her fingers trembling with barely contained rage. Steel stood before her, his tattoos contorted by the fear and anger masking his features as he explained that they'd lost her *again*.

"How is that possible?" Wolfe's nose twitched, a scowl taking her features. Her hold on the *suggestion* she exuded slipped with her heightened emotions. "Your men have equipment, helos, transports. How hard can it be to find a handful of children *on foot?*" She spoke through clenched teeth.

Before her, Steel's beady gaze found the floor, embarrassment building in his ruddy cheeks. "Deepest apologies, ma'am. They are more powerful than we anticipated. We lost two men. The ones who located them..." His lips twisted into a scowl. "They were shot down. By the time our men arrived, the children were gone."

Wolfe closed her eyes and sucked breath into her lungs. Now was not the time for this. She had to leave for the capital in a few days. She needed the girl. Needed *something* to show for her efforts these past months.

Progress with the current test subjects was slow going. She'd hoped a younger batch, the children from the city, would lead to different results.

Keith wasn't working hard enough. None of the Blue-Stars were. They treated this like a job, not a mission. The Black-Stars as well, acting as though their stunted soldier's minds were worth more than the researcher. Putting their egos ahead of their purpose.

All of them, letting caste dictate how much they accomplished.

She didn't have time for it.

"Ma'am?" Steel's voice carried a tremor.

Wolfe's eyes snapped open. She released the paper that had been in her hand when he'd delivered the news. It hit the floor in a crumpled ball. She stepped around her desk and strode the length of the office toward the captain of her personal Black-Stars.

"I leave for the capital in a few days, Steel." She was shorter than the man, but her heels put them at eye level. He wilted under the force of her stare. "We are expected to have results to report. Progress to share. If this facility is to keep its funding, you must do better. Be better. Be who I expected when I brought you into this venture."

He nodded, swallowing hard. "Of course. We know what direction they were headed. My men will find them."

"Find *her*," Wolfe growled. "I care less about the others. Kill them if that's what it takes."

"Yes, ma'am." A glint returned to the captain's eye. An outlet for his sadistic nature was all it took to recharge his enthusiastic efforts to please her.

"Go." Wolfe waved a hand. "Send Keith in, and alert me the moment you locate her."

Steel saluted, turned on his heel, and strode out the door.

"Did you catch all of that?" Wolfe murmured.

In the far corner of her office, standing silent in the shadows of two bookcases, a figure gave a soft "yes" of confirmation.

"I can't bring you this time."

The shadow shifted but remained quiet.

"If we have her by the time I must leave, you can join me. If not…" she shook her head, "I don't want to remind the Chancellor of our failures."

Silence permeated the office. Wolfe crossed to the viewing window on the far wall, looking down at the series of open topped exam rooms below her. The children they'd captured were powerful. Strong.

Not strong enough.

Her fellow council members were like sharks in the water, and the lack of progress she'd had in Dolor was as good as blood. Even Lectius, who'd worked with her to develop their new strategy for weaponizing the Alters, had been distant during their calls. He seemed reluctant to share information.

This meeting had to go well. Which meant she needed something to go right before she left.

A knock sounded on the office door.

"Enter," Wolfe called out, not turning from the window.

"You wanted to see me, Ms. Wolfe?"

Keith's overly confident voice grated on her nerves. The man was smart, but intelligence alone wouldn't get him the grey gemstones he so desperately craved. Nor would it gain him favors with his fellow researchers. Wolfe had heard enough chatter to know what the others thought of him.

He needed something to go right as well.

"How goes the research?"

"Well," he crossed the room slowly, joining her at the observation window, "we've been able to identify most of the subject's abilities, though pinning down the reason or trigger for activating them has eluded us so far."

"Eluded you," she said without looking at him.

"Yes, ma'am. The older ones who might shed some light on the matter have been reluctant to share their experience."

"Do you think that has something to do with what you did to Elaine?" Wolfe turned in time to enjoy seeing the color drain from his already pale face.

His lips parted, but no sound came out.

She held up a hand. "You needn't explain. I'm not angry about what you did; I'm disappointed you learned almost *nothing* from it. And I hear she's too far gone for further experimentation?"

He gave a short nod. "We believe anything further will result in the loss of her life. But we can—"

"No." Wolfe pursed her lips and returned her gaze to the window. "I had things to say to that girl. Questions." Barely contained fury caused her to clench her hands again to stop them from shaking.

"Ma'am?"

"She was..." Wolfe shook her head. "Never mind. Set aside gemstones for a moment and tell me about the serum."

Keith shifted, his arms flexing as he clenched his hands behind his back. "We aren't quite prepared for a trial run yet."

Wolfe's nostrils flared, and she finally turned. Her grey eyes narrowed as she took in Keith. "I want results. Get it ready."

He nodded, his head jerking in a stiff bow as fear flashed through his eyes. "Yes, ma'am." He hesitated then, "Would it be prudent to begin sifting through the camps? We might find more willing subjects among the White-Stars."

Wolfe's eyes narrowed. "We could. It would take months for the suppressant to wane from their systems enough to identify a power. And, as you're well aware," she sneered, "the Alters who present power earlier are significantly stronger than those born in the camps."

Keith swallowed. "Of course, just a thought."

"For future reference," Wolfe said, her voice cold, "I do not enjoy repeating myself. We will continue to take them from the camps as it becomes necessary. Do not let it become necessary."

"Yes, ma'am." Keith nodded.

"I'm sure you have plenty of work to be getting on with."

There was dismissal in her tone. Keith left the room, closing the door behind him.

Wolfe's shoulders sagged. She put a hand to the chill glass, leaning on it as the bravado left her body, replaced with a rush of anxiety. Her forehead pressed against the window, and she closed her eyes.

Footsteps barely broke through the buzzing frustration in her mind. A scarred hand rested tentatively on her shoulder.

The two stood for a long moment. Wolfe breathed in and out, letting the fear and fury wash over her in waves, encompassing her so she might shrug it off when it came time to face the predators circling her.

Chapter Fourteen

Mendax

Anthony kept Juliana's hand in his as they walked the remaining hour or so to the outskirts of Mendax. Her grip was weak, face pale and tread unsteady. More than once he caught her around the waist when she tripped on her own feet.

"That took a lot outta yeh," he murmured into her ear as the others pulled ahead.

Jane and Tommy walked at the front of the group with Taz and the twins right behind them. Luna hadn't exaggerated when she said she didn't need help. Her gait was as strong as her sister's.

Jason kept to the middle. He'd held a ball of flame in his hand for a long while after they left the crash site, his gaze scanning the skies above them.

Daisy had offered to help Juliana, until she'd caught sight of her hand interlaced with Anthony's. Her hazel eyes had met Anthony's and that knowing smile he'd grown so fond of when they were children crossed her lips. She'd taken Juliana's pack and gone to walk with Cho.

Anthony caught her glancing at them from time to time, still smiling as though she'd seen this coming from miles away. He stuck his tongue out at her the last time she'd turned back.

Then Juliana had stumbled again, and his focus returned to her.

"It's all right," she said, her voice as low as his. Her gaze darted to the others, her free hand clenching and unclenching for a few seconds before she shook out her fingers. "She was really hurt. Close to—"

She bit her lower lip and met his eye. "I've been so angry with myself for not going with you, not being there to heal May but now I think if I had..."

"She said as much when I wanted tah get yeh. Said yeh'd kill yerself healin' her."

Juliana nodded. "I don't want it to come close like that again."

"Me neither." He tightened his arm around her waist, the warmth of her body reaching his fingers through her shirt. "Do yeh think it'll change as yeh get stronger? Yeh've already made a lotta progress."

She was silent for a moment, focused on her footsteps. "I think so. That's what May said, right? I'll get stronger as long as I keep working at it, and don't overexert myself."

Anthony nodded. After another few steadying steps Juliana pulled away and took his hand again.

Juliana seethed. The frustration heating her blood was the kind that comes when one knows they are wrong, understands that someone else is right, and is forced to come to terms with the situation entirely too quickly.

She was not helping them get into Mendax. Nor was she helping them get out. She was doing nothing while Cho, Daisy, Taz, and Jane went in. She was doing nothing while Anthony prowled the perimeter of the half-mile wide man-made lake. She was doing nothing while Nova, Claire, and Jason waited at the exit point to make sure their friends got out.

Juliana glanced at Tommy and Luna, both nearly as furious as she was. Tommy's cheeks were stained with salty tear tracks. Jane had been firm with him, pulling him aside and speaking in harsh whispers. Luna, too, had fought her sister, though less quietly.

Juliana's pride hurt. That was maybe the most frustrating thing. She'd taken something of a leadership role in the group and had expected that to mean people would listen to her. But the moment she'd wanted to go into Mendax with the others she'd been shut down. Not even Daisy had been on her side. Her own petulance was pissing her off more than any of the valid points her friends had made.

She sank against the tree trunk behind her, still a bit dizzy from the long trek to the lake.

Another pang of annoyance bounded through her at the weariness in her bones. Of course, they'd all been right. But that didn't stop her from being mad about it.

Still, watching the sun set on Mendax wasn't an unpleasant sight.

She and the others sat on a cliff a little way from the lake, a smattering of gold-leafed trees keeping them hidden. To the north a trio of buildings hugged the shore. Tall, soft colors, wide windows, with glowing signs on each of the four sides claiming which caste was welcome. Blue, Black, and Grey all vacationed here: families, couples, individuals looking to shed the weight of the real world for a little while.

Behind the main towers, a collection of smaller buildings provided housing for the lower castes who worked at Mendax in weekly shifts. A parking garage, kitchen, mess hall, and a multitude of other small buildings hosting the necessary essentials to support the resort, sat far enough away to be inconspicuous and not intrude on the upper castes' peace.

Little eateries and shops surrounded the three towers at street level. Places for Blues, Blacks, and Greys to spend their money and time when they grew tired of the carefully designed nature elements.

Across the lake from Juliana, the Mendax forest glistened in the evening light. Reds, golds, and purples bounced off the specifically designed trees. Orbs began to glow along the meandering trails as night approached.

She swallowed as a few people moved in the trees. She hoped Anthony would stay out of sight. She'd walked those trails. Gaped at the animals, the rainbow-colored birds, the trees she'd once considered towering.

The idea of it now sent a roll of disgust through her. It was unreal, contrived. A pale attempt at the natural beauty she'd only discovered a few months ago and had fallen entirely in love with.

She missed the stream and the clearing in the woods outside Abredea. She missed reading to Jimmy. She missed Naya's stern voice telling the children to stay out of the fountain and May cackling when they refused to listen.

It was odd.

There were a hundred things she was glad to be rid of. Daisy's father, the guards, the children who picked on Taz whenever they thought he was alone, the hunger, the fear...

Not that the fear was gone. It had shifted, that was all.

"There they go." Luna's voice was tight. Pine needles and fallen leaves crunched under her feet as she moved beside Juliana.

The two focused on the miniature city below them. Shadows moved along the edges of the lower caste dorm-style buildings.

"It should be simple," Juliana breathed. "As long as they stay out of sight, and Taz remembers what I taught him."

Luna cast her a side-eyed look. This had been the biggest concern with leaving Juliana behind. She was the only one with practice driving a vehicle. Taz had helped with the food truck they'd stolen, and she'd walked him through each step before they'd made their way down the cliff. But tension gripped Juliana as the shadows disappeared from sight.

A few minutes passed before the anxiety in Juliana broke down her reasoning. She pushed to her feet. "I'm going to check the road."

"You said people don't usually come in this late." Luna stood as well, more stable on her feet than Juliana was at the moment.

"I can't sit here doing nothing," Juliana snapped. She bit her lip and flashed an apologetic grimace at the girl.

Luna heaved a sigh. She nodded. Without a word she returned to Tommy, took his arm, and the two of them followed Juliana through the trees and down the side of the raised cliff that overlooked Mendax.

It didn't take long to reach a spot where they could see the main entrance. Mendax, like Tornim, had one road leading in and out that connected it to the main thoroughfare cutting across this region of Pangaea.

Without speaking it aloud, Juliana knew they all hoped the Black-Stars would continue their search south and skip the route leading to Mendax. What purpose could their group have in visiting a populated vacation site?

But the road was still a danger. Nova, Jason, and Claire would be at the gate, ready to open it, or keep it open, if the people running things shut it for some reason. Mendax wasn't like Tornim—everything was open for the most part. Juliana had visited more than once with her family and had yet to see the gates for the road closed.

Night continued to fall, blanketing them in darkness. Little lights glowed from within the heart of Mendax, and the three towers glistened with the caste colors. As the evening grew late, sounds of laughter and shouts echoed off the buildings.

The road below was hidden in the black, blending with the tall waving grass and rolling hills. Luna glanced at Juliana more than once, but Juliana kept her eyes on the expanse before them. This wasn't hurting anything, and it made her feel useful.

Cho stood rigid against the grey concrete brick pillar behind him, breathing deep and nearly choking on the thick air in the parking garage. They'd made it in and gotten past the handfuls of lower castes in Mendax buzzing around like bees tending to their queens, fulfilling their superiors' orders.

He'd struggled against the churning disgust pressing against him as they passed a group of teenagers barely older than Jane, berating an Orange-Star woman about the color of the flowers she'd put in their room. They were the only upper caste people in the worker's area, and Cho wondered if they'd come all the way just to harass the poor woman.

Taz and Daisy held their mental wards well as they moved by, though he'd felt the stirring of discomfort and pity. Jane had been the one to surprise him with her burst of anger. She'd caught his eye, grimaced, and strengthened her mind, but not quickly enough for him to miss the bitter pain she pushed down.

"We can't do anything," he whispered to her as they snuck glances into the garage. "If anyone sees us—"

"I know." She cast her usual dismissive glare at him. "I didn't do anything, did I?"

The anger in her tone wasn't for him. He knew it and let the blades in her voice bounce off. Daisy and Taz exchanged a look before Taz spoke, his nervous fingers twisting together.

"I... I... I didn't like seeing that ei... either." He reached out and Daisy took his hand, giving a gentle squeeze barely visible in the dark. "Reminded me of the guards in Abredea."

Weight settled on Cho's chest. The four from the camp had shared a little about what life was like outside of Tornim. Haven hadn't been easy, but even in Agora none of them had been treated like less than the other lower castes going about their day.

He clenched his jaw. "None of us like it but—"

"We know." Daisy cut him off, reaching up with her free hand before stopping a few inches from his shoulder. She gave a little shake of her head and dropped her arm. Her voice carried a softness that went beyond tone. "Maybe someday things will change, but we have priorities right now. Getting to your family and getting them out."

Cho nodded, grateful for the words and the offer of comfort.

To his surprise, Jane nodded as well, her body tense but expression determined. "Right." She turned from their little hiding space behind the pillar and glanced out at the rows of vehicles sheltered in the dark garage. "Let's get this done."

They slunk forward.

If only it could be as simple as the story Taz kept telling them about hijacking a food transport. Juliana had filled them in on the most important differences. It was one of her arguments for joining them—someone was going to need to drive.

"There," Taz hissed. He pointed a narrow finger at a small office against the far end of the open-air building. Pale yellow light shone through the petite office window. A figure shifted within, casting a shadow on the concrete beyond the office. "Jules said the keys'd be there, right?"

"Yeah," Daisy murmured back. "How do we pick the transport?"

Cho squinted at the collection of colorful small cars around them. Most were similar to the ones he'd grown up seeing higher castes driving. His heart sank, nerves pounding as the seconds ticked by. Each moment here was a moment they might be caught.

"Cho."

He glanced at Jane. She pointed into the shadows along the farthest wall.

He followed her, trying to step as quietly as possible in this echo chamber. A row of trucks sat along the wall. They were massive things in an assortment of styles; some had canvas covering the backs, others were solid the whole way across with slits for windows where Black-Star troops rode.

"How did you see this?"

Jane pointed again, toward the ceiling this time. Above them, stamped into the pillars rowing off the section, was the symbol for the Black-Star caste. A shield, or helm, he'd never been sure. Black and ominous, it clearly marked the space where Black-Stars were meant to store their rides.

"Wha... wha... what is it?" Taz whispered.

Jane raised an eyebrow at him. "That's the symbol for Black-Stars."

He cocked his head, confusion in his gaze.

Jane sighed, gritting her teeth. "How about we fill you in on the artwork later?"

Cho tensed, but Taz huffed out a silent chuckle.

"Right, job tah do."

"Which one?" Daisy took a few steps down the line, eyeing the various styles.

Cho followed her until they reached a medium sized truck. The cab was smaller than the others but looked as though it would still hold everyone. "It might be a tight fit after Dolor, but this one looks good."

Taz nodded. "Keys then?"

Jane hurried forward, locating the identification tag on the windshield that Juliana had told them about.

Taz stayed with the truck. The other three went to retrieve the key.

"I'll need a distraction," Jane muttered. "If someone's in there I need them looking away while I go in and find the key."

Daisy nodded. "I might be able to help with that."

A smile twitched at the corners of Cho's mouth. "What do you have in mind?"

She flashed him her full grin. "I've been practicing, you both just have to make sure your wards are up strong."

Jane gave an incredulous squint.

They reached the windowed wall and crouched against it. The figure was still moving inside the office.

"I can get in this way," Jane said, pointing to the solid concrete behind them. "Won't be able to see until I get in there, but that won't be a problem. Looks like a couple steps forward and then I go left till I come out."

"About that distraction?" Cho looked at Daisy.

"Right." She sucked in a deep breath. "Stay here."

Cho opened his mouth, to ask more questions or object, he wasn't sure, but Daisy was already slipping along the wall. She ducked out of sight, just below the window, and pressed a hand against the wall.

Cho sucked in a breath at the same moment she did, slamming effort into his mental defenses. A split second later, a wave of emotion hit him.

Terror.

Pure, unfiltered fear that he was able to recognize and shunt back rather than let engulf him. Jane gasped. He shot her a worried glance, but she only curled her lip and growled, clenching her hand at her side as her shoulders shook.

There was a yelp. The shadow in the window grew close and then the door burst open. The person didn't stop long enough for Cho to make out their appearance. They darted into the darkness, sprinting toward the garage exit as sobs echoed through the building.

Daisy returned to Cho's side as Jane disappeared through the wall.

"That was..." Cho began, lost for words as the lapping waves of fear slowly subsided.

"Thanks." Daisy's voice cracked. She brushed a hand across her cheek, and Cho realized with a clench in his gut that she was crying.

"Hey, are you... what's wrong?"

She swallowed, palming away a fresh set of tears seeping from her hazel eyes. "I don't know how to do it without feeling it yet." She straightened. "How long do you think we have before they come back?"

Cho shrugged and stood as well. "No idea. But we should get out of here as quickly as possible."

"Agreed."

They both turned as Jane melted back through the wall, a set of keys dangling from her middle finger and a victorious grin splitting her lips.

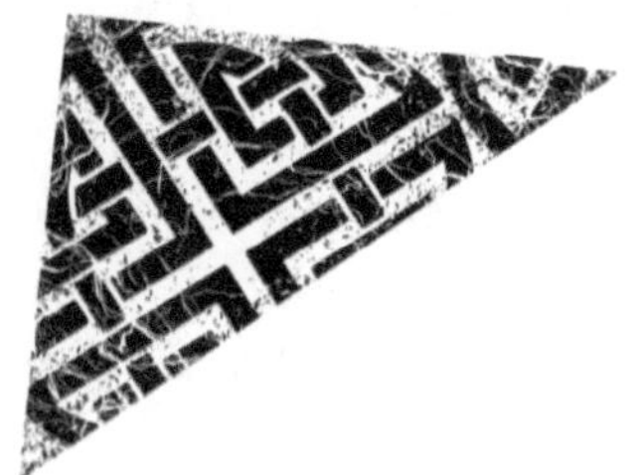

Chapter Fifteen

Allegi - 25 Years Ago

B renna waited patiently as the Orange-Star across the counter poured something vaguely akin to stew into a bowl. A slice of bread accompanied the bowl on her tray, along with a cup of water that would be too small to quench her thirst.

The woman slid the tray to her without a word, but she gave Brenna a look that she'd grown accustomed to as more members of other castes joined the facility. They knew little of the work being done which didn't help their opinions about serving White-Stars. Even if what they were serving could barely be called food most of the time.

Brenna chewed her lip, and bit back the remark she'd been wanting to make to this woman in exchange for the last week of dirty looks. Instead, she offered up her usual smile and carried her food across the large, mostly empty hall to her usual table under the long window.

The tray was heavy. Heavier than it had been a few years ago, when her arms had been thicker, her bones less brittle, and her mind less tired. What she did was necessary. Important. So, she offered up no complaint. No qualms as gifted individuals from various experiments were brought to her for their physical ailments to be healed.

She was doing good for Pangaea. More good than her sister ever would as a doctor. More good than her parents had ever done in their pathetic lives, wasted on their need for finery and status.

"Brenna."

She jerked from her reverie. Theo's tray slapped onto the table, and he sank into the chair across from her. He, too, was thinner than he'd been a handful of years ago. It was only the two of them left from that old group. The others had succumbed to their powers, blasting themselves into oblivion or fading to nothing as their gifts ate them from the inside out.

Brenna smiled. "Theo. How are you? I haven't seen you in a while."

He met the smile with a brief one of his own, but it faded quickly. His brow furrowed, and he picked at the beige sleeve of his White-Star uniform. Brenna's was similar in design, though Wolfe had insisted upon adding a black ring around the upper arm on each side—to indicate her usefulness in the facility.

"Have you wondered why that is?"

Brenna shrugged one shoulder, digging her spoon into the bowl before her and pulling up a chunk of what she assumed was some kind of vegetable. "I imagine you've been busy. I know I have." She gave him a conspiratorial smile, blew on the bite, and plunked it into her mouth.

His frown deepened. "I've been..." He glanced around, fear flashing across his face. His voice dropped an octave. "I've been helping the others," he whispered.

Brenna set her spoon against the edge of the bowl. "As have I." She cocked her head at him, confusion pooling in her chest. "Theo, are you all right?" She reached across the table and rested her hand on his.

Her heart fluttered, as it had each time they'd made contact since they'd met. A handful of stolen kisses, over a year ago, did nothing to calm the excitement in her gut when she saw his face.

"You're so thin," she murmured. She glanced at his plate. "Are you eating?"

Her fingers traced the lines of his hand, the bones protruding underneath thin skin, veins bulging and blue.

Theo looked as though he were about to pull away, but he leaned forward instead, his other hand covering hers. "Brenna, have you seen yourself? You're as thin as I am. It's not the food, it's the strain. They have us using too much of our gifts. They're..." he swallowed, again glancing around in a way which raised the hairs on Brenna's neck.

"What's wrong?" she demanded softly.

The mess hall was empty apart from the kitchen staff, bustling in and out all the way across the room.

"We're alone," she said. "Speak freely."

A hollow laugh broke from him. He did pull away then, the absence of his hands leaving hers cold and exposed. "Alone? Brenna, we haven't been alone since they loaded us onto that shuttle."

She licked her lips, raising a hand to her mouth that she might bite the nerves out of her cuticles. "What are you talking about, Theo? You're not making sense."

Another laugh. One that brought a sharp intake of breath into her lungs. He sounded strange. Different.

"There are cameras everywhere, Brenna. There isn't a place to 'speak freely'. There hasn't been in years."

She heaved a sigh, understanding finally reaching her. "Theo, that isn't some big secret you've uncovered." She smiled, hoping to lessen his stress and the fear on his face. "We've known about the security cameras since day one."

He shook his head. "You don't understand. It's more than that. Why do you think our friends left?"

Something flitted through the back of Brenna's mind. A memory of Wolfe giving her the horrible news of what had happened to Tonya, burned to death when her power raged beyond her control. Too far gone for Brenna to be able to help.

She shook her head. "They died, Theo. Why do you think I've been so busy? I'm trying to help Ms. Wolfe find a cure, for her and for us."

Theo's dark eyes, those pools of comfort she'd found in the early days at Allegi, before her power had emerged and she'd been shifted from experiments with the others to her own, more serious tasks, narrowed. "They died? Simple as that?"

"What do you want me to say?" she demanded, her voice rising as heat filled her chest. No part of her wanted to think about the horrible ways their friends had expired. No part of her wanted to relive the moments Ms. Wolfe had explained the urgency of their mission. "I'm sorry it happened? I'm angry about it? I wish things were different?"

Her hands shook on the tabletop, and she clenched them together in her lap. Her appetite, raging only moments before, was gone.

Brenna's voice trembled. "I miss them, Theo. I miss them every time I see some stranger in their rooms, in their clothes." Tears pooled in her tired eyes. "I know you miss them too, but..." She shook her head. "This ends when the Greys find what they're looking for. It ends when we can go back to our homes and live our lives."

Silence stretched between them, long and painful as Theo stared at her. She took him in during the space between words, reading the lack of sleep from the black circles under his eyes, the days without showering in his oily curls. He had to be as tired as she was.

"Brenna." Theo shook his head, deep sadness in his gaze as he leaned across the table. "I can't stay here. They've gone through so many of us, and I won't be the next one."

She shook her head, still lost.

He sighed. "Trust me, will you? Trust me that I was right all those years ago. We aren't here to help them." He glanced again at the walls, a settled sort of defiance in his gaze. "We're here to be used and discarded. That's why they keep having you heal us, Brenna, so we don't expire before they get what they want."

Brenna opened her mouth, but he held up a hand.

"I won't argue it with you. I don't want that. I just wanted to tell you before I leave. And I wanted to see if you might come with me."

Brenna stared out the window of her room, clenching her teeth against the sight coming up the drive.

This newest batch of people with powers weren't coded White-Stars. They were too young for the Coding at all. Their little legs stumbled at the pace kept by the Black-Stars, and a few of the older ones picked up the younger to carry them toward the building.

She spun from the window, strode across her room, and hurried to Wolfe's office on the far side of the facility. Her knuckles rapped softly on the door.

"Enter," came the muffled response.

"Thank you," Brenna said as she cracked the door and slid into the room. "I don't mean to bother you, Ms. Wolfe."

"Not at all." Wolfe smiled up at her from a grand, dark wooden desk. A stack of papers, glass tablets, and knickknacks took up most of the space. Plush armchairs rested before it, inviting and warm as the hearth on the side wall. "I was just finishing compiling this last round of notes. Come, sit."

Brenna nodded with a smile and sank into one of the armchairs. "I noticed the newest batch of Alters have arrived."

"Yes." Wolfe exhaled, relief clear on her face. "Finally. We can get back to the usual schedule now."

Brenna's blood chilled in her veins. The thought of it, healing various injuries on multiple children every day with no break, sent a pang of uncertainty through her.

"Ms. Wolfe, I don't want to speak out of turn, but I'm worried about running these tests on children. It seems... cruel."

Wolfe's grey eyes narrowed. She tilted her head a fraction and studied Brenna for a moment. "Cruel? You believe what we are doing here is cruel?"

The wounded expression on her mentor broke Brenna's heart. "No, of course..." she stumbled over the words, hesitating. "I only meant to say that children might not be able to sustain the kind of tests we run the way adults can."

Wolfe nodded, the hurt morphing into regret. "Indeed, it will be dangerous. Dangerous," she met Brenna's eye, "but necessary. The fastest way to get everyone, the children included, back to their homes and families is to accomplish our goals."

"Have they changed?" Brenna's voice was small, quiet. It was a question she'd wanted to ask for weeks, maybe months, but hadn't gotten up the courage.

"What?"

"Our goals." Brenna swallowed. "Have they changed? Are we still searching for a cure for your people? Or is there something else going on as well?"

Wolfe rose from her chair, the usual pencil suit immaculate and pressed. The neat white and gold was a sharp contrast to the baggy beige pants and shirt Brenna wore.

The Grey-Star rounded the desk and settled into the seat beside Brenna. "Are you asking me if I've given up on this?" She pressed a delicately manicured finger to her gemstone.

Brenna shook her head, stringy locks of blonde hair flopping this way and that. "No, of course not. I simply, well I think we all expected this to take a few years, but we've passed that mark. If we are searching for something else, trying to accomplish something else, I think it would benefit the other White-Stars, the test subjects, if they knew."

Wolfe leaned in, reaching out and smiling as Brenna took her hand. Her warm, soft fingers caressed Brenna's frail skin.

"We have multiple aims at this point, Brenna. We must. To continue receiving funding for our research, we had to promise things beyond curing my people and stemming the flow of Alters' powers."

Brenna nodded, her jaw tight as that old flame of letdown and shame burned within her. Why hadn't she been told? Was Wolfe questioning the trust she'd so generously given? Tears pooled in her eyes.

Wolfe gave a pitying smile. "Don't think that I am unaware of the value you provide here, Brenna."

Brenna closed her eyes, inhaling the praise as she bit back her tears.

Wolfe patted her hand. "I trust you more than any other in this facility. You are my right hand. Without you," she exhaled a mournful sigh, "I fear we would have lost many more, and our progress would be much slowed. You ensure that the White-Stars are able to return to testing sooner. You give us invaluable time."

Brenna bit her lower lip. Her fingers twitched within Wolfe's hands. "I'm not sure I can do it with the children. I'm not sure I'm strong enough to send them back to testing if they're... when they're hurt."

Her fingers went cold as Wolfe pulled away, leaving Brenna with numbing grief in her chest.

"If we want to send those children back to their homes, without them being a threat to everyone around them," Wolfe shook her head, disappointment in her features, "then I need you to *do your job*."

Brenna flinched at the ice in her words. She ducked her head. "Of course," her voice trembled. "I'm sorry, Ms. Wolfe, I didn't mean to—"

"It's all right," Wolfe cut in, rubbing a hand across her forehead. "I don't mean to be harsh with you, Brenna. I'm simply overwhelmed as of late. Please excuse me, I have much to get done."

Brenna nodded, taking the dismissal with as much grace as was possible in the moment. Tears would come once she closed the door behind her, but for now she put on a strong face for her friend.

"I understand. And I'll do better."

Wolfe gave a small smile, pressing her hand to Brenna's cheek and stroked with her thumb. "I know. I'm proud of you, Brenna."

Chapter Sixteen

Allegi - 25 Years Ago

Brenna wiped sweaty hands on a damp rag and tossed it into the bucket in the corner of her workspace. It was a sterile room with a comfortable white cot and a chair against one wall, a desk against the other, and a tinted observation window on the third. The door was open, a pair of Black-Stars patiently waiting outside while Brenna finished healing one of the newer test subjects.

She knelt, examining her handy work with pride. The boy had fallen outside, scraping his leg from ankle to knee. Clean new flesh, slightly pink, sat where the wound had been. It hadn't taken much out of her, but she still needed to steady herself when she stood. She'd been light-headed the past few weeks.

"Out of the way," an urgent voice shouted from the hall outside.

Brenna patted the boy's shoulder and scooted him off the bed. "Better get going, sounds like I have another patient."

The child, who had been extremely quiet during the healing, gave her a shadowed smile and darted into the hall to the waiting Black-Stars.

Mere moments later came the grunting, shuffling sounds of someone being half dragged, half carried.

Brenna cried out in shock as a man was brought into the room and laid onto the cot.

"What happened?" she gasped, staring in horror at the oozing, scorched flesh obscuring his features.

He was a White-Star, the evidence in the barely visible gemstone on his temple, as well as the clothes he wore. But beyond that, she didn't recognize him through the burns and swelling on his face, the bruises on his arms, and the charred clothes.

"Heal him," a Black-Star—one new to Allegi—barked.

She gave the man a hard look. "It helps to know what happened to the patient."

The figure on the bed moaned, and Brenna disregarded the Black-Star. She rushed to the man's side.

"Shhh," she murmured, sinking onto the stool beside the wounded man. "I'm going to make it better. It'll be all right."

"Don't..."

The word was so muffled by the cry of pain that came after, Brenna was sure she'd misheard.

Closing her eyes, she focused.

The vibrancy of her power had dimmed over the years. A mark, no doubt, of the effort gone into keeping everyone in Allegi healthy and whole. She might not be able to do anything for disease, sickness, or mental illness, but she'd stopped well over a handful of deaths so far. This man would be added to that tally.

Blue light pooled in her palms. Tendrils sank together, warm against her flesh. When her hands were full, she brought them to the man's burned face, making a point not to touch the tender flesh as light sank into his skin.

It took a long time, and more effort than she'd expected. The man was bloodied beyond the burns; his nose was broken, ribs cracked, bruises clotted his blood throughout his body. She imagined a fire had done it, causing structural damage that had led to a fall.

She bowed her head after a time, eyes still shut as she pulled more and more energy from herself into the healing. Warm liquid trickled from her nose to her upper lip, and she licked away the drop, tasting blood.

And then, it was done. Her power, what little was left, folded back into her. She sank forward onto the bed, eyes still closed, and rested her head on her forearms.

She needed food. Sleep. Maybe a blood bag given the amount of liquid that stained the front of her uniform. But she'd saved a life. She'd brought a man back from the brink.

In the distance, as though coming down a long tunnel, the sound of sobbing reached her. Brenna sat up breathing slow, deep breaths and opened her eyes. Her heart slammed into her ribs.

"Theo?" she whispered. Her hands went to him, touching him this time, tracing his arm up to his face.

His weeping face.

He stared at her, eyes hooded and dark. He was thinner than the last time she'd seen him, when she'd declined his offer to leave. When she'd walked away from his confession that he didn't want to go without her.

But he'd left anyway. He'd been gone for weeks, maybe months. She couldn't be sure with all that had been going on in Allegi.

"What are you..." Brenna licked her dry, cracked lips. Her fingers brushed against his cheek, and he winced as though it burned him.

Tears flowed freely, and his lips trembled as he took her in. "Why?"

"What?"

He sniffed and shook his head, face etched with pain, fury, betrayal...

Confusion rocked through her as he pushed her hand away.

"Why did you do it? Why bring me back?"

"I—"

Her words were cut off by footsteps in the room. Black-Stars, the ones who had brought him in, marched to the bed.

"He needs rest," she said quickly. "Get him to a new room immediately, and have some food brought up."

They ignored her. The Black-Star nearest her angled past and hoisted Theo by his armpit. The two of them dragged him off the bed.

He was standing now, at least. Holding his own weight though she knew he'd need several days to recover.

"Theo—"

She was going to offer to visit. Suggest coming by his room that evening with a snack and an ear. She wanted to hear about where he'd been, what had led to his injuries.

But she didn't get out more than his name before he turned to her, his expression twisted.

"You should have let me die, Brenna."

She gaped, unable to form words before he and the Black-Stars left the room, letting the door swing closed behind them.

A few minutes later the door opened again, and Brenna was broken from the swirling vortex of confusion and sadness she'd been drowning in.

"Ms. Wolfe." She moved to stand, her vision went black, and she collapsed back into the chair, blinking furiously.

"Darling, don't trouble yourself," Wolfe's voice overflowed with affection.

A hand rubbed Brenna's shoulder. At the same time, a second set of footsteps moved deeper into the room.

"Give her a moment," Wolfe said. "As you can imagine, such work is draining."

There was a murmur of affirmation. Several seconds later the darkness coating Brenna's vision faded to spots, blurs, and finally she was able to see again.

Wolfe knelt before her, grey eyes warm with pride as she scanned Brenna's face. "Are you all right? That was quite the feat."

Brenna sucked in a breath and pulled back the tears threatening to fall. "Thank you," she murmured. "I'm all right. I just need some time, and I'll be fine."

"That was quite impressive."

Brenna's gaze followed the voice, sharp and clear as the runoff of a freshly melted glacier.

A woman stood at the end of Brenna's desk. Her hair was up, twisted into a bun at the base of her neck with wisps of curls framing her face. She wore a dress, the lines and colors as flattering as Wolfe's pantsuits, but more feminine and delicate. The grey gemstone on her right temple was decorated with a thin silver chain, dangling from it to a piercing in her nose.

Recognition prickled within Brenna.

The two Grey-Stars spoke, their voices distant to Brenna's exhausted mind. She caught excitement, preparation, plans, dreams, and goals being formed as she tried to concentrate. Tried to push the image of Theo's distraught face from her brain.

After a while, the strange woman left, giving Brenna hope that she might return to her room to rest soon.

Wolfe stood, offering an arm which Brenna took gratefully. They walked together, Brenna leaning on the taller woman as they made their way through Allegi's wide halls toward the private rooms.

"You did very well," Wolfe said.

"Thank you," Brenna repeated.

"Ms. Collette will speak to her husband. With the support of the Chancellor, we'll have our funding back up in no time."

Brenna nodded, the words barely piercing her foggy mind.

"Are you sure you're all right, dear?" Wolfe's brow furrowed as they arrived at the door to Brenna's chambers. "I'd hate to think we're overworking you."

Brenna shook her head, aiming to clear it but only succeeding in making herself dizzy. "I'll be..." She swallowed down her rising nausea. "I'll be fine. Really. I'm glad to help."

"I know you are." Wolfe smiled down at her. "I knew you were special, Brenna. From the moment I saw you, I knew. This will do great things for us all. I promise you."

Brenna nodded, waited for Wolfe to disappear down the hall, and shut the door as a sob caught in her throat. She fell onto her bed, weakness of mind and body overcoming her.

In seconds, she was unconscious.

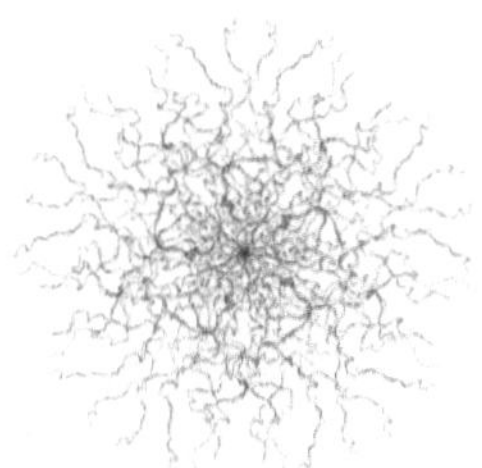

Chapter Seventeen

Dolor

K im couldn't sleep.

She needed to; she knew that. She needed to keep up her strength like Ichi and Samaira. She needed to be strong like Jane would be if she were here. Like Luna and Nova would be.

But they weren't here. They were gone, and Elaine was crying and not talking, and Ichi was quiet and tried to smile sometimes but...

She sniffed, rubbing the back of her hand under her nose and wiping it on the rough clothes they'd all been given their second day there. It seemed so long ago. Kim had lost track of how many times the Black-Stars had come to the room, dragging her friends from cages, taking her and running every kind of test until she could barely move. Until her body ached with burns and bruises and weariness pulled at every bone.

She glanced at Elaine. They were in the same cage, Elaine asleep in the corner, her braids draped over her face, frayed and dirty. Kim wanted, more than anything, for Elaine to open her eyes and see her, for her to sit up, recognition in her gaze, and pull her in to cuddle. Sing her a lullaby.

Ichi said she'd get better when they escaped.

But weeks had gone by already. Weeks, and no escape. No help. A few of the children hadn't come back from their experiments the last few days. Kim might have been afraid, but the feeling was so familiar she barely noticed it anymore.

She scooted closer to Elaine, leaning against her as she'd done back in Haven during story time. Elaine shifted in her sleep, raising her arm just enough for Kim to squeeze in and bury herself in her lap. Just enough for her to pretend.

The door to the cage room burst open. Kim jerked from Elaine's arms, alert and anxious. It was late, later than usual for the Black-Stars to be coming for anyone. The light in the window was almost gone.

A rush of dread and shame rose in Kim. Dread, at the possibility of being chosen for whatever horrible thing they wanted. Shame, at the idea that she'd prefer if they chose someone else instead.

Black boots marched down the row of cages and came to a stop before Kim's. She whimpered.

They unlocked it, and she panicked. With a squeal of protest, Kim latched onto the side of the cage, clawing toward the still sleeping Elaine. A fist came down, slamming into her tiny forearm, and she yelped with pain. Her fingers released the bar. The Black-Stars pulled her free of the cage, clutching her arm too tight as she stood barefoot in the center row.

"Who else?"

A familiar voice sent a chill down Kim's spine. She swiveled, spotting the Blue-Star responsible for Elaine's condition.

The Black-Star holding her turned around and dragged her toward the door as her legs scrambled to keep up.

"Ahh." Keith's wicked face broke into a grin. "The troublemaker." He jerked a nod at the cage where Samaira stood, facing him with the furious expression that hadn't left her features since they'd arrived.

"You wanna take me out of this cage?" Samaira growled. "Come on, let's see what you're made of. Get close to me, see what happens."

A chuckle broke out among the terrified children as Keith took a full step backward. His pale face flushed. He snapped his fingers at a pair of Black-Stars by the door.

"Get her out and let's go."

Samaira chuckled humorously as Keith hurried down the row and out the door.

Kim's anticipation, the fear gripping her heart, loosened a little as Samaira stepped out, an arm held by each Black-Star. She frowned down at Kim.

"Stay close, yeah?"

Kim nodded, already being pulled ahead of Samaira and out the door into the blinding light of the white hallway. She angled her head, craning her neck to see Samaira. There had been talk among the children from Haven, rumors about the outbursts of flame Samaira had used to hurt their captors.

Electricity crackled along Kim's knuckles. She may be small, but if the opportunity came along, she'd show these people what happened when they hurt her friends. She'd help.

"None of that now," Samaira said in a low voice.

Kim glanced up, meeting her eye. Samaira's face was marred, scabbed scrapes and fading bruises consuming most of her smooth dark skin. The injuries hadn't been so visible in the darkness of the room. Her gaze darted to Kim's fingers. Kim followed the movement, clenching her fist to stem the flow of little bursts of lighting growing in her palm.

"Do what they say." The words came through clenched teeth, but Samaira gave a firm nod.

The tightly curled, rose-like knots of Kim's hair bobbled as she nodded back. The Black-Star holding her arm jerked. She faced forward, still struggling to keep up with her short legs and bare feet.

She expected a turn coming up, but they continued forward. Apprehension built in Kim's stomach. After several minutes, they finally stopped. The Black-Star holding her let go, and Kim backed up until she felt Samaira's legs at her back.

"Stay close," the flame thrower said again.

Kim nodded.

The door opened, and the Black-Stars holding Samaira pushed both of them into the room.

It was built like the exam rooms but larger. There were three chairs here, positioned in a row against the side wall. The ceiling curved into a dome shape above them. A door stood open on the far side of the room, clear night air gently flowing in. Glowing orbs adorned the white walls. White, apart from suspiciously dark stains that carried a ruddy hue.

Kim's body trembled of its own accord. A whimper escaped her, then another. A string of them, frantic, almost sobs that she couldn't stop as she took in the sight before them.

Jacob, her friend with glowing blue skin, was no longer glowing. He lay on the ground near the far wall. His eyes were open and blank, skin grey and shriveled.

A pair of Black-Stars carried the body of another child through the door leading outside.

Kim's nose burned. Tears flowed down her cheeks. Behind her, Samaira had gone still. Kim pressed into her, half turning to bury her head into Samaira's chest.

A split second passed. A moment of quiet. Stillness. Terror.

Then the room erupted.

Kim barely had time to process the movement as Samaira's strong hands grabbed her shoulders and shoved her away. She fell, sprawling onto the tile as heat flared. Screams filled the room. The men at the exterior door dropped the body and rushed back toward them.

Kim scrambled backward, away from the fire in Samaira's hands. Flames flew, blasts slamming into Black-Star uniforms as Samaira whirled.

More were coming, storming in from the hallway.

"Go," Samaira shouted. She whirled and slammed her fist across a man's jaw. Her knuckles left scorch marks on his skin as he staggered back screaming.

Kim stared up, frozen.

"Go, Kim." Samaira's sharp voice split through the hesitation, the fear. "Run."

Kim clawed at the ground, finding purchase and launching herself up and out. She sprinted past Jacob's body, past the body of another friend, carelessly dumped on the ground. She glanced back as alarms rang out through the complex.

Samaira met her eye, flames blazing around her, and smiled.

Black-Stars descended, and the woman was lost from Kim's sight.

She turned and raced into the darkness.

Wind whipped at her face and clothes as she sprinted across a dark grassy field. Behind her, alarms and shouting echoed through the night air. She didn't stop. Didn't hesitate. Didn't turn back.

She reached a fence and scrambled up, her bare feet shuddering at the cold metal. Coiled wire was strung along the top. Blade-sharp squares of metal sliced at her arms and legs as she climbed over and began the descent. Her foot slipped. She fell.

Kim's ankle twisted under her, and a sharp cry burst from her lips.

Adrenaline pumped through her veins. Fury and fear and confusion and uncertainty, all of it swarming through her mind as she forced herself up, forced herself to keep going.

The grass had ended at the fence. Kim's feet ached as she hobbled over dirt, dry leaves, and sticks. Woods surrounded her. Darkness spread in every direction.

Forward. Keep moving forward.

Run.

That's what Samaira had said. Run.

So, she ran.

Time escaped her. Distance meant nothing. There was only pain and ache and fear and movement.

Eventually her ankle gave out, and she stumbled to a stop. Kim leaned against a thick, gnarled tree trunk, breathing heavily, and clutching a stitch in her side.

She had to be far from Dolor by now.

She sank to the ground, trying to examine her leg in the dim light of stars poking through the dense forest canopy. Her ankle throbbed.

Her vision blurred. She rested her head against the tree. Just for a moment. Just a moment to close her eyes and then she'd go again.

Rustling woke her. The sound of footsteps through the underbrush, accompanied by voices, low and fervent.

Kim bolted to her feet, winced at the pain in her ankle, and scrambled behind the tree. Someone was coming. She glanced around, surprised by the light which had overtaken the forest. The dim grey sunrise gave her options.

A tree, a few yards away, with low enough branches that she might...

Barely a moment later she'd stepped as silently as possible, reached the tree, and pulled herself halfway up. The view below sent a rush through her head, but she was out of sight. Handfuls of dry, golden-brown leaves barely clinging to the branches obscured her and her vision.

"This way." The voice was low, gruff. She recognized it enough to place the owner as a Black-Star, but she didn't know his name.

"Check again." A woman this time, also a Black-Star. "The rock formations around here interfere with the signal. I don't see any sign of her."

Chills went down Kim's dark limbs. Fear clenched like a vice around her chest as her mind flashed back to their second day in Dolor. Everything had happened so fast. They'd handed out a change of clothes, taken them a few at a time to the exam rooms, and...

Kim stared in horror at the small scar on her forearm where a tracking device had been embedded in her skin. She'd forgotten. Hadn't given it a second thought compared to the half-dozen other wounds she'd sustained since they arrived.

She glanced down. The Black-Stars had stopped a few yards away, glancing around.

"Looks like it stopped around here."

Tears beaded in Kim's eyes. She stuffed two knuckles in her mouth to keep from making a sound.

Then she paused. She pulled her hand out, examining her fingers. She touched, gently, the core of electric white light within her.

Small lines of electricity sparked across her knuckles.

She looked at the scar on her arm. Fear built within her. Fear at the pain to come, the threat of getting caught, the worry of what was happening to Samaira—if she was still alive.

Kim could *not* be caught. Not after what Samaira had done to get her out.

She closed her eyes, inhaled, and moved her left forearm between her right thumb and middle finger. She thought of Elaine. She thought of Cho, Luna, Nova, and the others who had been killed rather than captured.

Anger overtook the fear.

Power overtook the anger.

A bolt of lightning arced between her fingers and slammed through her arm. The pain was more than she'd anticipated. She bit down, slicing through her bottom lip as she clenched her teeth to stop from shouting.

Her vision blurred as she collapsed against the tree trunk behind her. Her left arm dangled, useless, at her side.

Below, someone swore. "Lost it. Frosted rocks."

"*Nacra*." There was a thump, as though someone had struck something. "She's going to be furious."

"Not on us. We didn't let the little brat escape."

Silence. Then: "Let's get back. See if they plan on widening the search."

Footsteps crunched in a direction away from her, sending a pang of relief through Kim's chest.

"Won't survive long on her own anyway," the man said, his voice fading as the Black-Stars strode back toward Dolor. "Not out here."

Kim didn't know how long she sat in the tree, knowing that climbing down when she couldn't feel her arm, and her ankle was swollen and purple, was a foolish thing to do.

She flowed in and out of consciousness until the sun was fully in the sky. The leaves above her splintered the bright beams of light, creating a patchwork of shadows around her. Birds twittered in the distance. Creatures rustled through the forest floor.

A shape came into view. Large, dark brown with tinges of red. It took her a long moment to recognize it as a bird. Long enough that the creature, nearly as big as she was, had swooped down and landed on a neighboring branch before it clicked.

"What're you doing here, birdy?" she mumbled. "This isn't a nice place."

Her eyelids drooped once again, the dark peace of unconsciousness looming close.

"Fly away." She swallowed, her throat dry, stomach empty, pain in every inch of her being. "Fly away."

But the bird didn't heed her warning. As she faded into darkness, it moved closer, seeming to grow larger before her eyes closed entirely, and she succumbed to sleep.

Chapter Eighteen

Dolor

Kim disappeared through the door to the outside. Samaira's rush of victory was channeled into the next blast. Flames slammed into Colby, and he went down howling.

Fear came next, even as she tried to shove it away to focus on the fight. Would Kim get away? How far was it to the edge of the complex? Were there guards?

So many questions unanswered, so many variables unaccounted for.

A boot slammed into her side, and she flew backward, barely catching herself before taking her stance yet again. On the ground, only a few feet away, lay Jacob's body.

She had to distract them. Keep them busy, stop them from searching for Kim. Give the girl a head start.

She covered half a dozen of the Black-Stars in scorching burns before she was overwhelmed. It would have been less, if it weren't for the food Abilene had snuck into the caged room early that morning. Sustenance did much for Samaira's power.

She sucked in heavy breaths, on her knees in the room where they'd murdered at least two of the children from Haven. Nothing they did to her now would matter, as long as Kim escaped.

Still, there was a tremor of fear within her as Keith strode forward. The Black-Stars on either side of her forced her shoulders into a stooped bow. They bound her hands behind her back, chained together with metal this time, palms together in an aching, uncomfortable position.

"I suppose you're pleased with yourself?" Keith hissed.

Samaira grinned, blood oozing from her gums. He was furious. Furious and scared. She could almost smell it on his weak form.

She spat, bloody mucus landing squarely on his shoe. "One less body for you? Yeah, I'm nacra pleased."

"Enough."

They pulled her shoulders back, yanking her head up to face him as he stared down at her.

He leaned in, fear flashing through those blue eyes. "You have no idea what you've done."

Footsteps clicked in the hallway beyond the room, and every person shifted. Samaira glanced around. Her brow furrowed at the sight; Black-Stars standing straighter, even with their wounds, and Keith trembling slightly as he eyed the door.

"What is this?"

A ripple went through the air as a woman walked through the door. Her heels were responsible for the clicking, her gemstones responsible for the shift in atmosphere. Lawrence trailed behind her, his expression grave as he took in the carnage of the room.

"Ms. Wolfe," Keith's voice shook. "This is the one I was telling you about before."

"Why is the alarm going off?" The Grey-Star's voice was quiet, soft.

It sent a shiver up Samaira's spine.

Keith swallowed. "We had an..." He straightened. "An incident. One of the subject—"

"Children," Samaira snarled, anger pushing past the strangeness of the situation. "They're children. Not 'subjects.'"

The woman, Wolfe, turned her cold grey eyes on Samaira. Her nose twitched. Her gaze shifted to the door behind her and understanding flashed across her face. She turned, scowling, to Keith.

"One of them escaped?" It was spoken as a question, but the tone and clench of her teeth left the room in silence.

Eventually, after a long moment of uncomfortable shifting, Keith nodded.

"Get this one in a cell." The Grey-Star exhaled; her eyes narrowed. "Immediately."

The others moved as one, hefting and dragging Samaira out of the room. One of the Black-Stars slammed the outside door shut as they left. The clanging sound filled Samaira's chest with hope. No order had gone out to search for Kim. Not yet at least.

They hurried down the outer hallway, Samaira barely keeping up with the combination of old and new injuries. Keith led them inward, away from the edge of the domed facility and toward the center.

A door opened. A light turned on, and Samaira blinked against the brightness. Keith halted, his gaze fixed on something in the room, and swore.

The room was lined with cells. Nothing like the cages the children had been living in, these were barred off chambers. The concrete floor and cold air raised the little hairs along Samaira's arms.

"What the frost are you doing here?" Keith demanded, stalking forward and giving Samaira a better view of the room.

It seemed she wouldn't be alone.

Abilene sat in the cell closest to the door, her knees pulled to her chest, hair a mess as though she'd run her fingers through it a hundred times. She bolted to her feet and rushed to the bars.

To Samaira's surprise, the Blue-Star's expression was twisted with fury.

"I had to try, Keith."

He scoffed, but the sound was weak, hurt. "You went behind my back. You went to Wolfe."

"You can't test experimental injections on *children*," she said through gritted teeth.

Samaira took half a step forward at this, the image of Jacob's limp body flashing through her mind. The Black-Stars jerked her back. They walked around Keith and brought her to the cell next to Abilene's.

"Clearly Wolfe disagrees. Or did you think I came up with that idea myself? I was ready to keep working on it. But she wants results."

"This *isn't* how to get them." Abilene's voice cracked. "You lied to me, Keith. You lied about all of it, and I... I won't be part of this."

The Black-Stars opened the heavy metal-barred door before Samaira.

"How about getting rid of these at least?" Samaira asked, her voice slurred because of the swelling of her cheek. She darted her head back, wiggling her fingers.

The Black-Stars shoved her into the cell.

"You'll be part of it, because you already are. I'm sure..." Keith's voice was strained, high. "I'm sure Wolfe will give you a few days to sort out your priorities, your allegiances. Then you'll return. Things will be back to normal."

Samaira scoffed, chuckling as she turned to look at the pair of them. "Yeah, she seems like a real forgiving woman."

She turned too far, and one of the Black-Stars backhanded her across the face.

Samaira slammed into the bars with a grunt. "Take these off and do that again," she growled as she straightened.

They said nothing, closing her cell and moving to flank Keith.

"You'll change your mind, Abilene." Keith smiled again. He reached toward Abilene's fingers clenched around a bar of her cell. "I vouched for you. I know you'll come around."

The woman pulled her hand away before he could touch her.

Samaira grinned, unsure why she was so pleased with this encounter, beyond that it was clearly causing Keith pain.

Keith backed away. He strode to Samaira's cell, and she rolled her eyes.

A flash of pain spasmed through her head at the action, but she held her chin high as he approached.

He leaned in, eyeing her bound arms with a sneer. "We will find that girl. And when we do, I'll let you watch while we test the serum on her. If all goes well, you'll be next."

Samaira lunged.

Keith was long gone by the time she reached the bars. He and the Black-Stars strode from the room, closing the door behind them. There was a sound of a latch locking, and then there was nothing but the cold.

Several long minutes ticked by. Samaira's fingertips grew numb and then her hands. By the time she couldn't feel her wrists she'd also gone lightheaded from the pain. She stumbled, leaning against the bars with nowhere to sit and no way to lower herself to the ground with her injuries and bindings.

"Here."

Her head snapped toward Abilene's cell.

The petite woman stood at the bars between them, something long and thin between her fingers.

"What?" Samaira's breath was shallow. The room spun and she paused until it straightened.

"Come here," Abilene said. "I can take those off." She gestured to Samaira's bound hands.

"Yeah?" Samaira huffed out a chuckle. "You'll free my hands? Willing to take that chance?"

Abilene's voice was low, her gaze steady as she met Samaira's gaze. "Your hands were free when I brought you that bread this morning."

This morning. A lifetime ago. And yet, she wasn't wrong. Samaira had been unchained when Abilene's small feet padded down the row of cages to hers. Her flames had been ready, a whisper away if the Blue-Star tried anything to hurt the children around her.

Instead, the woman had unwrapped a cloth and pushed bits of bread, cheese, and grapes through the thin gaps in the cage. She'd been silent. Uttering not a sound as she took in the sleeping children around them.

Samaira had refused to acknowledge the Blue-Star's expression. The dawning understanding that had broken across Abilene's soft features. The horror in her bright blue eyes.

Those same eyes were on her now. Waiting. Determined.

Samaira walked to the bars, unsteady on the even floor. She turned, a low growl rumbling from her throat at the requirement of putting her back to someone.

She barely felt what was happening, but when the chains fell away and she was able to bring her arms before her, pain flared through them.

Samaira gasped, hands clenching as her nerves shrieked their discomfort.

"It's the blood, flowing back into your hands."

"I don't care," Samaira snapped. She stepped away from the bars, turning to face Abilene as the woman set the chains on the ground and returned the thin metal instrument to her hair. It was a pin, Samaira realized. A silver pin with a little black bird on the end, looking as though it were flying through Abilene's hair.

"I just mean," Abilene said in a slow, patient voice, "that the pain will stop soon."

Samaira scowled. She paced the cell for a few minutes, but her injuries were many and eventually she found herself leaning against the wall with her arms crossed over her chest. Abilene had been right. The pain in her wrists had gone fairly quickly.

"Did she really escape?"

Samaira darted a glance at Abilene. The woman was curled into the corner beside Samaira's cell. The concrete wall had to be as cold on her back as it was on Samaira's.

She didn't answer right away. The question rolled through her mind, conjuring horrible scenarios in which Kim was caught, tortured, killed… all because Samaira told her to run. Then she thought of Jacob again. Of the serum Keith had mentioned.

"I hope so," she finally muttered. "Kid always was quick. I don't know what's on the other side of this." She jerked her head at the walls around them. "But if there's a way out, she found it."

The tremor in her voice startled her. She gritted her teeth.

"There is."

Samaira turned, arms falling to her side as she stepped closer to Abilene.

The other woman nodded, still curled against the wall. "There's grass, a stretch of field they keep maintained, then a fence. After that is forest for miles and miles. There's the main road, and a few old, overgrown streets to nowhere. But as far as getting out of here," she waved a hand around the room, "that wouldn't have been overly difficult. Not if she's good at climbing."

Heat filled Samaira's chest as tears filled her eyes. Relief broke over her in waves, painful and heart shattering. Hope sprouted, grew, and blossomed before her at the thought that at least one of them might survive this.

She sank down the wall, knees to her chest, and hid her face from view as the sobs she'd held at bay for weeks finally broke through.

Chapter Nineteen

The Wilds of Pangaea

The sounds of laughter from the back of the truck filled Juliana with an inordinate amount of joy. They'd done it. The truck was theirs. The trackers were disabled. The road was clear, and the sky was blue.

Taz had driven for the first portion of the night, Juliana dozing beside him in the cab in case he needed her help with anything. He hadn't, and the six or so hours of sleep she'd gotten before the sun peeked over the horizon had left her feeling whole and healthy again. When they'd stopped for a snack break, she'd taken the wheel.

Even their dwindling food stores couldn't diminish the sense of accomplishment they all felt at achieving this necessary step on the road to rescuing the children from Haven.

Juliana fiddled with the wheel, glancing at the energy gauge and trying to calculate how far it would be to Dolor. It was a tricky situation. They knew where it was on the map, but getting there meant finding the correct turn-off, following it without being seen, and parking somewhere hidden but with the opportunity for a getaway.

She was grateful for the abandoned roads crisscrossing the southern portion of Pangaea. Old streets, long crumbled and overgrown, would serve them well... if they made it out of Dolor unscathed.

The bubbling happiness within her dimmed.

As her thoughts turned dark, the window slit between the cab and bed of the truck slid open.

Taz's sandy blond head poked through, and he flashed her a wild grin. "Yeh doin' all right up here?"

Juliana nodded. "We might have to stop soon to let it recharge faster, but for now, we're looking good."

"Excellent."

He slid the window further to the side and, amidst Juliana's snorting chuckles, worked his gangly limbs through until he sprawled next to her on the bench seat. The chatter from the back was clearer now. Anthony and Jason were taking turns regaling the younger children with more and more far fetched stories about their various adventures.

Taz slid the window shut.

Juliana raised an eyebrow. "Is everything all right?"

Her friend fidgeted in his seat. "I wanted tah talk to yeh, if yeh don't mind?"

"Of course." Juliana furrowed her brow. "What's wrong?"

"Not wrong, r...r...really," he muttered. His hands twisted in his lap and his gaze seemed fixed on a point out the front windshield. "I just... Cho told us how amazin' Daisy was in Mendax. And Anthony can go all wolfy anytime he wants."

Juliana chortled. "I won't tell him you said wolfy."

Taz's grin in response was short-lived.

"What is it, Taz?" Juliana glanced at him before returning her eyes to the flat road before them.

"Yeh can heal people, Juliana."

She caught the worry in his voice and thought she understood where this was going.

"And wha' can I do? Nothin'. I've got no power showin' up. How'm I supposed tah help when we get tah Dolor?"

"Taz—"

"I wanna be able tah help."

The desperation in his voice and the pinch of his forehead, brows drawn together in anxiety, struck her heart.

"Taz..." Juliana hesitated. She often forgot how young he was. He and Daisy both were nearly adults in Abredea, but they'd be considered children for several more years in Tornim. This needed a tender touch. "You drove this thing out of Mendax. You helped get me back to my feet after Luna. You, me, Daisy, and Anthony? We're in this together. With the kids from Haven, sure. But the four of us left Abredea together. You..."

She broke off, emotion closing her throat for a moment. She felt Taz's gaze on her, felt him clinging to her words. Clearing her throat, she continued.

"You're a big part of what made Abredea different for me. Different than I thought it was going to be. Without you, without Daisy, I don't think I'd have changed enough to make the decisions I did in time."

"Yeh mean goin' through the fence and gettin' the medicine for Jimmy?"

"That and standing up to Steel. Refusing to..." She pinched her lips closed. The truck sped along, oblivious to her thundering heart.

She hadn't told him and Daisy about Steel's offer all those months ago. Anthony knew, but only because she'd felt the need to warn him. She'd turned Steel down with no remorse. Yet even being offered the opportunity to turn on her friends felt shameful.

"Steel asked me to watch Anthony."

She glanced at Taz in time to see his eyes widen. He stared at her, then looked back out the window.

"It was after you and Daisy became my friends. It wasn't difficult to turn him down. But if you hadn't..." Her throat caught again, and she took one of her hands from the wheel, reaching for his.

Taz took it, squeezing with clammy fingers.

"If you hadn't been *you*, I don't think we'd be here right now."

She let him go, returning her focus to the road. They rumbled along in silence for a few minutes. Eventually, Taz broke it.

"Do yeh think I have power? A gift or somethin' that'll show up?"

Juliana gave the question the thought it deserved. The cab was quiet again as she went through the stories May had told her and Anthony, as well as the information Cho and the others had shared.

"Most people don't show any hint of being an Alter until their twenties." She brushed a strand of hair behind her ear. "I think yours will show up when we need it. And," she grinned and leaned over, nudging him with her shoulder, "if it doesn't, you're still you. And we need you, Taz."

He smiled that wide smile of his and rested his head against the seat. They rode in silence for a long while. Long enough that the energy gauge began to concern Juliana.

She was near pulling over, when a sign on the side of the road caught her attention.

"Uh oh," she murmured.

Taz jerked awake, wiping a bit of drool from his chin. "What is it?"

"Might be nothing," Juliana said, tapping a knuckle on the window between them and the bed. "Might be a problem."

Cho slid the window to the side as he, Anthony, and Jason clustered around it.

"We're coming up on a fueling station." Juliana gestured at the dash, where the little arrow was nearing the empty symbol.

"What's that mean?" Anthony asked.

"We need to recharge, but there might be others there."

"Excellent," Jason growled.

Juliana gave an exasperated sigh. "We need to save our strength for Dolor. If we can find the right route, we should be able to get there sometime this evening."

He muttered something under his breath, and Cho shot him a glare.

"What do you suggest we do?" Cho said.

"We should recharge at the station. It'll be faster, and speed is a goal here, right?"

"Right."

Juliana chewed on her bottom lip. "How much equipment is back there? Uniforms, weapons, that sort of thing?"

"Not much in the way of weapons," Jason replied. "But there are a few blades, helmets, jackets, and a couple tarps and blankets."

Juliana nodded. "I think I have a plan."

"'Course yeh do," Anthony said. Even with her eyes on the road, she heard the crooked grin in his words, and it brought a smile to her face.

They pulled onto the shoulder of the road for a moment; just long enough for Juliana to zip into a jacket and secure a belt and blade around her waist. Jason did the same, also donning a Black-Star cap. It wasn't the full helmet, and the bottom edges of his gemstones were visible, but he'd stay in the cab. With any luck, the stop would be quick and quiet. The only travel on these roads that Juliana knew of was members of the upper caste members from the southern cities heading to Mendax.

It went about as quickly as Juliana planned. They stopped; most of the group remained in the truck. Juliana, hair pulled down around her face, Black-Star jacket zipped to the neck, and blade at her side, did the relatively simple job of plugging the transport into one of the charging docks. It was fortunate no one was around, as she'd never done it before, and the process involved a small amount of guesswork.

A twenty-minute timer popped up on the screen. Juliana went back to the others to let them know, and then strode over to the small, unmanned shop where people could purchase snacks and water.

The machines didn't accept the handful of coins Taz still had from Abredea. Juliana supposed that shouldn't have been a surprise. The higher castes rarely relied on physical currency.

Still, she banged on the side of the machine, craving one of the bars of chocolate nestled safely behind the glass.

Nothing happened.

Her mind ticked off the list of supplies they still had. There weren't many.

She gazed around the charging station. Theirs was the lone vehicle, but another five charging docks were ready to service the higher castes who came through. She stood under a beige colored awning, the machines before her sporting a display of chocolate, chips, protein bars, and more. The smallest held rows and rows of chilled glass bottles of water.

Uncertainty gnawed at Juliana. This was the main road, a charging station where others were sure to stop. If not today, then sometime soon.

Her stomach growled. She went to get Jane.

A moment later the girl was pressing her hand through the glass case holding the water.

"All of it?" Jane muttered as she pulled a bottle out, handed it to Juliana, and stuck her arm back through the door as though it were made of mist.

"Would that be too much?" Juliana tucked the water into a bag, weaving a thin blanket between it and the other bottles so none would break.

Jane shook her head, frowning in concentration. "It'll take me a few minutes."

Juliana glanced at the charging station. "We have time." She watched as Jane pulled more from the machine. "How does it work? Going through things?"

The girl gritted her teeth, and for a moment Juliana thought she wasn't going to answer.

Jane passed another bottle to Juliana. "It's harder to do things like this," she said softly, her focus on the task at hand. "Where part of me has to change, but another part stays the same."

"So, it's you that changes, not the surface you go through?"

Jane grunted an affirmative. She took the last water bottle from the machine and switched to the snacks. "With this," she took a handful of bars from their shelf and one slipped through her fingers, landing on the bottom part of the machine, "I have to keep my hands solid enough to hold things, but allow my arms to go through the glass. Otherwise..."

"You'd get stuck."

Jane let out a humorless laugh, pulling her arms free and plopping a handful of food into one of the bags laid out on the ground. "That's a best case scenario. If I'm not careful I could lose a limb."

Juliana inhaled a sharp breath, wincing. "That's..."

"Horrifying." Jane reached in, grabbed another chunk from the very top row, and gave Juliana a smirk. "Yeah."

The bags at their feet were nearly full. Jane held up a finger, and Juliana leaned in to look. The tip of her left pointer finger was missing.

"What–"

Jane interrupted with a shrug. "I wasn't careful."

Juliana nodded, her lips pursed with worry as Jane returned to work.

They took it all. Juliana darted back to the truck twice for additional bags to store the month or so's worth of snacks the higher castes enjoyed on trips. When it was done, she split open a package with her teeth, snapped the bar of chocolate in half, and handed a piece to Jane.

She raised an eyebrow at Juliana then chuckled and ate the thing in one bite.

They returned to the truck, cracking open the door to the back so they could talk while they waited the remaining few minutes for the truck to charge.

"We need to figure out where to go from here," Jane said with a stretch.

"Agreed." Juliana met her gaze with a nod.

Anthony traced his finger along the map spread out on the floor of the truck "Looks like there's just the one road. Should lead us there then, aye?"

Juliana shook her head. "I doubt it. This is a secret facility. It won't be on the map."

"But we have an idea where it is," Cho broke in. He looked at Anthony. "If someone were able to move through the woods in this location," he pointed to one of the red dots on the map, "they might find a way in."

Anthony grimaced, but Juliana caught the hint of his mischievous grin as well. "I suppose yer talkin' about a four-legged someone."

Jane snorted at that, and Daisy let out a string of giggles that brought a smile to Juliana's face.

Jason reached in and clapped Anthony on the back. "It's you or me, and if it's me that just means burning the forest down till we can see what's going on."

Anthony gave Jason a sarcastic glare. "Sounds all right to me." He winked at Claire. "Yeh just gotta take this one with yeh to put it out after."

Claire flushed to the roots of her hair.

"All right," Juliana said, glancing over to the charger. "We should be good to go in a minute or two. I'll try and find us a spot off the road where we can stop. I think," she craned her head and Anthony turned the map so she had a better view, "we should only have a couple more hours on the road."

A couple more hours had been an understatement. The region of forest where Dolor was supposedly located began earlier than it was labeled on the map. Little saplings and sprouts led them slowly from grasslands to forest. The road they were on remained clear, sunlight streaming down where tree branches had been cut back to avoid them falling and blocking the way. Either side of them, however, was nearly as dark as the woods outside of Abredea.

"This might be trickier than we thought," Juliana muttered to herself.

Anthony glanced over from the passenger seat. He'd switched with Taz after the recharge, claiming he wanted to be able to get a good view of the road and where they might pull off.

That was probably true, but he'd also confessed simply wanting to be nearer to her. She'd grinned and told him the same. That was several hours ago.

"Yeah." Anthony nodded. "It's a dense one. Prime for some dangerous stuff if we're not careful."

"What do you mean?"

"What Jason said, about burnin' it. Wouldn't be a far-off worry in a place like this." He gestured to the sides of the road where the forest floor was littered with leaves, needles, and branches. "A spark, Jules, a spark'd light this place up."

Her lips twisted to the side as she thought over what he said. "No one lives out here."

He met her eye for a moment.

She gave half a shrug and continued. "According to the maps, and everything I was taught in Tornim, there aren't any... innocent people in this area."

A shadow passed over Anthony's face. He nodded. "We don't have a clear eye on how large this forest is. But it's somethin' to keep in mind."

"Yeah."

"How much—" Anthony broke off and leaned forward, his gaze fixed ahead of them.

A shadow sped through the air toward them. Juliana squinted—was it a bird?

The thing rocketed at the windshield and, just as Juliana was about to slam on the brakes, it swerved to the right, avoiding them by a hair. Adrenaline jolted through her system. Her hands tightened around the wheel.

"What the frost was that?" Juliana gasped. Before she'd finished the question, the thing flew back again, aiming straight for the windshield.

She pumped the brakes, but it dodged right. A few seconds passed as she and Anthony gazed around.

"Looked like a bird to me," Anthony said. "Nacra strange thing tah do though."

They exchanged a glance. Juliana's gaze slid past him, and out the window.

"It's back," she murmured.

It was a bird. No longer flying head on, it was easier to distinguish the shape of the thing. Its massive wingspan was stretched out beside Anthony's window as it flew alongside them.

"It was slowin' yeh down," Anthony breathed. He bent slowly, lifting his bow from where it rested by his feet. After positioning it in his lap, he reached up and gave a gentle rap on the window to the bed of the truck.

Taz popped his head through. "Yeah?"

Anthony didn't take his gaze from the creature. "Get Cho and Jason."

Taz bobbed a nod and darted away. A few seconds later the other two leaned toward the window.

"There's a... bird out here." Juliana winced at the foolishness of the sentence. Apprehension stirred in her, and her fingers twitched against the steering wheel. "It's behaving strangely."

"Nacra odd is what it is," Anthony said, his gaze still fixed on the thing.

It shifted, darting out in front of them again, this time flying ahead of the truck, its red tinged tailfeathers doing a good job of blocking Juliana's line of sight.

"What is this?" Jason asked.

"That'd be why we brought you two up here," Anthony said. "Tah ask if yeh know what's goin' on."

"You're the first person we've met who can change shape." Cho squinted through the window, blocking Jason's view as he leaned forward. "But it isn't impossible for that to be..."

"That's a person?" Anthony demanded.

"Maybe?" Cho didn't sound convinced.

The hawk glanced back at them, its bright yellow eyes meeting Juliana's again. It slowed, angling to the right. Almost on instinct, she did the same.

"There," she said.

The others followed her gesture. A few yards down the road there was a split. A turn off nearly entirely obscured by the forest. But at one point it had been a street. Juliana's heart hammered in her chest. It was unlikely they'd have seen this side road without being slowed and directed by the creature flying ahead of them.

"Do we..." Cho began.

Juliana was already turning the wheel, and the question died in his throat.

"This is what we needed, right?" she confirmed as the truck left the smooth paved road and jerked and bumped down the crumbling asphalt of the turn off.

"Yeah," Anthony said. He glanced at her and reached out a hand, resting it reassuringly on her knee.

"Hold on," Jason called to the others in the back.

The truck groaned, branches broke, and paint scraped as they maneuvered past the first set of overgrown thickets. It was rough and slow going. The forest had nearly retaken the road.

Still, each careful maneuver around a fallen branch or dangling limb increased Juliana's sense that they were doing the right thing. They were nearer to the possible location for Dolor now and, if the map Cho had was correct, they were finally heading in the right direction to find it.

After nearly a quarter of a mile, the crumbling asphalt made a sharp curve. The turn, and the way most of the branches were bending and bouncing back in her side mirror, suggested this was a spot they weren't likely to be found.

"Here?" Juliana murmured to the others, glancing back at Jason.

He nodded.

"Yeah," Anthony agreed.

Juliana hit the brake, and the truck came to a sharp halt in the center of the road.

The hawk, still flying ahead of them, took a minute to notice. When it did, it flew back and landed on the hood, staring at Juliana.

"This is so strange," she whispered through clenched teeth.

The thing looked oddly comfortable on the truck. Its wings, massive things tinged with red as dark as the tail, draped loosely at its sides.

"Be careful," Anthony growled. He leaned back and said in a hoarse whisper, "Jason, go round the left."

There was a grunt, then movement and the sound of the back of the truck opening.

The hawk cocked its head to the side, still staring at Juliana. She reached for her door at the same time that Anthony reached for his.

"Is that a bird?" one of the twins piped up from the back.

Juliana stepped out of the truck slowly. Her heart thundered in her chest. Finding another free Alter here, so close to a place where the Haven children were being experimented upon, felt like a suspicious coincidence.

"What do you want?" Juliana left the door open, keys in her hand as she moved forward.

Footsteps sounded behind her. A glance at the driver's side mirror showed nearly everyone had piled out behind Jason and were following him to the front.

"Who are yeh?" Anthony asked from the opposite side. "And why are yeh here?"

Juliana jumped back as the thing spread its wings in a loud swoosh. It soared a few feet into the air and landed out of sight on Anthony's side of the truck.

Fear hit her. She gave a shout and rushed around the hood just in time to backpedal as a naked man rose from the ground, gave Anthony a grimace, and said, "Can I borrow some pants?"

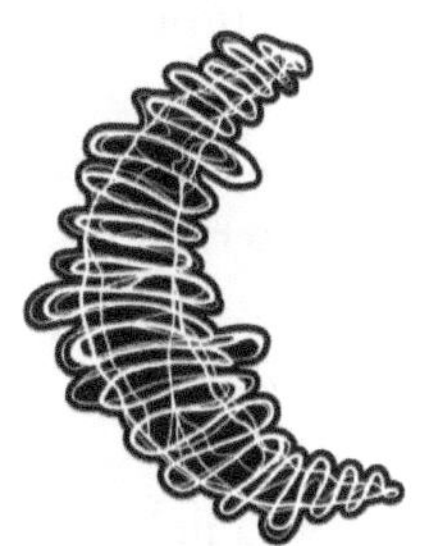

Chapter Twenty

Forest near Dolor

J uliana tapped her thumb against her fingers, the steady rhythm calming her nerves. "Name," she said, her voice tight.

The bird-transformed-into-a-man hadn't spoken since offering a gruff thanks for a pair of Anthony's jeans.

"Hawk."

Jane scoffed. Cho shot her a warning look, and she scowled.

"Little on the nose, yeah?" Jason snickered.

Cho rolled his eyes and cast a pleading look at Juliana. She stepped forward as the man pulled one of Jason's spare shirts over his head.

"I didn't name myself," the stranger snapped. His voice was rough, coarse as though it hadn't been used in years. His lip curled on the right side; the result of a thick scar etched from the corner of his cheekbone to the edge of the lip. The unmarred skin of his face was coated in freckles. He looked to be around Jason and Anthony's age, in his early twenties, though it was hard to tell through the layers of dirt. He was incredibly thin.

Juliana put up a hand. "Name aside," she faced the man, her gaze sharp, "what are you doing here? What do you want with us?"

He stalled, one hand ruffling his mess of red hair, the other straightening his shirt. "I thought that would've been obvious."

"Enlighten us," Anthony glowered. He stood at Juliana's side, half a step behind her, but close enough for her to feel his presence.

"You're going for Dolor. I'm going to help."

"Why should we trust you?" Jane spat. She'd tucked Tommy behind her legs after he'd refused to stand with the twins and Claire at the back of the group. The boy clung to her, staring at the man with wide eyes.

Juliana read the fear on her face, masked by anger. She lightly touched Jane's forearm.

The girl's gaze darted to Juliana, a fresh sneer in place.

Juliana looked away, facing Hawk. "She asks a valid question. We don't know you."

"We don't have time for this."

"Make time." Anthony took half a step forward, a dangerous promise in his voice and expression.

Hawk licked his lips, pale green eyes darting from one member of their group to the next, as though looking for some kind of ally. Finally, he settled on Cho. "Some of you are from Tornim, right?"

Cho blinked. He glanced at Juliana, and she gave the slightest dip of her head. He looked back to Hawk and nodded.

"One of your people needs help. I—" He broke off with a strained choke as Jason slammed him against the side of the truck.

The flame thrower's forearm pressed into Hawk's windpipe, cutting off the air and the words.

"*Jason*," Juliana said.

"Who?" Jason hissed.

Juliana gritted her teeth. Jason's free hand took on tinges of red, heat emanating from his person.

"Who do you have? Where are they?"

"Jason," she shouted this time, her voice ringing through the forest around them, echoing off the thick canopy above.

He jerked back, breathing heavily as he shot her a glare. Cho moved forward. His fingers settled on Jason's arm for a brief moment as he turned his attention to Hawk.

The stranger was doubled over, rubbing his throat and wheezing. "Little girl," he choked out. "Don't know her name. Came for help before she woke up. She's hurt."

He coughed, but the sound was muffled by the cries of the twins behind them.

Juliana inclined her head toward Cho, wondering if he wanted to take the lead.

His attention was torn. Jason was still fuming, struggling to keep a hold on the fire within.

"How far?" Juliana asked.

"Close," Hawk said. He coughed again and spat on the cracked asphalt. "We can walk. This is a safe place for the truck."

Juliana and Anthony exchanged a glance. He gave an almost imperceptible nod.

"Lead the way then." Juliana gestured for Hawk to show the way. "And if you try anything, the guy with fire coming out of his hands will kill you."

It was a slight reassurance to hear Jason huff out a chuckle at her words. They gathered their packs and hurried after Hawk.

"Why didn't yeh try tah talk to us?" Anthony asked.

He and Juliana led the group, trailing a few feet behind Hawk in case he made any dangerous moves. Juliana kept her hand near the Black-Star blade from the truck that she'd attached to her belt, glancing behind them often to make sure they didn't lose the others.

Anthony would be able to handle the bird man if it came to that. Juliana's concern lay in losing sight of their friends, someone getting lost, or this whole thing ending in an ambush.

Her stomach twisted into knots at the thought. They were so close to the kids' family.

"I don't…" Hawk hesitated, glancing back at them as his face twisted in what appeared to be discomfort. "I don't talk much."

"Familiar," Anthony drawled, giving Juliana a smirk.

She grinned, recalling her early time in Abredea.

"Still," Anthony continued, "might be good tah learn, as flyin' at trucks doesn't seem like the smartest thing in the world."

"You'd know all about being smart," Hawk mumbled, his words barely audible as he stomped through the underbrush, "making someone angry enough to throw you off a building."

Juliana froze.

Anthony took another step before the words sank in and he stopped as well, fury and confusion in his dark gaze.

"How do you know about that?" Juliana asked, her voice deadly low.

Cho stepped up beside her, curiosity in the furrow of his brow as he held up a hand to slow the others.

Hawk turned, grimacing at his mistake as he faced them. "I was there." He glanced at Cho.

Juliana followed his gaze. Her fingers tapped against the hilt of her short knife.

Cho's face had gone white as a sheet. "After the raid?"

Hawk nodded. "I've been watching all of you for a while now."

"Why?" Anthony's hands were clenched into fists, his eyes narrowed with suspicion.

The stranger ran a hand over his face. "Can we discuss this when we get to the girl?" He met Juliana's eye. "She needs healing."

A flurry of unease rippled through Juliana. "How long? Answer that, and we'll finish this conversation after we get to the girl."

Hawk tensed, the veins in his neck popping. He was a lean man, not as muscular as Jason but with a wiry look about him. His human stature reminded Juliana of his bird form.

"There's a Grey-Star." He spoke through clenched teeth, as though each word caused him pain. His thumb brushed against his inner elbow. "A woman. I've been watching her for a long time, and then she—" he broke off, his eyes flitting back to Juliana. "Since your Coding. That's how long I've been keeping an eye on the lot of you in the camp." He looked at Cho. "Less, for you all. Just before the raid, that's when I found out about you."

Juliana's mind raced. Questions, theories, fears, tumbled through her brain, at odds with the knowledge that they needed to get to the girl he'd spoken of.

"Why?" Cho asked. A split second later he shrank in on himself, staggering half a step back and breathing hard.

"Cho?" Jason pushed forward, reaching out before clenching his hand into a fist. "Are you—"

"I'm all right," Cho panted. He stared at Hawk.

A long moment passed, both Jason and Anthony glaring at the strange man before them while Cho and Juliana exchanged a look and a nod.

"Let's go." Juliana gestured forward. "You'll fill us in when we get there."

It wasn't a question, but Hawk nodded, turned, and hurried through the trees.

"Want to walk back—" Jason began.

"Yeah," Cho said before he finished the question. "Can we... can we lag behind a bit, just for a couple minutes?"

Juliana met his eye. "You sure you're all right? Are you hurt?"

He shook his head.

She hesitated. "Don't fall too far back."

Cho bobbed his head, but it was Jason's firm nod and understanding gaze that convinced Juliana to keep moving.

She followed Anthony and Hawk through the woods, the others trailing behind as Jason and Cho drifted to the rear of the group.

Daisy hurried up beside her, soft fingers grazing her shoulder. "Are you all right?"

Juliana shook her head without meaning to, collected herself, and nodded. "I will be, after we get some more answers."

"Since your Coding," her friend murmured. "Does that mean that woman, Wolfe..."

"Must be," Juliana said. "I'm curious why he's been watching her."

"Cho said they think a Grey-Star is running things at Dolor, right?"

Juliana swallowed, silent for a minute as they pushed branches out of their way and trudged deeper into the forest.

"It has to be her," she finally said. "May thought her interest in me had something to do with Alter powers. That must be what connects all of it."

"That means she's the one who ordered the raid on Haven?" Daisy's voice was strained.

Juliana reached out and the two clasped hands. Juliana gave a squeeze to ease the trembling of Daisy's fingers.

"It means she's the one with answers." Juliana stared ahead, watching Anthony prowl through the woods with ease. "It means if we want to be free of all of this, we need to find out what she wants."

Ten minutes later, the group emerged from the thick brush into a small clearing. It was as beautiful as the one Juliana missed so much from Abredea, but without the clear stream of fresh water. And on the far side, crumpled into a ball against a tree trunk...

Luna and Nova gasped at the same time. They sprinted across the space, arriving at the little girl's side at the same time as Jane. The twins held back tears, gently stroking the unconscious girl's shoulder and back.

Jane whirled on Hawk. "What did you do?"

He stared her down, a nearly identical stubborn anger in his expression. "She escaped. I didn't do this." He gestured as the girl stirred.

Juliana moved forward. She needed to look at the injuries and figure out how long the healing would take. She'd already noted a handful of cuts across the girl's dark skin, scraped up bare feet, and a painful discoloration around one of her ankles.

"What—" the girl let out a yelp and scrambled back against the tree, only using her right arm. Then her midnight gaze found Luna and Nova. She burst into tears.

Cho and Jason pushed past and hurried to her side. Tommy followed them, flickering in and out of visibility.

"You're... you're... you're..." the child choked on her sobs, gasping the words as she took in each face. "You're dead. Am I dead?"

Luna and Nova had melted into tears as well. Jason glanced back at Juliana and Anthony, his brow pinched together in desperation.

Claire stood awkwardly, holding her arms as tears flowed down her cheeks. Daisy went to her, put an arm around her shoulder, and pulled her close.

"Juliana," Cho said, his voice tight. "Can you—"

"Of course." Juliana hurried forward, and the others split apart to make room for her. She knelt and bit back the emotion building in her throat. "Hey, you're not dead, little one. And neither are they."

The girl's lower lip trembled, tears mixing with the dirt and snot on her face, as she stared up at Juliana. The presence of a stranger, someone not from Haven, seemed to calm her initial terror.

"What's your name?" Juliana asked, her voice as soft as the nights she'd read Jimmy stories until he fell asleep. Those evenings felt like a lifetime ago.

The girl didn't answer. The realization that she, and the others, were alive, brought forth a fresh wave of tears.

"Kim," Jane answered from behind them. The usual acid in her voice was gone, replaced with a combination of relief and grief that was somehow worse. "Her name is Kim."

"Kim," Juliana met the girl's eyes, "I'm going to take a look at your injuries, and try to make them feel a little better, is that all right?"

She barely nodded, her focus pulled again to the others. She reached up toward Jason, still only using her right hand. He knelt. Kim traced the scruff on Jason's face. "Samaira…"

He sucked in a breath, his face hardening.

"She told me to run. I didn't… I didn't wanna leave them, but she said to go."

Juliana's heart cracked in two. She glanced at Jason as she gently lifted and examined Kim's left arm. The man blinked back tears and gave a sharp nod.

"Juliana's gonna patch you up, and then we'll get 'em, kid. We'll get 'em out."

He rose, turning from the group and striding across the clearing with rigid steps.

"This is going to take some time." Juliana looked at Kim. "Are you comfortable? I need you to try and stay still."

"Here." Luna dug through her pack and within a minute she and Nova had laid out a padded surface of cloth for Kim to rest on.

"Food too," Cho muttered. "Do you need space?"

Juliana shook her head, barely listening as she knelt beside the girl. "Just time."

"Yeh 'ave it," Anthony's voice cut through the blur of her concentration, and she felt his presence behind her. A hand touched her shoulder. "Don't go too far, yeah?"

"This isn't like before." Juliana put a hand on Kim's shoulder. "I'll be careful."

Everything faded. Juliana closed her eyes, diving for the orb of blue within and pulling it forth. This *had* to be different. She couldn't drain herself with every healing. She had to learn halfway measures—getting people stable and then letting them rest and heal on their own over time.

First, she had to assess the damage. Juliana frowned, lightly biting her lower lip. She focused on her power, letting it build and grow within until she felt the warmth tingle from the top of her head to her fingertips. She opened her eyes.

A soft gasp escaped her lips. The world was different. The colors were sharper, and strange. Luna and Nova, sitting on their knees a few paces away, glowed with pale lavender light lining their bodies.

Juliana looked down and, with another jolt of awe, saw her own hand outlined in soft blue. It was the same shade as her power, but different than the tendrils she could call forth.

Kim was outlined in white, an electric color that reminded Juliana of warm summer storms.

Juliana looked up and out, marveling at her friends. Cho, crouching beside Jason, was lit up with gold, and the flame thrower was a bright red/orange. Anthony stood with Daisy and Taz, his gaze darting back and forth between Juliana and Hawk.

Juliana's heart leapt at the black outline around him. A shadow of darkness, warm and comforting, like the depths of a warm blanket, coals in the heart of a fire.

Daisy was ringed with pale pink, and Taz... Juliana's eyes widened at the rainbow of light sparking from her friend. Where the others' auras were soft and muted, his was vibrant, shooting off in little sparks.

A handful of new questions blossomed in Juliana's mind, but there was work to be done.

She returned focus to the girl before her and, with this strange new vision, noted clusters of angry darkness in her arm and ankle. They weren't warm like Anthony's power. They were an absence of light, a void. She prodded them with a tendril and winced at the pain, almost despair, she felt.

Kim's ankle was fractured, the fibula cracked in two places. That would take time to fix. Her arm was burned, scorch marks on both sides and nerve damage spreading from her fingertips to her shoulder.

The cuts and bruises were simple enough. They'd heal on their own if Juliana was too drained from the major injuries to deal with them.

She focused on the ankle first; mending the bone as sweat beaded on her brow. The swelling shrank, but she stopped short of fully eradicating the bruising. Shifting to the arm, she started with the biggest problem, pushing her tendrils of light through each nerve strand until the darkness was gone.

Kim's fingers twitched.

Juliana sat back on her heels for a moment, breathing deep as she analyzed her own energy. The orb of her power was still bright. It swirled and danced, eager to be used.

Her lips curved into a grin, and she went back to work, healing the electric burns that marred Kim's arm. She shifted, shrinking the bruising on the girl's face before she stopped.

Juliana sank down, wrapping her arms around her knees and resting her head on her forearm. "I'm done," she sighed.

Anthony was at her side in an instant. He passed her a water bottle and she drained it eagerly. "How d'yeh feel?"

She nodded. "Better; a lot better than last time. Just need a few minutes I think."

She glanced at Kim, a soft smile curling her lips at the girl's closed eyes and gentle breathing. She'd fallen asleep. Luna and Nova scootched closer, one on each side as they draped their arms across her middle and cuddled her.

"Well," Cho cleared his throat, "that was unexpected. What now?"

Chapter Twenty-One

Dolor

Samaira wasn't sure how much time had passed. She'd fallen asleep at some point, woken to the sound of Abilene crying, and rolled over to try and block it out. The sniffles kept her awake, and eventually, she'd scooted to the corner where their cells met.

The two sat, half leaned against each other through the bars, for a while longer. Long enough that Samaira fell into another fitful doze.

It was midway through the night when the door banged open. Heels clicked against the concrete floor, and Samaira jerked away from the corner, from Abilene. She settled in the middle of the wall, aiming for casual and unbothered.

She doubted it came across with the tension in her muscles, the clenching of her hands, and the flaring of her nostrils.

The Grey-Star was in the middle of speaking as she strode down the walkway toward Samaira's cell.

"...gone within the hour if I'm to get there on time. I expect the three of you to handle this, the way *I* would handle it. Is that understood?"

The men who followed her—Keith, Lawrence, and another Black-Star with a shiny bald head and dagger-like tattoos lining his face—made noises and nods of agreement.

"They're still headed south, ma'am," the Black-Star said. "This little," he sneered at Keith, "*setback* shouldn't affect our plans. We have men watching the road between Tornim and the bridge."

"You think they'll go so far south?" Lawrence asked, his deep voice reverberating through the stark room.

The Black-Star scowled at him. "You deal with your men, Lawrence, I'll deal with mine."

The captain of the Dolor Black-Stars didn't respond but turned his attention to Wolfe. "Ma'am, are you certain you want to expend resources tracking the child down?"

Samaira's blood went cold.

Wolfe studied him for a few seconds, her appraising eye seeming to shrink the man. "If you haven't found her by morning, call it off and return them here. I'd rather cut *one* loose than risk them all escaping because of your lack of men."

The other Black-Star let out a derisive snort. Wolfe turned her stormy gaze upon him.

"Apologies, ma'am," he muttered.

"This won't affect our plans either," Keith cut in. He bobbed his head toward Wolfe. "We have a stronger test subject; I'll have good news for you before you land at the Capital, ma'am."

Wolfe gave a sharp nod. Her gaze strayed down, eyeing Samaira.

Heat sparked in Samaira's chest. "Don't look at *me*," she sneered. "I'm not calling you ma'am."

As Wolfe's nostrils flared, a chuckle was quickly muffled in the cell next door. Samaira glanced over, as surprised as the others looked. Everyone's attention turned to Abilene, hands over her mouth, looking shocked at her own laughter.

Silence hung like a potent stench for a moment. Then Wolfe pivoted away from Samaira to stand in front of Abilene's cell.

"It's a shame." Wolfe's voice was soft, deadly.

Unease crept up the back of Samaira's spine and made her inch closer to Abilene, though the bars were still between them.

"She'll come around, Ms. Wolfe." Keith swallowed. His usually snide expression was fearful as he glanced from Wolfe to Abilene.

"Oh, I don't think so," Wolfe said. She stared down at Abilene who, to her credit, didn't shrink back. Instead, the little woman rose to her feet, chin held high as the Grey-Star appraised her. "Reaching out to your family? Running to tattle on Keith here when he was ready to begin the second round of serum tests? And," she let out a derisive chuckle, "sneaking food to the test subjects?"

Keith's eyes were wide. He glanced at Lawrence. The big man gave a brief nod.

Keith turned to stare at Abilene with hurt on his face.

Samaira watched the woman as well, her throat dry with fear.

"Keith had such high hopes for you." Wolfe sighed with a shake of her head. "Pity you won't be reaching them, and a pity you brought your family into it."

At this, Abilene's defiant expression wavered. "What do you mean?"

"This is a *covert* facility." Wolfe glanced at the new Black-Star, who watched the exchange with something like greed on his face. Lawrence looked at him as well, his face smooth and unreadable as stone. "We have people who handle information leaks."

"I didn't tell them where we are," Abilene spluttered. "I only—"

"You only informed them," Wolfe said with a curl in her lip, "that this was not what you expected, and that if they were able, they should look into the ethical practices of a certain Grey-Star on the Council." She spoke the last of it through her teeth, her rage finally visible.

Samaira stepped toward the Blue-Star's cell. Her heart hammered as Abilene's face went from pale to a sickly blue color, tears enlarging her eyes.

"Please." Abilene shook her head. "They don't know anything."

"Enough."

Wolfe turned from her and faced the men again. "You have your orders. I will make contact when we land. You all understand the consequences of continued failure."

"Yes, ma'am," the three men returned in near unison.

Without another word to the prisoners, Wolfe clicked out of the room, her footsteps fading down the hall.

A long moment passed before Lawrence faced the other Black-Star. "How many men are you sending out?"

The bald man scowled and cast a glance toward Samaira. "Hardly a discussion to have in front of prisoners and traitors."

Lawrence's face remained expressionless. "Only if you plan on them escaping, but very well. I expect you to leave a contingent here, on the chance you're wrong about your timeline. And given the likelihood of them slipping past you again."

A guttural sound emitted from the other Black-Star's throat. His features twisted, murderous fury darkening his eyes. "I will do as I see fit with my men." He turned to Keith, nearly spitting his words at the man. "Keep control of your experiments for the next few days. My men," he darted a glance at Lawrence, "will be *busy*."

Keith's nose twitched, his usual sneer threatening to return, but he inhaled and seemed to settle himself. "Of course. I'll update you with any progress."

"No need," the Black-Star said with a dismissive wave of his hand. "I don't care about your little science project."

He followed Wolfe out of the room.

Keith clenched and unclenched his hands at his side. He glanced at Abilene and seemed to steel himself. He faced Lawrence. "I need a squad tonight."

Lawrence's eyes widened a fraction. "Tonight?"

"Yes," Keith hissed. "Did you not hear, Ms. Wolfe? Send them here at once."

There was a pause as Lawrence appeared to grapple with being given a command by a Blue-Star. After a quick look at Samaira, he strode out the door, leaving the two women alone with Keith.

Abilene's tears had overflowed, spilling down her cheeks and shimmering like little crystals in the white light of the room. Her body trembled.

"Hey." Samaira cleared her throat, not knowing what to say, how to say it, or if she *should* say anything with Keith there. Still, she approached the bars and offered out her hand. "I'm sure they'll be all right. That Black-Star has other stuff going on. Your family won't be his priority."

Abilene's response was a choked sob. She met Samaira's gaze, her eyes full of a pain so familiar that it clenched Samaira's heart. She took a step toward the bars.

"We have limited time." Keith's voice broke the connection between the two.

Samaira scowled at him, his words injecting fear into her veins.

"Get her out," he barked toward the door.

A squadron of familiar Black-Stars moved into the room. They opened the door to Samaira's cell. Flames licked at her fingertips, but her energy had not returned from Kim's escape. In swift movements, they had her hands back behind her back, chained into that awful position.

Keith hesitated as the Black-Stars made for the door.

"You could have been so much more." He shook his head at Abilene. "*We* could have been more. Instead, you're a traitor, and you'll die as one."

It felt like a bucket of ice had been dumped over Samaira's head. She craned her neck, reaching to see Abilene as the Black-Stars pulled her from the room.

The woman had straightened, her chin back at its defiant height. The fear was well disguised, but Samaira could see it in her eyes.

And then the door closed, and she was lost from sight.

They marched Samaira to a familiar exam room. The Black-Stars strapped her arms to the chair, oddly comfortable after the chains, and remained in the room. They lined the walls, even blocking the tinted observation window from Samaira's view.

Keith entered a moment behind the rest of them, his blue coat back in place, as well as the snide look of superiority. Another Blue-Star trailed along behind him, pushing a cart laid out with supplies.

Samaira swallowed.

"Limited time," Keith murmured. He glanced at the other Blue-Star.

The man, a wispy thing with curly brown hair and watery eyes, nodded. They began fiddling with the vials on the cart.

"Larger dose this time." Keith lifted a large syringe.

Samaira's pulse sped up. Her breathing came quick as fear clogged her thoughts.

"Hold still."

It was a command she'd never obeyed in her life, and one she continued to ignore. She fought as they pinned her arm in place. Fought as Keith flicked the barrel of the syringe. Fought as he found a vein and plunged the needle into her flesh.

The swirling liquid flowed into her blood. Keith passed the syringe to the other Blue-Star, who left the room not long after. A handful of the Black-Stars followed him out.

Keith leaned against the wall, watching Samaira and checking the glass tablet in his hands.

Samaira twitched. Tingling spread the length of her arm. Tingling, and then something else.

It burned.

Nacra, did it burn. Like those days in her childhood when she and Jason were still learning to control their fire. When they scarred their hands, wrists, and arms with the heat of flames they didn't understand.

She understood her flame now. Understood the thrumming heat that was constantly within. She'd tattooed over the scars. Not to hide them, but to remind herself of how much control she owned over herself.

It felt like those tattoos were melting. Like the flames within were fighting every inch of her skin to escape.

A scream ripped from her throat. A sound she'd refused to make in this horrible place, but couldn't stop now.

Nor could she stop what came next.

Keith's eyes went wide as flame erupted from Samaira's hands. Even with her palms pressed against the chair, fire shot out, hitting the ground, and roiling out like waves. He took a stumbling step toward the door. "Make her stop."

The remaining four guards moved in.

Samaira barely noticed their approach. She was distracted by the roaring heat consuming her inside and out. A small sliver of her, a tiny piece that wasn't being burned alive, knew what was about to happen.

"Don't—" she tried to say. Tried to warn them, as little as they deserved it.

It was too late.

The flames burst from her arms, her torso, her core. Screams surrounded her. Screams and charred cloth and flesh. The door slammed closed.

She went fully within. Abandoned the outside world and attempted to huddle within her own mind until it was done. Until the fire finished consuming her. Until she was dead.

Samaira.

"Ichi?" she gasped the word, barely able to breathe. "How are you…"

I've been practicing. Can't hold this for long. What's happening?

She couldn't speak. Couldn't connect thought to words. So she showed him. Flickering images of Kim, the Grey-Star, the syringe. The fire.

You have to breathe, Samaira.

She shook her head, tears turning to steam on her cheeks. Her body wouldn't survive this much longer.

Breathe.

The strength of the command did it—slammed the years of Ichi's protection, training, and discipline into the forefront of her mind. She gulped in a breath. It seared her lungs.

Again.

She did it again. The intensity of the flames lessened.

Pull it back, Samaira. Find the core, find your wards.

"I can't." Her voice was hoarse, cracked and barely audible to her own ears.

You can. It's inside you. Find it.

Samaira dove into the well that was herself. Down, through the raging flames that encompassed her mind, and to the very center of her being. Her heart sank as she saw the golden box she'd spent over a decade perfecting. Its ornate designs, secure foundations, hopeful shimmer... all melted away into a pool of nothing.

She was surrounded by untamed fire.

A box won't work for these flames, Ichi said.

She felt him, a shadow of his presence in her mind.

"A cage," she murmured.

A cage.

Samaira built. Built and crafted and pulled together her power within. It hurt, pain beyond anything her physical form had experienced.

Seconds ticked past. Ichi stayed with her a little longer, his shadow self giving careful instruction, helping her weave together a cage to contain the beast her power had become.

As she worked, the flames consuming her burned themselves down to embers. They flickered and spun, spitting sparks with the promise of returning soon to reap more chaos and death.

When it was finally done, and the flames were contained, she opened her eyes.

The stench of death hit her nostrils before she spotted the bodies on the floor. The Black-Stars who had surrounded her were gone. Burned to a crisp where they stood.

She was nude, her clothes burned away as well. The restraints around her wrists had melted, leaving angry red welts on her dark skin. The tattoos on her hands were ruined, the intricate designs pocketed with scorched and discolored ink.

Her arms were marred with burns, but the rest of her was unscathed. She rose on shaky legs and stepped away from the chair. Ash fell from her with each movement.

Every motion hurt. Even now the embers of her power fought for release from the cage she'd created.

Samaira clenched her teeth, struggling to focus. The room had been destroyed; the tinted window peeling, the paint melted in places, and the little cabinet in the corner still smoking. She opened the cabinet door and took a spare Blue-Star coat from it. She'd finished pulling her arms through, wincing as she did so, when the door to the exam room burst open.

Keith stood in the doorway, his face alight with success. He barely noted the bodies on the floor.

"Alive. Good. And that display will do wonders for our next set of projects. Well done."

Fury pounded through her skull at his words, so intense it nearly numbed the pain for a few seconds. She bit back tears, watching him, horrified.

"You'll do it again?" Samaira gestured to the men she'd killed. Her voice was rough and hoarse, each word a sharp pain in her throat. "After *this*?"

He waved a hand and scoffed. "*This* was the goal. Now, I trust you'll accompany me back to your cell without much fuss? I don't need to test the serum again tonight, but I will if you force my hand."

Samaira took half a step toward him, unsure how she'd kill him, but certain she'd be able to end his life before anyone stopped her.

Footsteps sounded in the hallway beyond, and Keith's eyes glinted. "You understand that I'm not the only Blue-Star in this facility. The others have their orders, should anything happen to me, the work *will* continue as planned."

Samaira pinched her lips to keep from retorting. The thought of one of the children going through what she'd just endured... or worse, reacting to the injection the way Jacob had...

She gave a single, sharp nod, and followed him from the room.

They didn't let her bathe, but she was provided with a new set of clothes before being locked back into the cell beside Abilene's.

"What..." Abilene's wide eyes stared at her in horror. "Your hands..."

Samaira shook her head, moving to the far corner and curling into a tight ball. The cage in her mind was a patch, a desperate attempt to control something that demanded freedom. It wouldn't last forever, and when it broke she didn't want to think of the destruction that would follow.

"Let me—" Abilene began.

"No," Samaira cut her off. Pain rippled down her throat. She shut her mouth, ducked her head, and closed her eyes.

For the first time since they'd been taken from Haven, any trace of hope within her was gone. The only thing left was bitter fury.

Chapter Twenty-Two

Forest near Dolor

Cho brushed gentle fingers across Kim's forehead. She was still asleep, flat on her back with Luna and Nova curled on either side like crescent moons, their arms draped across her torso.

Her dreams were erratic. Rapidly shifting from calm to crazed, anger and fear twisting like dark storms. She slept fitfully, emotions coming off of her in waves.

Now was not the time to be proud of himself, but he was. The days on the road, training the new members of their group, being in the open air and away from the city... it had changed him. Changed his power.

The walls in his mind, and the thick chest hidden behind them, were strong. His power caressed the edges of both yet when he let it out, he had more control over the way it behaved with the emotions of others.

Even after feeling Hawk's burst of furious pain at the question of why he'd been following the Grey-Star, it hadn't taken as long as expected for Cho to pull his power away.

What had caused his reaction was yet to be discovered. Cho was waiting for Juliana to broach the subject. He didn't want to be close to the man when it was brought up again.

They'd agreed to take a rest once Juliana healed the worst of Kim's wounds. Tommy leaned against Jane, playing with a string of flowers Daisy had put together for him. Claire was with them as well. Jane talked her through different ways to handle overexertion of her powers. The low murmur of their conversation reached Cho, and a small smile crossed his lips.

Juliana and Anthony sat with Taz and Daisy. They snacked on a bit of food, talking quietly while Anthony traced spiral patterns across Juliana's knuckles. He leaned in and whispered something, his lips almost touching her ear.

Cho looked away, cheeks growing hot as his gaze found Jason. He was brooding again; the mischievous smile Cho had been surprisingly relieved to see had vanished at Kim's mention of Samaira.

Anxiety coiled in Cho's stomach. Jason's mental wards were as strong as ever. The worry Cho felt came from his own concern for their family and for his friend.

Jason glanced up. His dark eyes caught Cho's, and Cho averted his gaze, face even warmer than it had been seconds before.

His sights landed on Hawk. The man hadn't sat still since they reached Kim. He was on the ground now, but his bare feet danced up and down, fingers twisting and fidgeting as though he weren't used to them.

Kim stirred on the ground, a low moan stirring her from fitful sleep.

Cho rose, careful not to disturb the children as he moved across the clearing and knelt by Daisy. "Hey, do you think you can help her?" He gestured toward Kim.

Daisy's smile froze in place for a second before the edges of her mouth turned down. "I, um... wouldn't that be intrusive? She's asleep."

Cho sighed and ran a hand through his hair. "Maybe, but she's not getting the rest she needs to heal."

He glanced at Juliana, who met his eye and nodded in agreement. "It would help for her to sleep until it's time to go."

Daisy glanced from Taz to Anthony. They both nodded as well. "All right. Just for easy dreams, yeah?"

"Yeah." Cho followed as Daisy rose, straightened her shirt, and went to Kim's side.

"I don't know how to contain it to one person yet," she murmured.

Cho knelt as well. "Luna? Nova?"

The twins both opened their eyes. Luna raised an eyebrow.

"Daisy is going to help Kim get some sleep. If you don't want to feel what she's going to give her, you'll want to move back."

The girls looked at Daisy. She gave them a small smile. "Nothing bad; I was going to do how I feel watching the sunset."

They exchanged a glance and then nodded. The two rested their heads again, draping their arms over Kim but keeping their eyes open.

"I'll be right here," Cho said.

Daisy's eyes widened in alarm. "But your power—"

He waved off her concerns. "I've gotten stronger. Besides, it'll be good practice."

She swallowed, but nodded and closed her eyes. A brief moment later the twinges of anxiety picked at the edge of Cho's mind. He frowned.

Daisy inhaled and let out a slow breath. The anxiety shifted. Warmth replaced it, the contentment that came with letting the sun wash over one's face before it dipped below the horizon. The wonder of a multicolored sky, the peace of safety, the satisfaction of a full belly, all swirled against Cho's wards.

He kept his shields firmly in place, allowing the emotions to caress him, but not take control.

Almost instantly, Kim's shifting and murmurs stopped. Luna and Nova, their foreheads pinched with concern, relaxed. The three of them began the steady rhythm of breathing that suggested easy sleep.

Cho's shoulders dropped. "Thank you," he murmured to Daisy.

She nodded, her mouth twisted in a small frown, and returned to the others.

He remained a moment longer as he stared out across the clearing. Jason's back was to a tree, his hands fiddling with something as brief sparks of flame appeared and disappeared from his fingers.

Cho turned to Kim, extending his power just enough to ensure that her dreams remained pleasant, or nonexistent. Anything but nightmares about Dolor.

The sun had fallen further, splitting the sky with reds, purples, and oranges. The thought of leaving his brother in that place for another night sent a thrum of unease and impatience down his spine.

Cho rose, careful not to disturb the children as he moved across the clearing.

Juliana noticed, standing as well, and leaned on Anthony as the two followed. Jason got to his feet after a few seconds and joined the other three in a small group at the center of their little oasis.

"I don't want to wait," Cho said.

His skin prickled with the heat of Jason's gaze.

Juliana raised an eyebrow. "You want to go in now?"

He heard the hint of incredulity in her voice.

Anthony put a hand on her shoulder. "I don't think we should be waitin' too long either, but we don't know what we're dealin' with yet."

"Let's find out." Jason gaze left Cho, darting to the man on the ground at the edge of the clearing. He stepped away from the group, raising his voice. "Time to ask our feathered friend what he knows."

Anthony and Juliana followed him, surrounding Hawk with varying expressions of suspicion. The man twitched at their approach.

"Yeh did promise answers," Anthony drawled. "Now's the time for 'em."

"It's not," Hawk muttered through clenched teeth. He didn't stand, merely stared up at the three of them. "Now's the time to get your friends out. Before *she* gets back."

There was a long pause. Cho's power flared at the edges of his mind. Strong emotions were rising, and his saffron gift wanted a taste.

"Who?" Juliana asked, crossing her arms over her chest.

Hawk's nose pinched into a sneer. "The Grey-Star. She left last night, after I found the girl." He gestured to Kim. "I didn't get the best look, but I know a handful of Black-Stars went with her. Another troop split off along the main road, probably lookin' for you. Their forces are less now. It's the time to go in."

Cho exhaled. They needed answers, needed to know they could trust this stranger. Cho cracked the wall in his mind, and saffron power bounded toward the opening.

Juliana, Anthony, and Jason kept their wards strong; the anger and suspicion painted on their faces remained secure from the whispers of yellow that leapt toward them. Hawk's emotions did not.

Cho frowned. He winced, pushing back the roiling fury within the man, and limited the flow of his power. "Why does this matter so much to you?"

The others turned. Jason cocked his head, brows drawn together in curiosity.

Cho gestured to Hawk. "He's got as much anger in him as you do, as we all do." He shook his head. "You don't even know them."

"I don't know 'em," Anthony interjected. "I'm angry too."

Jane stepped up, leaving Tommy with Claire as she strode over to join Cho. "You know us," she growled.

Jason looked down at Hawk. "What's your stake in this? Why are you after the Grey-Star."

Hawk let out his breath in a low hiss. "Well, I'm not *now*, am I?" he demanded. "The smartest time to get Elaine and the others is tonight, while she's gone, so I—"

He froze.

Cho, Jane, and Jason moved forward as one. Cho's insides rippled with nerves. He loosened his grip on the saffron light, letting the tendrils swirl around the fear Hawk was emitting. The fear and the still rumbling, never ceasing anger.

"How the frost do you know her name?" Jane demanded through gritted teeth.

Flames appeared in Jason's hand.

Hawk swallowed, his freckled skin going pale.

"Let's take a breath," Anthony murmured to Jason.

Hawk hadn't left his seat beneath the tree, but his fidgeting came to an abrupt halt.

Cho shuddered at the tension in the air. He called back his power and sealed the crack in the wall within his mind.

Anthony cut the air with his hand, looking hard at Hawk. "Start at the beginnin' and tell us everythin'."

Jason uttered a guttural sound. Rage and fire danced in his eyes, reflecting the flames in his palm.

Cho reached out, biting the inside of his lip to steel himself. His fingers closed over the phoenix tattooed across Jason's dark skin.

Hatred, terror, and panic roiled under the man's fierce demeanor. Cho inhaled, reinforcing the barrier between himself and Jason. At the same time a flash of surprise went through the flame thrower. His dark gaze stuck on Cho's hand, still resting on his warm skin.

Cho bit harder, not wanting to feel Jason's emotions, not wanting to read them in such a strained moment. Not wanting to intrude on his friend's privacy. He let go, his saffron latching onto one last hint of something before he shook it off and clenched his fist.

"He gets it," Cho said, his words directed toward Jason. "There's fear in there too, now." He turned his gaze upon Hawk, and there was a tremor in his voice as he spoke again. "How do you know her name?"

Hawk flexed his hands, the long fingernails chipped and dirty. He sucked in a ragged breath and stared at the blades of grass between his feet.

"I was six when I started growing feathers. They sprouted from my skin when I got scared. I was scared a lot. Eventually my mum got tired of hiding them from dad, and instead of letting him find me like that, someone took me away."

Beside Cho, Anthony ran a hand over his own forearm. The vivid image of black fur sprouting from the skin flashed through Cho's memory.

Juliana reached out, not looking at Anthony as she took his hand in hers.

Cho shifted back to Hawk.

"I got sent to a place like this." He gestured vaguely into the forest, and his jaw went tight. "It was all right at first. Blood samples, simple tests. There were others like me. Kids with... with *potential*, they said. We had rooms early on, beds and clothes, and..." he drifted off, a storm of emotion in his green eyes.

Cho swallowed and took half a step back. Even locked away, his power felt the waves of pain coming off Hawk.

He briefly registered Jason's gaze on him again. Cho gave a small nod, but the concern on the flame thrower's face didn't fade.

"After a few years it got bad. We started losing people. They said it was necessary. 'Acceptable loss parameters.' Some of the older kids, the ones who'd been kind to me, taken me in, taught me to read..." He paused again, several seconds ticking by as he clenched his jaw and his fists. "They decided we had to go."

He met Cho's eye. "Elaine was one of them."

Silence permeated the clearing for a long moment.

A storm of thoughts swirled in Cho's mind. Elaine's memory loss, the collection of scars on her inner elbows that she hid with flowing sleeves, Ichi's mention of the Grey-Star, and his fear of unlocking more than Elaine could handle.

Cho's mouth went dry, and a weight sank in his chest like a stone in water. Jane's expression reflected the emotions within him, equal parts confusion and horror. Jason clenched his fist, extinguishing the fire.

Hawk cleared his throat. "I was young still, only ten or eleven when it happened. They burned it down. Ran. I got... I got separated from the others. Found myself in a city, being hunted by Black-Stars."

A sneer tugged at the edge of his mouth. "They can't fly. I got away, but I never... I never found the others. I never knew what happened to them until..." He looked at Cho again.

Realization blossomed in Cho. "You were following the Grey-Star."

Hawk nodded.

"You saw them take Elaine and the others out of the city."

He nodded again.

"And then you," Cho frowned, more memories stirring, "you followed us. Into Grigoria."

Hawk picked at the edge of his nails. "*You* were her family more than I was by then. I saw that you got out, and I had to make sure you were safe. For her."

Cho's eyes burned. Jason turned and walked away, but Jane remained by his side, frozen as tears slid down her cheeks. She stared at Hawk, and Cho knew she was picturing Tommy, imagining what would happen if he were separated from her in such a way.

Silence fell again, interrupted by occasional sniffles.

Juliana wiped her cheeks and straightened her shoulders. "That doesn't explain how you knew about Anthony falling. You've been watching us as well."

Hawk's lip curled and he glared up at her. "Didn't I just say I've been watching the Grey-Star—"

"Wolfe," Juliana supplied.

He gave a jerky nod. "Wolfe. I followed her to Tornim when she came to your Coding."

"Do you know what she wants with me?" Juliana asked in a low voice.

Hawk shook his head. He turned from her, finally pushing to his feet as he faced Cho again. "I've waited long enough to find her. I won't wait any longer to get her out."

"Neither will we," Jason growled a few paces away. He was wearing a track in the grass, striding back and forth across the clearing.

Cho's veins thrummed with nerves. His usual anxiety, that beast which had grown docile the further they were from Tornim, reared up in his belly. But he nodded, met Jason's gaze, and hardened his resolve.

"We go in tonight."

Chapter Twenty-Three

Dolor

"We know next tah nothin' about the complex," Anthony said.

Jane scowled at him. "We know they have our family."

Anthony nodded. "Aye, but we oughta have a plan before we run in." He glanced at Juliana. She'd have something in that head of hers, some idea already forming.

Sure enough, she met his gaze with a slight grin, her fingers tapping against her thumb in that way he'd grown so used to. "We need to figure out where to get in. Somewhere as close to the room the children are being held as possible. A spot with thin walls, right Jane?"

The younger girl blinked, a flash of surprise briefly replacing her twisted expression. "Yeah. If we can find a route that only goes through one wall, I should be able to move everyone out without us needing a door."

Anthony grinned.

"We can't go now," Juliana said. Her gaze flicked to Jason as she said it.

"Why the frost not?" he demanded. He stepped toward her, Jane beside him as the two of them stared Juliana down.

"Because," her voice was steady, but her bright eyes flashed, "it's too early in the night. There's a strong chance people are still awake, eating dinner, wandering the halls, checking on prisoners..." She raised her eyebrows and pursed her lips.

Jason's lip curled. "I'm not waiting, Juliana. For all we know my sister could die if we wait."

"We could *all* die if we rush this, Jason." Her reply was low.

Anthony clenched his jaw. He understood the desire to run in now, but Juliana was right. He glanced at Hawk. "Yeh said they're experimentin' on the kids?"

Hawk slowly shifted his gaze to Anthony. "Yeah. At least, that's what they were doing when I was at a similar facility."

Anthony caught Juliana's eye as he looked back at Jason. "They won't kill her."

A flash of anguish went across Jason's dark face. "How do you know that?"

"Because," Juliana took a step toward him, her voice firm, "if Samaira is half as strong as you, she's one of the most powerful Alters they've ever seen. They won't kill her. They need her."

Silence fell for a few seconds. Anthony's heart hurt for Jason. If it was Naya or Jimmy in there... he understood the internal struggle his friend faced.

"I don't like waiting," Cho muttered. He met Jason's eye. "But if our chances of success increase by giving it a few more hours..."

Jason said nothing. He watched Cho for a brief moment then nodded.

"Frost," Jane grunted. "Fine, but we can make a plan at least."

"What's the biggest obstacle?" Daisy wondered aloud.

Anthony gave her half a grin. "I'm just guessin' here, but probably the Black-Stars with guns."

Even Jane cracked a smile at that. Jason's lip twitched.

"Actually," Juliana took up tapping again, her fingers brushing against her thumb in quick movements as she began to pace, "I think the biggest issue will be security cameras."

Cho groaned.

"They'll be everywhere," Juliana continued. "And if we want to get in and out without them noticing until morning—"

"We'd need to disable them," Anthony finished.

Juliana nodded with a grimace. "But I don't think that's even possible."

"We're in the middle of nowhere," Jane said. She ran her fingers across the bark of a tree. "How are they getting power?"

Juliana's eyes widened, a glint returning to them. "Good question." She turned to Hawk, and her fingers rested on Anthony's arm. "Can you two do some scouting? There will be solar panels on the roof, but see if you can find a large inverter. It'll be massive for a complex as big as you've described. It's how they transform solar energy into electricity, make it usable for the facility. If we can shut it down..."

"The power will go out," Cho said, something close to hope in his voice. "Will that cut the cameras?"

Juliana shook her head. "Not likely. Even if they do go down it will only be for a few seconds. They'll have a backup generator, but it'll be a distraction at least. It might disrupt things long enough for us to get in and out, and if not, it'll hopefully pull the attention of some of the guards."

"That's brilliant." Anthony grinned. He squeezed her hand and turned to Hawk. "Let's get this done before it gets too dark. Give us time to plan when we get back."

The bird-man jerked his head and strode into the trees, taking off his borrowed shirt and tossing it onto the forest floor.

Jason scowled.

"Is everyone on board with this plan?" Juliana looked at each of them in turn, only the twins and Kim not part of the conversation as they were still sleeping on the far edge of the clearing.

Anthony reached for one of her hands and gave her fingers a light squeeze.

Jane nodded. "We take out the power."

"And get our family back," Cho murmured.

Jason nodded, crossed to his shirt, and plucked it from the ground with a glare into the dense forest.

Anthony prowled the edge of the woods, his heightened gaze fixed on Dolor. Lights were ablaze on the southwestern side of the complex, but the rest was cloaked in shadow.

The fence entirely surrounded the oval-shaped building, a cleared patch of ten yards or so between it and the encroaching forest. Anthony stalked through the trees, staying out of view of the occasional clusters of guards wandering the perimeter.

He stopped just short of the entrance, hidden by the trees and the late evening light. A gravel road led away; he assumed it connected with the main road that led through Pangaea.

Guards were posted on either side of a closed sliding gate. The gravel drive circled a fountain, grass framing either side and sloping down to join the massive stretch of greenery between the fence and the actual building. Anthony had spotted walkways, clusters of trees, and benches throughout as he'd circled the perimeter.

There was a line of vehicles parked just inside the fence. Black-Star trucks, from the look of them, though not as many as there were spaces for.

Anthony's head twitched as his ears picked up chatter from the guards at the front gate.

"... glad we're done looking."

"Waste of time, she can't survive out there on her own. She's probably dead already."

A low growl rumbled in the back of his throat.

Shapes moved at the front of the building. Massive glass doors, which poured light onto the front lawn, opened. More Black-Stars stepped out, their features blurred from such a distance, but their uniforms impossible to miss.

He sniffed, a familiar scent distracting him for a brief moment. His hackles rose. He couldn't place it, but the wolf knew a threat when it smelled one. Anthony clamped down on the snarl he wanted to unleash, and instead backtracked into the trees.

He went slow until he'd gotten well out of earshot, then broke into a run. His powerful legs propelled him through the forest, leaping fallen logs, branches, and bushes, and taking him north parallel to the fence.

Something swooped overhead, and his attention caught the massive bird soaring through the air on the other side of the fence.

He snorted a wolfish laugh and sped up.

They raced to the northern arc of the fence, and Anthony skidded to a halt.

Hawk angled up, his figure becoming a pinprick in the sky as he drifted over the top of Dolor.

Anthony's sharp eyes watched him for a moment. Then he returned to skulking along the fence, focused on finding the big metal box Juliana had talked about.

He paused only a few seconds later. There it was, a massive grey rectangular box a few yards from the complex. His head cocked, a faint buzzing making his fluffy ears twitch.

Ahead, the hawk made another circle, crossing in front of the nearly full moon that was just cresting the tips of the trees to the east. Anthony filled his lungs with the chilly evening air and darted into the trees.

"Someone will have to stay outside the building," Cho muttered.

Anthony finished tugging his shirt over his torso and glanced toward the children on the ground. Luna and Nova had woken while he was gone, and Kim was up now as well. The little girl munched on a handful of nuts from the charging station.

Jane sat against a thick tree, Tommy stirring from his nap on her lap. The others had grouped together, running through the various plans they'd come up with while Anthony and Hawk had been gone.

Darkness had fallen. Only moonlight illuminated their little clearing.

Jason crossed his arms. "A handful of people if we can manage it. The smaller our number going in, the less chance we're seen."

"Agreed," Anthony said. "And it'll be important tah have someone ready tah help the little ones when they get outside."

"If it's like the last facility, Black-Stars'll be patrolling the inside. Even at night." Hawk clenched his hands. He'd arrived back a minute after Anthony, quickly tugging on a pair of pants before joining the planning.

"We'll be quick." Juliana glanced at Jane, who nodded. "In and out, and back to the truck. Kim said there's only one door to the room they're being held. We can keep them out long enough."

"We could cut the fence," Hawk said, stretching his neck and glancing toward the sky. "But if those two," he pointed to the twins, "can hover people over it, the Black-Stars won't know where to start the search."

"What about the g... gr... grass?" Taz cut in. "Footprints?"

Anthony's lips twisted as he thought for a moment, then shook his head. "There are patrols, like Hawk said. Black-Stars stomping all over the lawn. Plus a dozen paths cutting through the grass. Maybe Luna and Nova," he gave them a nod, "can lessen the impact, but I don' think that'll be a problem."

The twins exchanged a quiet look and nodded back.

"I may be able to leave a trail headed the wrong way," Hawk glanced at Juliana and Anthony. "Get in a truck and steer it up the road, crash it into a tree or something and transform. I can meet you somewhere."

Juliana shook her head. "That's a last resort scenario. I don't want anyone going off on their own. We stick with two groups. One creates a distraction, and hopefully shuts down the cameras for a few minutes, and the other goes in for the kids."

Jason nodded. "Agreed." He unfolded his arms, casting a look toward Cho. "Non-active powers should stay behind; kill the inverter, keep a lookout, and get everyone to the transport."

Anthony took half a step back as a ripple of frustration flickered across Cho's face.

"I'm going inside to get them, Jason." The tone was a new one. Anthony didn't know Cho could sound so assertive.

Jason's eyes narrowed.

Anthony glanced at Juliana. He didn't bother asking if she'd stay with the outside group. He didn't want that lighting blue glare turned on him.

"It'll be safer for the ones who don't go in," Jason murmured. "They can make a break for it if something goes wrong."

Cho's expression hardened. He gave the slightest shake of his head.

"I'll stay behind," Taz broke through the mounting tension, and all eyes shifted his way. "Outside, to disable the electricity thing."

Anthony raised an eyebrow at his friend.

Taz shrugged. "I don't have any kinda power, active or not. But I know where we are, I know how tah get to the transport, and I don't expect I'd be much help on the inside."

"You'll need someone with you," Juliana said. "Breaking the box won't be easy."

"We'll be there," Luna piped up.

Nova nodded. "We can go with Taz, cause the distraction, then meet everyone from Haven at the fence after Jane gets them through the wall. We'd need to be there anyway, to get them over a bit at a time."

"Kim can stay with us too," Luna added. "She doesn't need to go back in there."

Kim's wide eyes sparkled with tears. "I might be able to help with the electricity," she said in nearly a whisper.

Juliana looked at the twins. "That, and she can disable the tracking devices as you're moving with the kids."

Their eyes widened, and Kim let out a small gasp.

"If you can manage it," Juliana said to the girl. "You'll need to short them out the way you did yours. Otherwise none of this will matter."

She sniffed and gave a fierce nod.

Anthony turned to Daisy.

"I'm coming in," she said before he even opened his mouth. "I can help."

Anthony pursed his lips. Beside him, Juliana's mouth twitched in a grin.

"Claire?" Cho looked to the quietest member of their group. "Do you want to stay with Taz? It'll be safer than going in."

She swallowed; ice hardened around her knuckles like it did every time she was nervous. "I..." She bit her lip.

Anthony crossed to her and put a reassuring hand on her shoulder. "It'd be a help," he said softly, "knowin' there's a safe spot for us when we get out. Knowin' someone who can chuck a blade of ice is there watchin' out for us."

The others nodded, and Claire's anxiety seemed to lessen.

"Yeah." She gave Taz a weak grin.

"No."

Anthony turned. Tommy standing beside his sister, glared up at her with a pouting lip and disobedience in his eyes.

Anthony's heart twinged at the resemblance to Jimmy.

"Tommy," Jane said in the gentle voice she reserved for him. "There was a warning in the tone, however. "You're staying outside."

"No," Tommy said again, louder this time. "It's not fair. I can help. I can—"

"Yeh are helpin'," Taz interrupted. He strode forward, flashing a crooked smile that brought a quiet chuckle from Anthony. "I need yeh here with me, little man. What happens when a Black-Star patrol comes sniffin' round the power stuff? We'll need that trick of yours tah keep everyone safe and hidden."

He knelt by the boy, putting a hand on Tommy's thin shoulder, and met his eye. The boy sniffed, suspicion in his gaze.

"I'm not foolin' yeh. I can't protect the others the way you can. Yer sister'll get 'em out. I need you tah keep 'em safe."

Tommy's attention was on Taz, but Anthony watched Jane.

Her hard expression slipped, and she looked years younger, closer to her fourteen-year-old self and less like an adult worn down by the world. Her lower lip trembled as she stared at Taz. Her eyes brightened for a brief moment before she blinked rapidly and cleared her throat.

"That's why?" Tommy glanced up at Jane. "To help everyone? Not to keep me out of the way—"

"No." Jane shook her head. "You're never in the way, Tommy. It's so you can help."

Anthony marveled at the steadiness of her voice given the multitude of emotions that must be playing within. But it worked. Tommy nodded and fixed Taz with a serious gaze.

"I'm ready. I won't let you down."

Taz chuckled and stood, putting a hand on Tommy's shoulder. "I know."

The next few hours were spent resting, rehashing the plan, and fidgeting. The lot of them were anxious at the magnitude of what they were about to attempt, but as Anthony went over the plan again and again, he thought they genuinely had a chance of getting the kids out and getting away before too much attention came their way.

The dead of night came. They donned warm clothes. Juliana opted for a Black-Star jacket that made Anthony cringe. She chuckled at him, looped her arm through his, and kissed his cheek.

They stayed close for a moment, enjoying each other's warmth. When she moved away to talk with Jane, both Taz and Daisy caught Anthony's eye in the silvery moonlight. Their faces were lit with mirth.

A bubble of happiness filled his chest as heat filled his cheeks. He smirked and rolled his eyes at both of them, then went to find Jason.

Eventually, the time came for them to make their way to the fence.

Hawk led the way, his eyes half-shifted to help his vision. He and Jason strode at the front, making more noise than Anthony was comfortable with, but moving silently compared to the others.

Tommy, who had been latched to either his sister or Taz since they'd left the lake near Abredea, scurried forward and tugged at Juliana's sleeve. She hunched a bit, listening to his whispers as they walked.

The second he was gone, Jane was at Taz's side.

Anthony, bringing up the rear of the group, caught her hissed words.

"If anything happens to him—"

"I won't let yeh down anymore'n he would," Taz interrupted, his voice equally low.

Anthony stifled a grin at the surprised hitch in her breath. A brief moment passed and then she gave a sharp nod and darted away to walk with the twins.

Then they arrived at the edge of Dolor, and a collective inhale and tension rolled through the group.

The fence lay before them, stretching as far as they could see in either direction. Ahead, the complex itself sat with a couple hundred yards of manicured lawn, winding paths, clusters of trees, and concrete benches between it and them. Faint lights shone from second and third story windows in the distance.

Anthony stepped up and reached out for Juliana's hand. She took it and squeezed, her pulse racing.

They kept a lookout for Black-Star patrols but, seeing none in the immediate area, they hurried forward. Wanting to spare Jane's abilities, Luna and Nova hovered everyone over the fence.

Anthony was painfully reminded of the chain-link surrounding Abredea as he landed on the other side. His skin crawled at being on this side of a cage again, and his wolf snarled within at the feeling of being trapped.

It helped that he knew the escape plan, and that he could see so well in the darkness. It wasn't just his eyes, he realized as they padded across the manicured grounds, hurrying between sections of trees to stay out of the open. Maybe it was the heightened state of awareness, but his hearing had grown more acute as well. The footsteps of his friends around him, the rustle of dry leaves as a light breeze blew through the trees, even the occasional voice in the distance that made him listen for potential threats.

He concentrated, took a breath, and felt the wolf within stir. He sniffed, and nearly sneezed.

An assault of smells hit him. So many were impossible to describe, to decipher. Even more were intensely familiar. The grass, trees, metal of the chain-link, dust from the concrete building, and his friends. Daisy's soft scent of dandelions, barely noticeable with his human senses. Taz, the dirt on his hands from playing on the ground with Tommy, sap on his fingers from running his hands across trees as they walked. Jane, the steel of her gaze also found in the smell of her sweaty hair, her heavy breaths.

Hawk carried the scent of a fellow predator, and it took Anthony a second of effort to stop the wolf getting distracted by the idea of a hunt. He shifted his focus.

Jason smelled of fire. Ash and soot and burning things, consuming.

Anthony caught a whiff of the same scent on Cho. The smell of sitting too close to a fire, along with the anxiety Anthony associated with Cho's twisting of hands and the way he pulled at the hem of his shirt.

And Juliana. Juliana stood out the most, to him and the wolf. His heartbeat quickened at her faint strawberry and pine scent, the sound of her breath, and the moment of acknowledgement that they were walking into danger. That *she* would be in danger.

The wolf within growled. *It'll be all right,* Anthony murmured internally. *We'll be with her; we'll keep her safe.*

His power settled, and he pulled back from it, returning his senses to normal as they slowed to a stop midway between their respective destinations.

Chapter Twenty-Four

Dolor

Moonlight cast the world in silvery shadows. Before them lay a long stretch of manicured grass. Little dots of trees, benches barely visible, ripples in the ground where gravel made paths through the lawn were scattered throughout the massive space.

Dolor itself loomed ahead of them. The structure was unlike anything Cho had seen before. The entire thing was a dome, the sides curving down until they touched the dirt, the top stretching to the equivalent of maybe three or four stories high.

They'd spent nearly thirty minutes walking through the forest before reaching the fence in order to arrive on the eastern side of the building. Thanks to Hawk and Anthony, they had an idea of what to look for. Thanks to Juliana, they had a plan. And thanks to Kim, they knew where the children were being held.

Cho exhaled through parted lips, his nerves thrumming like taut strings that had been plucked.

"The main doors are on the opposite side," Hawk whispered. "Big glass things, a helipad, trucks, and the drive that connects to the main road."

"Glad you two checked it out," Juliana said just as quietly.

Cho nodded, the motion lost to the others as they moved forward across the grass.

"Split up?" Jane murmured, a slight tremor in her voice.

"Yeah," Juliana said.

Cho glanced at Claire. She'd barely just discovered her power, barely gotten her head around the idea that her parents were ready to send her away, barely known the peace and love Ichi and Elaine had built in Haven.

Frost, she'd nearly died as they'd snuck out of Tornim.

"Hey." He met her eye as she looked up at him. "Be careful, yeah?"

She nodded, and a hint of the incredulous smile she'd worn when he'd confronted her in Agora so many weeks ago returned to her lips. "What, is this dangerous or something?"

Cho huffed a silent chuckle. "You're spending too much time with Jane."

"Heard that," Jane hissed.

"It's time." Juliana took Taz's hand for a second. "Get the power down and get back on the other side of the fence. Quickly as you can. Hawk will be able to see you when we get out. Don't wait for us here. Short out the trackers and then get to the truck. Make sure you do the trackers first."

Taz nodded. "S... s... see you soon."

He and the others darted away through the grass, making their way to the large black box just north of where they'd paused.

"Let's find them." Jane stepped to the front of the group. Her lanky form was stiff with the same tension they all felt.

She was the key to their plan, and the weight of it had settled, however she tried to hide it, on her shoulders.

Jason and Anthony flanked Jane. Daisy joined Cho in the center of their group, and Juilana trailed behind with Hawk.

Low lights were visible within Dolor. The ground floor was entirely obscured by the domed wall, but there were windows on the second and third floors. None were particularly bright, but there was a steady glow from what, Juliana told the others in a hushed whisper, were probably hall lights.

Cho's gaze was fixed on the wall, scanning its surface in the dark for the slitted window Kim had told them about.

"There," came a hushed whisper from Anthony.

Cho looked where he pointed. There was a gap, a section of wall where the evenly sized windows stopped, and all that was left was a stretch of blank concrete curving around the building.

Blank concrete and one thin slit.

No light came from within. Whatever room that was, with the window high enough that it could have been on the second floor, was pitch black.

They hurried to the wall. Jane caressed the surface. She extended her hand, pressing through, and then brought it back.

"Not too thick," she said. "I can bring us all through."

Juliana opened her mouth.

"When it's time," Jane snapped quietly.

Cho gave a stern frown and held the expression until she looked at him. She rolled her eyes.

"Any minute now," Anthony murmured.

Jason crossed his arms. Tension rolled off the man in waves. Not from his mind, his mental barriers were as strong as ever, but from his tight shoulders, his furrowed brow, and the little sparks visibly dancing from the tips of his fingers even as he tried to hide them in his clenched fists.

Time seemed to stretch.

There was a thunk in the distance. Everyone looked north. Jane took a few steps, her body rigid with worry.

Cho almost said something, but Juliana stepped toward the girl.

"Taz will keep him safe, Jane."

"What if he doesn't listen?" Jane's voice trembled. "What if he tries to come help?"

Juliana stepped into Jane's eyeline. "Tommy's a good kid. He knows the plan. Besides, Taz has plenty of practice dealing with people who don't want to listen." Her gaze darted to Anthony. Jane followed the look, and a smirk broke her thin frown.

"Hey," Anthony whispered, dry humor in his tone.

A split-second later, Jason put up a hand. "They did it."

A chill went down Cho's spine. He turned. Along the dome, just before it rounded off and blocked their view, the little windows were dark.

"Give it a second," Juliana said as Jane hurried toward the wall. "They'll probably do some sort of prisoner check when something goes wrong."

"It's all dark," Jason muttered. "Can she stick her head in?"

Juliana grimaced.

"Not anymore." Hawk pointed. They followed his gesture to the thin slit nearly a story above them. It glowed with dim blue light.

"Emergency lights," Juliana breathed. "The backup generator is on already. Just give it another minute, Jane. Then you can check."

"How long do we have before Black-Stars get to the inverter?" Anthony wondered aloud.

"If either of you see them coming," Juliana glanced from him to Hawk, "Jane will pull us through."

The anxiety of waiting clenched Cho's stomach into knots.

"I'll hear 'em before we see anythin'."

They waited in silence. After a moment, Jane pressed a hand to the wall, stuck her face against the concrete, and her head disappeared into the surface.

It was a disturbing sight.

She darted out a second later. "You were right," she huffed with a glance to Juliana. "There are two Black-Stars in there."

"Did they see you?" Sweat trickled down Cho's spine, the cold night air doing nothing to cool him amidst the heat of anticipation.

"No," Jane shook her head, "they were walking away from me. Toward the door, it looked like. It's... it's bad in there."

"The others are back at the fence." Hawk squinted into the darkness.

A collective rush of relief went through the group.

"How long do we wait?" Cho asked. He sucked in a breath, releasing it slowly as he bolstered the walls in his mind.

Not long. Barely a minute passed before Jane checked again. She popped back out, reached for Jason's hand, and waited as they all connected.

"Fast," Juliana murmured. "We *have* to be fast."

Cho clamped a hand over Jason's forearm. A buzz raced across his skin, but he held on, aware of the danger of losing contact with Jane.

Cho was struck hard with the scent of stale air. A mix of fear, mold, sweat, and other things he didn't want to identify saturated the massive space they'd stepped into.

The ceiling was high, stretching past a normal first floor and arcing into darkness. Along the walls, orbs of pale blue light glowed.

Cho trembled as his internal mental wards strained. The darkest emotions he'd ever experienced slammed through and around him, a whirlwind of tortured pain.

Daisy's gasp was the loudest. Juliana cursed under her breath, and Anthony stumbled in horror, planting a hand on one of the cages.

They were surrounded by them. Crates to hold the children, some as tall as Cho, some significantly smaller. Outrage pulsed like a heartbeat radiating from the group.

Cho forced more power into his wards. The saffron glow within him was drawn to the fury, the sadness, and the pain permeating the room.

Wide eyes took them in. Murmurs began. Confused whispers that sounded like a leaky gas pipe as they spread through the room. Then...

"Cho?"

Cho's stomach lurched. The familiarity of the voice, the reprieve from his unacknowledged fear that he'd never hear it again, simultaneously crushed him and lifted a weight he'd been carrying for weeks.

He turned. At the end of the middle row of cages stood Ichi. Cho practically flew.

Footsteps hit the ground behind him and, as he skidded to a stop before his brother, Jason halted beside him.

"How is this..." Ichi gaped at him, horror and hope playing across his face, his worn, drawn face.

Cho had never seen him like this. It looked like he *had* died. Died and been reborn as a frail, thin, skeletal version of himself.

"This isn't possible," Ichi muttered. His brown eyes were fixed on Cho, pain bleeding from them. "You can't be here."

"I'm here, Ichi." Cho's voice was thick with tears. "We're here."

"We're getting you out," Jason said through gritted teeth.

"This is impossible." He shook his head, tears pooling in his eyes as he glanced at Jason and back to Cho.

"It's not," Anthony drawled. He drew close in Cho's periphery, but Cho only had eyes for his brother. "We need someone at the door," Anthony said.

Jason disappeared.

"Yer family's been looking for yeh a long while. It's time tah go. Let me get 'im out, Cho." Anthony's gentle voice was enough for Cho to take a step back.

Anthony knelt, pulling a few long metal instruments from his pocket.

"No time," Jane snapped. She strode toward them, her face already pale.

At the far wall, a dozen children had been pulled from their cages. They huddled together near Daisy and Hawk.

Jane reached through the bars of Ichi's cage, gripped his arm, and pulled him through.

"I thought..." Ichi stared between them with wide, disbelieving eyes.

Juliana cut him off. "Cho, is this everyone?"

A thud interrupted his answer.

They all wheeled around, terrified gazes on the door. Jason was leaned up against it, keeping the thing closed with sheer strength. Hawk darted past, joining Anthony as the two hurried to help.

"Cho?" Juliana barked.

"No," Cho shook his head, biting back the fear clenching his chest. His power writhed within. He turned to his brother. "Where is Elaine? Samaira?"

Ichi blinked. Whether it was the shock of seeing them, the results of his treatment in Dolor, the obvious lack of nutrition, or the cumulation of all of it, he inhaled and shoved his struggle down. His eyes cleared. "Elaine is there." He pointed and Jane, pulling out the last child in the row, sprinted over.

"We can't hold it," Jason called from the door.

Juliana pushed past Cho, rushing to Anthony's side. Ichi gave another shake of his head and followed her. Cho joined him.

The dim blue light of the room illuminated Ichi's thin arms as he raised them before the door. "Only two right now."

"Let 'em in?" Anthony grunted. "Tie 'em up?"

"Not quite," Ichi's lip twitched, rage burning in his gaze.

"I can take one." Hawk darted a glance toward Ichi.

Cho's brother nodded. "And I can take the other."

Jason sucked in a breath. Another surge of weight slammed into the door, knocking the three men holding it back an inch.

Juliana stepped to the side. "Now."

Hawk, Jason, and Anthony jumped back. The door fell open and two Black-Stars lost their footing on the way in. One recovered, gun at the ready.

The other landed on one knee. Before he rose there was a flash of steel, light glinting off the metal. Hawk stepped away as blood poured from the man's open neck.

Juliana moved to shut the door.

Cho watched the Black-Star holding the gun. She had a ponytail high on her head. Sleep-deprived eyes darted from the man on the ground to the nearly two dozen loose prisoners around her. The muzzle of her gun dipped down.

Ichi hissed, a low stream of air escaping his lips. Cho's brow furrowed as blood dripped from his brother's nose.

The Black-Star grunted. Her weapon fell from her hands.

She collapsed a second later; the blood that poured from her ears, eyes, and nose took on a purple hue in the blue light of the room.

"What…"

"No time," Juliana barked. "More will be here any minute. We have to go."

Cho swallowed the questions, the horror, and took his brother's arm. "Where's Samaira."

Jason darted forward as well. His eyes were wide as he stared at Ichi.

Ichi shook his head. "I don't… they took her, last night. Her and Kim—"

"Kim escaped," Juliana said. "She's with the others, waiting for you. Is Samaira alive?"

Ichi looked from Jason to Juliana with hesitation.

"Is she?" Cho demanded, his skin buzzing with nerves. Waves of Jason's anxiety washed over him, but his mental shields held.

"She was last night."

"We don't have time for this," Juliana breathed. She looked back at the door. There was no way to keep it closed from the inside.

"We leaving, or what?" Jane called from the far wall. Something muddled her voice, exhaustion, and what sounded like tears.

Jason let out a growl, turning from the others and striding toward the door.

Cho caught hold of his arm. "Don't."

"Get off me, Cho." Jason's expression darkened. "I'm going to find her."

"No," Cho said, his voice fierce. His heart slammed against his ribs as a furious combination of terror and determination thundered through him. "*We* are going to find her."

Anthony stepped forward with a nod and put himself between Jason and the door. Cho blinked back tears as Daisy and Juliana approached as well.

"I have questions," Juliana said. Her expression was sharp. Cho finally caught a glimpse of the rash anger Daisy had laughed about a week ago. "Things we *need* to know if we want to be free. We find Samaira, maybe some answers. But we have to get them out first."

She gestured to the huddle of children against the far wall. Cho spotted the outline of Elaine, leaning hard against Jane.

Cho released his hold on Jason's wrist and shook the mild burning from his hand. "We won't leave without her, Jason. I promise."

"I'll take them," Hawk said. He cleaned the blade of his knife on his pants and tucked the steel back into his belt. He met Jason's eye. "Get your sister. I'll make sure they get to the others."

"We'll meet you at the truck," Juliana said. Her voice was steady, no hint of the fear leaking from her wards.

Cho nodded. "Hurry."

Ichi watched Hawk's back as the man hurried toward Jane and the children. Conflict marred his expression as he looked back at Cho. "I can't leave without you…"

Anthony stepped to his side. "We'll keep an eye on 'im," he murmured. "Get yer people to safety. We know where tah meet yeh."

Ichi gritted his teeth and, for the first time Cho could remember, an influx of emotion rolled off his brother. Pain, fear, indecision, all amplified as Ichi put a cold, thin hand to Cho's cheek.

Anthony clasped Ichi's shoulder. "Yer worried about yer brother, I understand. But yeh haven't seen him these past few weeks. He's strong. Kept people together. Kept them safe. Kept 'em focused on rescuin' the lot of yeh."

"It's time." Jane's growl echoed down the dark chamber. A second later nearly a third of the group vanished.

Cho met his brother's gaze. One of his dark eyes was bloodshot, a vessel had burst when he'd killed the Black-Star. Blood still dripped from his nostril.

"Get them to safety. I'll see you soon."

It was a scramble of movement from then on. Cho walked Ichi to the others and watched Jane take him through with the last group. Hawk had transformed on the other side, Jane told them, and was prepared to lead the children to the fence.

Pale and panting as she was, she'd shot down Cho's suggestion to go with them.

"You're exhausted," Jason snapped, gesturing at her as she slumped against one of the walls.

"Yeah," she spat back "How do you plan on getting Samaira out of the building without me, exactly?"

"Bigger problems." Juliana stepped between them.

Cho turned toward the door as the sound of pounding footsteps reached his ears.

"Frost."

Chapter Twenty-Five

Dolor

Anthony stood to the side of the door. It was going to open inward. Black-Stars would attack them any second now.

Cho had released his power and let it sprawl as far from him as possible. He'd counted six before doubling over and sinking into the shadows to regain control.

Anthony's palms were sweaty. One hand clenched his uncle's old blade. The other held a long metal rod he'd taken from one of the Black-Star bodies. A shudder went down his spine. He reminded himself that these people were torturing children.

He glanced back at the rows of cages. A growl rumbled within at the thought of Tommy in one of them.

They had to do this.

His stomach churned.

Jason stood a few feet from the door, flames ready in his open palms.

Daisy stared at the door with concentration splashed across her face. She was their secret weapon. A surprise of terror that would, hopefully, knock the Black-Stars off balance when they burst in.

Juliana insisted on being beside Anthony. The knife she'd taken from the truck was in her hand. Jason had run them all through a few drills on the hand-to-hand combat he and Samaira used, but none of them had any real experience with a blade.

Jane leaned against a row of cages, a gun in her hands, her face paler than usual.

It would have to be enough.

Footsteps staggered to a stop on the other side of the door.

"Ready?" Anthony's whisper seemed to echo through the now empty room.

Daisy nodded.

He inhaled, pouring effort into shielding his mind.

The door burst open. Light flooded the room at the same time hollering Black-Stars piled in.

Daisy shunted her power toward them.

Anthony winced as terror whispered against the trees protecting his mind. It was strong, the kind of fear that locks a person in place, freezes them to their bones.

Or causes them to flee.

Pride swept through Anthony for a second as half of the Black-Stars scattered. Their pounding boots faded down the hall. Another cowered against the door-frame, sobbing frantically.

The remaining two soldiers attacked.

Fire hit the first, flames engulfing his face as Jason leapt at him. The flame thrower dealt another blow that sent the Black-Star staggering back. He slammed into the cowering man, and they fell in a tangle of limbs.

Jane fired. Her shot went wide.

Anthony darted forward, slicing down with his knife. The blade dug in but not far enough. The Black-Star whirled, slamming her thick-gloved hand across Anthony's face.

His vision blurred.

Juliana rushed past him and sank a fist into the woman's stomach. She raised her blade, prepared to strike.

Something barreled into her. Jules and another guard tumbled to the ground with cries of pain.

Anthony lunged. He pressed the metal device against the Black-Star who'd hit him and flicked a small switch at the handle.

The woman screamed. She fell to the ground twitching and spasming.

Anthony jerked back. He shot a quick, alarmed look at the weapon in his hand, then rushed to Juliana's side.

She grunted, rolled, and shoved the Black-Star off. He was dead, her knife planted firmly in his chest.

Juliana reached up, and Anthony pulled her to her feet.

The fight was over. Jason and Jane had each felled a Black-Star. The uniform on one was still burning. The other had a gaping hole in his gut that painfully reminded Anthony of May's death.

"Yeh all right?" he huffed, glancing at Juliana.

She shook her head. "Not really. You?"

He didn't respond, moving to the Black-Star he'd electrocuted and kicking her over so she faced the group. She was the only one in the room still alive.

Jason stalked toward the downed soldier, fire at the ready "Door," he snarled, reminding the others of their continued danger.

"Wait." Anthony put up a hand, stepping between the man and his prey.

Cho hurried around the two, tugged a body through the doorway, and slid the door closed. "We can't stay here."

"We also can't go running in blind," Juliana said. She met Anthony's eye with a nod before her focus turned to the woman on the ground.

She was tanned, with curly brown hair in a tight bun at the back of her head. A mixture of anger and fear glinted in her eyes.

"Fine," Jason said through gritted teeth. He closed his hand, the flames disappearing and returning the room to a dull blue glow. "Be quick."

"Don't move." Anthony bent, plucking the shock stick from the Black-Star's belt. He took a thick pair of nylon handcuffs as well.

Juliana reached down, grabbed the woman by the shoulder of her jacket, and yanked her onto her knees. "Hands out."

Jason scoffed. "Why bother? They know we're here. We don't have time for this."

Anthony glanced at the man, and then at the bodies on the ground. "We don't need tah kill her right now. We need answers. If she can provide 'em, maybe she lives."

The Black-Star's vicious breaths shifted. A hint of hope glinted in her eyes as she looked from Jason to Anthony.

Cho stepped toward them from the shadows. "Get her tied up. She'll answer our questions, and then she'll go in a cage until someone comes to find her."

Juliana stooped and grabbed another of the metal shock sticks. Anthony frowned as he surveyed the guards. There was an odd lack of plasma guns on the bodies.

Anthony bound the woman's hands. A heavy silence weighed down the room. Anthony worked to slow his breathing. Not from the effort of the struggle, but from what else they'd have to do to get Jason's sister out of Dolor.

Bloody images flashed through his mind. The hot metallic taste of blood seemed to coat his mouth before he shook out of it.

"Where is the woman who can control flames?" Juliana crouched before the Black-Star, her voice low.

The Black-Star's eyes, oddly green in the blue light, darted to Jason. Something like understanding seemed to flash across her face.

"You won't find her," she breathed. "The complex is massive."

Jason growled, but Juliana held up a hand.

Anthony sidestepped, positioning himself just out of the Black-Star's line of sight. He stood behind her right side in an attempt to be a threatening presence. He tucked his uncle's knife into the small leather sheath on his belt.

Juliana cocked her head. "That's *why* we haven't killed you."

The Black-Star looked at the pungent, smoking bodies around her.

Juliana snapped her fingers, drawing attention back to herself. "Tell us where she is. How to get there. And if there are any more children still alive in Dolor."

The woman's swallow was audible. "You weren't…"

The fear was palpable now. Cho's expression twisted as he inhaled deep breaths and backed further from the woman. Daisy stepped in front of him, a physical shield against the emotions.

Anthony clenched his fist. How much time did they have before another set of Black-Stars showed up? How many were in the facility? He looked at Juliana, but her gaze was fixed, furiously, on the woman.

"We weren't what?"

"You weren't supposed to be here yet," the woman gulped.

Cold seeped into Anthony's chest. "What do you mean?" he asked from the shadows behind her.

Juliana's breath caught, but she steeled her expression. "Where is she? Answer that, and then we'll revisit our unexpected arrival."

The Black-Star scoffed, a tremor of fear in her voice even as she responded with scorn. "Nothing unexpected about it. Captain knew you'd show up in the next couple of days. Don't know how you made it past the patrols, though."

Anthony caught Juliana's eye this time. Worry furrowed her brow.

"Enough of this." Jason strode forward, flames reappearing in his hand. "Where is my *sister*?"

The Black-Star's head turned. She eyed the fire, now large enough to engulf her head with a flick of Jason's wrist, and sucked in a breath.

Anthony looked down at the metal stick in his hand, tracing the rubber grip with his fingers. The wolf paced the clearing in his mind.

"If she's still alive, she's in the holding cells in the center of the facility."

Jason's stony expression flickered. "What do you mean, if she's still alive?"

The Black-Star leaned away from the flames. "Keith, the uh, the Blue-Star conducting research… he needed a subject for something new Ms. Wolfe wanted done."

Anthony glanced at Juliana. Her breath hitched for the briefest of seconds. Her eyes narrowed, a scowl turning up the edge of her mouth. "He used Samaira."

The Black-Star nodded.

"How do we get to the center of this complex?"

The woman shook her head, another scoff coming out of her. "You can't. We're everywhere—"

"Right," Juliana interrupted, "you knew we were coming; we get it. This thing is an oval, correct? What is the fastest way to the center."

Silence.

"Tell us," Juliana said in a deadly low voice, "and you might keep your life."

At that, Anthony put a hand on the Black-Star's shoulder, his nails elongating just enough to cut through her jacket and dig into her skin. He leaned down, drawing on every ounce of disgust for the Black-Stars in Abredea who had nearly killed him, and the ones here, who *had* been responsible for the deaths of innocent children already, and muttered in her ear.

"Yeh think yer being brave, not tellin' what we wanna know. It's not bravery. It's foolishness. That man," he didn't need to point, her head swiveled to look at Jason, "is ready to watch you burn. And we won't stop him."

The stench of her fear wafted into his nose. He straightened as she opened her mouth.

"Head—"

Voices shouted in the corridor.

Anthony whirled, gut clenching as his teeth elongated without his command. He grunted, shoving the wolf aside, and touched the metal end of his weapon to the back of the Black-Star's neck.

He hit the button, and a buzz of electricity tickled his palm.

The Black-Star spasmed and fell to the ground, twitching.

Anthony rushed to the door, wedging his shoulder against it just as someone attempted to slam it open.

Juliana and Jason joined him. The three leaned on the door hard, but it wouldn't hold for long.

The others grouped around them, Cho moving beside Jason to help.

"What do we do?" Jane put a hand on the wall to steady herself.

"Run?" Daisy asked, voice firm but face pale.

Jane straightened her shoulders. "I can get us through the wall."

"I'm not leaving," Jason spat. The door cracked an inch, and he rammed his shoulder into it, forcing it back into place.

"None of us are," Juliana said.

Anthony glanced at her as another slam shuddered the door. "Yeh've got another plan?"

"Always." She grinned at him, only a hint of uncertainty in her eyes.

They were surrounded. Black-Stars marched them down the hallway toward the front of the complex.

A dozen Black-Stars had arrived at the door to the cage room. A dozen men and women stormed in to find their group waiting to be taken. The pain of surrender had played violently across Jason's face, but he'd gone along with the plan.

A large Black-Star with a rich dark brown complexion, a deep voice, and the insignia of a captain had held off the soldiers as a few made motions to get revenge for their fallen comrades.

"She needs them," was all he had said before ordering that the group be bound and taken to the front of the facility.

Anthony glanced at Juliana as they walked. She'd been right, of course, a fight wouldn't have ended well for them. Not with the Black-Stars' numbers, Jane's drained power, and so many of them without weapons.

Instead, they allowed themselves to be captured in the hopes that they'd be brought to the holding cells the Black-Star had told them about. They'd find Samaira, Jane would rest a little longer, and then they'd flee. They'd be gone before the sun came up.

It was a good plan.

Except for the gnawing unease in Anthony's gut. The feeling that they'd forgotten something important, that they were missing a piece of this puzzle.

They walked for nearly ten minutes, following the curve of the building and keeping tabs of the doors and halls they passed. The corridor ahead of them turned sharply to the left. The exterior wall shifted from white to the dark of glass windows at night.

Juliana met his eye, and he read the same unease in her expression. He tilted his head. She gave the slightest of shrugs before the man behind her gave a shove to the small of her back and she stumbled.

Anthony snarled and whirled, anger banishing his nerves in a rush of heat.

"None of that, boy."

He froze. Horror gutted him as he turned back to the central lobby.

Standing in the center of an additional half-dozen Black-Stars stood Captain Steel. His twisted dagger tattoos curled up his pale skin. A gnarled scabbing wound cut through his forehead.

A reminder of their last interaction. When Steel had murdered Anthony's grandmother, Anthony thought he'd returned the favor.

But Steel was not dead. His mouth twisted into a victorious sneer. "Excellent work, Captain Lawrence."

The man who'd led them down the hall gave a shallow nod. "Seems they managed to get past every one of your patrols, Captain Steel. Has Ms. Wolfe been informed?"

Steel's sneer wavered. "Not as of yet. I'll contact her shortly. Once I get the girl to a secure location."

Anthony jerked forward, pushing Juliana behind him. The wolf within uttered a low growl as fear and fury went through them both. "Don't you touch her."

Juliana exhaled, her breath warming the back of Anthony's neck.

His muscles were tense, locked as he held his wolf in check. The temptation to transform and bury his teeth into Steel's neck was almost overpowering. But the certainty of what would happen to his friends kept him at bay.

"Perhaps we should move them *all* to a more secure location. The cells have more than enough room." Lawrence moved past Black-Stars and gestured out the clear glass doors. "We do not know how many others may be coming. The children are gone. Escaped. The inverter is down, and we are on back-up power if you haven't noticed."

Steel bristled but kept his focus on Anthony. "Send a patrol out to find them. They can't have gone far. And get someone making repairs."

Irritation flashed across Lawrence's face before his expression smoothed. "I already have men on repairs, and there is a squad searching for them as we speak."

Anthony's blood went cold. He thought of Taz and the others, silently hoping they'd made it over the fence before anyone had gone looking. The forest was dense, there was a chance...

A Black-Star with no eyebrows and peeling ruddy skin jogged in from the far end of the lobby where the corridor continued past their sight.

"No sign of them, Captain," he directed at Lawrence.

Steel's scowl deepened. He looked at his fellow captain. "This is your responsibility, Lawrence. Handle it."

The larger man hesitated for a brief moment, looking as though he'd like nothing more than to crush Steel where he stood. Instead, he named several Black-Stars, halving the number of soldiers in the lobby, and sent them to join the search of the grounds.

Steel stepped closer to Anthony as guards bustled about. "Thought you wouldn't see me again, did you? Thought I wouldn't come for you after this?" He pointed to the wound on his head, fingers shaking with anger.

Anthony took a shuddering breath, rage driving away any humor he might have used to release his own tension. "I thought I'd finished the job," he growled. "Thought yeh were dead."

Steel stepped again, and his gaze flicked to Juliana.

She was tucked behind Anthony. Her hands were bound, but she brushed her fingers against his arm, a silent reminder that he wasn't alone.

He wasn't. The knowledge rippled through him. Jason stood to his left, watching the encounter with sharp eyes. Behind them, Cho, Daisy, and Jane waited. Ready, he knew, to act if he or Juliana made a move.

Not alone, but still surrounded. Still inches from the man who'd tried to kill him. Still counting on the plan that would get them to a cell near Jason's sister.

Anthony's mouth curved into a half-grin.

"What are you smiling about, boy?" Steel said. "You're going to die here. You *and* your friends."

"Yeh've had trouble killin' me in the past." Anthony glanced behind the man.

A rush of cool, fresh air hit Anthony as nearly half of the Black-Stars drew their weapons, pulled open the doors, and disappeared into the night.

Steel snarled at Anthony's words and leaned in close to hiss, "You're not worth the time they'll spend cutting you open to find the wolf."

Anthony reared back, preparing to slam his forehead into Steel's smug nose.

Juliana got there first.

Anthony had no idea when she'd freed her hands. Her fist slammed into Steel's jaw with a loud smack of knuckles on flesh.

The man staggered back and Juliana, huffing and shaking out her fingers, gave him a savage glare.

"Touch him," she panted, "and I'll kill you myself."

Steel spat. A mix of blood and saliva landed on the pale tile floor.

The Black-Stars around them moved in. One grabbed Juliana's arm, jerked it behind her back, and forced her forward into a stiff twisted angle. She struggled against him, her face pinched in anger.

Anthony lunged and was stopped in his tracks by the force of the other captain's hand on his chest.

Daisy hurried toward the fray as well, her bonds also missing as she clenched her small hands into fists.

"Enough." The deep thrum of Lawrence's voice echoed throughout the space. He looked at Steel. "We need to put them in the holding cells."

Steel rubbed his jaw, his gaze catching on Juliana for a second. He scanned the rest of them, a glint of cruelty in his eye. "We don't need them."

Juliana struggled harder. The others did as well, Black-Stars piling forward to keep them contained. Multiple hands clasped Anthony's biceps and, were it not for the strength of his wolf, he'd be held in place. As it was, he barely managed to move a foot closer to Jules.

"Ms. Wolfe's orders, and the experiments—"

Steel cut off Lawrence's words with a slash of his hand and a glare up at the man. "As long as your men find the others, it won't matter. I was left in command of this facility. Not you."

Lawrence's face hardened. He gave a sharp nod. "Your orders, Captain?"

"When you have confirmation of capture, get rid of them."

Fear seeped into Anthony's bones. He watched as Juliana's face fell, horror widening her eyes as she looked from him to Daisy and the others.

"No." She turned her gaze on Steel. "Don't do this. We have power, all of us. Wolfe would want us alive."

Steel chuckled. "Don't look so worried. She has different plans for *you*."

Daisy strained against the Black-Stars holding her. Anthony did the same, to no avail, as Steel jerked his head and the men holding Juliana began dragging her away.

"No," Anthony shouted. Lawrence sank a fist into his stomach. He grunted and doubled over, still struggling to get free of the Black-Stars' grasps.

Lawrence looked down at him with a cold stare. "Silence."

"Frost that," Jane retorted. She slipped through one of the hands gripping her, but her face blanched, and she didn't get free of the other. "Let her go you nacra piece of shit," she snarled at Steel.

Steel's grin widened. "Contact me when it's done," he directed at Lawrence, tapping his left ear as he turned and strode ahead of Juliana and the Black-Stars holding her.

Juliana strained, her gaze catching Anthony's for a split second that wrenched his heart apart. Then she was torn away, pulled down the corridor, and out of sight.

Juliana shouted. Screamed at the men holding her. Cursed Steel a hundred times until her voice became an echo from beyond.

In the lobby, Anthony was silent. His jaw locked in place as he stared up at the Black-Star tasked with killing them.

He would not get the chance.

The wolf within was near bursting. Fury permeated every inch of him. *Wait,* Anthony inhaled, his eyes fixed on the Black-Stars. He needed a moment, a handful of breaths to transform and rip the throat out of the captain.

No, that would take too long. He needed to get part way there. Let the wolf sneak through until it would be too late to stop him.

Lawrence lined them up against the lobby desk, not bothering to re-tie Daisy, Cho, and Jane. Jason glanced at Anthony as they shuffled over.

"Give me the signal, and we go," he said, his voice barely a whisper.

Anthony gave a slight nod to show he'd heard. He positioned himself beside Daisy, hoping he could at least shield her if it came to that.

Fur pushed against the fabric of his shirt.

"Your men won't find them," Daisy said as the Black-Stars stepped away, guns raised. She glanced at Anthony, and he gave a slight nod.

"How did you get loose of your bindings?" Lawrence asked. He looked from Daisy to Jane, who still had a strip of nylon hanging from her wrist.

Anthony twisted his hands, positioning his fingers along the edges of his wrists. His feet morphed uncomfortably in his shoes.

"Wouldn't you like to know," Jane snapped.

The big man chuckled. "I would." He crossed the lobby, moving behind the handful of remaining Black-Stars as they formed a line in the center of the space like a barrier between them.

"Don't kill us then." Cho's fear sent a tremor through his voice. "Like our friend said, the Grey-Star would want us alive."

Lawrence gave a solemn nod. "That she would."

He unholstered the plasma gun at his side.

Anthony shifted, putting himself in front of Daisy. His heart clenched with fear, but his nails extended, the edges becoming sharp claws. His teeth did the same. His jaw began to elongate.

Lawrence raised his weapon.

Anthony sliced through a strip of his bindings. He wouldn't be quick enough. He'd seen how fast a plasma bolt moved.

Lawrence fired.

The Black-Star in front of him crumpled, plasma burning a hole in his back.

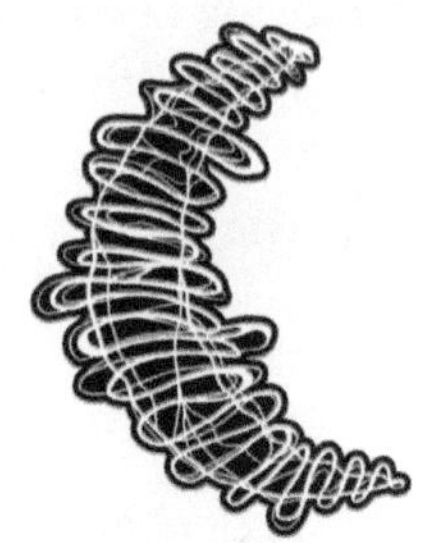

Chapter Twenty-Six

Dolor

Juliana's heartbeat thundered so loudly she could barely hear anything else. The Black-Stars on either side of her, a man and a woman with close shaved haircuts and worn uniforms, clenched her arms tight enough to cut off circulation.

Her blade was still hidden, tucked into her waistband. She'd used it to slice through the nylon while the two Black-Star captains argued in the lobby.

Her captors hadn't bothered to re-bind her hands. Not that they needed to with the way they were holding her.

Steel strode ahead of them, looking back every now and then with such triumph on his face it made Juliana sick. Her feeble meal from earlier that night rose in her stomach.

She swallowed it down. The time might come for that kind of distraction, but it wasn't while they were halfway up a stairwell and her friends had weapons trained on them.

She'd stopped struggling when they'd reached the stairs. Better to act compliant, wait for the Black-Stars to let their guard down. It was increasingly difficult.

Fear snapped at her like an angry animal, barely kept at bay. She tried to talk it down. She knew Anthony, knew her friends. Cho was smart, Jason stupidly brave. Jane too stubborn to die, and Daisy...

Tears blossomed, unbidden, in her eyes. Her lips curled in fury at the emotion escaping her control. Focus. Daisy... Daisy was too kind. Too full of the potential that had been squandered by her piece-of-shit father and the life she'd been born into. She couldn't die.

This line of thought only served to fuel Juliana's rage—a better alternative to the paralyzing fear that had begun to creep through her.

Her friends would *not* die. She wasn't done planting kisses on Anthony's full lips. Wasn't done tracing the stubble on his jaw when they were alone. Wasn't done with the warmth of him, pressed against her as the nights grew colder.

Steel's fingers snapped in front of her face. She flinched, and he chuckled.

"Don't ignore your betters, girl. Wolfe will be beyond pleased to see you again, little moon. She was so hurt when you fled the camp."

Juliana's lip curled in disgust. "It's called Abredea. And we didn't flee our home. We left your cruelty."

Steel's smile faltered.

"And your stupidity," Juliana spat.

They'd reached the top of the stairs and, as her saliva hit the tip of Steel's shoe, his palm slammed into her cheek.

The Black-Stars behind her held fast as her body jerked to the side.

She grunted. Pain radiated down her jaw and neck. "How angry was she?" Juliana continued, tasting blood along her gums. "When you told her how he beat you? Made a fool of you?"

A low rumble emanated from Steel's throat. His face reddened, his tattoos darkening as fury twisted his features.

"How about when you told her we were gone?" Juliana asked viciously. "When you told her you *failed*?"

He struck again, backhanding her this time as the Black-Stars made faint noises of protest.

"What?" he snapped, spit flying from his mouth.

Juliana slumped, leaning on her captors more than necessary.

"Sir," the woman said, tightening her hold, seeming to try and pull Juliana back upright. "Ms. Wolfe wants her alive, correct? Unharmed?"

Splashes of sanity flickered in the captain's eyes as he straightened. He gave a sharp nod. "Correct, Harkin. Get her to the office. Once she's secured, we will contact Ms. Wolfe with our news."

Juliana moved slowly. She purposely stumbled a few times, causing the Black-Stars on either side of her to exchange worried glances.

They reached a large wooden door when the faint sound of a plasma gun firing echoed up the stairwell.

Juliana jerked. Panic laced her limbs as she tore herself from the grips of the Black-Stars, their nails raking her skin. Without thought, without breath, she turned and sprinted toward her friends.

Another shot split the air. She cried out, fear engulfing her.

It wasn't too late. She could get there. She'd heal them. She'd—

Juliana was yanked backward by the long braid at the base of her head. She hit the floor with a yelp of pain, but scrambled to her knees, desperate to get to the stairs.

Steel's face interceded her view, his lips curled into a menacing smile. Her braid was still wrapped around his fist, a point he made clear by jerking her head backward.

"It's too late."

"No," she huffed out, trying not to sob. "It's not."

"They're dead," Steel murmured, his mouth too close to her ear. "Listen."

The other Black-Stars had reached them. They took hold of her again, lifting her to her feet as Steel released her hair.

She kicked. Twisted her head around and bit down on the hand of the man holding her. She thrashed with everything in her.

Another shot rang out, then a fourth, fifth, and sixth. She couldn't break free.

Fury pooled in Juliana like water in a dam. Her body had gone numb, her thoughts replaced with a soft buzzing sound. She stopped struggling. Stopped fighting. Stopped listening.

Steel turned them back toward the office with glee. He spoke as they walked, the Black-Stars pulling her along as she took stumbling steps to keep up.

There was nothing left in her but a boiling rage she'd never experienced before. Images flashed through her mind. Daisy handing over the first book Juliana borrowed from her. Cho leading them through morning meditation. Jason with a mischievous grin on his face as he cast fireballs into the air for Claire to practice shooting ice at. Jane's tender expression when she looked at Tommy.

Anthony, framed by the forest, his dark eyes looking into her like he was seeing her for the first time. Like he finally understood her. In the same moment she realized she finally understood him as well.

Steel was going to die.

That was the promise she made to herself as the Black-Star opened the door to Wolfe's office. As they moved her inside and sat her in one of the armchairs before the desk. As they closed the door, and Steel got on a com device, victoriously telling whoever was on the other end to have Wolfe contact him after the council meeting.

He would die. And so would the other Black-Star captain, the researchers who tortured children, the guards who facilitated it, and Wolfe, the woman who'd ordered everything.

Juliana had no plan, no notion of how to achieve her objective. But she'd kill them for what they'd done. She'd kill them all.

"Keep your weapons on her," Steel barked when he finished his call.

Harkin and the other Black-Star had taken positions at the door, seemingly taking Juliana's vacant stare and lack of struggle to mean she was done fighting back.

They exchanged another glance when Steel turned to face Juliana, and moved away from the door as they drew their guns.

"I'm going to kill you." Juliana looked up at Steel, and the cold in her gaze caused his prideful expression to falter.

He recovered quickly, the sneer returning. The other Black-Stars didn't look as sure.

Juliana met each of their gazes in turn. "Each of you. I'm going to end your lives. Everything you've ever done will be for nothing. Worth nothing."

Harkin licked her lips, adjusting the grip on her weapon as she looked at the other guard.

"Quiet," Steel snapped. "You have no weapon."

"I have power," Juliana whispered. Her mind had started up again. The buzzing remained, but now it was like an engine was running.

Survive. The first step was, seemingly, already accomplished. They hadn't killed her. Wouldn't because Wolfe wanted her. The second step was to get free of the guards. Get her hands on the blade tucked into the folds of her clothes without anyone noticing.

Step three was burying the blade in Steel's eye.

The Black-Stars took half a step back at her words. She'd spoken softly with a promise in her tone, and she raised her chin to sell the bluff.

The man swallowed, and Harkin's gaze darted to Steel with unease.

"I know your power." Steel raised his eyebrows as though entertained. "You don't scare me, girl."

He strode behind the desk and bent. After clicking a few buttons, he flipped the clear glass monitor around to face Juliana.

Her smooth surface, the cold calm she was trying to emote, cracked a fraction as her own face stared back at her. It took barely a second to place the scene. She was in Abredea's town square. Children sat on the steps before her, their proportions odd because of the camera's angle. The Juliana on the screen let out a silent laugh and ruffled a familiar boy's hair.

The image changed, and Juliana swallowed. She, Daisy, Taz, and Anthony stood in the forest. Her finger reached toward Daisy's lip and, within a moment, her friend's bruise and cut were gone.

Juliana's breath caught. More images flashed across the screen. Earlier moments of her life in Abredea. A life she'd thought was free from this kind of surveillance. She watched herself walk with May, hug Naya, hike Jimmy up onto her back and run him around the square.

She watched Wolfe arrive. Saw her ascend the steps to the town hall and step inside.

"You remember those moments, don't you?" Steel asked, his voice sickeningly smooth.

"What is this?" Juliana's voice trembled.

"This," Steel grinned, "is why I came to the camp in the first place. You."

The images flashed again, this time a zoom-in on Juliana, rain pounding down from above as she stared up in horror at Anthony's beating. Steel hit a button, and the image froze with Anthony midair after being shoved from the balcony.

"We thought you'd manifest here," he said. "If there was ever a time to activate healing powers, this was it." He chuckled. "Your failure to help him was almost enough to pull the plug on the whole operation, but she knew." He wagged a finger, the evil glint returning to his eye. A flicker of a scowl crossed his face. "She knows everything, it seems. She knew you'd have it."

His gaze slid past Juliana, looking into a dark corner of the office.

Juliana breathed heavily. His words, these images, they twisted every moment in Abredea. The pain her friends had suffered... it was all to get her to manifest her healing abilities. And now, they were dead because Wolfe wanted *her*. The whole thing had been a trap.

Because of *her*.

Footsteps padded on the soft carpet of Wolfe's office.

Juliana turned quickly as a figure emerged from the darkness, and her heart nearly stopped. This wasn't possible. After everything, this was...

"Mom?" she breathed.

Chapter Twenty-Seven

Dolor

Anthony halted mid-transformation. The pain of holding back the wolf gutted him. But he did it.

The other Black-Stars turned, confusion slowing their movements as many lowered the guns they'd been pointing at Anthony and his friends.

"Sir?"

Lawrence shot again. The blast slammed into the one who'd spoken, and she flew back a foot, collapsing to the ground.

"What's—"

"Questions later," Anthony growled as Cho turned to him. "Fighting now. Grab a gun."

His hands were free. The combination of wolf's nails on his human fingers was painful, but they'd done the job. He turned to Jason.

The man held out his wrists, and Anthony sliced through his bindings. Then the flame thrower went to work.

Jane darted forward and grabbed a metal shock stick from a fallen Black-Star. She plunged it against another's back. He collapsed in spasms.

Three of the guards were on Lawrence, trying to take him down without killing him. The other guards turned toward the group.

Flames slammed into one, propelling him into the window. It cracked, spiderwebs of glass spreading from where the man's skull had hit.

Anthony sprang at another, his claws digging into the soft part of the man's neck. Blood sprayed across his clothes and splattered the tile floor in a mockery of art.

Anthony wheeled around as the body was still falling.

Cho and Daisy disarmed the youngest looking Black-Star. Cho held his gun to the man's head. The Black-Star knelt with his hands raised, radiating fear and confusion.

Jason's flames scorched the uniform of another man as he gripped him by the jacket and slammed his head against a tall pillar.

Jane darted to the side as one of the remaining guards directed his weapon at Cho. She brought the metal end of the rod to his neck, pressed the button, and he fell in a fit of spasms. She did not release him until the charred scent of burned skin filled the air.

There were two left, both still on Lawrence. Each was using their full weight to force down an arm. Their frantic voices called for him to "be still," "calm down," "Captain, please" until finally one of them turned to Anthony and the others and desperately demanded, "What have you done? Release him from this."

Anthony strode forward; the fear and fury of Steel taking Juliana empowered his wolf and poured strength into his muscles. He twitched slightly at the discomfort, but brought his arm up nonetheless. He struck, his hand closing around the man's neck as claws pierced flesh and the Black-Star's scream was cut short.

"It's not us," he muttered, his eyes locked on the final man as Lawrence shook him off and backhanded him across the face.

Lawrence lifted his gun from where it had fallen to the floor. In a swift movement, he took aim and ended the Black-Star's life before he could plead for mercy.

In the seconds of quiet ticking by, Anthony backed up, his gaze never leaving the Black-Star captain who had saved them. He reached the others and let himself glance at Jason.

The flame thrower looked back at Anthony and raised an eyebrow. Daisy, stifling her heavy breaths with the back of her hand, hurried to Anthony's side.

Cho remained before the only conscious Black-Star, his stolen gun pointed at the man's chest. His eyes darted to Anthony and the others, then to Lawrence. "Why?"

"They were going to kill you," Lawrence said in his deep drawl.

"Yeah." Jason's face was tense. "Those are your orders. So why help us? Why kill your own men?"

"Better yet," Jane snarled, "why not help us earlier, *before* they took our friend?"

Lawrence inhaled and let out a breath through wide flared nostrils. "There is much you do not know."

Anthony nodded. "Why don't yeh fill us in, then? And quick." He gritted his teeth and flexed his arm as the strength of the wolf faded. "We've got rescuin' tah do."

The captain strode across the room and stopped just short of Cho. Anthony moved forward, but Jason got there first. He stepped in front of Cho, flames roaring in both of his fists.

Lawrence cocked his head and then turned his gaze away from them. He pointed his gun at the Black-Star on his knees and killed the man.

Anthony's tongue went dry. Bile rose in the back of his throat and he watched, the adrenaline of the moment no longer serving him, as Lawrence went to each of the fallen soldiers in turn and ensured that they were dead.

Even Jason looked uneasy at the brutality. He kept himself in front of Cho, eyes on Lawrence as the man straightened and holstered his weapon.

"Now, a quick explanation and then you have work to do."

Anthony frowned. He glanced down the hall where Steel had dragged Juliana away. Apprehension tightened like a hand around his throat.

"You have minutes until this facility is crawling with Black-Stars," Lawrence said, his voice a low rumble. "I chose to wait," he glanced at Jane, "because until now, we were badly outnumbered and, until now, the cameras throughout this facility were still up and running."

Anthony exhaled. "Why aren't they now?"

Lawrence's gaze cut to him. "I disabled them. With a timed switch to ensure I'm not blamed when it's discovered that they are down. I wouldn't have needed to if you'd left with the children."

Jason opened his mouth, but Lawrence held up a hand.

"I understand why you did not." He looked the flame thrower in the eye. "Your sister is being held in the center of Dolor. Take the left hall, first right, and follow it until you reach the only door barred from the outside."

Jason nodded, his chest sagging.

"Where did they take Juliana?" Daisy stepped forward, and Anthony moved automatically to keep her within reach. "*Why* did they take her?"

Lawrence shook his head, his expression shifting to frustration and confusion. "I don't know why Wolfe wants her. I have not yet earned that level of trust." He cocked his head and gestured to the bodies littered around them. "I doubt I will be able to stay much longer after this. As far as where, Wolfe's private office and quarters are down the right hall, up the first set of stairs you come to, and then the second door on the left."

Suspicion warred with relief within Anthony. He glanced at Cho and caught the flash of a frown on the man's face.

"Why should we trust you?" Cho asked, his voice low but firm. "Why do this?"

The Black-Star stared at the ceiling for a long moment. When he looked back at them, his eyes were bright with determination and commitment. "I do this because it is my assignment. There are few who would have been able to infiltrate at this level."

He moved toward them. Jason and Anthony squared themselves in front of the others. Anthony's heartbeat had yet to slow.

Lawrence's lips twisted into a rueful smile. "As far as trust, maybe this will calm your suspicions." He reached out his left arm toward them, turned his palm upward, and tugged his sleeve up to his elbow.

Anthony's brow furrowed. A tattoo was embedded in Lawrence's skin, an inch or so above his wrist. A set of mountains, surrounded by a thin circle, with a trio of birds flying through.

Anthony glanced at Jason. The man shrugged.

"What's that supposed to mean?" Anthony asked. He looked again to the hall where Juliana had disappeared. Time was not on their side.

Lawrence shook his head and pulled the sleeve back down. "Ahh, I thought... never mind then. You should trust me because you must. There is no other option."

"You'll help us get out?" Daisy asked.

He huffed out a chuckle. "I've done as much as I can. Even this will be... difficult to explain." He frowned for a moment. "Actually, it might be better to fully destroy the place. That will help cover your tracks. And mine."

"Destroy it?" Cho asked.

Lawrence nodded. "Burn it down."

Jason's lips curled into a tight smile. "I can make that happen."

"As can I," Lawrence said. "The generators won't be too difficult to overload. If you get things started on this side of the complex we may be able to cause enough damage that I can maintain my cover." His gaze darted to Jason again. "That reminds me, give me a good hit, will you? Right across here," he traced his jaw, "and make sure it burns."

Jason shrugged and, before anyone else had moved, called forth a ball of fire and slammed his fist into Lawrence's face.

Laughter bubbled from Anthony's chest as the Black-Star reeled back, biting out a curse.

"Get going," he said after a moment of rapid blinking and wincing. "You don't have long." He reached out, taking hold of Jason's arm. "When you get out, head south. Make for the mountains at the edge of Pangaea. If I'm discovered, I'll try to meet you there. If not," he gritted his teeth, pausing as though struggling to make a decision, and then shook his head, "if not, you should still find help there."

"Wh—" Cho began.

"I can't tell you more than that now. Not while there's a chance of you getting captured." Lawrence shook his head. "I'm going to the control room. With any luck I can redirect the Black-Stars on patrol and steer them away from your escape. You'll only have a few minutes once I overload the generators. Leave through these doors. Stay off the main road."

"We'll be quick," Anthony murmured. His mind whirled with the events of the last few minutes, but gratitude for the man before them eclipsed the less savory emotions. He put a fist to his chest as they did in Abredea to show respect.

To his surprise, Lawrence did the same.

Then, with a sharp nod to the others, the Black-Star drew his gun and jogged away down one of the halls.

"Where to first?" Cho asked, shifting the weight of the gun in his hand.

Jane moved toward one of the bodies and, taking a weapon from the corpse, looked at Anthony. "We don't have time to go together."

Daisy's eyes widened. "Split up? Is that a good idea?"

Anthony heaved a sigh and rubbed a hand across his forehead. "No, but it might be our only option. Yer sister," he looked to Jason, "and Juliana are pretty far apart, it sounds like. Not to mention the squad of Black-Stars searchin' for our friends as we speak. The longer they wait for us at the truck, the more likely they are tah be spotted."

Jason nodded, but his jaw was tight.

"I don't like this." Cho crossed to Anthony and met his eye. "We owe Juliana. I'll go with you." His voice shook at the end, hands clenched at his sides.

Anthony shook his head. "Find yer family. We'll get Jules, and we'll meet back here. Then we all go together." He shifted his gaze to Jason. They exchanged a weighted look of determined purpose.

"We'll wait for you," Jason said. He clapped Anthony's shoulder and the two exchanged a brief embrace. There was a resiliency they shared. An understanding that this *had* to happen. That failure for one meant failure for the other.

Anthony stepped away, plucked a couple of weapons from the floor, and jerked his head at Daisy. "Yeh ready?"

She didn't speak or nod. Instead, a ferocity he'd never seen in her before gleamed in her wide eyes. She turned and marched ahead, leading them down the hall and toward Juliana.

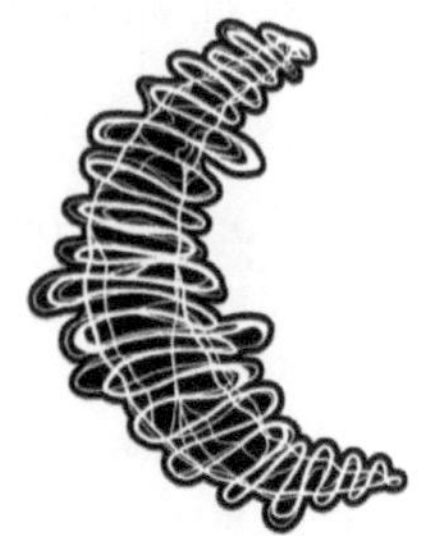

Chapter Twenty-Eight

Dolor

The woman before Juliana certainly *looked* like her mother, but not the mother she remembered. The woman was pale, thin and emaciated, her eyes wide and sunken, hair longer, darker, and braided into thick tangles.

"This can't..." Juliana's head spun. There wasn't enough air. She tried to stand, to go to the woman, but Harkin pushed her back into the chair. Confusion filled her, overflowing in tears that glistened down her cheeks. "Mom?" she asked again.

This couldn't be possible.

"Not quite," Steel said with a snide chuckle. "Juliana, meet your aunt."

A flood of relief. A swarm of memories. A burst of pity for the person before her.

"Brenna?"

The woman shrank in, her eyes darting from Steel to Juliana in rapid, scared movements.

"What did you do to her?" Juliana demanded.

Steel shrugged. "I di—"

Whatever he'd been about to say was broken off as he held a hand to his ear. The other Black-Stars stilled as well; expressions furrowed with concentration.

Juliana took the opportunity to hiss to the aunt she'd thought was long dead, "Are you all right?"

Brenna's wide eyes, dull compared to Juliana's mother's, darted back to Steel. Juliana nodded, looking at the man as well. None of this was all right.

"How is that possible?" Steel demanded, his smug expression melting into rage before their eyes. He rose and strode across the room.

The other Black-Stars watched his movements.

"Sir." Harkin moved from her spot behind Juliana's chair, following him into the center of the office with a side-eye at Brenna. "If the runaways disappear and the prisoners are killed, Ms. Wolfe will—"

The door slammed open.

Juliana's heart nearly burst.

Daisy was on one knee in the doorway, a gun in her hands. She took aim and missed, her plasma bolt slamming into the window behind Steel.

Anthony stepped around the doorway. He carried a gun as well and had better aim. A bolt of plasma slammed into Steel's left arm.

The man yowled with pain.

Juliana lunged from the chair, but the Black-Star snagged her arm and ripped her backward.

"Anthony," she shouted, half unsure he was really there. Really alive.

Both of them. Still alive. The relief was a splintering pain in her chest.

"Jules," Anthony drawled as he stepped into the room, weapon pointed at Steel. His gaze darted to Harkin.

"Daisy, you got that one?"

"Yeah." Daisy rose to her feet, her gun trained on the woman.

"You don't have anyone," Steel spat. He looked at Juliana.

She trembled with fury and relief, the Black-Star's grip on her arm cutting off circulation, his weapon digging into her gut.

Harkin drew her weapon as well and took a few steps back toward Juliana.

"Don't," Anthony shouted. "Move, and I kill him."

"You tried to kill me before, boy," Steel snarled. "It's harder than it looks."

"Sir," Harkin kept her gaze on Daisy, "what would you like us to do?"

Steel scrunched his nose, a shallow grunt echoing through the room as he examined his wound. "If they make a move, kill her."

"But sir," the other Black-Star's grip loosened, "Ms. Wolfe—"

"I gave you an order," Steel shouted.

Juliana felt the flinch of the man holding her and fear stirred in her stomach.

Steel advanced toward Anthony and Daisy.

As he did, Brenna slunk back into the shadows, her eyes wide with terror.

Daisy kept her weapon pointed at the Black-Stars holding Juliana, but her gaze flicked to Anthony. "What do we—"

Steel reached them, stopping a few feet from Anthony.

Juliana cursed and jerked in the Black-Star's grip to cover the movement of her hand toward her waistband.

"You want her to die, boy?" Steel raised his right hand, touching the gemstone on his temple. He stepped again and Anthony's gun bumped against his chest. "Shoot me. You can watch *her* bleed to death too."

Anthony's brow furrowed in a flash of anger and conflict. His gaze darted to Juliana as he slowly lowered his weapon.

"Don't," Juliana shouted.

Harkin slammed the butt of her gun into Juliana's stomach. She doubled over in pain, staying a few seconds longer than necessary.

She looked up just as Steel slammed his shoulder into Anthony.

Anthony stumbled back.

Daisy yelped and swung her gun toward Steel.

He grabbed the muzzle with his right hand, yanked it from her grasp, and chucked it across the room. Daisy rushed him. Steel swung, fist connecting with her face and knocking her backward. He kicked at the side of her ribs. She fell and hit the ground hard.

Juliana shouted again, an incoherent cry as her friend's head cracked onto the floor. She made to move forward but the Black-Star holding her tightened his grip.

"Now," Steel growled, snapping his finger at Harkin and pointing to Daisy.

The Black-Star turned her gun on the girl.

Steel advanced on Anthony. "Drop the weapon, or they both become scorch marks on the carpet."

Anthony's face trembled with fury. He gritted his teeth, glancing at Daisy and Juliana before tossing his gun on the ground.

"We've done this dance before." Steel's hoarse rumbling voice reached Juliana in the tense silence of the office.

Brenna cowered in a far corner, nibbling at the edges of her nails.

"Didn't end well for you." Anthony shifted, planting his feet in defiance as anger flashed in his eyes.

"This time is different." Steel grinned. He put a hand on Anthony's chest and shoved.

Anthony stumbled back a few feet but regained his balance.

Steel was there again, shoving harder. Anthony slammed into the wall beside the open door.

Juliana glanced from the Black-Star with his gun aimed at her stomach to the other, who's gaze was on Steel even as she continued to train her weapon on Daisy.

She could get one, maybe even both of them, distracted for a moment. But would that do any good with Anthony facing Steel without a weapon?

Steel leaned into Anthony and shoved his forearm against the shorter man's throat.

"No," Juliana cried out. She struggled against the Black-Star, fear curdling in her gut.

Anthony's hands flew to Steel's forearm, nails growing long and sharp as his face reddened and his breaths became shallow. He scratched at the man, claws digging into the thick fabric of Steel's jacket sleeve.

"I'm going to watch the life leave your eyes," Steel snarled. "Then I'll kill the girl."

Anthony's eyes flicked to Daisy, inching toward them on the ground, blood oozing from her forehead.

Juliana screamed. The Black-Star holding her gave a shake, and she stopped fighting back her tears. Nausea built in her stomach at the sound of Anthony's ragged, forced breaths.

Steel pressed harder. Anthony went to his toes, claws finding purchase on Steel's arm. Blood dripped from the wounds. Still the man didn't release him.

Daisy crawled closer, reaching out a hand toward Steel.

Harkin lifted her gun.

Juliana wretched.

Harkin jerked back in disgust as vomit splashed onto her pants.

Juliana spun. Her fingers were clenched around the knife she'd managed to pull free.

She buried the blade into the gut of the Black-Star holding her. The squelching sound was barely audible over the wail of anguish that split the air behind her.

Juliana whirled.

Anthony clambered up from where he'd fallen to the ground.

It was Steel who'd cried out. He was doubled over, pain and sorrow etched across the lines of his face. Tears flowed freely as he sucked in shuddering, gasping sobs.

Anthony looked as confused as Juliana felt.

Then Juliana noticed the reason for Steel's strange behavior.

Daisy lay on the ground at Steel's feet. Her hand was wrapped around his calf, and she was curled into a ball, tears pouring from her eyes as she too, heaved heartbroken sobs.

Juliana refocused and ripped the blade sideways as she pulled it from the Black-Star. He went down, dropping his gun as his hands desperately tried to catch the blood draining from his body.

She swung again, but Harkin was ready. The Black-Star blocked, and pain reverberated down Juliana's arm. She turned, kicking out to catch the woman in the knee.

Juliana spun away, darting toward Anthony as he bent and picked up his gun. He spun, face still red and neck swollen.

There was a crackle. A burst of plasma whizzed past Juliana's ear. She leapt, pain searing her shoulder, and landed on the ground a few feet from Daisy.

Another crackle as Anthony fired back. His bolt struck Harkin in the chest. She fell backward and slumped against the desk for a few seconds before her smoking body slid to the floor.

"Can't... longer," Daisy groaned from the ground. Her face was pale with effort, eyes red from crying.

Steel began to straighten.

Anthony strode up, his face set, gun ready.

Steel's gaze darted frantically from his fallen soldiers to Anthony. He spun, stumbling out the door and dodging to the side as Anthony fired off a shot.

A blast of plasma skimmed Steel's side. A yowl filled the corridor beyond the office.

"No," Anthony furiously hissed, rushing to the doorway. He fired again, and then darted back. A bolt of plasma hit the doorframe just behind his head.

Steel's footsteps didn't falter in the distance.

"Frost," Juliana snapped. She hurried to join Anthony by the door. It only took a quick glance to see that Steel was gone. He'd vanished around a bend in the hall, blood dripping in his wake.

She stood frozen for a few seconds, torn between her friends, answers, and the desire to track him down and fulfill her promise. Daisy moaned.

Juliana backed away from the corridor.

Anthony turned, looking as furious as she felt, and slammed the door closed with a loud crack.

Then there was silence.

Juliana faced her friends. She sucked in a disbelieving breath before hurrying to Daisy's side and helping her up. Once she was standing Juliana threw her arms around her and held her tight.

Daisy squeezed her back with a weak grip, tears dripping onto Juliana's shoulder.

"Hey," Anthony's voice was hoarse.

Juliana turned in time to see him wince and tenderly poke at his throat. She released Daisy. Her hands fell to her sides as overwhelming, heart-stopping relief flooded her.

She pawed at the tears streaming down her cheeks.

He said it again, more concern in his voice this time. "Hey, are yeh all right?"

She shook her head, emotion clogging her throat.

Anthony put a hand on her shoulder, ducking into her line of sight with a ghost of his usual crooked grin. "Jules."

She sucked in a breath. With another small shake of her head, she gave him a weak smile. "Thought I was the one who gets you out of trouble." The joke lost its effect as her voice broke and another rush of tears poured from her. "You came for me."

"Always," he murmured, pressing his forehead against hers for a brief moment.

Heat, a molten mixture in her core, ignited at the word. She settled herself with clasping his hand, the logical side of her knowing that now was not the time for a 'thank you' kiss. Or an 'I can't believe you're not dead" kiss.

"We have to go," Daisy said.

Juliana turned to her. "The others? They're—"

"They should be all right," Anthony cut off with a nod. He winced again.

Daisy eyed him. "Stop talking until Juliana can look at your throat." She turned toward the door.

"Wait." Juliana hesitated, relief fading as her mind began functioning again.

Steel had said... well, he'd said many things. But the implication behind his words hadn't fallen on deaf ears.

"I need answers." Juliana met Daisy's gaze. "*We* need answers, especially if we want to get somewhere safe after this."

Daisy sighed with a glance toward the door, but she nodded. "We have to be fast. The others will be waiting for us after they get Jason's sister."

A jolt went through Juliana's stomach. She wheeled around. In the far corner of the room, huddled so tightly into the dark shadows that she was barely visible, was her aunt.

"Brenna?" Juliana asked quietly. She released Anthony's hand and stepped toward the woman. "Are you... were you kept here? As a prisoner? Like the children?"

"Who..." Anthony's question faded to silence as Brenna rose.

She took a few trembling steps forward and nodded in quick, tiny movements. "I—" she broke off, her gaze darting about frantically.

"It's all right." Juliana took another step toward her, extending her hand. "We aren't going to hurt you. There aren't any more Black-Stars."

"Jules," even with the quiet gruffness of his voice, Anthony's tone was wary, "who is this?"

She answered without looking back, keeping her sight on Brenna. "This is my aunt."

The other two were silent for a long moment.

"Juliana," Daisy whispered, "how can you know that? You never met your aunt."

Juliana glanced at her friend, eyes glistening with tears. "She's my mom's twin. I thought," she shuddered, "she *was* my mom when I first saw her."

Daisy ran a hand across her mouth, eyes wide. Then she nodded. "If we want that information, we need to move fast."

"Right." Juliana gave a reassuring nod to Brenna and hurried around Harkin's body to Wolfe's desk. "Steel showed me—" she grimaced, "he showed me images from Abredea."

Anthony crossed the office in quick strides, his brow furrowed.

Juliana pointed to the screen as he came around and stood behind her. "Look. These numbers in the corner."

The images flickered through slowly, a pre-set collection that followed her past six months in order. Her entrance into Abredea was marked with a scribbled, *stressor #1.* The next image, one of her gardening with May, contained a short sentence, *nutritional packet decrease day six, stressor #2.*

They continued in that way, each moment since Juliana's arrival, each painful strife, added pressure, instance of failure, was marked as though it were some kind of test. Some experiment.

A familiar image came on the screen, the one Steel had boasted about before. The one of Anthony falling to his near-death on the steps of town hall.

A little red *stressor #8* was in the corner.

Juliana's stomach roiled.

"I..." she swayed, dizzy. "He wasn't lying."

Anthony's hands closed around her shoulders. "Jules, don't..."

"It was my fault," she whispered.

Another click. The image of her healing Daisy. Someone had circled the blue light coming from her finger nearly a dozen times in red.

"We need," Juliana shook her head, trying to clear it of the pounding guilt, "we need to find out what they're trying to do here."

"Juliana," Daisy had crossed to the door and waited for them, weapon up and ready in her hands, "we don't have time."

"One more minute." Juliana exited the images, typing frantically on Wolfe's keyboard. "We need *something*, Daisy. Somewhere to go and get away, or at least some reason for all this."

Files filled the screen. Blueprints for structures similar to the one they were in, as well as scans Juliana recognized from her Blue-Star training—it felt so long ago. They were human brains, subject numbers beside them.

Juliana frowned, her mind working to understand what she was looking at. She clicked open more documents. Robotics research. New weapons technology. Mind control.

"Juliana," Anthony muttered. He put a hand on her shoulder.

"Wait." She threw up her hands, the idea hitting her so hard she was frustrated she hadn't thought of it before. "Here." Juliana wrenched open Wolfe's desk and dug through the drawers until she found what she was looking for.

"We *have* to go," Daisy warned.

"I know," Juliana said. "A few more seconds." She plugged in the device and clicked a few buttons. A little bar began to fill up on the screen.

She turned, flushed with adrenaline and success. Anthony raised an eyebrow.

"This'll download the information. When we find a safe place, we can look at it later."

"Jules," Daisy hissed. "We have to go now."

"I—"

"Not that," Daisy snapped with a wave of her hand. She pointed to her ear where Steel's com device sat. "They're coming."

"Nacra," Juliana growled. She yanked the storage device from the screen, shoved it in her pocket, and rushed after Anthony toward the door.

He halted halfway there and glanced at Brenna. "Hey," he croaked, "yeh don't have tah stay here anymore. Yeh can come with us. Yeh'll be safe." He flashed his half-grin. "Safer, at least."

Brenna gave a jerky nod.

A rush of admiration, of gratitude, sank Juliana further into whatever warmth had taken over her senses. She took his hand again, and the two of them followed Daisy and Brenna to the door.

As they crossed the threshold Juliana paused again, a rush of anger striking her senses. She glanced at the trail of blood leading to wherever Steel had fled like a coward.

Smoke filled the air above them, and her lip curled.

Her gaze cut to Anthony. "He'll keep coming."

Anthony shook his head. "We don't have the time. Cho and the others are waitin'. From the smell of things, Jason did his work. This place ain't got long."

She gave half a shrug, rolling her shoulders uncomfortably. "I don't like it."

Anthony shuddered, a tremble going through his hand and up her arm. "Neither do I. But it's a problem for another day."

Juliana glanced down the corridor once more, then looked at Anthony and nodded. "Let's go."

Chapter Twenty-Nine

Dolor

Cho kept to the back of their group. Jason raced ahead, a single ball of fire at the ready in his palm. Jane hurried along between them.

The cages had drained her, so much so that Cho worried how long it would take her to bounce back. Frost, he wasn't even sure she *would* bounce back. The thought scared him. They relied so much on her power.

They rounded another corner and came to a halt before a long corridor.

"There," Jason hissed, pointing to a door in the center of the hall with a thick metal beam barring it closed.

They rushed forward.

Jason reached for the bar, but Cho threw out a hand to stop him. "Give me a second, let me check what we're dealing with."

Jason grimaced but nodded.

Cho reached out with his power. Saffron tendrils flowed through the door, mere metal not enough to stop their thirst for emotion. He wasn't able to distinguish which individuals felt which emotions, but he knew enough to get an idea of how many people were inside.

His power sparked. It swirled and danced and thrived in the wretched agony and raging fury it found.

Cho staggered back as the emotion sprang into him. He reeled, planting his hands on his knees as tears forced themselves from his eyes. His heart beat wildly, adrenaline flooding his system. Sucking in breaths, he closed his eyes and concentrated on releasing the pain, anger, and hurt from his power's sticky grasp.

His body shook, chills running down his spine until a warm hand settled on his back. Cho pressed into the palm, the steadiness it provided. He inhaled again, pushing the last of the emotions from his defenses and locking his power back into its chest.

Jason's hand moved to Cho's shoulder as he straightened. Their eyes met, a jolt going through Cho at the realization that Jason's emotions weren't encompassing him. The man must be pouring energy into his mental wards, for the purpose of comforting him.

Cho swallowed and turned his gaze to the door. "It's bad in there. Not many people, but there's so much anger." He shuddered, darting a glance at Jane. "And pain."

Jason's jaw tightened. "Cho, get the bar. Jane, you open the door. I'll be ready to handle anything that comes out."

They went to work. Cho hefted the bar. Jason braced before the door, his hands full of fire. At his nod, Jane yanked it open.

They moved in.

The smell was nearly as bad as the room where the Haven children were kept. Cho gagged, swallowed, and breathed through his mouth. The stale taste made him twitch.

They were bathed in darkness; the only light was the fire in Jason's hands.

It would have been quiet, were it not for a scrambling sound the second the door opened. A figure darted toward a shadowed row of bars to their right.

There was an intake of breath.

Jason stepped forward, but it wasn't her. His flames illuminated a short woman with tangled blonde hair and blue gemstones glistening on her temples. Her wrinkled and dirty coat marked her as a researcher.

Why was she in a holding cell? Cho moved toward her to ask, but as the light brought Jason's features into her sight, she gasped.

"You're..." her mouth fell open in shock, and she darted away.

Jason snarled, following her as much as was possible with bars between them. She disappeared from view as they reached another cell, fading into darkness beyond the light of the flames.

"Hey," the same voice said, her voice gentle.

Cho stepped up beside Jason. Jane remained at the door. She kept it cracked enough to let in a pinch of light and avoid them getting trapped inside.

The dark was encompassing.

"You've got to wake up." The low murmur barely reached them. "Samaira, wake up."

Jason's breath hitched. "Samaira?" he called out.

The hope in his voice dragged a hook into Cho's heart.

A pause. Silence ticked on longer than Cho could stand. Then, shuffling, dragging footsteps. A figure, taller than the Blue-Star, clung to the bars as they moved toward the flames.

Cho gulped.

Samaira was alive, but barely. Her skin was ashen, blood matted into her singed hair and clothes, burns marring her hands, wrists, up to her elbows. She stared at them, mouth parted in disbelief.

She sucked in a quick breath. Then another. Tears blurred her eyes, cleaning tracks of soot and dirt off her cheeks. She shook her head, limbs trembling.

"Can you…" Her words caught, choked in the back of her throat before she looked down at the Blue-Star. The petite woman stood at her side, the bars between them, her arms pushed through a gap in the bars so she could help hold Samaira upright. "Can you see them?" Samaira whispered.

Cho's heart ached at the disbelief in her words.

"They're here," the woman replied, putting a hand on Samaira's shoulder.

Samaira flinched. Her gaze landed on her brother, and she couldn't seem to look away. She stepped forward, and he did the same.

"I'm here, Samaira." Jason closed a fist, putting out one of his fires as he reached toward his sister.

She shook her head, tears pouring in earnest. "I can't…"

There was a crack, and Samaira jerked back.

"Sorry," Jane muttered, rushing toward them. She'd propped the door with something. "Didn't think it'd be that loud." She came to a stop on the other side of Jason. "We have to go."

"Right." He nodded. "Get her out."

Jane reached her hand toward Samaira as well, but the woman flinched and pulled her hands to her chest.

"I need to touch you," Jane said gently.

Samaira closed her eyes, nodded, and stepped forward.

Jane reached through the bars, took hold of Samaira's shoulder with a grunt, and muttered, "Come on."

The effort on her face brought another wave of concern through Cho's gut. When Samaira was free Jane released her and hunched over, panting.

Jason's twin leaned on the bars, staring at her brother's face. "How are you alive?"

"Not now," Cho said. He gave Jason a quick glance.

His friend's brow was furrowed in worry, alert eyes taking in every injury on his sister. There were many.

"We have to meet the others," Jane agreed. "Let's go."

Cho turned with her, making for the door.

"Wait."

Cho glanced back. Samaira had stopped at the first cell, her hands on the bars as she gazed in at the Blue-Star.

"Samaira?" Jason's voice was quiet, a warning and a question in his tone.

"We can't leave her here," Samaira murmured.

"The frost we can't." Jane scowled. Her pale face was shiny, sweat trickling down her temples.

"She's a Blue-Star," Cho said softly. "Doesn't she work here?"

Samaira shook her head. "She comes with us. She..." every word appeared to be an effort, "she saved my life."

Jason's lip curled in a snarl. "How many children did she torture?"

Samaira growled, a hint of her old self poking through. "It's not like that, Jace. She comes with us."

"I don't like it—"

"You don't have to," she interrupted.

Cho's eyes went wide. Jason blinked; hurt splashed across his face before he recovered his scowl.

"Samaira..."

"They'll kill her," Samaira snapped.

"Good riddance," Jason responded. The fire in his hand grew larger.

Cho stepped forward, putting himself between the twins and gazing up at Jason. "We can take her with us for now. When we reach the others, we'll get what information she has to offer, and decide what to do from there."

Jason's expression was mutinous. He glared from Cho to Samaira, and then to the woman behind bars who'd been watching the exchange with wide, fearful eyes.

Cho moved his head between Jason and the woman, catching his friend's gaze. "We don't have time for this. We have to meet the others. We have to go."

Jason swallowed and, after a second, the flames shrank back down. He nodded.

"Frost me," Jane uttered through gritted teeth. "Someone get the door then."

Cho hurried back to her, holding the door as she pulled the woman through the bars.

The Blue-Star wiped her palms on her coat. "I'm—"

"Introductions later," Cho said firmly. "Come on."

Despite Samaira's protests, Jason threw an arm around her waist and helped her stagger out the door and down the hallway.

He paused and Cho met his eye. "He said to burn it down, right?"

Cho nodded.

Jason kept one hand around his sister. The other filled with flames and, with a grunt of effort, Jason coated the corridor behind them with fire as they ran. When the walls had caught, the ceiling paint cracking with heat, he closed his hand and focused on Samaira.

The Blue-Star kept up easily. Cho hurried ahead, glancing back every now and then as heat pressed against their backs. The woman watched Samaira, concern etched in her furrowed brow and the thin line of her pursed lips.

Lawrence had done whatever he was doing well; they didn't run into any Black-Stars on their way back to the lobby.

Samaira gasped as they hurried toward the array of bodies scattered across the floor. Vicious rage wrinkled her nose and upper lip as she gazed down at them.

"Hey," Jason frowned at her, "what is it?"

She glanced at him, the scowl shifting back to relief, and then a small wry smile. "Wish I'd been here for this. I owed a few of 'em."

Jason's sly smile curled his lips, dark eyes glinting in a way Cho had almost forgotten.

Cho inhaled through parted lips, the sight of that smile bringing more happiness to him than he'd thought it could.

"Where are they?" Jane asked. She sagged against one of the pillars near the door, looking into the darkness on the other side of the glass.

Cho bit his lip. "We'll give them a few minutes. They'll make it."

She raised an eyebrow at him, then cocked her head and gave a grudging nod. "Yeah, I bet they will."

The crackle of flames grew louder from the hall. In the distance, something shuddered and burst. The building shook.

Jane darted away from the pillar as cracks crawled up the stucco.

"Who are we waiting for?" Samaira looked at her brother. "Where's Ichi and the others?"

"They're out," Jason replied. "As for the rest, I'll fill you in once we're out of here."

Jane met Cho's eye. "What about the Black-Stars? The ones who went to find them?"

"They're taken care of."

Cho nearly leapt out of his skin. He pulled the plasma gun from his waistband and wheeled around, searching for the familiar, yet disembodied deep voice that had answered Jane's question.

"There." The Blue-Star pointed to a small com on the wall next to the door.

"Lawrence, that you?" Cho asked, taking a step toward it.

"Yes. The ones sent for your friends haven't found them. They're on the north end of the complex. A handful went down with one of the generators. The rest should be busy with the fire. But a patrol is coming from the main road to assist Steel. If you leave now, you should make it to the fence before they arrive."

"Lawrence?" Samaira demanded, fury etched on her face.

"Explain later," Jason growled.

She glared at him.

"Got it," Cho said. He glanced toward the far hall, where Anthony and Daisy had disappeared in their search for Juliana. "How long do we have?"

"Nacra if I know, just hurry. The control room is going up, I'm about to leave. Get going. And be careful."

Cho sighed. He exchanged a look with Jason.

"We have to wait," Jason said.

Cho nodded. "I know."

Seconds later, footsteps echoed from down the corridor. Cho and Jane aimed their weapons toward the sound.

Anthony, Daisy, Juliana, and a frail-looking older woman rushed into the lobby, skidding to a stop as they noticed the weapons.

Cho and Jane lowered their guns. Cho tucked his back into his waistband with a sigh of relief. "You made it." He glanced behind Juliana at the woman. She met his eye for half a second before looking at the ground. "And you've brought an extra as well."

Juliana nodded, huffing. "Who's this?" She gestured to the Blue-Star.

"Introductions *later*." The exasperation in Jason's tone almost made Cho laugh.

Instead, he grinned. "The way is clear, let's get to the others."

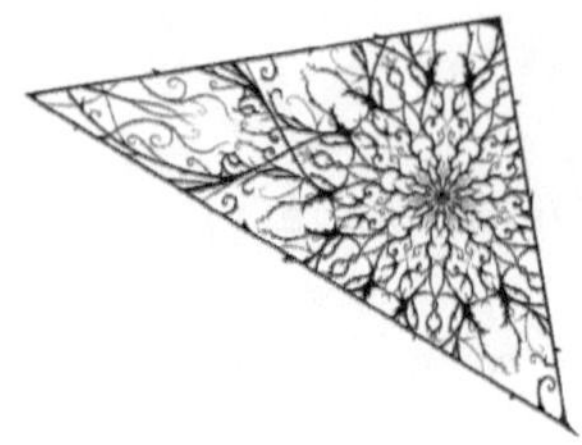

Chapter Thirty

Capital City - Pangaea

The Capital was an undeniably lovely place.

Wolfe hated it.

The smell of the ocean, the vastness of each district set in rings around the government center, the flurry of activity, and the constant nagging of what was and what could have been... she hated every minute of it.

The helo landed on the outskirts of the Grey-Star district, a few short miles from the coast-line. From there, Wolfe and her entourage were driven to the capitol building in elongated black vehicles painted with the Council emblem.

They passed vast homes, towering apartment complexes decorated with flowering vines and glass panels, and dozens of empty playgrounds.

Wolfe's gut clenched. The shift happened so long ago. It was hard to believe there had been a time when her sole purpose had been to cure the sterility that plagued their people. Others had taken up that fruitless mission. People who didn't know or understand the threat of the Alters, of their meddling neighbors. People who had small minds, small plans.

She checked her com. Nothing from Lectius, as expected after his silence for so long. His assistant had been their only point of contact for the past several months. Still, she'd hoped his lack of communication was an error on his part, not deliberate malice.

Her gaze darted to the Black-Stars sitting across from her. They were trusted soldiers, but they weren't her usual guard. It wouldn't be wise to air her grievances with fellow Council members to them, or within earshot. The upper echelon of Grey-Stars had ears in every corner.

A slight buzz drew her attention back to her device. A message from Keith lit up the palm-sized glass in her hand. She stuck a bead-like com in her ear and his voice, overly excited as usual, drew a smile across her lips.

The serum worked. Perhaps not exactly as planned, but they'd made progress. Progress she could discuss during the meeting.

"Of course, limiting access for Orange and Green is a long-term goal."

Wolfe's focus drifted as the councilor a few seats down her droned on. They sat at a circular table, meant to impress upon them the equity of their station. The effect was somewhat lessened by the ostentatious presentation of the Chancellor's chair. Those on either side of her sat a little straighter, smug in their stations.

Wolfe's seat had shifted over the past few years. She'd begun at Collette's side, complicit in her plans long before her husband—the previous Chancellor—had died. Now she sat across from her cousin and old friend, watching as the most powerful person in Pangaea listened to a greasy man discuss the pros and cons of shifting the lower castes into cities of their own.

"Pardon me."

This drew Wolfe's attention. Councilor Arturus had remained silent for most of the pre-meeting brunch and the meeting itself thus far. He was by far the oldest among them, nearly a hundred and twenty. Grey hair draped down his back, segments braided with ornate jewels matching his long beard.

All eyes turned to the old man, and a few of the newer council members exchanged snide glances that did not escape Wolfe's notice.

"I believe my colleague here," Arturus gestured to the man who had been speaking, "is forgetting some of our earliest learning in primary."

A low chuckle went around the group. Wolfe raised an eyebrow, her gaze darting to Collette to gauge how the Chancellor was taking this interruption. The woman had leaned back in her throne, a slightly amused smile twitching at her lips.

"I'm sure I don't know what you mean," Councilor Gan replied, his voice forcefully cool.

"We inherited this land, this world, from a fallen society." Arturus's voice was gruff and dry. His manner of speaking, almost as though he were trying to enunciate past his overgrown grey beard and mustache sent a brief cringe through Wolfe. "Many of us remember our lessons as young Greys preparing to rule Pangaea. We mustn't fall into the traps of previous cultures. The steps we've taken in the past hundred years have already fractured the fragile system of gemstones put in place all those generations ago."

A ripple of unease went around the circle. Wolfe looked again to Collette, whose smile had dropped into a thin line.

Wolfe kept her expression neutral, but silently uttered a thanks to the old fool. He was setting up her announcement perfectly.

"Are you suggesting a problem with the caste system?" Lectius asked from his seat to the right of the Chancellor. His smooth skin, still youthful at nearly fifty, and slicked back blond hair reminded Wolfe of Keith. All the cocky arrogance of a man with too much intelligence and not enough wisdom to know what to do with it.

"Never." Arturus licked his lips. "Never, Councilor Lectius. The peace and order instilled through our efforts are incalculable in their value. However, as a student of history, my purpose on this council is to warn when we approach mistakes that have been made in the past."

"Mistakes."

The breath seemed to leave the room as Collette finally spoke, her gaze fixed on Arturus.

"Yes, Chancellor," he said, his ancient voice unwavering. "Mistakes made by those who work for us, below us. The same sort of prejudices that led to the downfall of civilizations that came before."

"Interesting." Collette nodded her head, her tone suggesting his input was anything but interesting. "We will be sure to take your wisdom into account, Councilor Arturus."

He inclined his head with the deference of someone who knew when they were being dismissed.

"Moving on," Collette said. Her gaze turned to Wolfe, who fought the urge to sit even straighter in her chair. "What news from Dolor, Councilor Wolfe?"

A grin still spread across her face as she clicked the tablet before her with a polite nod to the Chancellor.

"Much news, Chancellor. Thank you for the opportunity to share the remarkable progress we've made these past few weeks."

Collette raised an eyebrow.

"The danger from Alters is palpable," Wolfe continued. "Their power rivals our own, and with so few Grey-Stars inheriting *suggestion*, it stands to reason that we must search for advantages elsewhere."

"You've had success at transfers then?" Lectius interrupted.

Wolfe disguised her scowl with a grin. "Not as of yet, Councilor. But we recently had a breakthrough I think many of you will find valuable."

Collette clicked her tongue.

Wolfe swiped the screen, and the images sent by Keith only an hour ago flew to the tablets of each councilor in the circle. "As you can all see, subject 1129 began with the ability to create and manipulate fire. A power we can agree would be highly useful in combat. However, there are limits. Her ability required long cool-down periods, and her will..." Wolfe grimaced, "is strong."

Her gaze flicked to Lectius. "You mentioned wanting to ensure my research was worthy of your collaboration, last we spoke."

Another ripple went around the circle. Collette turned her head to Lectius, a raised eyebrow suggesting she hadn't been made aware of this.

The councilor's irritated expression shifted, morphing into a benign smile as he gave a polite nod for Wolfe to continue.

"I think you'll find this," she brushed the glass again, "is worthy of further collaboration."

Low gasps went through the room. All of them, Wolfe included, watched as subject 1129 was buckled to the chair, injected with the serum, and experienced something like a seizure. A moment later flames erupted in the room. The Black-Stars assigned to guard her were incinerated in seconds.

The fire grew, blazing orange and blue, lighting up the faces of each councilor. Even Collette, who had so vehemently demanded Wolfe narrow her focus to Juliana, exhaled with a greedy smile on her face.

"Excellent," the Chancellor murmured as the flames dimmed and the screen went dark. "The subject *survived* the process?"

"Very much so," Wolfe confirmed with a nod. "So much, in fact," she turned to Lectius, "that I wish we'd continued our joint venture. It would make the next few steps easier to accomplish."

The councilor's shoulders slumped just enough to send a rush of satisfaction through Wolfe.

"Speaking of your research," Collette turned to the man, "perhaps you should fill us in on your recent progress. Then the Council can determine if your time is better spent on private research, or on furthering the Dolor agenda."

The meeting ended. Another was scheduled for the next day, but for now, the councilors were hard at work demolishing a decadent buffet prepared in their honor. Attendants stood in far corners of the room, ready to swoop in with fresh drinks and clean plates. Other Grey-Stars, governors, and state officials not quite at the level of the Council, were in attendance as well.

If it weren't for the recent success in Dolor, Wolfe would have hated every minute of it. As it was, there were chunks of time when she found herself alone at a tall table, irritated by the cuffs of her dress and the lack of pant-legs she was so fond of. Still, the frustration was somewhat muted by the moments when council members approached her with praise. Their eyes were alight with the same greed that Collette had displayed at the prospect of wielding flames with their own hands.

Wolfe had shut off the video before they'd seen the burns coating 1129's arms. That was a problem for another day.

There were no Blue-Stars in attendance. Unfortunate, as Wolfe had hoped to bend the ear of Lectius' assistant a bit more. The girl had promise, drive similar to Keith, but without his debilitating ego and flair for needless dramatics. She also had access to all of Lectius' work and a grievance with the man that Wolfe was curious to learn more about.

"Well done."

Wolfe turned, lifting a flute of bubbly liquid in a faux salute. Lectius raised his in return, then leaned against the marble-topped cocktail table.

"You've made a fool of me, Wolfe." He said it lightly, a breezy conversation between friends. Darkness flashed in his eyes.

"Hardly more than what you made of me at the last meeting. Promising to work together, guaranteeing a level of cooperation with no follow-through. You slowed my work, Lec." She kept her level tone as well, but her throat was tight. Frustration, anxiety, fury from the past several weeks were at a breaking point.

Besides which, she desperately wanted to return to Dolor before the girl and her little friends showed up. There was time, of course; their troop was on foot. It would take them a few more days, at least, to get to Dolor.

But the stress of waiting almost made her want to alert the Council of the situation so she might request additional Black-stars to aid in capturing the runaways. Almost.

As poorly as previous attempts had gone.

Her own supply of private soldiers was dwindling. Not something that needed to be shared in this shark's den, so she'd make do with Steel.

Lectius scowled. He was younger than her by a few decades and had grown up with limited peers. His inability to disguise his thoughts was an unhealthy trait common in this newer generation of Grey-Stars. They didn't hide their emotions as well as she did.

"Had I known you had made significant progress, I'd have been eager to continue our joint venture."

"And how were you to know," Wolfe turned to him, lowering and sharpening her voice, "anything about my progress when you refused to communicate with me?"

He winced, then bristled. "No matter. I will have my people meet you in Dolor when you return, and we will continue our work as though it had never been interrupted."

Wolfe scoffed. "Don't bother yourself. I will bring my subjects to you."

"Ahh yes." He sneered. "Always the strictest secrecy around your work, Wolfe. Part of why you have trouble making friends."

Her grip on the glass flute reached a dangerous tension, and she made a concerted effort to relax her fingers. "No need to concern yourself with my social life, Lec. I have plenty of people I trust."

He ran his tongue across his teeth, a malicious grin spreading his lips as he gazed around the crowded room. "Of course. I see you left your pet at home. A shame, though probably for the best after what happened last time."

Wolfe's lungs went cold with blistering fury. She opened her mouth, but her words were cut short by a buzzing in her ear.

Without a word to Lectius, she clicked a button on her com and walked away to take the call.

Her pace quickened at the sounds of shouting, footsteps, crackling, and panting on the other line. "Captain Steel?" she hissed.

A few heads turned her direction, but she made it to the grand double doors and stepped through, finding a quiet room several yards down the hallway.

"Ms. Wolfe," Steel responded, his breath heavy. "We have a problem."

Wolfe sank to the ground as Steel filled her in on the evening's events. Fear and rage circled in her chest, thrumming adrenaline through her body with no outlet for it.

Dolor was gone. Burned to the ground by those nacra children. They weren't supposed to arrive yet. They'd stolen a transport somewhere—she'd deal with that little tidbit of information harshly, but not until the rest of this was taken care of.

"Who knows?"

"You're my first call, ma'am." Steel grunted and sucked air through his teeth as though someone was binding a wound. "We believe they're heading south."

"How?" Wolfe uttered through clenched teeth. "How did you let this happen?"

"I don't know, ma'am. I don't understand how they overpowered Lawrence, but most of his unit are dead. Our resources have been halved."

Wolfe pinched the bridge of her nose so hard her nails slightly bent the wrong way. "South... Find them, Steel. Find out how they escaped. And keep it quiet. This *has* to stay quiet until I am able to do damage control. If the council finds out—" Her breath caught there, the control over her trembling hands slipping as her gaze darted to the closed door leading to the hallway.

"Of course, ma'am."

"Salvage what you can. Move to our secondary site, and for the love of Pangaea, find that frosted girl before I decide you aren't worth keeping alive."

Steel audibly gulped. "Yes, ma'am."

Silence fell between them. Wolfe hardly noticed. Her mind whirled between seething fury and frantic planning.

"There is something else, ma'am."

"What?" she snapped.

"They uh, they didn't leave alone."

Wolfe's gaze zeroed in, focused on a painting of mountains on the far wall. "What do you mean," she asked with slow, deliberate words, "not alone?"

Chapter Thirty-One

South of Dolor

Juliana drove for hours. Cho felt her exhaustion before she commented on it. The sky had grown light, the colorful sunrise filling his heart as it filled the horizon.

The others were in the bed of the truck, squashed together but comfortable enough. And safe. That was part of what had put them to sleep, the dip that came from a sudden loss of ever-present terror. He had felt the fear slide away even with his power locked safely behind his walls.

Jason sat with them in the cab of the truck. His hands shook in his lap, the simmering effects of rage and over-exertion clear in the trembling as well as the lines on his face. Dolor had burned. They'd seen the flames rising above the treetops, shooting sparks even higher into the night sky as they'd roared away down a long-forgotten road.

Cho rested a hand on Jason's arm as dawn crested the hills to the left.

The trembling slowed and, though Jason didn't look at him, Cho thought he felt a purposeful swell of gratitude through their physical connection.

Anthony had refused to leave Juliana's side, resulting in a rather cramped cab barely wide enough for the four of them. His hand was on her thigh, their fingers intertwined anytime the road was straight enough for her to drive one-handed.

They drove south, roaring past hills and valleys, small wooded areas, and even the occasional neat rows of fields as they skirted two of Pangaea's larger farming cities.

Their path was clear. This reassurance was proven time and again as Hawk swooped beside the driver's-side window and gave very non-bird-like nods.

He'd avoided the bed of the truck. Even after they'd gone past what they figured was the most dangerous section of road and didn't need his bird's eye view, he didn't rest. It made their movement faster. There were increasing mazes of overgrown streets and towns as they went further south, and Hawk was able to guide them on a more direct route.

Ichi had always planned on them going south. Had planned on taking advantage of the old roads and buildings long forgotten. Cho and Jason's combined knowledge of these plans, along with the map Carthik had given them and

Hawk's help, led them on a winding journey that was less likely to be spotted by any Black-Stars who might be searching for them.

"We won't reach the Mavi river today," Juliana muttered as she cast a glance at the dashboard.

Cho had no notion of what the little buttons and lights meant, but he knew vehicles ran on solar energy. They could run on the power it gained as they went through the afternoon, but it would be a slow pace.

"Better tah stop soon and start up again in the mornin'." Anthony nodded. "We can find a place tah camp. Get some food in everyone." He glanced at Jason as he said this. "We could all use a rest."

They stopped to orient themselves and decide on their next move. Anthony finally relinquished his spot next to Juliana as he and Hawk darted down a side road to find them a good place to rest for the remaining hours of afternoon and through the night. He left his pants behind, folded neatly on the hood of the truck.

Cho fought back his grin as Juliana's cheeks reddened.

His own went red a minute later when Jason jumped from the cab and stretched, the muscles in his back pulling his damp, sweat covered shirt tight.

Cho coughed and faced the road.

Juliana grinned over at him. "So, that went about as well as we could have hoped, right?"

He nodded, then cleared his throat of the lump that had blocked it and took her comment as a good excuse not to watch Jason pace in agitation beside the truck.

"I'm worried about what waits for us next."

She met his eye. "This Lawrence guy?"

He nodded again, picking at the edge of his shirt. "You weren't there when he… he shot his own men in cold blood. Murdered them, Juliana."

He looked up just in time to catch her face go pale. Her fingers clicked together in a rapid pattern.

"We all have blood on our hands from Dolor," she muttered.

Cho shook his head. "That's not what I meant. We did what we had to do; I know that. Frost, it's *my* family we rescued. Don't think for one second I regret anything we did to get in or out of that nacra place."

Her cheek twitched. She cast him a glance and dipped her head. "You're worried he might betray us as easily as he did the Black-Stars in Dolor."

"He didn't seem to be an Alter," Cho explained. "I don't understand his motivation to help."

"You said he showed you a tattoo?"

Cho nodded. He, Jason, and Anthony had filled Juliana in on the events that had occurred in the lobby of Dolor. Then she and Anthony had told them about Steel, his second attempted murder of Anthony, and then his rapid escape as Dolor went up in flames.

Cho had been left to share what happened with Samaira. Each time his sister's name was mentioned, Jason grimaced with an expression of betrayal.

Juliana bit her lip, giving a slow shake of her head. "I don't know what it is, but that sounds so familiar. Mountains and birds?"

"Surrounded by a thin circle," Cho confirmed. "I've never seen the design before."

Juliana frowned. "It doesn't sound like anything May told us about, but she died before she was able to tell us much."

"I'm not sure how much it matters," Cho said, rubbing his chin and stifling a yawn. "We'll only *possibly* see him again if his cover is blown. Said to keep heading south and he'd find us. Whatever that means."

Juliana snorted as his yawn morphed into a grin. "That only gives him several hundred miles to search."

"Assuming we don't find somewhere safe before that."

"We have been making pretty good time." She covered her mouth as a gaping yawn stretched her lips wide. "I'm sorry we can't keep going this afternoon."

Cho shook his head. "Don't be. We all need a break, and I need to talk to my brother."

Juliana nodded. Her lips drew in a tight line, and she gave the smallest shake of her head. "I can't believe we all got out of there."

Cho didn't respond. He'd barely started wrapping his mind around their success. It didn't seem likely, even possible, that they'd done it. Gotten their family.

"Well," he murmured, "we aren't done yet, are we?"

They exchanged a glance, and he could see on her face that she knew he wasn't just referring to finding a place to hide.

A few minutes later, the shape-shifters returned from their search. They'd found a spot.

Juliana started the truck up again, Jason jumped back into his seat, and they followed Anthony's massive black wolf form down a rough asphalt street until they were surrounded by trees.

Cho pressed his forehead to Ichi's, heat filling him, the relief almost too much to bear. Tears squeezed from his eyes and when they finally broke apart, Ichi was crying as well.

They made introductions but halted abruptly as Elaine stumbled from the bed of the truck.

Ichi and Samaira shared the burden of explaining what the Blue-Stars had done to her. Cho's heart nearly shattered at the sight of her dazed eyes, looking past everyone she loved as though they were uninteresting blades of grass.

She radiated fear. The barriers in her mind were gone, shattered as Cho's had been all those years ago when she and Ichi had saved him. It was only when Ichi was beside her, his fingers firmly interlaced with hers, that she calmed.

Juliana settled her aunt at the edge of the camp with a fair bit of distance between her and the nearest children. Then she patched up the worst of the children's wounds, with a promise to take care of the rest, and make an attempt to help Elaine, after sleep and some food.

Abilene stuck by Samaira's side, the two going around with a med kit from the truck and doing what they could outside the realm of healing powers.

Anthony and Jason excused themselves to go hunting. Cho gave Jason a curious frown before he left, but the flame thrower just shook his head, a grimace still fixed on his face.

Hawk went after them a short time later. He hadn't spoken to Ichi or Elaine. He'd barely looked at them.

They'd need to talk about it. All of it. The connection between Hawk and Elaine, the Blue-Star Samaira had brought, Juliana's aunt, their next steps...

There was much to discuss, to decide.

At the moment, none of it mattered to Cho. He stayed close to Ichi, keeping his brother in his sights at all times. He helped settle Elaine against a blanket covering a crumbling log. He tended to the little ones, their eyes still wide and afraid for the few minutes before they satiated their hunger and passed out again.

Before long, sleeping bodies covered the ground in their camp. Juliana paced among them with Daisy at her side, healing the residual nerve damage in each child's arm from where Kim had disabled the trackers. It was slow work, but she'd gotten just about everyone. Weariness dragged at both women as Juliana finished with the last child.

They would cut the destroyed trackers out, someday. Juliana had reassured Cho and Jason that they were inert, but no one wanted to keep the Grey-Star tech in their bodies. It would take a clean space, pain killers, a sharp blade, and stitches afterward. All things that weren't available at the moment.

It was still good to know it could be done.

Jane clutched Tommy to her, sitting before one of the three fires they'd built. Taz was sprawled beside them. He had a satisfied smile on his face and gave Cho a nod when their eyes met.

Eventually there wasn't anything left to keep Cho busy. He settled by the same fire, snug beside his brother, leaving space for Jason when he returned.

Juliana stumbled over a moment later, her arm draped around Daisy as the younger girl scolded her.

"It's time to sit, Jules. Don't fight me on this."

Juliana's lips twitched into a grin. "I wouldn't dream of it."

Daisy rolled her eyes, gave Cho an exasperated look, and helped lower Juliana beside Elaine.

"Hey, Ichi," Jane said, her voice uncharacteristically soft.

He turned his attention to her, one hand interlaced with Elaine's.

Jane glanced down at Tommy, then took a breath. "Back there, when the guards came in and you... you handled that Black-Star by yourself."

Ichi nodded, his face paling.

"What stopped you doing that before?"

Cho's chest tightened. He fiddled with the edge of his shirt, anxious about the answer and the pain the question clearly brought to his brother.

Ichi flexed his hand at his side, his gaze shifting from Jane to the fire dancing between them. "Retribution."

Cho winced, his lips pressed together as understanding dawned.

"I used my gift when we first arrived. It was... I miscalculated. I knew what would happen if..." He broke off.

There was no need to finish his thought. Cho glanced at Jane, who wore regret for a moment before tightening her grip around Tommy and focusing on the fire.

They sat in silence for a few minutes. Weight settled around them as though the darkness of the night were a heavy blanket.

Tommy yawned, stretching and clipping Jane in the jaw with his hand. She yelped, he laughed, and the tension faded a bit.

"So, little brother." Ichi stretched forward, forcing himself out of his sunken expression. He rolled his neck and extended his legs. He seemed unable to keep his limbs folded for more than a second. "What's next?"

Cho's gaze flitted to Juliana. She was looking at him as well, studying him. He briefly inclined his head and gestured for her to answer his brother's question.

Ichi raised an eyebrow but turned to her as well.

Juliana cleared her throat. "Searching the office was unhelpful for our current situation. Maybe something I pulled will help us someday, but for now, we have very limited options." She sighed with a grimace. "There are more research facilities to the north."

Ichi leaned back, his eyes wide with alarm. Cho held up a hand to steady him.

Juliana dipped her head in a brief nod. "Nothing like Dolor. These belong to others. Wolfe's notes were simply noting them and the kinds of research they're doing. That, combined with the information Carthik gave you... we *need* to head south. In spite of the possibility of running into Lawrence."

She glanced at Daisy and Taz before meeting Cho's eye. "There are mountains there. Snow-capped peaks that protect the border of Pangaea."

"Why does that matter?" Jane asked.

Cho swallowed. His dreams of late had been plagued with mountains. Filled incessantly with towering rock, evergreen trees, and snow. He didn't understand the dreams, but he knew he wasn't alone in having them.

Juliana had told him about hers during a meditation session not long before they found Hawk.

"There's something there," Cho murmured.

Jane's gaze snapped to him.

"What do you mean?" Ichi asked.

"I've had..." Cho grimaced. "I've had dreams about a set of snow-capped mountains. Juliana has too."

There was movement beside Ichi and all of them glanced at Elaine. She'd shifted, her gaze still distant, staring blankly into the fire. But she'd put her hand on Ichi's forearm, her fingers squeezing his skin.

"The mountains?" Ichi's voice was low as he looked at her with all the concern in the world.

Elaine blinked, and her head dipped in a shallow nod.

"Have you had the dreams too?" Juliana's voice was gentle.

Elaine didn't respond. Her hand remained on Ichi's arm, though her grip loosened. She continued to look into the fire.

Across from them, Tommy gave Jane a worried expression. She held him tighter.

"South then." Ichi nodded. "That means crossing the Mavi River. Not a simple task. And when we get to these mountains? What then?"

"Lawrence might be there, but I don't know how much we want to trust him." Cho fidgeted uncomfortably. "If he can get us to a safe place..."

"If he was lying?" Jane asked in her usual stern voice. "If he *is* there but tries to take us back? Or somewhere worse? Maybe he's working for one of those other research places." She glanced at Juliana.

"If he doesn't show, we keep moving as planned," Juliana said. "If he is there, we can talk about it then. And if he tries to take anyone..."

"He dies."

The low rumble of Jason's voice made Cho whip around. The hunters had returned. Hawk had a rope draped over his shoulder, half a dozen fish strung on it. Anthony had done the same with a few rabbits and smaller rodents, and Jason carried Anthony's bag, full to bulging with what looked like onions and other wild-grown vegetables.

Jason lowered the bag from his shoulder and set it beside the fire with a louder thump than was necessary. He settled beside Cho with a huff as his gaze traveled to a fire a few yards away.

Samaira had stayed with Abilene. The two were bent beside the flames, Abilene gently prompting the still-awake children to eat a few more bites and drink more water. Samaira's arm went around her shoulder as Abilene, who had yet to eat, straightened and swayed on her feet.

Cho lifted his hand, the temptation to reach out and take Jason's was strong. He knew the relief it would bring, the sense of warmth, of calm even amidst Jason's anger. But Jason shifted away, clenching his hands around his pulled-up knees and looking at Ichi.

"They filled you in?"

Ichi nodded.

"Did you do a check on the..." Jason's hand clenched and a wave of frustration broke through his wards.

Cho's power jumped at it, but he pulled it back quickly.

"The new people," Jane finished for him, her gaze darting to a figure at the edge of their little clearing. Juliana's aunt had opted to stay away from the fire and had barely spoken a word since their escape.

Ichi shook his head. "Not yet, I..." his jaw tightened. "I don't have the strength for it right now."

"I can get a read tonight," Cho offered. He glanced from Juliana to Jason. "If everyone is all right with that."

Juliana nodded. "I trust you Cho, and I want to know what's going on as much as anyone."

Jason grunted in what sounded like the affirmative. Behind him, Anthony clapped a hand on his shoulder.

"I'm off tah take care of this," Anthony said. He waved his catch and moved away from them, toward the least occupied fire.

Hawk followed him without a word to the others.

Jason remained, to Cho's relief, but his mood didn't lighten.

Juliana groaned as she stood. Daisy moved as well, but Juliana shook her head. "Rest, I'll be back in a few minutes."

Cho held up a hand as Ichi went to rise. "I've got this, Ichi. Stay with Elaine."

His older brother gave a surprised blink but nodded, his expression shifting to gratitude as he looked down at his love.

Cho followed Juliana to Samaira's fire first. The children around the flames were already fast asleep. The sun had barely left the sky, its colors still painting the blue horizon in an array of purples and reds. Winter was on its way, the fallen leaves cushioning their camp was evidence enough, but the air had also taken on a frigid temperature in the evenings.

"Hey," Samaira muttered as they approached.

She sat against a rock, Abilene nestled beside her in an intimate cuddle. She must have just finished helping the little ones.

Cho blinked. "Hey."

"Thanks for getting us out," Samaira said. Her voice was thick, with emotion or the aftermath of her ordeal, he wasn't sure. She glanced at the fire he'd just left. A wave of sorrow rolled up, licking at the wall of his power. He pushed it back and crouched by her side.

"Don't forget your wards," he said gently. "I can feel it all right now."

She grimaced and inhaled through her nose. A moment later the residual fear and sadness faded.

"You're here for her?" Samaira glanced down at Abilene.

The petite woman sat up, a yawn stretching her mouth wide as she glanced from Juliana to Cho.

Juliana nodded. "To get a read. On your friend, and on my aunt."

Abilene's eyes widened, and she darted a look at Samaira.

"Just to keep everyone safe," Juliana said, her voice kind but firm. "Tomorrow Ichi will go into your minds a little. To make sure you aren't going to betray us."

Abilene sucked in a breath, releasing it as she clenched Samaira's knee. "All right." She looked from Juliana to Cho. "What do you need me to do?"

Cho smiled, trying to channel calm reassurance. "Just sit here. Think about Dolor. Think about the Grey-Stars, the Black-Stars, us. Think about Samaira."

Samaira's dark gaze flicked to meet his for a brief moment, and she raised an eyebrow. He gave an apologetic shrug, hoping she didn't think he was being overly invasive. This was important.

Abilene nodded and straightened. She pursed her lips, taking on a look of determination.

He opened his mind, let his power out of its box, and pushed it toward the Blue-Star.

A jumble of emotion hit him. A collection of swirling colors and feelings that didn't seem to go together in any logical way.

Then again, how logical was emotion?

In the distance, as though coming through a long tunnel, Cho heard Juliana speaking.

"Focus on Dolor first. Think about the people you knew there."

Unease. A nervous anxiety that crawled into Cho's gut as hard as he tried to keep himself free from it. There was more, twinges of happiness, pride, but those feelings had faded within her in the last few weeks. He felt their lingering presence, but as Juliana spoke again, they disappeared entirely.

"Now the Black-Stars and the Greys. How do they make you feel? You don't have to answer out loud."

But Abilene did, and her words matched the fear that flooded her. "Scared. It felt like they were always watching. Any misstep, any act of what they thought was rebellion..." her voice caught.

Cho nodded, his eyes still closed.

"Now us," Juliana's voice took on a harsher tone. That protective sound Cho had become accustomed to when she defended Daisy, when she spoke of plans and strategies, and when she told off Jason and Anthony for doing something dangerous.

Confusion muddled much of Abilene's other emotions. Flashes of fear, unease, sympathy, pity, concern... but none of the rage Cho was looking for. None of the anger or hatred he'd have expected from one of the people tasked with hunting them.

He nodded again.

"Now me," Samaira murmured.

This wasn't muddled. It was as sure and solid as stone, as fixed and entrenched as thorny vines wrapped in and around an ancient tree.

Admiration flowed through Abilene. Pride, then worry, a surge of desire, of joy, and...

Cho flinched at the strength of the emotion. He'd felt it before, with Juliana and Anthony in the early days before they'd learned warding. But the suddenness of it now stirred something in him. A memory, a flicker of awareness that he'd felt this before, somewhere.

Love.

Abilene was hopelessly, completely in love with Samaira.

Cho pulled away, plucking the saffron strands of his power from the vibrancy of Abilene's feelings.

He swallowed hard, settling back on his heels and then butt as he wiped sweat from his brow and focused on steadying his breaths.

"Well?" Juliana asked.

He squinted up at her. She stood at Abilene's side, one hand clenched tight around the hilt of her blade.

He gave a weak grin. "She's with us." He glanced at Samaira, reading the question in her eyes even as he noted Abilene blushing to the roots of her hair. "As long as Samaira is with us," he said softly, his smile growing, "she's with us."

Samaira's lower jaw jutted to the side in a look of slightly embarrassed exasperation. She lightly shook her head, but then gave him a grateful nod.

Juliana's grip on the blade eased. She met Cho's eye. "You need a minute?"

He nodded, heart still thundering through his chest at the strength of Abilene's feelings for Samaira. He breathed in deep and tried to recall the moment that the same feeling had danced across the periphery of his power.

It had been so brief. He remembered not understanding it. Not knowing what it was he'd felt and not caring in the moment. It had been warm.

He frowned. Why would an emotion be warm?

But the feeling. The flicker that darted out of the person who had held him…

His gaze drifted to where he'd left Ichi and the others. Jason stared through the fire, watching them closely. It took a moment for him to notice Cho looking at him. When he did, Jason turned his focus to the flames.

"Brenna next?" Juliana asked a few minutes later as Cho rose and dusted off his pants.

He nodded.

The two of them crossed the clearing. Darkness had fallen now, the colorful sunset turned deep blue in the time they'd spent with Samaira and Abilene.

Brenna was by herself, partially hidden by an overgrowth of tree branches and so far from the fires that the area was nearly black.

Cho's eyes took a moment to adjust. He followed Juliana, kneeling when she did and releasing more of the saffron strands usually tucked away in his box.

Ichi might call it unethical—or at least would have before everything happened—but Cho wasn't waiting for Brenna's permission the way he had with Abilene. Samaira at least knew the woman, trusted her. Juliana had never met her aunt and, prisoner or not, they had no idea how long she'd been in Dolor.

Abilene had told them she'd never seen Brenna before, which suggested she hadn't been locked up like the others.

"Hey," Juliana said softly.

"Marissa." Shadow stirred as Brenna moved forward. She was crouched, folded together like a spider before she got a better look at Juliana and sank back to the ground. "Not Marissa."

Disappointment oozed from the woman. Cho allowed his tendrils of power to read the emotion, but kept them on a tight leash.

"No." Juliana gave a sad smile. "I'm your niece, Juliana. My mom is your sister. She misses you very much."

Cho's gaze darted to Juliana, wondering if that was true. Most city people would have been eager to forget a White-Star in the family. Brenna's gemstones were as dirty as the rest of her, but they glinted with the same pearlescent color as Juliana's.

"She... she remembers me?"

Disbelief. Not quite shock, but definitely doubt. As though Brenna thought Juliana might be lying.

Juliana sucked in a wince. "She does. She told me about you after my Coding. She said you were always good at making friends."

Brenna scoffed. The sound was so loud compared to her previous words that Cho jerked.

"No friends."

Bitterness. So tart Cho pursed his lips.

Brenna's gaze flitted past them. The bitterness grew, sadness along with it and something else Cho couldn't quite describe. Something close to anger, to shame.

Juliana raised her hands, palms out in an appeasing gesture. "That's fine. I didn't have many friends either, until them." She waved a loose hand toward the fires.

There was silence for a moment.

Juliana swallowed, lowered her hands, and settled onto the ground. "You could come over with us, you know. Get warm? You don't have to stay in the dark."

Definitely shame now. A rush of it that made Cho grit his teeth to keep from experiencing the emotion himself. He pulled his power in a bit, reducing the intensity of Brenna's reactions.

"We have a few questions," Juliana murmured. "Would you be all right answering them?"

Brenna's gaze went from Juliana to Cho and back. Then she nodded.

Juliana smiled. "Excellent. Let's start with Dolor."

Fear. A rush of fear and fury and terror and disgust. Loathing, muddled with pride.

Cho put a hand to his forehead, trying to press the emotions out of his mind as they threatened to overwhelm him.

"I don't like that place," Brenna muttered.

Juliana nodded. "And Wolfe? You were in her office. Are you familiar with her? With what she was doing?"

Another wave of roiling feelings. Cho rose, requiring a physical step back to keep his walls from cracking. There was so much: fear, anger, pride, yearning. What felt like decades of emotion crashed upon him.

"Cho?" Juliana's voice came from far away. Distant.

Darkness overtook him. Another slam of multiple competing emotions struck. His walls splintered.

"Cho!"

He barely heard her. Barely heard Brenna's mumbling apologies, her voice frantic and unsteady. He staggered backward, tripping on the uneven ground and wheeling.

Something caught him. Strong, steady arms gripped him and pulled him upright with a rough shake. Worry overtook the storm of Brenna's emotion. The darkness dimmed and another flash of the emotion he'd recognized in Abilene split through the remaining panic.

Then wards went up. The physical contact, and the strength of the emotions that came with it, faded as Jason let him go and took a step back.

Jason was speaking. Cho's ears rang as he inhaled, shook his head, and winced against the piercing pain now throbbing in his temples. He tried to focus.

"—did she do?" Jason demanded, fury barely tempered in his voice.

"I don't know," Juliana responded, her tone filled with concern as well. "Cho, are you all right?"

He blinked again and was finally able to take in the space. Juliana stood a few yards from Brenna, one hand held up to stop the woman moving closer, and the other pressed against Jason's chest to stop him from advancing on Brenna. Her brow was furrowed, lips pulled in a tight line.

"I'm..." Cho shuddered and licked his lips, his mouth suddenly dry. "I think so."

Jason looked away from Brenna as Cho spoke. The fire in his hand diminished slightly. "Are you?"

"Thirsty," Cho muttered. He tried to still the trembling of his hands, clenching them into fists and then extending his fingers out.

Ichi had rushed over as well. He put a hand on Cho's shoulder, all the concern of an older brother apparent on his face. With his wards in place, strong and steady, there was no transfer of emotion from the physical contact. "Cho, let's get you sitting down."

Cho nodded and turned away. He reached up a hand and rested it on Jason's bicep. "It's fine, Jason. It wasn't on purpose."

Jason's eyes were brighter than he'd seen before, the dark pools that so often held laughter or rage seemed wider than usual. With his flames still in hand, Jason gave a sharp nod.

Juliana dropped her hand, relief splashed across her face. Still, Cho heard her speaking to Brenna as Ichi guided him away.

"Stay here. I don't know what that was, but we all need a few minutes. Keep your distance."

There was more, but it was lost in the distance and bustle as Cho was settled beside the fire. He was already so warm. His cheeks were flushed, sweat matting his hair to his head.

Ichi knelt at his side, hand remaining a steady presence on Cho's shoulder.

"Here." Taz appeared on Cho's other side with a container of water.

Cho guzzled half of it down. The liquid cleared his throat and eased the heat in his face. "Thanks."

Across the fire Jane watched him with wary eyes; Tommy had fallen asleep on her lap.

"What happened?" Ichi asked.

Cho drained the last of the bottle, his chest still heaving. "There was so much." He glanced over to Jason. He stood a few yards away with Juliana, the two in the midst of what appeared to be a heated discussion.

"Is she w... wi... is she a danger?" Taz murmured, his voice low in Cho's ear.

Cho shook his head, shrugging at the same time. "I don't know. She's not well, I know that. But I couldn't get anything definitive."

Ichi nodded. His expression was twisted, pained as he rubbed Cho's arm. "I'll take a look in her mind tomorrow. I'm—" he tightened his jaw—"I'm sorry I can't tonight."

A weak smile crossed Cho's lips. He looked up at his brother. "I'm fine, Ichi. I'm just glad you're alive."

Ichi smiled as well, wrapping his arms around Cho and pulling him tight. The two sat that way for a long while.

When they finally broke apart, Ichi returned to Elaine's side, and Cho curled against his bag by the fire, eventually falling into a deep sleep.

Chapter Thirty-Two

South of Dolor

Abilene fell asleep at Samaira's side. The relief of the escape, the tension of the drive, Jason's reaction to the Blue-Star... it was enough to collapse Samaira as well, if she hadn't been so worried about what her powers might do in her sleep.

She couldn't make a flame. Each time she thought to pull forth a spark like she'd done as easily as breathing since childhood, her power surged within. It promised more than a palm-full of warmth, it promised destruction. Death.

She closed her hand after the sixth attempt, biting back the tears in her eyes. They were on the run. Hiding from anyone who had survived the fire in Dolor, not to mention what was likely a swarm of Black-Stars headed their way, and she had nothing to fight with.

Then there was Jason.

Her nose itched, gaze drawn to where Jason stood. He'd taken up watch in front of Ichi's fire, a continuous ball of flame in his hand, his focus darting between the old woman they'd rescued and the trees surrounding them.

He'd come for her. Same as she would have done for him.

She'd thought he was dead.

Samaira closed her eyes, pressing palms against her lids until she saw spots. She was in so much pain; from the beatings, the serum, the escape, and none of it hurt as much as the thought of her constantly laughing brother unable to smile at her.

She shifted, adjusting Abilene on their blanket so she could get up without disturbing her. The smaller woman stirred, her pale eyes fluttering open. Her gaze sought Samaira, as evidenced by the relieved exhale when their eyes caught.

"Is everything all right?" Abilene asked.

The softness of her voice cut into Samaira and sent a ripple of calm through her.

"Yeah." She smiled. "I'm just going to talk to my brother. Help with the watch."

Abilene straightened, blinking sleep from her eyes. "I can help too."

Samaira's grin spread. "You could. But you should sleep."

"Are you sure?"

She nodded.

Abilene squinted for a brief moment, but a yawn broke through her stubbornness. Her delicate fingers brushed against Samaira's arm, and she laid back down, pulling a thin blanket over her shoulders.

It had happened quickly, the intensity of what Samaira felt for this woman. She couldn't leave her, not knowing what Wolfe had been willing to do even before the lot of them had escaped. If they'd left her there…

She'd be dead. Simple as that, and it was what Samaira had told herself as Abilene had helped her across the grassy lawn, steadied her as Luna and Nova levitated them over the fence, and joined her in the bed of the already full-to-bursting truck. It's what Samaira had repeated in her head as they'd driven off, away from the terror and pain of the last few weeks. Away from death for them all.

It might have been the moment Abilene shifted her attention to the others that Samaira had felt more than a stirring in her chest. When they'd been driving for a little over twenty minutes without the sound of plasma bolts, helos, or other signs of a chase, and Abilene had removed herself from Samaira's side to check on the wellbeing of the children around them.

She hadn't had to do it.

All but Sky winced away from her touch. The little girl remembered the food Abilene had snuck them.

Even so, she'd spent the better part of an hour digging through the supplies stuffed into racks above their heads, going from person to person spreading as much burn ointment as she could find over the wounds where Kim had disabled their trackers, checking the children for additional injuries, and trying to get them to drink from the bottles of water the girl, Daisy, had offered everyone.

Samaira had watched until her eyes drifted closed. When the truck came to a halt and she awoke, Abilene was by her side again, holding her hand.

Samaira inhaled, enjoying the smell of the fires as she took unsteady steps toward her twin brother.

His gaze darted in her direction as she drew near. He looked away again when he saw who was coming, his face stiff.

She sidled up, sticking her hands into the pockets of the pants he'd leant her. "I had it, you know."

She forced down her grin at his double take. He glanced at her, his brow furrowed.

"What do you mean?"

She shrugged. "You didn't need to rescue us. I had it handled."

The sound that emitted from him brought malicious mirth to her belly.

"The frost you did," he snapped, indignant.

She let out some of the humor in a low chuckle and cocked her head. "Ichi and I had the place mostly mapped out. We were about to set our ingenious plan into action."

Jason's lip curled. "You were in a holding cell in the middle of Dolor covered in injuries. You really expect me to believe you were on the verge of escape?"

Samaira nudged his shoulder with her own and winked. "No. But I've missed messing with you."

There was a brief pause before a shadow of her brother's smile flickered across his face. He gave a dry chuckle and shook his head.

"I've missed you too," he muttered.

A knot of tension eased within her. "I thought you were dead, you know? We all did."

His jaw went tight. He clenched his hands, the ball of fire disappearing into his fist. Samaira put a hand on his arm. To her relief, he didn't pull away.

Another moment passed, longer this time as Jason's mouth twitched and shoulders shook. Eventually he turned to look her in the eyes, her hand falling away from him.

"We thought you were dead too. When we escaped Haven, we thought all of you..." He shook his head, tears leaking from the corners of his eyes. "I saw you fall, Samaira. I held your body, and I thought I'd never see your eyes open again."

She swallowed, an invisible weight heavy on her chest. The pain of losing him rose up in her mind, the memory of it pulling tears from her eyes as well.

"I'm here, Jase." She put a hand on his cheek, giving a gentle pull until he leaned forward and pressed his forehead to hers. They stood there, skin to skin for a minute before he pulled away.

"Seems like you found some comfort there." His gaze darted toward the fire where Abilene was sleeping.

Samaira's nose curled. A flash of irritation swept through her. "She was in a cell too, Jase. For helping us. Helping *me*."

He scoffed. "And how much damage did she do before she decided to develop a conscience? How many of our friends did she hurt before she fell for you?"

Samaira's breath caught.

Her brother stared at her, his mouth curled into a furious sneer. "How much did she hurt you before you fell for her?"

Samaira was already shaking her head, heat rising in her gut and trickling down her limbs as she glared at him. "Don't."

"Tell me," Jason snapped, pointing toward the fire as his voice rose. "Tell me how you can see the gemstones on her temples and bear even looking at her?"

The heat grew to an inferno. Samaira's power pressed at the bars of the cage in her mind, begging, demanding, to be released. She clenched her hands, inhaling through her nose and breathing out through pursed lips.

"Jase, that's enough. You weren't there. You didn't go through what we did—"

"Because of *her*," he shouted.

People around the camp stirred. The two keeping watch by the truck noticeably looked their way.

"It's because of her, and nacra people *like* her that you were taken in the first place," he hissed.

Samaira shook her head. Her hands trembled at her sides, but she had a hold on the unstable power in her mind. Tenuous, maybe temporary, but a hold nonetheless.

"You have no place to judge me for wanting to get her out," Samaira murmured.

Jason blinked, seemingly taken aback by her uneven yet quiet tone. He cocked his head, concern cutting through the anger on his face.

"The Grey-Star threatened her family, Jase." Samaira inhaled again. More tears burned in her eyes, not from emotion, but from the effort of keeping her power in check. "They're probably dead. Because she told them about us, told them about Dolor, and tried to stop what was happening there."

Jason took a step toward her. He put a hand on her shoulder, brows now furrowed with worry. "Samaria?"

She stepped back, causing his hand to drop before he felt the heat thrumming through her skin.

"I'm sorry," he growled. "I can't trust her, but I'll keep a lid on my attitude while she's around."

Samaira nodded. She swallowed, wincing at the heat already in her throat. It was as though her body was being consumed by the flames within. She needed water. Needed to dive into a pool of ice and let it ease the burning.

"Samaira, what's—"

"Get me when your watch is done," she interrupted. "I'll take over 'til morning."

He called to her again as she walked away, but she barely heard it through the roaring in her ears. She strode past the fire where Abilene lay.

Huddled around a pile of embers lay a handful of the children who'd been rescued from Haven. Luna and Nova were there too, a sight that brought a smile to Samaira's lips. Beside them slept the girl Cho had rescued before everything went to shit.

The girl who could create ice.

Chapter Thirty-Three

South of Dolor

Anthony's fingers were interlaced with Juliana's. He'd left her side twice since Dolor. Once as a wolf to find this clearing, and again when it became clear they'd need more to eat than what they'd managed to put aside in the truck.

He didn't want to be far from her. Not after nearly losing her to Steel.

His lip curled at the thought. The man was a coward. Juliana was right—he needed to be ended permanently.

Still, Anthony's gut did a somersault at the thought of taking more lives. It had come so easily in the moment. When it was to protect Juliana, or Daisy, or one of the others, he pulled a trigger and swung a blade without a second thought. Afterward though...

He'd volunteered for the first watch for a reason. He wasn't looking forward to his dreams.

"Hey." Juliana leaned into him. "Are you all right?"

They sat on the tail of the truck; the glowing remains of the evening's fires at their back and a dark road in front of them.

Jason watched the other side of their camp. He watched Juliana's aunt, a woman they were all still very unsure of. Another thorn in the growing headache of worry in Anthony's mind.

He copied Juliana's movement and draped his arm over her shoulder, letting her tuck into his side. "It's all gotten complicated."

She chuckled mirthlessly. "That feels like an understatement."

Her tone drew a smile from him. He rested his cheek on her blonde hair. It was dark with ash and dirt. Soot stuck to their arms and, while they'd found time to change into clean clothes, blood still stained their hands.

"Abredea was easy," he murmured. He stared into the trees, gently pulling on his wolf's sight to give himself an edge against the darkness. "Didn't feel that way at the time, but it was. Find enough tah eat. Stay outta trouble—"

Juliana snorted, but he continued.

"I worried about Naya and Jimmy, Daisy, Taz, the rest of 'em, but there was a routine to it. I didn't realize how steady things were 'til—"

"'Til I showed up?" Juliana asked.

It was his turn to chuckle. "Nah, 'til everythin' happened with Steel. That's when things started gettin' complicated. And now," he squeezed her torso, pressing into her solid form as though it were the only thing holding him upright, "it feels like we're in a storm, Jules. An' I don't know how tah see past the clouds."

She tapped her fingers along his arm, repeating that pattern he'd grown so familiar with, but on his skin instead of her own thumb.

"We have a destination," she murmured. "That's something."

He heaved a sigh. "It is. The matter of gettin' us all there alive isn't gonna be as simple as we hope, though."

She shifted against him. "You think Lawrence is going to betray us?"

Anthony lifted his head from hers and scanned their surroundings. "I don' plan on us runnin' into him again. I'm more worried about Steel still bein' in the world. Steel, the other Black-Stars, that Grey who's after yeh. Besides all that, where are we goin' when we reach the mountains? From what yeh've said these aren't like the ones back home."

Juliana shook her head. "They're different, Anthony. Massive. Like nothing you've ever experienced before. We'll probably be able to see them after we cross the Mavi River."

"And there's supposedly somethin' there?"

She shrugged against his body. "I've had these dreams since I got to Abredea. Snow-tipped mountains consuming the horizon. I don't know what we'll find when we get there, but there's a part of me that breathes easier knowing we're headed that way."

He squeezed her again. "I understand that. I just wish we knew what was comin'."

She took a deep breath, a yawn breaking through her exhale. He grinned down at her, his wolf's sight letting him watch the flutter of her eyelids as she struggled against exhaustion.

"You should get tah sleep," he murmured. "Yeh drove the whole way here."

Juliana shook her head. "I'm fine."

"Yer a bad liar."

She laughed. "I'm a fantastic liar; just," she turned and gave him a rueful grin, "not with you."

Heat stirred in him at the look in her eye. Her hand brushed against his chest, and he inhaled a sharp breath.

"Really, Jules," he said through gritted teeth, "yeh should get some rest."

"You're right." Her voice shifted, taking on a low, husky tone that caused a lump to form in the back of Anthony's throat.

He put a hand over hers, keeping it pressed to him. "It happens."

She smiled, leaned closer, and pressed her lips against his.

The warmth of them, the feel of her body molded perfectly against his in their little section of dark forest, chased away the worries that plagued his mind. He sank into her kiss. His eyes closed, the wolf inside of him growling appreciatively as Juliana shifted to get closer to him.

Time stretched as the troubles of the world fell away. In the back of his mind, the stack of odds against them teetered on its base. It would fall. Probably soon, and they'd be back in a frantic state of running and hiding and trying to survive. But for now, in this moment, all he cared about was the feel of Juliana's lips pressed to his.

Footsteps broke them apart. Footsteps and the realization that they were meant to be keeping watch. Anthony stroked Juliana's cheek. The small scar on her skin marked the day she'd saved his life. His thumb lingered on the pale strip of white.

She yawned. "Who is taking the shift after you?"

"I'm not sure. Daisy maybe," he replied with a stretch.

Juliana grinned. "Come find me when you're done?"

Heat rushed through him again. He nodded, her hand falling away from his as she stood and strode away from the truck toward the collection of fires behind them.

"Am I in... int... interrupting?" came Taz's unsteady sarcastic drawl from the side opposite where Juliana had left.

"Shaddup," Anthony growled, unable to keep the laughter from his voice.

Taz swung around the truck and plopped down beside Anthony on the tailgate. "Seems like things are goin' well with the two of yeh."

Anthony's face grew warm. Taz was nearly seventeen, not a child, and had been secretly pining for Daisy as long as Anthony could remember. It wasn't like this was the first time they'd talked about relationships. Still, the warmth crept up to the roots of his hair.

"Yeah," he murmured, pulling his feet up onto the bumper and resting his arms on his knees.

Silence fell for a moment. Taz leaned in, nudging Anthony's shoulder. "Well..."

"Well what?"

"What's it like?" he demanded.

Anthony huffed out a laugh. "Kissing?"

Taz scoffed. "Being in love, yeh idiot."

Anthony's eyes went wide. The wolf inside growled, a deep and low rumble that was very much like the sound of approval it had made when his lips were locked with Juliana's.

"I..." Anthony swallowed. "I don't think I've thought about it."

Taz grinned, his white teeth glinting in the light of the moon. "It's gotta feel nice, knowin' she loves yeh back."

Anthony did a double take and blinked at his friend. "What?"

Taz laughed, throwing back his head with a true guffaw at Anthony's expense. "For someone with extra fancy eyesight now, yer still blind as ever."

"What's that mean?"

"Yeh never picked up on it when the girls 'round Abredea had a likin' for yeh." Taz chuckled, waving a hand through the air. "I'm surprised yeh figured it out with Jules."

Anthony flushed again, the heat more intense this time as tingles went down his spine. "She, uh, she kissed me in May's garden. That's when I figured she liked me."

Taz nearly fell off the truck.

Anthony glared at him until the laughter faded, and even then Taz had a smile on his face, not likely to leave anytime soon.

"Yeh've gotta be tired," Anthony growled pointedly. "Don't yeh wanna get some rest before tomorrow?"

Taz nodded, a few seconds passing as his features sobered, and he turned to face Anthony. "I wanted tah talk to yeh about somethin'."

"'Course." Anthony frowned. Taz rarely looked this serious.

"I think I can still be useful."

Anthony blinked, confused. He squinted at his friend. "Whaddya mean?"

Taz shook his head, blond hair flapping into his eyes. "The rest of yeh have power, Tony. Yeh've got abilities like nothin' we've ever imagined. And these kids," he gestured behind them, "they're even stronger."

Anthony lowered his legs and turned to lean against the wall of the truck to look directly at his friend. His brows drew together in a frown. "What does that have tah do with anythin'?"

Taz gave an uncomfortable shrug, his gaze darting away. "I w.... w... was feelin' maybe not the best way about it for a while."

"How long?" Anthony asked, worry in his tone. "Why didn' yeh tell me?"

Taz rolled his eyes. "I know yeh. I know the way you were thinkin' about yer own wolf ability for a while, and I didn't wanna add tah that."

Anthony sighed. "I've never got too much goin' on tah not wanna hear about your worries, Taz." He leaned forward and put a hand on Taz's shoulder.

The boy shook his head, a grin splitting his face as he pushed Anthony's hand away. "That's what I'm sayin' though. I'm not worried about it anymore. I was..." his expression turned sheepish. "...jealous for a while. But after Dolor, after helpin' get the little ones out while the rest of yeh went for Juliana and Jason's sister... I didn't just help. I was important."

Something clenched in Anthony's heart. A combination between pride and pain. Pride for his friend's accomplishment and the knowledge that he had, in fact, been vital to their success. Pain at the thought that Taz had considered, even for a second, that he didn't matter as much as the rest of them.

He waited, watching as Taz's eyes got even brighter, the gemstones on his temples swirling with color.

"I can make a difference," Taz continued. "I can help get us somewhere safe and keep us safe, even without being able tah do what the rest of yeh can."

He looked at Anthony, the wild grin on his face so bright that Anthony couldn't help but smile back.

In a quick motion, Anthony pushed off the truck and rocked toward Taz. His arm looped around his friend, pulling Taz to his side in a tight, one-armed hug.

"Of course, yeh can." Anthony swallowed, his throat tight. "Yeh know it doesn't matter to us if yeh have power or not," he said, half a question as he worried that Taz *didn't* know. That maybe Taz thought everyone looked at him differently now because of everything they'd been through in the last two weeks.

Taz nodded, looking away, but Anthony leaned around and caught his gaze with a hard look in his eyes.

"Really, Taz. Yeh have tah know we don't care if yeh have a power or not. We love yeh, same as we always have." Anthony watched closely, keeping a sharp eye on Taz's reaction to this.

Taz gave a hard swallow, a shadow of the pining he saved for those moments when it was only him and Anthony and he poured out his heart about Daisy, flashed across his face, but it was quickly replaced with a smile.

"I know."

Anthony squinted hard enough that Taz chuckled again.

"I know, Tony. Really, I do."

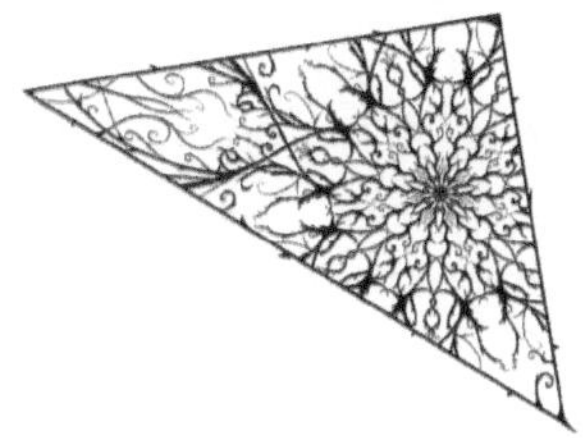

Chapter Thirty-Four

Capital City

"I have it handled."

The Chancellor scoffed. Scorn laced her features as she strode back and forth across the vast circular office she claimed. Her movement cast shadows across the carpet, interrupting the stunning view of the sunset through a series of rounded glass windows.

Wolfe swallowed, resisting the urge to clench her hands together. Nothing physical. Nothing that would show her weakness. Instead, she straightened. "We know they are going south."

"Really?" Collette snapped, whirling and fixing Wolfe with all the intensity of her grey gaze. "You know a direction on the compass? Congratulations. Do you know *where* they are? Will your Black-Stars reach them before they find the rebels?"

A shudder ran down Wolfe's spine. She remained quiet.

"You have no idea." Collette slashed the air with her hand. "You know nothing."

The words echoed around the room for a long moment. Finally, Collette's heavy breaths steadied. She straightened, running a hand down the agitated lines of her silken shirt.

"You're done, Minerva. The Council has decided to go a different direction. Lectius will take over the Black-Stars under your command. You are to return to Dolor—what's left of it—and deliver your research to his compound by the end of the week. I'm giving you time so you might grieve your position and prepare yourself to work at his side."

It was odd, the things Wolfe thought of as her life crumbled around her, brought low by the Chancellor's words. She wondered, briefly, who had betrayed her. Ultimately that didn't matter.

She'd gotten so far in the past forty years. She'd accomplished so much.

She'd been so close.

Collette was still speaking, something about Wolfe's place on the Council. Not that it mattered now. She wouldn't be returning to the Capital again.

She stood silent as her future was laid out in excruciatingly mundane detail.

It would not be hers.

Collette finished the admonishment, and Wolfe convinced her body to give a short bow before leaving the chambers.

She strode down the immaculate hallway, heels clicking against the tile floor as the veneer coating her emotions began to crack. The Black-Stars she'd brought took up positions at her flank. The normally comforting movement brought a hiss from her lips.

No one could be trusted anymore.

Still, they walked with her all the way out of the capitol building, through the overly decorated gardens, and to the helipad where her ride was waiting.

Wolfe watched Capital City disappear from view as the helo rose into the air and headed southeast.

She was on her own now. No back-up from the Chancellor. No help from the Council.

It had all fallen apart.

A slow smile curved the edge of her mouth as the realization set in; she was done. No one expected anything of her. If she followed the Chancellor's orders, Lectius would shuttle her away to a confined laboratory. He wouldn't work *with* her; he'd stifle her every move.

No. She was better alone. So, alone she'd be.

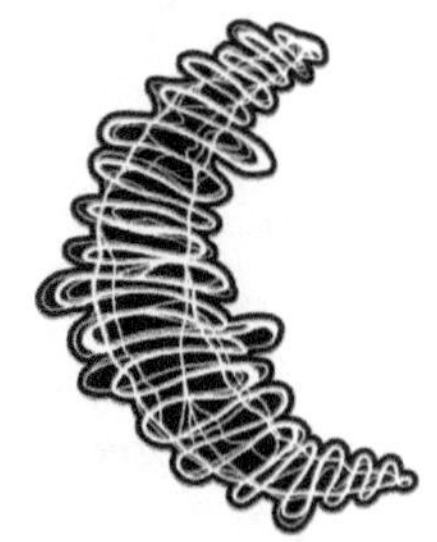

Chapter Thirty-Five

South of Dolor

Dawn's light woke Juliana. A concerning thing as it was coming later and later each day. She'd been cold the first half of the night, until Anthony's watch had ended and he'd found her like he promised.

His warm body was still pressed against her when she opened her eyes. His hand draped over her torso, fingers entwined with hers.

She loosened them, shifting out from under him and standing slowly to not wake him. Taz would drive a chunk of the day today; Juliana stretched out some of the ache in her back, but it was still there.

Most of the children were still asleep, likely getting their first actual rest in a long time. The fires had burned out completely, nothing but coals within the ash.

Juliana lifted her hands. They were as clean as she could get them between leaving Dolor and falling asleep last night. The rest of her was still covered in soot and blood.

"There's a creek not too far."

Juliana jolted, turning and putting a hand to her chest as Jason's eyes met hers. He sat against one of the massive wheels of the truck. Bags had settled under his bloodshot eyes. A grimace had taken up residence on his face since they'd fled Dolor. It had deepened with Cho's reaction to Brenna's emotions the night before.

Juliana looked away, scanning the forest edge for her aunt. A bundle of cloth curled against a tree-trunk.

"She hasn't moved," Jason said, again seeming to read Juliana's mind.

She pursed her lips. "Been watching her all night, have you?"

He met her gaze with no apology in his eyes. "Yes. She hurt Cho, Juliana."

"Not on purpose."

He shrugged in a 'may as well have' gesture. "Doesn't matter. She's unstable."

Half a smile ghosted across Juliana's face. "More than the rest of us, you mean."

This got a reaction. Jason's jaw jutted to the side as a grin bloomed and wilted on his face. "I'm serious. There's something off with her."

"It would be worse if there wasn't."

He raised an eyebrow.

Juliana crossed to his side, leaning against the edge of the truck. "She's been Wolfe's prisoner for... we don't know how long. If she was all right, nothing wrong with her, we'd know she was there willingly."

"She could still have been."

Juliana bit the inside of her lip. Her fingers tapped absently beside her leg. "True. But the way Steel spoke to her, it wasn't like she worked for him. It was like she was..." Juliana gritted her teeth, "one of the White-Stars back in Abredea."

"I don't—"

"I'm not saying we should trust her," Juliana broke across his words.

Jason clicked his tongue. He rose to his feet, glowering at her. "Good." His gaze flicked away but not toward Brenna.

Juliana followed his look. His twin lay on a thin blanket near one of the fire pits. Under her arm, which was draped remarkably like Anthony's had been, slept Abilene.

"Ahh." Juliana pursed her lips. "So this isn't just about Brenna."

A low growl sounded from the back of Jason's throat.

Juliana studied him for a moment, a little furrow in her brow as she met his gaze once again. "Do you trust me?"

The man blinked. He tilted his head, hesitated, then gave a gruff nod. "I do."

"You know I was like her." Juliana's voice was low now. She'd taken a step closer to Jason, a familiar guilt burning in her gut. It had faded, drowned out by the sense of purpose brought by rescuing the children and helping her new family. Now, after everything they'd discovered in Wolfe's office, it was back with a vengeance.

"A Blue-Star?" Jason asked.

He hadn't known. None of the Haven children had asked what caste Juliana came from, and she hadn't volunteered the information.

She nodded. "My parents are influential. I had a lot of potential before the Coding. If things had gone differently... I might have been sent to Dolor a few years down the road."

He scowled. "You'd have left. The minute you saw what they were doing, you'd have left."

Her mouth twisted into a bitter grin. "I saw what was happening in Abredea for months before it clicked that it was wrong."

Jason shook his head. "This is different, Juliana. You're my friend; she's my sister. And she's with that—" he broke off in a grunt, letting out a frustrated gesture that was accompanied by a flash of flame.

Juliana nodded. There was little left to say. His anger would subside, eventually. In the meantime, Juliana followed his directions to the small stream a few yards into the trees.

She scrubbed her skin clean, splashing the ice-cold water onto her face and running wet fingers through her hair. It wasn't much, but it was a thousand times better than before. When she was done, she sat on the rocks at the side of the creek, watching it flow.

She could have been there. In Dolor. As an experiment or a Blue-Star. What would she have done in Abilene's position? Would she have done something to help sooner? Or would she have been blinded by Wolfe's *suggestion*, blinded by her own ambition, blinded by what she'd grown up believing?

And if Anthony hadn't accidentally killed that Black-Star outside of Abredea? If they'd stayed... Wolfe knew her powers had emerged. Would the Grey-Star have continued trying to win Juliana over, or would she have forced Juliana to go with her?

Her throat went tight at the thought of that dark room, the ceiling an empty stretch of black, children crammed together in cold cages.

She thought of the Wall around Tornim. The fear that gripped her each time she'd gone through it.

She thought of Anthony's hand, clenched tight around hers the last time they'd gone through. Together.

Juliana sat awhile by the water's edge. Her stomach roiled with hunger, guilt, and that rush of heat she felt whenever she thought of Anthony's arms around her.

Footsteps crunched on the fallen leaves behind her. Daisy approached with a small wave and sat down beside Juliana.

"How do you *always* find me?" Juliana chuckled.

Daisy smiled. "Jason told me. Everyone's awake. There's a little bit of food left for you, but we need to get going."

Juliana nodded. "I know. I've just been..."

"Lost in your thoughts?"

Juliana exhaled. "Yeah." She leaned to the side, settling her head on Daisy's shoulder. "There's a lot to think about."

"Want to tell me?"

Juliana was quiet for a bit. "I do, but I don't want to put anything on you."

"Jules, you're my best friend. There's nothing you can't tell me."

Still, it took another minute for Juliana to speak. When she did, her fears at what she could have become had it not been for the Coding, and her worry about where they were going and what might happen to them when they got there, poured out of her. The heart-clenching terror she'd felt when Steel had pinned Anthony to the wall, his life draining away because she'd been caught. Her concern that she wouldn't be able to do anything to help Elaine, and that

Cho and the others would hate her for it. Her worries about Anthony and Daisy and Taz and not being able to protect them, heal them.

She spilled it all across the rocks and the river as Daisy rubbed little circles into her upper back. When it was all out, the fear and worry and even bits of anger she still felt at herself, Daisy offered a hand and pulled the two of them to their feet.

"Jules, I need to say this, and you need to hear it. You're a good person. A genuinely good person who does good things. We all know it. You don't have to prove anything to anyone. If you can help Elaine, that's wonderful. If you can't, it's all right."

Juliana swallowed, wiping away the tears that had dripped down her cheeks. "I thought I'd lost you and Anthony and the others."

Daisy pulled her close, tucking her head into Juliana's shoulder and squeezing her tight.

Halfway into their drive to Mavi, the river that split Pangaea into two pieces, they stopped for a long lunch break. Food was running critically low. They were too far from the main road for charging stations, which meant they needed to rely on the sun, and they couldn't steal any food from the dispensers.

Instead, Anthony ventured off once again, with Taz and Jane this time, to hunt in the plentiful forest surrounding them.

Juliana sat on the ground across from Elaine. Ichi had settled her onto a soft patch of grass and draped a blanket over her shoulders like a shawl.

That was another thing they needed Juliana realized as the other children from Haven nestled themselves around Jason's fires—clothes. Elaine shivered in her thin grey long-sleeve and matching pants. Ichi tugged the blanket tighter, wrapping an arm around her shoulder as he looked at Juliana.

"How are we doing this?"

Juliana licked her lips. "I was going to ask you. You can get into her mind?"

Ichi nodded. "But I run into a block. It's like rubble built up into a wall."

"I'll get a read on the injuries first," Juliana said. She breathed in, letting the air out slowly as she put her hands on Elaine's knees, and closed her eyes.

A delicate silver locket glowed in her mind's eye. Blue light sparked from the seam; Juliana brushed her hand across it, and the locket swung open, releasing her power.

She opened her eyes as warmth flowed through her limbs. Blue light seeped from her fingertips, and her eyes took on that odd multi-color vision. Elaine glowed bright before her, gold emanating from her dark skin.

But there were patches of darkness. The spot on her temple, still wrapped in dirty gauze, her fingernails, two of which hadn't grown back yet, and her eyes...

Ichi's eyes glowed with a soft silver light, matching the color surrounding his skin. Elaine's were dark.

Juliana reached out and touched Elaine's fingers. The woman pulled back, but Ichi put his hand on top of hers. Her shoulders dropped, the tightness of her features easing as he held her hand out for Juliana.

Blue tendrils laced their way around Elaine's fingers, caressing the patches of ruined skin where her nails had barely started growing out again. Juliana couldn't replace the nails. Well, maybe she could, but she had no idea how to, so she settled for easing the pain.

In a swirl of light, the red, swollen skin shrank down and smoothed over. It barely took a moment, and then Juliana turned her attention to Elaine's temple.

She'd been nauseous when Ichi told them all what happened. When she removed the bandage and saw the extent of the damage, it was a struggle to keep from gagging.

Gemstones reflected a person's emotions until the Coding. Even after, they were still tied into the part of the brain that dealt with such things. When Elaine's had been pried from her head, the technicians hadn't bothered to cut the connection. They'd ripped it out.

The wound was scabbing over, but patches of infection slowed the healing process. Juliana did her best, forcing red-tinged pus from the gaping hole while Daisy dabbed at it with a clean cloth. Tendrils of blue eased in and around the bloody mess, soothing the skin and sanitizing the wound.

Elaine was still as a statue. Juliana winced repeatedly, forcing her breakfast to stay in her stomach as unbidden images of this happening to her, to Taz, to the others with gems, tore through her mind.

She released Elaine after doing what she could for the wound. She hadn't healed it entirely, but enough to ease the pain and kill the infection. She had to save her energy for the other part of her and Ichi's plan to help Elaine.

Taz brought her water, and a piece of cooked meat still hot from the fire. Juliana downed them both before facing Ichi again.

"I'll follow your lead. I've never done anything like this before."

Ichi nodded. "Maybe you can heal as we go. I'm not sure how much of this is the trauma, how much is the past, and how much is the physical damage."

Juliana rubbed her hands together. "Let's go."

Tendrils of blue floated between herself and Elaine, pressing into the woman's smooth forehead as Ichi, sitting beside his lover, closed his eyes.

The sensation of Ichi's power threw Juliana off for a moment. A silver wisp pushed from him, seeping into Elaine's mind as Juliana watched. She followed, the blue light of her power trailing in his wake.

Juliana's throat caught. Her gift illuminated Elaine's mind, putting the jagged chunks of darkness into stark contrast. It was like a building—even a city—had shattered within her head. Chunks of black hid Elaine's golden light, keeping it pinned down. Outside of her head but below her skin, tar-like strands of... *something* stemmed from her skull, followed the curve of her neck, and settled into the muscles and nerves of her upper back.

Juliana exhaled. Ichi was in there, his silver mist just visible to her odd vision. She pushed her power deeper.

Elaine winced.

Juliana pulled back, her stomach twisting as tears formed in the woman's eyes.

"Does it hurt?" Juliana whispered, unable to imagine it not hurting given the extent of the darkness consuming Elaine's mind.

Eyes still glazed and distant, Elaine nodded.

"Where is the worst?" Juliana put a hand on her knee, giving a gentle squeeze.

Elaine pressed a hand to the fresh bandage Daisy had just finished applying to her temple.

"Inside?"

Elaine's head dipped in a slow nod.

Juliana reached up. She touched Elaine's forehead and breathed. The darkness resisted her light, fought against it as she brought blue energy to unknot a clump of shadow just behind Elaine's temple.

Juliana was sweating by the time she was done with just that knot. Sweating and shaking and breathing heavily as she struggled to get her regular vision back. Her power had taken over more than she was used to. Even as drained as she was, it didn't want to be put away.

Taz caught her as she drifted sideways. "Jules?"

"I'm all right," she muttered.

Before her, Ichi had opened his eyes again, tears flowing from them as he cupped Elaine's cheeks and kissed her forehead.

She'd responded to Juliana, given her an idea of where to start, but that appeared to have been a single moment of lucidity. Her gaze was still distant, her expression blank.

"Let's get yeh some rest," Taz said, his wary eyes fixed on Juliana.

The two retreated from Ichi and Elaine.

"I think you're driving the rest of the day," Juliana grunted. Her head throbbed, pain pacing across the back of her eyes.

Taz chuckled. "I was hopin' yeh'd say that. I like it."

Juliana chuckled, ceasing quickly as spikes drove through her temples. "I need to sit."

He brought her to the bed of the truck and helped her step up so she could lean against the side. Her eyes were half-closed, and she almost didn't hear Taz tell her to wait there while he went to get some water.

"You're using too much."

Juliana jolted, a fresh ache running down her neck.

Brenna sat in the far end of the truck bed, near the cab. Her eyes, the same blue as Juliana's mother, but bloodshot and wide, watched her.

Juliana swallowed. Her mind called forth the last memory of her mother, holding her as they said goodbye after the Coding.

Tears filled her eyes as the recollection brought a shadow of her mother's comforting arms. She could almost smell her parents' distinct scents, expensive lilac perfume for her mom and the starch of pressed lab coats for her father.

"Girl."

Juliana shook her head, blinked back the tears, and focused on her aunt. "It's Juliana."

"Yes, Juliana. You told me that."

Juliana nodded. Her heartbeat quickened as Brenna moved toward her. Cho had spoken about his experience with her emotions, and Ichi had verified that her mind was so scrambled it was impossible to make out intent. Both had said they didn't find anything malicious within her, but Juliana was still wary.

Her aunt settled against the bench on the opposite side of the truck.

"You've been in here since we stopped?" Juliana murmured. She pressed a hand to her forehead, wishing the throbbing would go away.

Brenna nodded.

"You should go outside." Juliana gestured to the expanse of greenery around them. Golden and russet-colored leaves littered the ground, but shoots of grass burst between them, still finding their way to sunlight.

"It's too loud." Brenna's head twitched back and forth in a rapid shake.

"Are you..." Juliana's brow furrowed, "are you all right?"

Brenna's gaze met hers. "You're using too much."

"Yeah." Juliana sighed. "You said that. I'm not sure what you mean."

"Your gift," Brenna said. She offered no other explanation, and Juliana didn't think she needed one.

She'd been overexerting herself since Dolor. So many of the children had been injured, so many malnourished and in pain.

"They're getting better," she said. "Not as many injuries to take care of now. I can't give up on Elaine though."

Brenna shook her head. "Too much."

A familiar stir of frustration rumbled through Juliana's chest. "Well, I'm not doing anymore today."

Her aunt nodded. "Good."

Juliana gritted her teeth. She filled her lungs and exhaled, keeping her lips pressed together to avoid saying anything.

Taz returned with some of the water they'd boiled that morning. Juliana drained it while he cast concerned looks at Brenna. Fidgeting with his hands, he timidly asked if she wanted anything to eat.

Brenna blinked at him. "That would be... yes," she stammered.

Juliana's heart ached at the realization that his kindness was what unbalanced her aunt.

Taz disappeared again, and Juliana leaned her head against the truck.

"How long were you in Dolor?"

Brenna's head twitched. She pulled a lock of dirty hair forward and twisted it between her fingers. "Long."

"Years?"

She nodded.

Juliana looked down at the bottle in her hands. "My mom never forgot you."

Brenna twitched hard enough to jolt the bench she sat on. Her head cocked to the side, uncertainty in her gaze.

"She thought you died." Juliana offered up a sad smile. "I think she'd have burned down Pangaea to find you if she had known what they'd done."

Tears pooled in Brenna's eyes. Juliana opened her mouth, but the woman's hands were shaking. She jerked again, as though her head was on an odd axis. She shifted, scooting forward and out of the truck.

"I didn't..." Juliana let the words fall away as Brenna scurried away. Juliana sighed, set the bottle down, and laid out on the dirty floor of the truck.

She closed her eyes, avoiding the urge to press her hands against her eyelids. She was already seeing spots. There was so much to do. Food, clothes, shoes, fresh water, a way to cross the river... the list kept growing. Her temples throbbed.

The interior of the truck was cool. A light breeze carried through the open end and out the tiny window leading to the cab. Even with the bright sunlight pouring in, it didn't take long for sleep to find her.

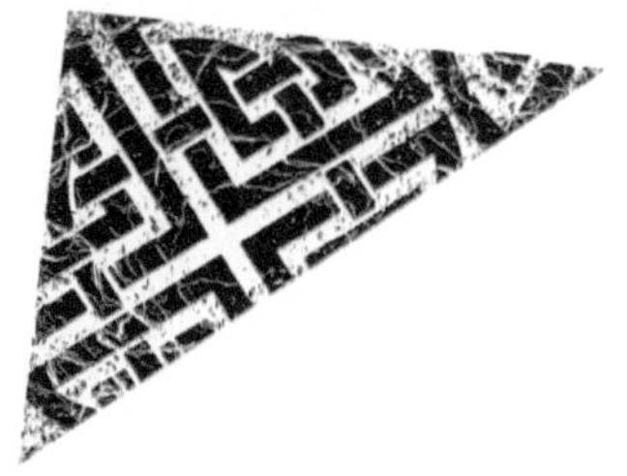

Chapter Thirty-Six

Allegi - Twenty Years Ago

B renna slept in bursts. Short periods of time between patients, with her head resting on the small desk in the corner of her lab, when she could succumb to the darkness that constantly called to her.

They were close. Wolfe kept saying it, and the new Blue-Stars who had joined them in the last few months agreed. Or so Brenna was told. Her freedom in Allegi had been limited since the incident with Theo, so she wasn't able to see for herself.

She jerked from her sleep. The memory of his tears was one of many things that haunted her dreams and woke her too soon. She still hadn't found out what happened that day, how he'd sustained the injuries, where he'd been when he'd disappeared for months. She also hadn't seen him since.

The Black-Stars offered no explanation, and Wolfe had merely said he was a traitor. His case was being dealt with by the Black-Stars. She was not involved and had no information for Brenna.

They'd gotten the funding from the Chancellor; Grey-Stars were supporting Wolfe's research again. Brenna only caught little bits of what was going on at the Capital, but it was clear allegiances changed frequently.

Brenna rose from the chair and strode to the door. "Is there anything else today, or can I go to my rooms?"

The Black-Star on the other side, an unnecessary guard Wolfe insisted upon for the sake of appearances, shook his head through the small glass window.

"No to which thing?" Brenna leaned her forehead on the cool metal of the door, frustration coursing through her.

"Stand back," he barked.

She jerked away. "What—"

The question was answered before she asked it. The door slammed open, a horrifying surge of familiarity bringing ice to Brenna's veins as a bloody man was dragged into the room.

The Black-Stars dumped him on the cot, pausing to tie his wrist to the edge of the bed before backing away.

Brenna stood frozen.

"Heal him," a burly bald man barked.

"Why?" She glanced from the Black-Star to the figure on the bed. "What do you want with him?"

The man's upper lip curled into a growling sneer. "Do as you're told."

"What do you want with him?" she asked again, her voice low as fear caused a tremor in her words.

The other Black-Stars moved further away from them, toward the door.

"I have questions. He has answers. Heal him."

Brenna swallowed and crossed to the cot. There seemed to be no need for the restraint; the man was unconscious. His face was recognizable, unlike with Theo. Blood marred his cheek and jaw. His free arm was broken in at least two places, and based on the swelling, he had a bruised eye socket. His breath was ragged, a whistling sound accompanying each inhale.

Those were just the injuries she could see. Her power would undoubtedly find more.

"What happened?" she murmured. "How did he get so hurt?"

"Like I said," the Black-Star uttered impatiently through gritted teeth, "he has answers. Didn't feel like sharing, so we *incentivized* him."

A pang of dread went through Brenna. She put up a hand, calling forth the spindly blue light from within. She didn't heal—yet. Instead, she assessed the extent of his injuries.

She winced, tears filling her eyes.

His ribs were broken. The bone had pierced a lung and he was bleeding internally.

He was dying.

Her hands shook.

"Fix him," the Black-Star barked.

She ignored him, her heart in a vicious war with her head. Theo's words echoed through her mind. *You should have let me die.* Pain overwhelmed her, tears pouring down her cheeks.

Her hands shook as she moved them from the unconscious man's chest. Brenna lightly caressed his forehead, allowing her power to dance around the superficial injuries on his face.

He twitched.

Her breath caught as his eyes opened. The man groaned, realization clearing the pain from his eyes.

He looked into Brenna's eyes and recognition struck her. He was one of Allegi's Alters. One of the older children who had arrived a few years ago. An adult now—at least, she thought so. Maybe years of experimentation had aged him the way it had aged her.

She'd healed him before; cuts and burns here and there. Nothing this extreme. Nothing that could have ended his life.

His face was pale. Each breath brought a wince of pain as his fear-filled gaze darted around the room. When it landed on the Black-Star, he whimpered.

Brenna clenched her jaw. "They brought you here to be healed."

The Alter's eyes fixed on her. His lips were trembling, tears pooling and running down his cheeks. He shook his head.

"I can fix you," Brenna said, barely moving her lips.

"Please—" The word brought too much pain for him to continue. He gasped; his damaged lung making it impossible to get enough air.

"I can heal you."

He shook his head again, tears running faster now.

He was fading fast. Brenna's power sensed it, reached for him, wanting—needing—to fix it. To heal him. To bring him back from the brink of death.

Tears dripped from her chin, dark spots appearing on the light grey shirt she wore. "Please, let me help you."

He closed his eyes, bright green disappearing behind thick lashes and caramel colored skin.

"Please," Brenna whispered.

He shook his head.

"Heal him, already," the Black-Star demanded.

Brenna nodded, bobbing her head as she took the Alter's hand and held it tight. He opened his eyes long enough for her to offer a smile she hoped would bring him some comfort. Then she squeezed his hand, and called her power back into herself.

The blue light faded, and with it went her ability to guess how long he had left. Minutes, maybe. Less, given his increasing struggle to breathe.

Relief splashed across his face, and a fresh wave of tears glistened in his eyes. He gripped her fingers, a link to the world he was leaving. Solace in the face of death that was coming so quickly now.

His last shuddering breaths were accompanied by a roar of rage.

The Black-Star grabbed Brenna by the shoulder and yanked her around.

"What did you do?" he shouted.

"He didn't want..." Brenna choked out the words, grief clogging her throat.

"I don't give a frost what he wanted." The man whirled, breathing heavily as fury reddened his pale face. He strode to the open door. "Get her to Wolfe."

Brenna's heart thundered in her chest.

A pair of younger Black-Stars strode in, gripped Brenna's upper arms, and led her into the hall.

"You're nacra lucky she puts such a high value on you," the bald man spat at her as she passed. His hand clenched into a fist, a threat of what would have happened if she weren't under Wolfe's protection.

Brenna swallowed. She allowed the Black-Stars to march her through Allegi. It wasn't far to Wolfe's office.

They knocked on the solid wood door. There was silence. Another knock, followed by a full minute of waiting.

"What the frost just happened?"

The three spun around. Wolfe strode toward them, her usually calm demeanor fracturing.

"Ms. Wolfe," one of the Black-Stars began.

"Leave us," Wolfe snapped.

He blinked, offered a short bow, and left, tugging the arm of his fellow Black-Star. The two of them hurried away.

Brenna faced Wolfe. "I'm sorry. I didn't—"

Pain slammed across the side of her face. She staggered back, a hand going to her cheek where Wolfe's palm had just struck. Heat seemed to blister her skin, eyes widening as tears threatened to pour.

"You disappoint me." Wolfe took in heavy breaths, shaking out her hand as her furious gaze bored into Brenna. "I thought you were better."

Brenna's heart crumbled, the pain of Wolfe's disappointment worse than being struck.

Wolfe shook her head. "I can't look at you right now." She turned, walking back the way she'd come with purposeful, long strides.

A sob broke free, then another, and before she knew it, Brenna was struggling for breath as she sank onto the rough carpet. She curled around herself, every part of her in pain and grief. Every part of her alone.

Chapter Thirty-Seven

Near the Mavi River

Cho carefully followed Anthony's footsteps through the brush. They were only a few yards from the road, far too close to the bridge gate for Cho's comfort.

It was a necessary risk. They had to scope out a way to cross the roaring river ahead of them. At its narrowest, there was a quarter mile between them and the other side, and that spot was another few days upstream according to Juliana, Hawk, and the map.

No, they would need one of the two bridges connecting the bottom half of Pangaea to the rest of the country.

Despite the need, Cho's apprehension clung to him. He glanced to the sky. Hawk's soaring shape cast a moving shadow across the trees. At least they had eyes above.

Jane and Taz hurried along behind him. They'd been eager to join the little scouting mission. Others had wanted to come, but there were a multitude of pressing issues that needed to be dealt with at the camp.

Juliana stayed behind to help Ichi with Elaine. They'd made progress in the days they'd been on the road. Each stop to recharge the truck came with another opportunity for Juliana to unknot—as Juliana put it—the darkness in Elaine's mind. Cho didn't entirely understand it, but the difference in Elaine was evident. She wasn't cured, or fixed, or back to normal. Cho privately doubted she ever would be; not with the trauma of what she had gone through. But now she had moments of lucidity. Minutes at a time when her eyes would focus and she'd recognize them, when she'd breathe easy and even smile.

He'd caught her humming a lullaby the night before. Elaine hadn't finished it, her voice had gone quiet, eyes distant and full of pain again.

Ichi wasn't handling it particularly well. It was part of why he wasn't on the scouting mission—he refused to leave Elaine's side. His realization that Juliana wouldn't be able to immediately heal Elaine resulted in a hushed, yet severe, conversation among himself, Cho, and Jason. Cho and Jason's insistence that Juliana was doing all she could, that she would continue to try, was met with desperate disbelief. It wasn't until Jane stomped over and hissed that Ichi 'pull himself together before the children heard him' that he'd calmed down.

The anger in Ichi's eyes pained Cho and filled him with worry.

Jason's dark eyes had met Cho's as the group departed, concern and regret mingling in his gaze. He wouldn't leave Samaira, or the others, alone with Brenna and Abilene. He didn't trust the newcomers any more now, after days on the road, than he had when they'd first joined the group.

Brenna wasn't doing much to help the situation. She kept to herself, staying in the truck when the others took breaks to stretch their legs and get a breather. The only person she spoke coherently to was Juliana. Most of the time her eyes were wide and fearful, her words rambling, and her movements sharp and twitchy.

Abilene was making an effort. Cho recognized it even as his own suspicion refused to fade. He'd felt her love for Samaira, and yet he couldn't get past the same hang-up that had a hold on Jason. She was a Blue-Star. She'd been in Dolor, been complicit in the pain and suffering their family had endured.

Still, her kindness to the children, her willingness to assist with every chore, and the admiration and affection in her gaze each time she looked at Samaira, was wearing him down. It was not wearing down Jason.

Samaira had surprised Cho by not volunteering, but he supposed she wanted to continue trying to smooth things over with her brother.

Daisy stayed behind with Tommy. He'd been less angry about being left this time. Cho credited Tommy's cooperation to Taz. The young man had spent the last several days praising Tommy for all he'd done to keep the children safe while the rest of them went to find Juliana and Samaira.

"Here should be good," Anthony whispered.

They came to a stop, Jane moving up beside Cho to get a better view of the obstacles in their path.

The bridge itself was a massive thing and spanned a wide gulch. Designed to connect the limited traffic from southern Pangaea's few cities to the capital and the rest of the country, it was wider than any road he'd seen. Massive concrete pillars held it up; two-dozen of them sank into the river at even intervals. Deep, rushing water roared below, the river wide enough that even from where they were, they could see white rapids in the distance.

Just visible at the other end of the bridge was a tall guard post, a twin to the one on their side of the Mavi.

"This feels like a lot of guards, right?" Jane asked in a dry tone.

Cho and Anthony nodded in unison. Over a dozen Black-Stars paced back and forth in front of the barricade blocking the bridge.

There was rustling above them. Anthony didn't move, but Cho jerked and stared up. Hawk, in his massive bird form, was perched on a thick branch above them.

"Are there more guards further downriver?" Anthony asked.

The bird let out a low squawk and bobbed its head.

"And upstream I'm guessing," Taz murmured.

Another squawk and bob.

"Great," Jane grunted through gritted teeth.

Anthony met Cho's gaze for a moment. Cho swallowed. They had to get across. There would be Black-Stars no matter where they were, but at least south of the river they had a chance of hiding in the mountains.

Mountains Cho *needed* to get to. He needed to see them, find out why they were in his dreams.

Anthony glanced at Jane. "Looks like a challenge tah me. Yer not worried, are yeh?"

Cho stifled his smile as Jane glared.

"No."

"Didn't think so," Anthony said with a grin. "Now, how're we gettin' through this mess?"

They stayed hidden in the trees for a long while. They counted Black-Stars, got an idea of patrol patterns, and watched a shift change. Eventually, the little scouting party retreated.

Hawk sprang off a tree, circling above for another few minutes before meeting them well away from the bridge and any patrolling Black-Stars.

"Well?" Jane snapped. "Ideas?"

Cho shook his head. "I don't think we should cross here. It's too heavily guarded."

"Won't the o… oth… won't the other bridge be the same?" Taz leaned against a rough tree trunk.

"More'n likely." Anthony nodded. "We've got two choices. Try to get through that mess," he jerked his thumb back toward the river, "or attempt tah cross on our own."

Cho's spine tingled with nerves at the thought. The river was deep, fast flowing, and wide. Even if they made it across with over a dozen children under the age of ten, there was no way they'd be able to bring the truck. That would mean walking from there on, which would make the multi-day journey stretch into a couple of weeks.

Jane said as much as Hawk fluttered to the ground and darted his gaze expectantly at Anthony. The man chuckled, pulled a pair of pants from the bag slung across his shoulder, and tossed them to the bird.

A few moments later a half-clothed Hawk stepped out of the trees. "Have you all decided how we're getting across yet?"

Jane scowled. "We were just trying to think of something."

"Is the other bridge this... bad?" Taz asked.

Hawk shrugged. "Do you wanna wait a day while I go check?"

Jane clicked her tongue against her teeth. "I doubt we have time for that. I don't suppose you have any bright ideas?"

Hawk shook his head. "I can get across just fine, but I've got no notion how to get everyone else and the kids across. Also," he glanced from Cho to Anthony, "your friend is there."

"What?" Cho's pulse quickened.

"The Black-Star from Dolor. Lawrence, right?"

Jane nodded.

"He's there."

"In what capacity?" Cho picked at the edge of his shirt.

Hawk shrugged. "Looked like every other guard. I was soaring close when someone called for him. Heard the name and figured it was probably the same guy. Dark skin, thick as a tree?"

"Sounds like him," Jane said. "Does that mean he kept his cover? If he's with the Black-Stars still?"

No one answered for a beat.

"It depends on how good a liar he is," Hawk finally muttered.

"So, what do we do?" Taz twisted his hands together, eyes darting around the group.

"We need tah talk to the others," Anthony said. "But I don't wanna put our trust in Lawrence, not after what happened in Dolor."

"You mean when he saved us?" Jane cut in.

Anthony gave her a hard look. "I mean when he murdered his men in cold blood."

"To get us out."

Anthony's jaw tightened. He let out a sigh through clenched teeth. "Yeah, but that doesn't mean we have tah trust him."

Cho bobbed his head in a thoughtful nod. He was torn. Lawrence's words had echoed what Carthik told them when they'd left Tornim, as well as his own dreams. But the man had facilitated Samaira's beatings. He'd commanded the Black-Stars in Dolor.

"Who said to trust him?" Jane said. "I'm saying we use him to get across the bridge."

Cho shook his head. "Good liar or not, I doubt one man would be able to get us through all those guards." He gave a limp wave, a defeated weariness dragging at his shoulders. "They take one look at us and they'll either start shooting, or take us all back to that Grey-Star."

"We'll figure something out." Taz reached out to put a hand on Cho's shoulder, quickly repositioned, and planted both hands on his own hips instead.

A grin broke from Cho at the attempt to comfort. "Thanks," he muttered.

Taz gave a half shrug, but his smile reached his eyes.

"What do we think from here?" Hawk directed the question to Anthony.

"Hunker down, stay a few hours, see what they do at nightfall."

"Could be they lessen the guard after dark," Cho agreed. "I imagine crossing at night is more dangerous."

"It will be if we're in a hurry," Anthony said.

A light, uncomfortable laugh went through the group.

"Stay the night?" Jane asked after a long pause.

Anthony shook his head. "I say we only stick around a few hours. See if they loosen up after dark, then we head back to the others."

"How do you plan on us getting back?" Jane crossed her arms.

A crooked smile, one that had been missing since they'd seen what was between them and their goal, reappeared on Anthony's face. He closed his eyes for a moment and when he opened them, they had taken on a yellow hue. "Some of us can see in the dark."

Jane rolled her eyes as Taz let out a chuckle.

"No fire, I'm assuming?" Cho rubbed his hands up and down his arms. The chilly day had only gotten colder with the slow descent of the sun.

Anthony and Hawk both responded at the same time. A fire was not a good idea.

So the group pulled their ragged jackets tight and huddled between the trees. They took turns keeping an eye on the bridge. Cho and Taz spent the sunset hour watching guard movements. Not much changed as night fell, though they were able to confirm that Lawrence was at the crossing.

"Could you find out if he's waitin' for us?" Taz whispered, crouching down again to get more cover behind a fallen tree.

"With my power?"

"Yeah."

Cho quirked his mouth to the side. "I could try, but it would mean getting closer, and my power being in range of all of them when I let it loose."

"That might be a bit much," Taz said.

"I'm thinking so." Cho swallowed. "I wouldn't want to have a breakdown so near that many Black-Stars."

Taz nodded fervently.

When the sun was gone, and the light with it, Hawk and Anthony took over the watch.

Cho lay on the squishiest patch of grass he could find and settled his head on his arm. The trip back to their camp would take a while, especially stumbling through the dark. Anthony and Hawk could see, but that wouldn't necessarily help Cho, Jane, and Taz avoid holes and sticks and thorny brambles. Resting before the trek would be good.

It was difficult to sleep. The ground was hard, he was used to that, but without one of Jason's fires keeping him warm it felt as though ice were seeping up through the dirt to soak into his skin.

He imagined light bursting from Jason's dark skin, his strong hands creating flames that chased away the cold. He imagined those hands catching him again, pulling him close, pushing back the cold another way.

"Hey."

Cho opened his eyes, flushing deep red, grateful for the darkness hiding his embarrassment. He was facing away from the others, curled into a ball while Jane and Taz leaned against a nearby tree.

Jane had spoken, but not to him.

"What's wrong?" Taz's usual energy was somewhat dulled by the sleepiness in his voice.

"Nothing." There was tension, stress in Jane's voice that almost made Cho turn around. "I just—" she huffed out a sigh—"I wanted to thank you."

Cho refrained from shifting. He stayed quiet, astonishment keeping him from interrupting the conversation.

"Me?" Taz sounded as awed as he had when he'd seen Tommy make something disappear for the first time.

Jane snorted. "Yes. You. The person I'm currently speaking to."

"Wh... wha...wha..." There was a grunt. "Why?"

Silence. Cho thought Jane wouldn't answer.

Then, "When we got out of Haven, Tommy and I ended up on our own. Black-Stars had us cornered. I thought we were done. Dead. But we made it. Since then I haven't..." She paused, and Cho didn't need the gentle laps of her pain against his wards to know she was hurting. "I haven't been as good a sister to Tommy."

"That's nacra stupid," Taz said.

Cho blinked and could tell from the silence that Taz's words had stunned Jane as well.

"It's not," she growled. "I've been great at protecting him, same as always, but I've been so... so scared of losing him..."

Cho poured a bit more into his mental shields. Jane was tired, more tired than he'd realized if her emotions were spilling out so strongly.

"I need to keep him safe, Taz. But I'm going about it wrong, and I don't know how to change it. He would have followed us into Dolor. I know it."

Taz was silent. Cho heard his movement in the rustling of leaves and twigs on the ground.

"He listens to you," Jane went on, "because you don't treat him like a child. You're his friend, and that's something I haven't been able to be in a long time. If you hadn't said what you did, the way you did, he'd have followed me."

Her intake of breath cut a slice through Cho's heart. He was one of Jane's closest friends, one of the few people she opened up to. But he'd never heard her this vulnerable before.

"So thank you. For keeping him safe."

A long moment passed. When Taz spoke again it sounded as though he was closer to Jane. His voice was low.

"Yeh don't think yer doin' a good job as his sister, but yeh are. And as far as keepin' him safe, I'm happy to. He's a sweet little guy. And yer—"

"Don't say I'm sweet," Jane growled.

Cho stifled a snort at the barely contained amusement in her voice.

"Wasn't gonna." Taz laughed. "But yeh are a better sister than most."

Jane swallowed audibly.

Their conversation faded, leaving only the sounds of crickets, wind through the trees, and the occasional call of nighttime animals. Cho was grateful for Jane's ability to be kind in that moment. Her harsh temper had caused friction with their friends from Abredea, but between this and her efforts to save Juliana, it seemed she was, if not welcoming, at least begrudgingly accepting the blending of their two groups.

Cho fell into a doze. It felt like mere minutes had passed before a wet nose was nuzzling his forehead. When Cho rose, Anthony, in wolf form, moved on to Taz and pawed at his forearm until he woke up.

The group made their way back to the others. It was a long trek, with Taz keeping a hand on Anthony's back while Hawk drifted through sky above the treetops. Cho and Jane stuck close, not wanting to get lost in the darkness.

Chapter Thirty-Eight

Near the Mavi River

I ce crawled up Samaira's arm. Little shoots of it hardened over her knuckles, sticking to the spots where her skin had scabbed and then scarred over the years. Juliana had healed most of her wounds, save the little cuts and bruises that didn't matter. The pain and damage from her outburst after the injection had all but disappeared. The only physical sign from that horrible moment was the ruined ink on her hands and wrists.

Someday she'd get the tattoos redone. If things with Jason ever got back to normal, maybe she'd get a phoenix like him.

Claire released Samaira's hand. "Is that better?"

Samaira nodded, leaving both hands flat for the time being. The ice had become all that held back the burning within her. Claire had been within reach for the past few days, silently offering her power whenever Samaira's twisted gift flared beyond her control.

At some point it would break free.

Samaira's stomach knotted at the thought. She swallowed and curled her hands into fists. The ice shattered, little pieces pressing into her palms as a chunk fell off her wrist. "Much, thanks."

Claire glanced around the encampment. They'd settled for the night a few miles from the river. There was plenty of room between them and the bridge, or so said Juliana and Jason.

Samaira's brother had latched onto the people from Abredea rather quickly, and with his anger towards Abilene still simmering at the surface of everything he did, he hadn't bothered to tell her why he trusted them so much. He'd kept his promise of reining in his animosity, but all that had done was keep him away from her.

Juliana's healing probably helped his trust, but Abilene had done what she could for the children as well. Not with power, but with her hands and her learning.

"When are you going to tell the others?" Claire murmured.

Samaira's gaze snapped to the girl. She inhaled, breathing through the light surge of panic that came with the thought of revealing what had been done to her power to the others, of what her brother, and her friends, would say.

"Ichi already knows," Samaira replied. It was half true. He'd helped her contain the raging flames as much as he could. Yet for all he knew they were still contained.

He'd been too busy with Elaine to ask if she had a handle on things.

Samaira glanced over at the two of them, sitting together as usual. Ichi hadn't left her side since their escape. The work of caring for the younger children, leading them through meditation, re-teaching them not to be afraid of their gifts, and keeping them fed had fallen on the rest of them.

Luna and Nova had jumped on the chance to help. The comfort they gave the little ones had led to the first peaceful night's rest the kids had had in a long time.

Cho was already leading the newcomers in mediation; it seemed the transition to guiding everyone was a natural one. He was patient with everyone and diligent in making sure people kept up their wards.

Samaira was impressed and surprised at his steady voice and assertive presence. She never would have guessed he'd gain so much control over his power. The boy had changed a lot since the raid on Haven.

They all had.

"Samaira?" Claire's voice was small, hesitant.

Samaira looked at the girl. Her eyes were icy white, frost dusting her lashes.

"Are you…"

She was so young. It hurt Samaira's heart to think of how little time Claire had gotten in Haven. She'd barely discovered her power when she'd nearly been hunted down for it. There was some small relief in the fact that she'd been among those who hadn't been captured.

"What?" Samaira blinked and shook her head. "Sorry, Claire. I'm… I'm tired."

The girl nodded. "I'll be nearby, if you need anything."

"Thanks," Samaira repeated. She rose from her seat on a smooth boulder. "I'm going to walk the perimeter until dark. I'll come find you before bed for another round if that's all right with you."

"Anything you need," Claire said, the worry in her gaze sending a flare of frustration through Samaira's chest.

She was a warrior. Not someone to be worried over. Not someone to be coddled. Still, she gave a grateful nod before striding away from where she and Claire had tucked themselves away behind the truck to avoid questions.

There were no fires burning this evening. They didn't want to risk it. Tonight, they'd rely on blankets.

Anticipation and anxiety rolled through Samaira's stomach. She glanced down at her hands. They were wet now, the ice melted. She wiped them on the dirty pair of jeans she'd taken from Jason.

Most of the children had managed to find something beyond the grimy grey uniform they'd been forced to wear in Dolor. It was only the smallest among them who hadn't been able to borrow something from their rescuers.

Even then, Samaira grinned as she passed Daisy sitting beside Tommy and Kim. She was teaching them to sew, something Elaine had begun doing before everything happened. They were reshaping a few pieces of clothes to fit Sky—the youngest of their group after Jacob's death.

Samaira's nose twitched as a different kind of burning filled her eyes. She glanced through the scattered trees in the clearing they'd found. Abilene was there, a few yards away dishing out watery soup and making sure people who had already been fed shared their bowls with those waiting to eat.

The temptation to go to her was strong. Those slim arms offered surprising amounts of comfort, the woman's voice a balm that soothed Samaira's anxiety. But she was busy, and Samaira wanted too badly for the children from Haven to accept and trust Abilene, so she continued on.

Brenna was at the edge of the wood, curled in a tight ball against a gnarled tree trunk. The bark matched the twisted expression on her face as she stared out at the forest.

"Did you get something to eat?" Samaira asked in a low voice. This, at least, she and Jason agreed on. Brenna was not to be trusted. She'd been a prisoner in Dolor far longer than the rest of them, so why was she unable to offer any sort of useful information about Wolfe?

"Not yet." Brenna's voice was rough and hoarse. Familiar in that it sounded as though she'd also spent long stretches of time screaming in pain.

"Make sure you do. It's a long ways yet to the mountains."

Brenna finally looked up at her, that odd jerking motion making Samaira flex her hands instinctively. "You worry for me?"

Samaira's nostrils flared as she inhaled. "I worry for us all."

Brenna didn't respond.

Samaira scanned the horizon, glancing behind them to make sure the others were still all right.

She swallowed. "What do you know of Lawrence, the Black-Star captain in Dolor?"

Brenna blinked her wide, sunken eyes. Her head tilted further; the angle almost made Samaira wince.

"I know little beyond the room where I was kept."

This did make Samaira wince. "How long were you there?"

"Long enough."

The wind whistled through the trees around them. They were far enough from the river that the sound of rushing water couldn't reach their ears. The sounds of the forest weren't familiar to Samaira yet; every snap of a twig caught her attention.

"He is loyal," Brenna said, interrupting the soft quiet.

"Lawrence?"

She nodded. "He has been there a long time. That much I know. And Ms. Wolfe trusts him."

Samaira chewed her bottom lip, frustration and unease growing.

"I heard others talking." Brenna glanced out toward the trees. "They want to find him?"

Samaira clicked her tongue against her teeth. There was a limit to how much she wanted, and was willing, to tell this woman. "We've been discussing it. Apparently, he helped get us out."

Brenna shook her head, fear flashing across her face so suddenly and so vivid that Samaira took a step back. "He works for Ms. Wolfe. He would not betray her."

There was bitterness in her words. A bite Samaira heard and felt herself at the thought of working with Lawrence. The man had let her be beaten half to death. He'd led the other Black-Stars as they tortured and experimented on herself and her friends. He was responsible for many deaths.

Within her, the core of her power sparked.

Samaira inhaled and let her breath out through her lips. Jason had been there when Lawrence supposedly helped them. As much of a frosted ass her brother was being, there was no one in the world she trusted more.

She swallowed down the rush of frustration that rose each time she thought of her brother the past few days.

"What comes next?" Brenna asked after a few minutes of silence.

Samaira, busy concentrating on calming down, barely looked at her. "We hope the bridge is clear. If not, the crossing will not be easy."

"You know the river?"

Samaira shrugged, her jaw tight. "I know without the bridge it will be nearly impassable."

Fear replaced the frustration, another pull on her power that sent a shot of stress down her spine. She breathed through it.

"I have been south before," Brenna murmured. "Once."

Samaira raised an eyebrow, glancing down at the woman.

"We took a different bridge. An older one, built a long time ago." Brenna looked up at Samaira, those wide eyes clearer and more lucid than she'd yet seen them. "They don't use it anymore. The old bridge. Not since this one was finished."

Samaira's forehead wrinkled as a comprehending frown overtook her features. "How far?"

Brenna shrugged, her bony shoulder protruding from beneath the grey cloth of her shirt. "Not terribly."

"Why didn't you say something sooner?"

Samaira jumped. Her heart raced at the sounds of Jason's voice and his footsteps coming through the trees to their left.

"How long were you standing there?" she demanded.

"Long enough you should have noticed me." He didn't look at her, his dark gaze fixed on Brenna. "Why didn't you say anything about the other bridge sooner?"

Brenna didn't meet his eye. She fidgeted with her hands, her voice returning to the hesitant, panicked tone. "I didn't..." her head jerked. "I didn't remember."

Jason scoffed.

"Enough, Jase," Samaira scolded. Pity stirred in her stomach. The woman's eyes had clouded once again, her lucidity lost to the fear that had taken over at Jason's words.

"We could have saved time with this information," Jason said. His eyes glinted with heat, ready for a fight.

Maybe that was part of it, part of why he couldn't get past Abilene. Part of what kept him from talking to Samaira. The two of them hadn't sparred. They had trained together almost every day in Haven. A test of their skill, practice, showing off for Jason and a chance to knock some of his cocky attitude down a notch for Samaira.

Her gut churned at the thought of what she'd do to him if they went flame to flame now.

Samaira took hold of her brother's arm and pulled him a few yards away. "She's barely aware enough to have a conversation, let alone pull up information from years ago when she didn't even know where we were going."

His lip curled. "It's dangerous to be on this side of the river, Samaira. Maybe we could have crossed already."

"Maybe," she growled, "and maybe you can have some empathy for once in your frosted life."

There it was. The line the two of them had been dancing around since the escape. The line Jason had tiptoed near, but never crossed.

She crossed it instead.

Samaira bit her lip as soon as the words left her, heat spreading down her arms even as regret swarmed her.

Jason didn't look wounded. His expression barely changed, but she knew her twin, and she saw it in his eyes.

"Jase—"

He held up a hand. "I'll get Juliana and Ichi. The two of them can decide what to do with the information."

"Jase," she said again, more desperate this time.

He had already turned and was walking quickly toward the others.

"*Nacra*," she spat. Tears dripped down her cheeks. She wiped them away with the back of her hand. With one more glance at Brenna, now rocking sideways, she hurried after her brother.

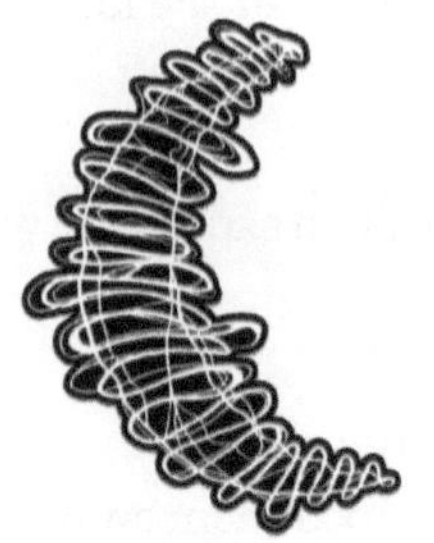

Chapter Thirty-Nine

Near the Mavi River

Juliana sat on the edge of the truck bed, her thumb dancing across the tips of her fingers, the other hand pressing against her chest to relieve a bit of the anxiety. There were decisions to make, plans to cement, and people whose lives depended on their success.

Anthony sat beside her, his hand rubbing circles into her lower back. The scouting party had returned late in the night, a few hours after Jason finished angrily filling her and Ichi in on what he'd heard Brenna tell Samaira.

According to Brenna, Lawrence wasn't to be trusted—he was loyal to Wolfe.

But there was an itch in the back of Juliana's mind about this. Why help them? Why do anything for them if he was loyal to the Grey-Stars? And yet, why be at the bridge? If the Black-Stars had found out what he'd done in Dolor, wouldn't he be hunted? If they hadn't, why would he leave his station?

She grimaced. May was a better judge of character than she was, a better judge of who to trust. A pang of intense longing shot through her; this would all be a thousand times easier with the old woman's wise words in her ear.

Juliana closed her eyes and breathed in the cold night air, filling her lungs in an effort to slow the vortex of thoughts whirling in her mind.

Lawrence was a problem to be dealt with later, or not at all, if they were lucky. If they could get across the river without anyone knowing...

The bridge was another anxiety on her mind. She'd checked the map and found no sign of another way across. It made sense if the thing was old and unused, as Brenna had said.

Which brought Juliana back to the issue of trust. She trusted Anthony, Cho, Jason, Daisy, Taz, and a handful of the others.

Yet she'd been the one who'd brought Brenna with them. The thought of leaving her aunt in that place was too horrible to consider.

She rubbed her hands across her face. This decision didn't rest entirely on her. It was one for all of them to make.

"Yer tense," Anthony murmured.

Juliana snorted. "Oddly enough, as it's been such a relaxing week."

He chuckled, the sound low and deep and sinking into her bones to drive away some of the stress.

"What're yeh thinkin'?"

She sighed. The words didn't come right away, but he waited, silent and more patient than she'd ever be.

"There aren't a lot of options, and none of them sound safe."

Safe didn't feel like the right word, but *safer* seemed accurate. If they made it to the southern end of Pangaea, they'd be safer.

"Yeah." He nodded, scooching closer and wrapping his arm around her. "Yeh talk to Jason?"

"He wants to take the old bridge, if it exists. I think he'd be fine with going to Lawrence, but Samaira is dead set against it. So is Ichi."

"Fair."

Juliana inclined her head. It was fair after all they'd gone through.

"I don't know how we'd even get to him with so many Black-Stars around." She heaved a sigh. "I don't trust Brenna. I brought her, but only because—"

"Yeh couldn't leave her," he finished for her. "Not there."

She nodded. "So the old bridge troubles me too."

"It'll be work findin' the frosted thing."

"Not to mention the condition it might be in."

Anthony shrugged, and Juliana raised an eyebrow. "Well," he said, "we've got a dozen powerful Alters with us. We can handle a bridge."

A grin split Juliana's worried expression, and she shook her head. "How do you always do that?"

He cocked a crooked smile, not needing to ask what she meant. "I only turn into a wolf for fun; my real gift is making yeh smile."

Heat stirred in Juliana's chest. She shoved it down. Now was not the time. Standing, she bent to kiss Anthony's smooth, warm lips before pulling him with her back to the others.

Hawk found the bridge.

The suspicion Juliana harbored about his loyalty had faded after he'd gotten the children away from Dolor, but directing them safely upriver alleviated the last of her concerns. He'd stuck close to her and Daisy, choosing to keep his distance from the ones they'd rescued.

Juliana hadn't asked him about Elaine.

The woman was still lost in her own mind. As much as Juliana had helped lessen some of the pain and as far as Ichi had gone to bring her back, she was still suffering.

Privately, Juliana thought Hawk might be able to help at this point. A face from a long time ago, a reminder of what Elaine had already overcome, might push her past whatever block remained.

The man kept his distance, however. In the rare times when Elaine was aware, Hawk would stride from the camp, shed his clothes out of view, and disappear into the air.

Juliana looked toward the darkening sky. The crisp evening air sent a shiver down her spine.

Hawk was now a small dot in the sky, soaring above them as he kept look-out.

"This looks precarious." Daisy's bubbly voice held more than a hint of trepidation.

The two stood at the precipice of a gorge, the water nearly thirty feet below them. The river here was nearly half a mile wide, one of its narrowest points. It churned violently below them.

The abandoned road they'd driven on to get here was poked and overgrown, a good sign for keeping out of sight. A bad sign for the condition of the bridge.

Juliana wondered how long it had been since Brenna had crossed here. "That's an understatement," she grumbled.

The mass of metal and concrete before them had visible cracks. The pillars holding it up seemed to have been partially eroded by the flow of water.

Daisy leaned forward, looking down. "It's so high."

Juliana's stomach clenched at the distance.

"What do you think?" she asked.

Daisy met her gaze. Tired eyes held a heaviness, one that permeated the air around them. It felt like a long time had passed since Abredea.

"We have to cross," Daisy said, resigned. "I'm with Jason on this one, being on that side of the river feels safer."

Footsteps crunched on the gravel behind them. Cho walked forward, picking at the edge of his shirt.

"Well?"

Juliana gestured with a tense hand. "It's not safe, not by a long shot. But we don't have a better plan."

Cho nodded. "Lawrence wasn't the only one who said we should go south. Carthik suggested we come this way also."

"I'm surprised you trust him." Juliana raised an eyebrow.

Cho shrugged; a twisted frown of conflict briefly crossed his lips. "He got us out of Tornim. Without him we'd still be stuck in the city."

Juliana nodded. Without the smuggler, Anthony's cousin would have died. Still, using the man to get medicine and trusting him were two different things.

"Besides," Daisy murmured, her gaze drifting to the horizon where the faint peaks of mountains had begun to grow in the distance, "we all need to see the mountains, right?"

Juliana glanced at her friend.

Daisy lips twitched to the side. "I've been having them too."

Weight pressed on Juliana's chest. Sharing dreams was a new level of strange.

Cho looked between the two of them. "We should ask the others, see if they're having the same dream."

"After we get across," Juliana said.

She turned and waved to the truck, idling in the middle of the cracked and crumbling street. Taz stuck his hand out the driver's side window and waved back.

Luna and Nova joined the three of them at the front. The small group walked, staying twenty or so feet ahead of the truck, testing the bridge for breaks or holes. Slowly, the vehicle rumbled along behind them.

There were a few places where the twins used their power to ease the wheels over gaps. Each time sent pangs of fear through Juliana.

Behind the truck, following on foot to keep the weight spread out, came the rest of the group. Hawk flew above them, Anthony bringing up the rear in wolf form. Jason followed as well, choosing to walk beside Anthony rather than his sister.

Tires rolled over the last few feet of the bridge, and Taz angled the truck to follow the sharp turn in the road. Samaira and Abilene walked at the front of the cluster of children trudging along after the truck. Each held a plasma gun, two of the few they'd stolen from Dolor.

Jason had balked at Abilene being allowed a weapon. It was something Juliana understood, but Abilene had opened her mind freely to Ichi. There was no malice there. Nothing but regret and a need to fix her past mistakes. So, while Juliana didn't want to damage her growing friendship with Jason, she'd stood up for the woman when it came up.

It had taken most of the day to reach and cross the bridge, but they pushed on, putting space between them and the river, until the sky above was entirely dark.

"Nothing ahead, not for a long ways," Hawk said as he pulled a shirt over his torso.

"Safe to stop," Anthony suggested, putting on his shirt as well. "There's no one on our tail, at least not that I can tell."

Hawk confirmed, and they set out to make camp.

Within an hour, four fire pits glowed with warmth. Children snuggled around the flames, covered with every piece of cloth they had. Juliana was grateful, yet again, for Anthony's warm body beside her.

Daisy sat curled on her other side, with Taz keeping her warm as well. Between the four of them, and the low fire, they managed to keep the cold at bay.

"We need food," Daisy murmured as they gazed out on the group.

Juliana nodded. "Tomorrow we can pull out the map. There are a few cities on this side of the river, maybe we can take another truck."

Taz's eyes lit up. "I could go for a p... p... peach pastry."

Juliana grinned. "Yeah, me too."

"I dunno." Anthony stretched, a groan interrupting his words. "Chocolate sounds good right about now."

"Hmmm," Cho murmured from his place across from them. "Hot chocolate."

A chorus of agreement went around the circle.

"With sprinkles," Tommy chirped. He was nestled, half laying on Jane's lap as she brushed her fingers through his sandy hair.

Daisy giggled, the sound easing Juliana's nerves.

"Coffee," Juliana murmured. She caught sight of Taz's wrinkled nose and laughed.

"Peach pastry," Taz said with a definitive nod. "You all can have everythin' else."

The conversation went on like that for a while.

Jason sat with them, laughing along as they made wild plans to somehow steal a full restaurant's worth of pasta. He left after a bit, settling at one of the other fires and fiddling with the strip of thin metal he'd routinely played with since they started this journey.

The rest of them talked about food, about spending days sewing, knitting, reading, drawing, or hunting. They envisioned what it would be like to be safe from the Black-Stars, from the cities.

Elaine was herself for a few minutes and shared her plans to grow a vast garden wherever they settled. Sky crawled into her lap, elated at having Elaine back even for a short time, and ran her hands along the ground, sprouting a collection of pale white flowers.

Eventually the conversation subsided, and Juliana fell asleep, Anthony's arm still around her.

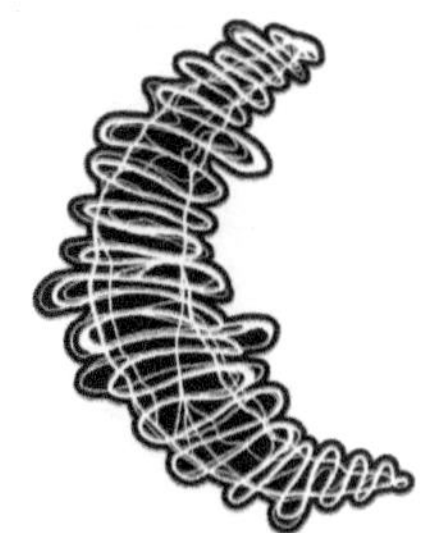

Chapter Forty

Southern Pangaea

The frigid snow-capped mountains she hovered above shrank from view. Juliana reached out a hand. They were so close...

She woke to someone shaking her shoulder.

"Juliana!"

It was Brenna's voice, and the sound of it brought her from sleep in an instant.

"What's wrong?" Juliana demanded, sitting upright and rubbing the sleep from her eyes. The sky was a dull grey, frosty dew on the grass and trees. The fires had died down, coals and embers sending thin trails of smoke into the air.

The others were still asleep.

"It's Anthony," Brenna murmured. Her eyes were wide, filled with fear, and Juliana hesitated, unsure if her aunt even knew what she was saying.

A quick glance, however, revealed his absence from her side. She was surprised the cold at her back hadn't woken her earlier.

"Where is he?" Juliana rose and stepped away from the others, her gaze sharply trained on Brenna.

"He's hurt. Bad." Brenna strode a few paces, turned to see Juliana standing still, and gestured vigorously. "Hurry."

Juliana's heart clenched at the words. She glanced around their camp. Anthony was gone, that much was true. His pack was beside hers, but his bow was missing.

"Where?" she asked, hurrying after Brenna with fear curling her hands into fists.

"He was hunting," Brenna said, her words hurried as she darted into the woods.

Juliana followed, joining Brenna on the road as the two of them jogged toward the bridge.

Juliana's blood raced. Her mind tumbled through a hundred horrible scenarios. "What happened?"

"Don't know." Brenna gestured again, and Juliana sped up. "Have to get back."

"Back?" Juliana's brow furrowed, unease growing.

"He's back," Brenna said, "toward the bridge. Quick."

Juliana gave a frustrated shake of her head, and hurried after her aunt, wishing she'd woken Daisy before they'd left.

Her heart pounded as they ran. Full minutes passed, trees thinning as they neared the open space between the scraggly trees and the river.

"Where?" Juliana panted. It didn't make sense for him to have come this far. There was no place to fish. Animals would be in the woods, wouldn't they?

Brenna turned around, and Juliana skidded to a halt.

The bridge was ahead of them, the sound of the water just audible from the distance.

"Brenna?"

Her aunt's eyes darted to Juliana, then to the road behind her. She twitched, her mouth twisting into a pained expression. "You have to come back."

Cold dread trickled down Juliana's spine. "What are you talking about? Where is Anthony?"

Brenna twisted her hands so hard her fingers went white. "You have to come back." Her head jerked to the side.

Juliana took a step backward.

"She'll be mad," Brenna said, her voice almost a pleading whisper. "You have to come."

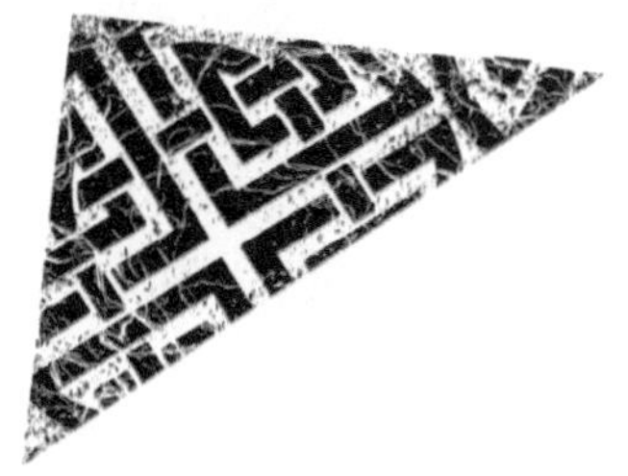

Chapter Forty-One

Allegi - Fifteen Years Ago

Angry pounding woke Brenna from an uneasy sleep. She sat up, head spinning simply from the effort of lifting it. She was at the small desk in her little lab. It had become her home years ago, the comfortable rooms in the distant wing of Allegi a faint memory.

The cot where she healed the injured served as her bed, the desk her workstation, the tight space her living area. Her food was brought in twice a day. There was nothing else now, only healing.

The door slammed open, and Brenna turned with a jerk. Two Black-Stars strode into the room, but neither held an injured person.

Brenna frowned, her mind muddled by sleep and hunger. "What's going on?"

"It's time to prove yourself."

She shuddered as Wolfe stepped into the room. The Grey-Star looked on Brenna with cold eyes.

"Come."

Brenna stood with a swallow. She followed Wolfe out the open door, the relatively fresh air in the hallway bringing her senses into slightly sharper focus.

The Black-Stars took up formation behind them, marching close enough to send a prickle down Brenna's spine.

They moved through the exam and experimentation sections of Allegi and into the softer, warmer living quarters. Wolfe led them to an open door but halted just outside it. She waved a hand and the Black-Stars hurried away.

Brenna looked at Wolfe, fear gripping her heart. "What am I to do?"

Wolfe's scornful expression softened slightly. She inhaled, weariness lining her features for a few seconds. "There is a prisoner inside this room. A man known to have worked with dregs of the rebellion. He knows the location of a few survivors, stragglers the Black-Stars haven't yet rounded up."

Brenna plucked at a cuticle, the pain sharpening her attention even more. Her hands were skeletal, the bones protruding against her paper-thin skin. She shivered in the chilly hallway air.

"He is dying." Wolfe caught Brenna's gaze and held it, her eyes blazing with intent. "He cannot be allowed to die. His information is vital, and there are..."

her jaw tightened, "important people watching. Do this correctly, and we might regain our status."

Brenna's brows twitched together at the word *our*. Hope bound through her chest and into her throat. She nodded and stepped into the room.

Black-Stars lined the walls. Each held a drawn plasma gun, the muzzles pointed at the floor. Their eyes were alert, gazes locked on their target.

A man lay on a tilted back, raised chair. His arms were cuffed to the metal armrests, his ankles chained together. A jagged slice marred his left shoulder, cutting deep into his chest. Despite the clear medical efforts of the Blue-Star hovering over him, blood pooled on the shining hardwood under the chair.

"Step away," Wolfe said to the Blue-Star.

He gave a hurried nod and retreated to the hallway.

Wolfe's heels clicked across the floor as she moved to Brenna's side. "I will be watching." She nodded to the pane of black glass against the far wall. "Make me proud, Brenna."

Brenna swallowed, and Wolfe left.

The Black-Stars remained, their guns at the ready.

Brenna exhaled through pursed lips, released her bloody cuticle, and placed her hands over the wound in the man's shoulder.

He *was* dying. Close to it, the light of his life as faint and flickering as the power within Brenna. She tugged at it, pulled it free from the core of her and stretched it to her fingertips.

The traitor under her fingers was wounded in many places. Externally, the bleeding gash was the worst, but inside there was more. His ribs were broken in several places, there was internal bleeding, and several bones were fractured.

Brenna urged her power forth, flushing it through him like a wave. The bleeding on his shoulder stemmed. Her hands shook. The room began to fade.

It was too much, but she couldn't stop. Ms. Wolfe was watching. She *had* to heal him.

Each beat of her heart was an effort, each breath a success over the darkness that slowly consumed her vision.

He wasn't well yet. He'd lost so much blood.

But she couldn't... her fingers were like ice, her breathing too slow, her heartbeat...

She couldn't hear it anymore.

Couldn't see.

Couldn't feel.

There was nothing left. Nothing but darkness.

Chapter Forty-Two

Southern Pangaea

Anthony strode through the forest with a dance in his step. A line of odd creatures dangled from the rope on his shoulder. They were near the size of rabbits, but with longer tails, shorter ears, and plumper bodies.

The vegetation was different as well, but there were enough wild onions he recognized that he was able to gather a few handfuls. He steered clear of the mushrooms. They were close, but not close enough to the ones he was used to for him to risk it.

This was enough. He grinned, the wolf within rumbling its contentment at the thought of soon being fed.

The sun had peeked over the edge of the horizon by the time Anthony returned to the group. He unslung his catch and set the bag of onions beside it. Most of the others were still asleep, though Jason was tending the fire with heavy bags under his eyes, and Taz was pacing at the edge of the clearing near the old road.

Anthony gave Jason a nod, which was returned, and walked over to Taz. "Nice mornin'."

Taz hurried the last few feet to Anthony and took his arm.

"What?" Anthony asked, his shoulders tensing at the worry on Taz's face.

"Juliana and Brenna left, and they haven't come back."

A furrow creased Anthony's brow. "How long?"

Taz shook his head, the mop of dirty-blond hair flopping over his forehead. "Ten minutes, maybe more."

"Did they say anythin'?" Anthony strode past his friend, heading toward the road.

Taz shook his head again, following. "I was just wakin' up and saw them go. Thought about followin', but Jason only just got up. I was about to let him know."

"Yeh didn't want tah leave without tellin' someone," Anthony grumbled. "That's smart."

Taz flashed him a worried look that Anthony returned. Jules was smart. Leaving without telling anyone wasn't something she would do.

Anthony wheeled, darted to Jason's side, and explained the situation. Jason agreed to stay behind and rouse the others. They'd be ready to leave as quickly as possible in case something was wrong.

The wolf within Anthony stirred. Something *was* wrong. The question was what?

"Yeh comin'?" Anthony said as he passed Taz at a steady jog.

Taz didn't respond, simply picked up the pace and hurried alongside Anthony as the two made for the road.

They reached the turn-off. Anthony sniffed the air, his wolf growling at the faint whiff of Juliana's natural scent.

"W... w..." Taz let out a shout of frustration as the words refused to come.

"Back toward the bridge," Anthony answered, assuming what Taz was asking.

The younger man nodded, and they sped down the road.

"Wolf?" Taz huffed as they ran.

"Not yet." Anthony kicked up the pace, ducking low hanging branches and skipping over potholes and fallen debris from the years of neglect.

If he changed now he wouldn't be able to speak, and he wanted to find out what was going on.

They moved around a long bend in the road and sounds of shouting reached their ears.

"Not on your life," came Juliana's fierce snarl.

Anthony sprinted the last thirty yards, cleared the forest, and screeched to a stop. Taz came up behind him, breathing hard.

Juliana stood at the edge of the road. In the distance behind her, the bridge they'd crossed the day before was visible. Brenna had her hands around both of Juliana's wrists, the bony fingers holding tight as Juliana jerked backward.

"I said let go," Juliana snapped. She twisted and broke free, turning and catching sight of Anthony and Taz. The relief on her face bathed Anthony in worry.

"What's goin' on?" He strode forward, his eyes narrowed at Juliana's aunt.

"You're all right," Juliana breathed, backing away from Brenna until she reached his side, a good twenty feet from the woman.

"'Course." He frowned at her.

Juliana's relief shifted to anger. She turned back to Brenna with a scowl on her face. "You said he was hurt."

Brenna's wide eyes darted from Anthony to Taz and back to Juliana. Darkness flashed across her features. "You aren't supposed to be here. She doesn't want *you*." Her head twitched and she focused on Juliana. "She wants you. You have to come back."

"Never," Juliana spat. She shook her head, hurt trembling in her voice. "I thought you were on our side. I thought you were with us."

Anthony took half a step forward, putting himself just ahead of Juliana in case her crazed aunt tried something violent. The hairs on the back of his neck were on end. The wolf within prowled angrily, furious at the sound of pain in Juliana's voice.

Brenna's hands trembled. She moved toward them, even as her head twisted to look at the bridge.

"That's enough," Taz said. "No closer."

Brenna glanced at him, and her lips drew together in a hiss. "You don't command me, boy," she said in a severe tone.

A low growl rumbled from Anthony's throat. He took another step forward.

"You have to come back." Brenna's voice was weak again, pleading and disjointed as it had been a second ago.

Anthony called up the wolf within and prepared to unleash it.

"We can help you." Juliana moved up beside Anthony, a hand out in a silent request for him to hold off. "Come with us. You don't have to be controlled by her anymore."

Brenna twitched again, her head jerking at an odd angle before she righted it and straightened. Her eyes brightened with lucidity. Her hands went to her sides.

The stillness was somehow more unsettling than her constant movement. She stared at them, her gaze serious and firm.

"Juliana, you need to come with me."

"No."

Anthony lightly touched Juliana's arm. "If yeh try to make her, we will have tah fight you."

"It isn't somethin' we wanna do," Taz added.

Brenna glared from one to the other, her expression twisting again.

Anthony pulled the wolf to the front of his mind. The woman's reaction to the situation had him more on edge than he'd been moments before. The wolf growled, ready to be released.

"You have to come. She'll be angry," Brenna said, her voice still oddly calm. Something sparked in her eyes.

Anthony's instincts told him to move back, but he took another step forward, trying to put himself between Juliana and Brenna.

"Then let her be angry," Juliana replied, her voice full of sadness.

Brenna twitched again. The air sparked.

"It'll be all right," Taz said. He stepped forward, putting up his hands to appeal to Brenna. "No one wants tah hurt yeh, we wanna help."

Brenna's gaze flicked to him. "You can't help me."

"We can," Taz insisted.

"Taz," Anthony muttered, a warning in his voice. He shifted, pushing Juliana back with one hand as the other began to transform. His arm burst with fur, claws lengthening. He moved toward Taz.

Brenna shook her head.

"We can," Taz said again. He took another step.

Brenna's hands rose, her fingers outstretched toward Taz. Her head rolled back. The sky above them crackled with electricity.

Anthony leaped. There was a roar of sound, like he was standing in the center of a storm. Darkness shot toward him.

Pain erupted in his chest, and he fell.

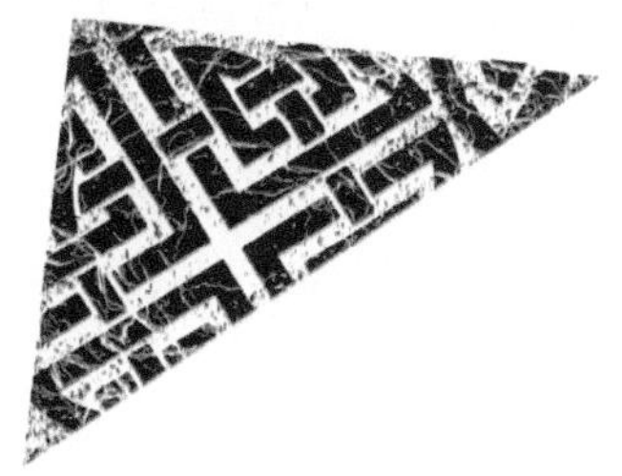

Chapter Forty-Three

Allegi - Fifteen Years Ago

Air slammed into Brenna's lungs with the force of a hurricane. She gasped, nearly crumpling, barely holding herself up as energy surged into her limbs.

Tendrils of life sped toward her. The Black-Stars circling the room stood frozen, each of them wearing matching horrified expressions as they gasped and, one by one, fell to their knees. Lines connected them to her, flowing colors of black, green, and blue that pooled in Brenna's palm.

Energy shot through her body, slamming into the traitor on the chair. He screamed.

The Black-Stars *should* have screamed. Their mouths were open, gasping in silent terror as one by one they collapsed. She felt their hearts stop beating.

Her head tilted as the final breath left the last one.

Her pulse returned, the beat steady and even, stronger than it had been in years. After a few breaths, she shook her head to clear the fuzziness in her eyes.

Everything seemed slow.

As she took in her hands, whole and strong, the emaciated pallor no longer revealing too much bone and veins, she caught the eye of the man before her.

He was still tied to the chair, staring at her with his wide green eyes. They were alert, filled with terror. There was no blood leaking from him anymore. He was whole and healthy and whimpering.

Brenna licked her lips. The dryness that had coated her tongue was gone. She took a faltering step away from the chair and swallowed.

The Black-Stars were dead. All of them.

No. There was one.

Brenna cocked her head at the man sheltered in the corner of the room. He'd dropped his weapon, his face pale with fear, hands shaking as he held them like a shield before his body.

She glanced up at the dark glass where Wolfe was supposed to be watching her heal. Instead, she'd watched Brenna murder a squad of soldiers.

Brenna would find out soon enough what Wolfe thought of this new development. In the meantime...

This power was different. New. Brenna flexed her fingers; within her, a roiling storm of energy waited for her to call it forth. It wasn't the frail ball of nearly depleted healing she'd carried with her before. This was strong.

This demanded to be used.

Brenna inhaled, the scents of urine and blood twisting her nose into a scowl. She extended her hand.

The Black-Star screamed as a mud and mold-colored ball of electric power slammed into his chest.

He crumpled.

The door behind her burst open. Brenna wheeled, hands at the ready as the power within her sparked with potential.

Wolfe stood in the doorway. A shudder of anxiety shot through Brenna, that familiar fear of being a disappointment.

Then Wolfe's expression broke into a warm smile. "You've done well, Brenna. This is…" her teeth clicked together as she took in the room. "Unexpected."

Brenna exhaled. Her hands went limp at her sides.

"Unexpected." Wolfe held out her arms and Brenna stepped into the embrace, her head resting on the Grey-Star's shoulder. "And impressive. I'm proud of you, and so are the others. Come, let's discuss what happens next."

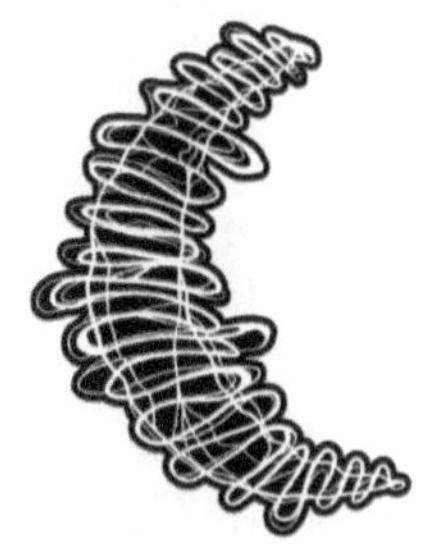

Chapter Forty-Four

Southern Pangaea

The thing that erupted from Brenna's hand looked similar to Jason's flames, but only in shape. The color was wrong; dark brown and green, like sludge.

Juliana's yell stuck in her throat. She reached for Taz as the power surged toward him. She wanted to grab him, pull him out of the way. He was too far from her.

And then Anthony lept in front of Taz and twisted energy slammed into his chest.

Juliana's eyes widened, icy fear filling every inch of her..

Anthony fell with a thud at Taz's feet. The world went quiet, the air thin and cold as Juliana raced to his side. She dropped to her knees and ran her hands over his torso.

The burst had hit his chest. A singed hole in the grey material of his shirt encircled a deep, gaping wound. The smell was not of flesh burned by fire, but something closer to acid.

Vaguely, Juliana caught sight of Taz moving to stand between her and Brenna. He was speaking. The words didn't reach her.

She plunged into herself, grasping her power and pulling it to the surface in a desperate rush. Her vision warped. Her hands trembled as tendrils of blue light exploded out of her, spreading across Anthony. The worst of the bloody mess healed before her eyes, veins and sinew stitching together.

He wasn't breathing.

Juliana reached to check his pulse, as she had done months ago when he'd fallen from a much larger height, when he'd crashed down onto concrete steps and survived. When she hadn't been able to heal.

She could heal now. She could fix this. She pushed more power into him.

Her fingers were dry this time, no rain falling on them, no blood. And yet she could not find his heartbeat.

Tears welled in her eyes. "No." Juliana gritted her teeth. She inhaled and focused.

In a blur of movement, Taz knelt on the other side of Anthony's body. He glowed with a rainbow of color. His gaze darted from Anthony to Juliana and back.

Anthony didn't glow. The warm black shine she'd seen each time she'd gone this far into her power was gone. Shadows, those dark voids of light, filled his chest and his head, almost blocking her light.

Juliana wiped her eyes, clearing her vision before putting a hand on his forehead. She called forth another wave of blue light. The shadows shifted but didn't leave.

She whimpered, fear clutching at her chest.

"You can do this," Taz's voice broke through the terror.

She met his gaze, tears reflected in his eyes as well. Her lips trembled.

He nodded. "Yeh've got this, Juliana. I know yeh do."

Juliana inhaled, shoving away the fear and pouring every ounce of herself into pushing the shadows from Anthony's heart and mind.

They moved. Little by little, inch by inch they seeped out of him and into the ground below. A shiver ran down Juliana's spine as the remains of her aunt's power oozed away.

When the last of the sludge was out of Anthony, her light flared again. Pain hammered her head as she poured energy into Anthony. A long few seconds passed.

"He's not—" Taz sniffed— "he's not wakin' up."

She shook her head. "This is wrong. Why isn't he..." She felt for his pulse again but found nothing. "Taz, why isn't he..."

Her vision was still influenced by her power. She looked from Taz to Anthony. The glowing black was still absent. Anthony's outline was plain, pale, lifeless.

Tears dripped down her cheeks. "This can't be happening." She sniffed, fury building in her chest. "This can't be..."

She dug deeper, pushed harder. There was more power inside her, she knew it.

Juliana drained the pool of blue light within, her head and heart growing faint as she poured every ounce of herself into Anthony, murmuring as she did so, begging him to return.

She lost feeling in her fingers. Darkness tunneled her vision. She couldn't breathe.

Something slipped.

Snapped.

Rushing filled her ears as the air around them went cold. Juliana met Taz's eyes, unease furrowing her brow as he stared back at her, tears flowing down his cheeks.

Against her will, her hand rose off Anthony's chest and extended toward Taz. Juliana frowned at her arm in confusion. Faint blue tendrils, the remains of her power, wove in and through her fingers. Her palm reached toward her friend.

Fear slammed through her. "*Wait.*"

Taz froze. His body stiffened. His chest constricted as the brilliant colors that had surrounded him pooled at his heart. The light moved, sliding from him like a strand of yarn and arcing toward her hand.

"No." Juliana shook her head, terror lacing her voice as confusion melted into realization and understanding.

Every muscle in her arm screamed in pain as she tried to pull it away, to stop the flow. She grabbed her extended wrist with her other hand and yanked down with all her strength. Her arm, that blue light swirling around her skin, didn't budge.

Taz's eyes were wide. He stared at her, tears still on his cheeks. His skin paled to a dull beige. The last of his rainbow light eased through Juliana's palm, down her outstretched arm, and into Anthony's chest.

Taz let out a soft exhale and, eyes still staring, tilted sideways and collapsed onto the ground.

In the same breath, Anthony gasped.

Juliana fell back, her hands falling limp and shaking.

"Nacra." Anthony coughed. He sat up, leaned forward, and retched.

Juliana stared past him; her gaze stuck on Taz.

Anthony groaned, wiped his mouth, and tenderly poked at the still ruined flesh of his chest. Scabs had formed, but his skin was red and inflamed. "What..." he looked at Juliana.

She was on her knees, her lips parted, horror frozen on her face. Shallow breaths did little to fill her chest. They did nothing to fill the gaping hole that ate away her insides.

"Jules, are yeh all right?" Anthony hurried to his knees and inched closer to her. "What happened? I was—" He shook his head, a hint of his crooked smile briefly flashing across his face— "in bad shape, yeah?" He swallowed. "Worse than bad. Yeh saved me." He pulled her in, caressing the back of her head before releasing her.

She was trembling. Cold and trembling and unable to speak.

"Taz." Anthony glanced around, a yelp escaping him as he spotted their friend's body. "Jules, he's hurt, unconscious. Can yeh..." His words faded as his fingers found Taz's neck. "He doesn't have a heartbeat." His voice became frantic. "Jules!"

She crawled to them, the dead grass scratching her palms. Taz lay on his back, his eyes staring blankly at the sky above them, shock etched onto his face.

Anthony scrambled, his hands moving to Taz's chest as he looked to Juliana. "Can you do something? Can you heal him?"

Juliana stared at her palms. The faintest hints of blue tendrils faded like smoke as she moved them toward Taz's body.

"I…" she inhaled just enough air to speak. "I can't."

Anthony shook his head. "No, this isn't—" he grimaced. "I was too far gone, wasn't I? You spent it all getting me back." He gritted his teeth, pain straining his words. "Taz…"

Tears flowed from Juliana's eyes. Her insides were melted, numb, an empty void of raging guilt and horror all at once. She opened her mouth, to explain, beg forgiveness, scream…

"Where's Brenna?" Anthony demanded.

Juliana blinked and looked around. Her aunt was gone. Taz had spoken to her, said something while Juliana tried to heal Anthony.

She met Anthony's eye for the briefest of seconds, struggling to form the words, to tell him the truth of what happened.

He pushed to his feet and shed the remains of his shirt with twisted fury on his face. "I'm going after her. She can't get away with this."

"Anthony…"

He darted away, morphing as he went. Soon a large black wolf ran across the open expanse toward the bridge.

A few seconds ticked by as Juliana stared after him, her confession stuck on her tongue.

A blast rocked the air. Ahead of them, the bridge shook, crumbled, and a massive chunk of it dropped into the roaring water below.

Anthony came to a halt, a furious howl breaking from him.

Juliana took Taz's cold hand in hers and closed her eyes. "Please come back," she whispered. "Trade it for me, Taz. Take it from me."

She went into her core, into the cracked and broken locket where she'd safely tucked her power. It was empty. All of her, empty. There was nothing to bring forward for Taz. She tried, tried to take her own lifeforce, trade it, make the exchange willingly unlike what her power had done to her friend.

What she'd done.

Stone formed in her mind. As grief and panic washed over her, the locket that had stored her gift melted into nothing and was replaced with a wall. Tall, dark, made from concrete and rock, it circled the space where her power normally sat.

By the time Anthony returned, snarling and furious even back in his human form, she had locked away the dregs of her gift.

"Jules."

She jerked at the touch on her shoulder. Anthony gazed down at her, his eyes red and swollen with tears.

"We have tah get back to the others. We have tah go. Brenna knows where we are. She'll get tah the Black-Stars soon enough, and we can't be here when she does."

Juliana nodded. That much at least, she understood. Taz was... gone. Dead. But the others didn't have to be. She could help get them somewhere safe and then... and then she'd be able to tell Anthony what happened.

No. She needed to tell him sooner. Now.

"Anthony, I—" The words caught in her throat when Anthony hefted Taz's corpse and turned to look at her.

The boy's gemstones were dull. Not quite grey, but a dimmed version of their usual brightness. She was struck with how young he was. He and Daisy spent so much time with herself and Anthony, she often forgot they were years younger. Taz would have turned seventeen that winter.

Anthony met her gaze, concern flashing through the grief. "Jules? Can yeh walk? Did bringin' me back take too much?"

She opened her mouth, closed it again, and nodded. "I can walk."

Anthony led the way, his footsteps heavy with the weight of their friend.

Juliana limped along behind, her body as weak as it had been the day she healed Anthony's hand so long ago. Her mind and heart, even weaker.

Chapter Forty-Five

Southern Pangaea

They were only able to bury Taz's body because of the twins. Luna and Nova used their levitation to pull dirt from the earth. They wouldn't have had time otherwise.

Anthony didn't like putting Taz in the ground. He'd have preferred Abredea's usual method of burning their dead. He could have been lifted to the sky, soaring on ash and cloud until the breeze swept him somewhere better, safe.

As Jason pointed out, his voice as soft and kind as Anthony had ever heard it, the Black-Stars would likely see the smoke.

So they buried him.

Sky grew an array of flowers over the top of the dirt, adding more color to Taz's death than he'd seen for most of his life.

Anthony stared numbly at the mound of earth. The fury within couldn't compare to the guilt ripping him apart.

Daisy touched his arm, and Anthony jerked. "It's time to go," she muttered, her voice thick with the tears that hadn't stopped streaming from her eyes.

He glanced behind her. The others were loaded up, Juliana behind the wheel as she was now the only one truly capable of driving. She hadn't spoken to him since they'd returned. Had barely spoken to the others as he'd explained what happened.

He couldn't blame her. If he hadn't died, hadn't been so far gone that she'd needed to use every ounce of her to get him back... she'd have had the energy to heal Taz.

Then again, if he hadn't leapt between his friend and the bolt of twisted darkness that came from Brenna's hands, maybe Taz would still be dead.

Or maybe Anthony would have gone completely wolf, and taken her down before she could hurt someone else.

His head ached almost as much as his heart.

"Anthony," Daisy said again.

He looked down at her. Her eyes were as red as his own, her voice ragged from the wails she'd released upon seeing Taz' body.

Cho had needed to leave. He'd been the first to realize what happened upon their return. His gasp, the stumbling steps backward as he fled the emotions pouring from Anthony and Juliana, stuck with Anthony. Almost as much as Daisy's screams.

"We..." Daisy cleared her throat. "We need to go."

She looped her hand through his arm and, without resistance, tugged him to the truck.

He stopped at the back. Cho was in there, and Anthony was nowhere near in control of his mental wards. He glanced at Daisy.

"Will you wait a moment?"

Her exhale was followed by a nod.

Anthony rounded the corner of the truck, stripped, and morphed into a wolf. The agony was still there, the pain and hurt and guilt and grief, but he sat within the treed clearing. His mind was protected by the strength of the beast.

He gently lifted his clothes between his teeth and returned. Daisy took the pants and shirt. She climbed up, and he jumped after her. Cho caught his eye and gave a grateful nod.

Anthony padded across the wooden planks of the truck and curled into a ball against the cab wall.

Jane slapped the window separating the cab from the bed, and the truck rumbled forward.

After a few minutes, Tommy rose from his seat beside Jane, plunked down onto the floor, and began scratching Anthony's head. Tears dripped into the fur on Anthony's back.

The ride was long and silent.

"How long until we reach the mountains?"

Anthony stirred from his sleepy haze, his wolf ears catching the low murmur of voices through the cracked window to the cab.

Jason was up there with Hawk and Juliana. He had been the one to ask.

There was a long pause before Juliana spoke. "We should reach the foothills by tomorrow morning if we keep this pace. The truck will be slower through the night, but we won't be able to use it once we get there anyway, so we may as well push it."

"We can't use it?" Hawk asked.

Anthony lifted his head, angling an ear to better hear Juliana's answer over the soft rumble of the tires.

"No. At least, I don't think so. There aren't any roads on the map."

"We're on a road not on the map," Jason pointed out.

Juliana let out a barely audible sigh. "Even with a road, it's likely it'll be unusable. With how often we've had to stop to clear the way... it won't be as easy climbing in the mountains."

"Think we'll be safer when we get to them?" Hawk's voice was hushed.

Anthony's jaws tightened at the thought of what Brenna might be telling Wolfe and the Black-Stars at that very moment.

"The Grey-Stars send people they don't like to the cities in the far south." Juliana said. "My father had a friend who was sent to Althea after he'd made a big mistake. Pangaea is less patrolled down here, wilder." Anthony caught the bitterness in her voice, "The camps down here have even less than Abredea."

"What's all that mean?" Jason demanded.

"It means there are less Black-Stars. It means they don't usually pay attention to what's going on."

"But they might be now." Hawk filled in the silence that followed. "Because of..."

"Brenna," Jason growled.

"Yeah." Juliana's voice was tight with what Anthony recognized as tears. "She knows about everything—"

Her words stopped, a sniff suggesting she had taken a second to compose herself.

The front was silent for a long minute.

"You know this isn't your fault, right?" Jason murmured.

The truck slowed a fraction. After a few seconds it sped back up, but Juliana didn't respond.

Anthony's chest tightened. His ears drooped as the three in the cab ceased their conversation.

Tommy had fallen asleep, his little body draped across Anthony's long form. He was reminded so vividly of Jimmy that the longing in his heart reached an intolerable level.

"Shh," Jane whispered from the bench beside him.

Anthony darted a look at her, only then realizing he'd been whining.

"We miss him too." Jane's jaw was tight, her eyes narrowed and her expression one of fury rather than sadness. "Once the others are safe," her gaze danced to her brother and back, "we'll find her. She won't get away with what she did."

Anthony huffed a breath out of his nostrils, a low growl escaping his throat as both he and the wolf dipped their head in agreement.

Chapter Forty-Six

Southern Pangaea

The reverberating grief that Anthony and Daisy were trying in vain to keep behind their mental wards shunted against Cho as the truck rumbled to a stop. He wasn't looking forward to Juliana joining them for a rest.

He planted his feet on solid ground and strode away from the cab before the others started moving. Dry grass crunched under his feet. They'd left the forest a few hours ago and while there were scattered clusters of trees here and there, the open space left Cho with a crawling feeling of exposure.

He should help set up camp. Anthony deserved a break, Daisy too. And he didn't want to think of how Juliana was doing. She'd done so much to keep them safe. Brought Elaine away from the brink, repaired the damage done neutralizing the tracking devices, saved Luna's life, and so much more.

Brenna's betrayal had hit everyone hard. As much as she kept to herself, she'd been a part of their escape. Part of their group. Someone they thought they'd helped save.

Juliana would be taking that betrayal harder than the rest, amplifying her guilt over Taz' death.

Cho shook his head, his power a whirling vortex of anticipation. It was hungry. If it could feed on Juliana's pain, it would.

He'd give her time to settle, and he'd give himself a few minutes to reinforce his barriers before facing the others.

He reached an outcropping of trees, just a handful with their peeling white bark a stark contrast to the orange-tinged sky. The sun approached the horizon earlier these days. It seemed like a lifetime ago that Carthik had snuck them out of Tornim.

The anger he'd felt back then, at the way Kendra had looked at Jason and their demand to keep him... he understood it now.

The realization had been coming on for a while.

Losing Taz had been the final coin tipping the scale of strain. Fear that the Black-Stars would catch up with them at any minute, the distance Cho felt between himself and Ichi, the constant worry about what would come next, and Taz's death; all of it finally peaked within him.

He needed to tell Jason the truth.

A flutter stirred in his stomach. He hadn't seen the flame thrower since they'd buried Taz. Cho had stood in the back, away from the emotional onslaught from Daisy, Anthony, and Juliana.

He'd wanted to be there for them.

The flutter dissipated as guilt rumbled through him. His power stirred within.

Cho inhaled, closing his eyes, and letting out the breath in a fluid whoosh. They'd be stopped for a time, an hour at least, to let the children stretch their legs, relieve themselves, and catch a break from the constant running. He had time to build up his walls.

They were intact. Sturdy and thick and containing his power better than he'd thought. The chest was there as well. He'd made some changes after the raid. The thing was no longer an intricate prison. Instead, the wood was simple with burned swirls patterned along the edges. They were there as a reminder of the occasions in which his power almost destroyed him. He'd been broken by it many times but never irrevocably.

The knowledge was like a light he held against the darkness. Cho touched the box in his mind, cracking it and letting the tendrils of saffron power circle him.

He'd been brought low so often, and there had always been someone to pick him up. To heal him. To bring him back from the brink.

His skin warmed at the memory of Jason holding him after the raid, his steady breaths centering Cho, pulling him away from the teetering edge of nothing. Cho's power sparked. It spun and arched and danced around the safe place he'd created for it in his mind.

It liked this feeling.

Cho smiled. He gently eased the tendrils back into the box, took a final meditative breath, and opened his eyes. Rising to his feet, he walked back to the rest of the group.

Ichi knelt beside Elaine, a hand on her arm and worry furrowing his brow. Cho sat a few paces away, forearms rested against his knees as his stomach twinged with concern.

Elaine's eyes were gold. Light shone from them, and from the tips of her fingers and the edges of her hairline. Her visions were usually small. Little glimpses of the future, a moment or two of time.

This was different.

"What is she seeing?" Cho murmured.

Ichi shook his head. "I don't know. I can't get past the block."

Cho huffed a frustrated sigh through his nostrils and grimaced. Elaine had been trancing for several minutes. That would be dangerous enough if she weren't already in such a fragile state.

"Can Juliana help?" Anthony asked from behind Cho.

He'd done well with his mental shields. Cho hadn't felt him approach.

Ichi glanced up, a brief flash of hope crossing his eyes. He nodded. "She may be able to. Together we might be able to find a way to break her out of it."

Anthony's features were tight, his eyes still red, nose ruddy and chapped from the number of times he'd wiped at it. He inclined his head and turned away.

Cho rose, gave Ichi's shoulder a squeeze, and hurried after Anthony.

"You know where she is?" Anthony asked as Cho caught up.

"Thought you did."

Anthony shook his head, a pained grimace pulling the muscle in his jaw taut. "I 'aven't seen her since we stopped. She darted outta the truck quick."

Cho frowned. "I figured she'd want to be with you. With all that... happened."

"I thought so too." Anthony's voice was quiet. His broad shoulders were hunched in, his head dipped in a way that showed the weight of his grief.

Cho knew that pain. He twisted the edge of his shirt, wishing he could lay a hand on Anthony's arm without the danger of collapsing under the man's despair. "I know how it feels, Anthony. And I'm sorry for what happened to Taz. We all are."

Anthony shook his head. "It was because of me. If I hadn't let Brenna join us, if we'd gone to Lawrence at the bridge, if I hadn't taken the blast—"

Cho swung around, putting himself squarely in Anthony's path with a hand hovering before the man's chest. "Don't."

Tears glistened in Anthony's dark eyes. "I did this, Cho. If I hadn't killed that Black-Star outside of Abredea..."

Cho pursed his lips, empathy eating his insides. He inhaled and met Anthony's gaze with unwavering intensity. "Your decisions didn't lead to this, Anthony. Only one of us can see the future, and she's catatonic at the moment. We do our best."

Anthony's jaw trembled. He pinched his lips together as tears slid down his cheeks. "My best wasn't good enough to save him, Cho. And now Juliana won't talk to me, and Daisy..." He broke off with a grimace.

Daisy had stuck by Jane and the others from Haven since Taz's death. As far as Cho knew, she hadn't spoken a word to anyone since they'd buried him. Her struggle was the opposite of his. He could imagine the effort it took to keep her emotions from spilling over and infecting everyone around her.

He'd go to her soon. He had to. For now, though, he'd give her time and space with the hope that it was what she needed to heal. Or at least to get past the first stages of the trauma.

"Have you had a chance to talk to her?"

Anthony rubbed his forehead. "I don't think she wants tah see me either."

"You have to know that's not true. With her power what it is, she probably thinks she'll cause you more pain. It's a hard gift to control when things are good. Right now..."

Anthony shook his head. "I've gotta—" He cleared his throat, his words clipped and tight. "Thanks, Cho. I've gotta find Jules."

Cho understood the desire for space and simply nodded. As Anthony continued his search, Cho went to find Jason.

The flame thrower stood at the edge of their clearing, his gaze fixed on the cracked road they'd used to get there. After a moment, Jason darted a glance toward the nearest cluster of bodies. Samaira sat there, one arm draped around Abilene's shoulders, the other snuggling Kim close.

"You could talk to her," Cho murmured.

Jason jerked and turned. "Since when can you sneak up on me?"

Cho didn't hold back his smirk. "I've been taking lessons from Anthony. Learning to move quietly."

"Yeah?" The smile didn't reach his eyes. "Anything else you've been learning from that bunch?"

A furrow creased Cho's brow. "What does that mean?"

Jason shrugged. "You've spent a lot of time with Daisy, and with Taz before..."

Cho blinked, confused. "What are you talking about, Jason?"

The taller man crossed his arms, uncrossed them, and strode a few paces away from the others. Cho followed, still at a loss for where this was coming from.

"We don't know them well enough." Jason muttered out the side of his mouth.

"Well enough for what?"

"For you to be falling for her."

Cho's jaw went limp. He swallowed, recovering from the sting of hurt in Jason's voice. He shook off the disbelief muddling his mind and moved further away from the others. Jason followed him into the trees, stopping only when Cho did, several yards out of sight of their little camp.

"I came to find you because we need to talk," Cho said after coming to a halt. "I need to..." He hesitated, his heart beating faster than it should in the moment, his power dancing at the emotions coursing through him.

The silence stretched too long.

Jason cracked his neck, his face tense. "I made you something."

Cho shook out of his frozen inability to form words. "You... what?"

Jason shrugged a shoulder and dug into his pants pocket. He pulled from it the piece of metal Cho had spotted at a distance from time to time on their journey.

He held it out.

Cho reached for it. The metal was smooth, and surprisingly warm. It was a thin strip, maybe an inch wide and four or five inches long. It was barely thicker than a few sheets of paper, and Cho marveled for a second at the way it felt in his hand.

Then he caught sight of the design.

"Ohh," he exhaled.

Spirals lined both sides, delicate and seemingly burned into the metal. On one side was an open book, its pages fluttering in an unseen wind. On the other, an intricate burst of flames burned in the foreground of a massive set of mountains.

Cho took unsteady breaths through his open mouth. "I... Jason, this is..."

"I wasn't sure what to put on the back." Jason shoved both hands into his pockets. "Then you started talking about those dreams, and I thought maybe—"

"It's stunning." Cho looked up at him. "You made this. For me?"

Jason shrugged again. "I got the metal in Tornim, just before the raid. It took a while to get the design right but..." He clenched his jaw, and his gaze turned to the ground. "I know you like books. It's nothing."

Silence fell again. Cho stared at the bookmark in his hands. His chest was warm, his fingers trembling as he traced the carefully carved—burned—lines.

Jason turned.

Cho's breath caught as the man took a step toward the others. "I need to tell you something."

Jason glanced back at him. "What?" His voice lacked the usual bite. It seemed almost fearful.

"I need you to know..." Cho swallowed, his mouth suddenly dry. He'd planned this, thought through the words, but now they were gone. "... that I... I'm..."

Jason faced him, dark eyes flashing in the low light.

"I don't feel that way about Daisy," Cho finally spluttered. "I feel that way about you."

Jason blinked. His arms, folded tight across his body, loosened. "*What?*"

"I get what you've been doing," Cho said, his words coming quickly now that the ice had broken. "Pulling Jane and the kids away so I could teach the others at the lake, helping control my power, when you caught me... You've been here for me since the raid—before the raid. I didn't see it. Now I do."

There was a long pause. The silence between them was only broken by the rustle of the wind and the chirping of evening birds. Jason turned away, staring out at the trees.

His forearms flexed, back and neck stiff. The carefree joker Cho had grown up with had changed so much. Catching glimpses of Jason's old mischievous smile, hearing the occasional burst of laughter, stirred more in Cho than he thought was possible.

He longed to see that smile now.

"How do you know?" Jason finally demanded.

Cho flinched away from the harshness of his voice. His fingers tightened around the bookmark. "What do you mean?"

Jason turned, agony blazing in his eyes. "How do you know what you feel isn't just one of the others, pushing it onto you? Juliana and Anthony, or Ichi and Elaine?"

Realization flooded Cho's expression. "I... I have enough control of my power, Jason. I know which emotions are mine and which aren't. *I* care for you," half a smile ghosted across his face, "more than I ever thought possible."

Silence descended again. A flurry of emotions flashed across Jason's face before he shook his head, jaw tight. "We can't do this. You're too young. You haven't even gone through the Coding yet."

Cho huffed out half a laugh, though the situation was anything but funny. "Neither have you."

"You know what I mean." Jason ran an agitated hand across his thick black hair. "It wouldn't be right, Cho. You're my best friend's brother."

Cho fought the burning in his eyes and took a step forward.

Jason moved back, shaking his head even as longing glinted through the pain on his face. "I can't—"

"I felt it, Jason."

The flame thrower paused, meeting Cho's eye for the first time since his confession.

Cho held his gaze. "Back in Grigoria. After the raid, when we thought they were gone. When you brought me back from wanting to..." He broke off, gritting his teeth as the memory of that pain wrapped an icy fist around his heart. "When you held me. I didn't know what it was, but I felt it."

"Felt what?" Jason muttered, his hands, normally so still, clenched and unclenched at his sides.

Cho stepped forward again, and this time Jason let him. Cho reached out, putting a hand on Jason's forearm. There it was again: warmth, comfort, relief from the anxiety that constantly plagued him.

Fear sat on the surface with pain, and longing. Then heat, the fire within Jason that had driven Cho's frigid despair away so long ago. And deeper, something more.

"I can't show you what I feel for you," Cho said, his voice low as he took another step closer. The two were a breath apart now. Cho's hand drifted, caressing the phoenix on Jason's arm before finding his hand.

Jason's breath hitched, and that apprehension, the fear, roiled over Cho. He let it, breathed it in, and squeezed Jason's hand.

"I can't let you feel mine the way I feel yours. So I need you to trust me." He looked up at Jason, meeting the man's dark gaze with a plea in his own.

Jason blinked away the moisture in his eyes and nodded.

Cho rose, pressing onto his toes as Jason tilted his head. Their lips met. Timid at first, because fear was still there. Cho released Jason's hand, cupped the man's face, and drew the two of them deeper into the kiss.

The fear melted. The emotions Jason had tried so hard to keep hidden rose to the surface. The flame thrower circled an arm around Cho's waist and tangled his other hand in Cho's hair.

Cho closed his eyes, releasing the barriers holding his power in place as Jason's love cascaded over him like a waterfall. It was pure and real and true and as Cho's power latched onto it, recognizing it as a match for the intensity of his own love, relief flowed through them both.

A long moment passed locked in the embrace. When they finally broke apart, Jason kept a hold of Cho's hand.

"I trust you," he said, catching his breath.

Cho grinned, heart still pounding as he squeezed Jason's hand. "I trust you back."

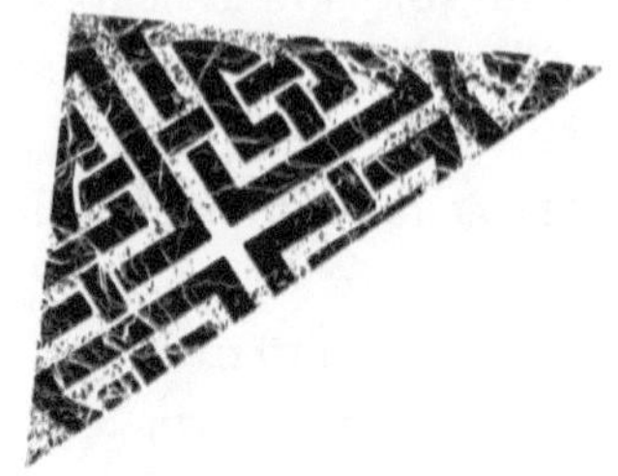

Chapter Forty-Seven

Capital City - A Few Years Ago

S he strode beside Wolfe, half a step back, gaze wary. The Capital was the power center for Pangaea, and a place Wolfe was loath to go on the best of days. This wasn't the best.

Brenna straightened as they stepped into the council chambers. Weapons were not allowed in this section of the Capitol building; it was too close to the Chancellor's rooms.

Steel, on the other side of Wolfe, was not pleased. His hand itched toward the empty holster at his side, and he disguised the action by smoothing down his pant leg.

The other councilors were already present. In the middle of the room, standing cuffed to a metal loop in the floor at the center of the hollow circular table, stood a pale man with sandy blond hair.

Scars marred his skin, fresh wounds beginning to clot on his face and arms. His eyes were defiant, taking in the well-dressed members of the Council with disgust twisting his features.

His temples were bare.

"Another one," Wolfe uttered in a low voice.

Brenna folded her hands behind her back, taking up the right space behind the chair Wolfe sank into.

All around them, the other councilors followed her example and settled into their seats, attendants assuming similar positions behind their superiors. Moments passed in silence.

After a time, Chancellor Collette entered from the hall that led to her own rooms. Low gasps circled the table.

The woman's usually immaculate clothes showed a hint as to the events earlier in the day. A bandage covered her left shoulder, the wrap visible at her side where it wrinkled the fabric of her shirt. Blood had begun to seep through.

"Chancellor," Wolfe whispered.

Brenna's gaze darted to the man, cold fury stirring in her chest.

"I will be all right," Collette said, lifting her right hand in a placating gesture. She stepped slowly to her chair and settled into it. Her movements were stiff, and though she did well hiding it, Brenna noted the wince as she sat.

"What is to be done with the traitor?" The councilor who spoke was seated a few chairs down from Wolfe.

Clamors filled the room. Many called for death, some for interrogation, some for a public example to be made, and others voiced their outrage at the act of someone attacking a Grey-Star. Wolfe remained silent, and Brenna knew that if the prisoner had any trace of power, she'd push to bring him back to Dolor for experimentation. After Allegi had been destroyed, they'd struggled to find enough Alters to make any headway with their research. Those few they'd found in the camps hadn't had enough power to freeze a puddle; the time it took for the suppressant to wean from their systems wasn't worth the effort.

Collette raised her hand again. The room went quiet.

"Tell these people why you came here," she commanded.

The chained man turned to look at her. His hands were stained red, her blood soaked into the cloth of his sleeves. "I don't take orders from you."

"We are Grey-Stars," said a younger councilor. Her ears and nose were decorated with fine jewels. They matched the bits of color pinned in her dark hair.

The man spat on the marble floor. "That means nothing to me. We don't bow to your castes."

A shiver ran down Brenna's spine. Wolfe had been speaking of people like this for the past few years. Strangers to Pangaea, men without gemstones, traitors. They were the reason Wolfe was sure they'd be able to secure more funding. Pangaea needed powerful weapons to face this threat.

Brenna clenched her hand, flexing her arm as hunger surged in her. Her power had been much changed. She was more alive now, healthier and stronger, but that strength came at a cost. A condition.

Silence permeated the space after the man's words. Shocked councilors, the ones not privy to issues of national security, were drenched in confusion and fear.

Wolfe raised her head, ignoring the man, and looked directly at Chancellor Collette. "I would like to put Dolor on the list of possible solutions to this problem."

A man across the table scoffed.

Brenna's gaze flicked to him, her eyes wide with warning. He was whole, strong, and well fed. His energy would keep her satiated for a long time.

Wolfe seemed to feel Brenna's attention shift because she reached back and put a hand on Brenna's forearm.

The warmth of her mentor's fingers steadied Brenna's emotions. She released her breath, returning her focus to the Chancellor.

"Interesting," Collette mused. She glanced at Brenna before fixing Wolfe with a sharp eye. "You believe you'll be able to get information from this man?"

Wolfe inclined her head. "I also believe he may be valuable for our research. Learning more about these... *things*, may help us discover how to utilize their abilities."

Low murmurs swept around the table again. The chained man jerked at his restraints, furious.

"Silence." Collette held up a hand, a wince pinching her face for a brief second. "I am inclined to grant Councilor Wolfe this request. We have enemies." She gazed around the table, meeting each councilor's eye. "More than expected. The rebellion quelled decades ago has reared its head once more. It seems a few of them managed to evade the extermination."

A few intakes of air, Brenna's among them, followed Collette's words.

"They are a danger to us all." Collette gestured to the man.

He shook his head, his lips twisted into a sneer. "You're the danger. The system is broken, Chancellor. Your attempts to remain in power put the people of Pangaea in danger. Your inability to step into the future keeps us prisoners. But no more." His chest heaved with emotion, tears glistening in his eyes. "We will not be chained."

Cracking sounded from above.

Steel moved first. His arm flew around Wolfe's torso, and he brought both her and the chair to the ground with a loud slam.

The Chancellor's guards were on her nearly as quickly. She was up and away from the table, Black-Stars blocking her from the man.

The other councilors followed suit, springing from their seats with cries of fear and confusion.

Only Brenna remained in place.

She watched, fascinated, as the ceiling cracked. Earthen brown roots grew at an alarming speed. They forced their way through the concrete, shattering lights and stone, reaching for the councilors and their guards.

The man in chains was crying. Blood dripped from his nose, mixing with his tears.

Brenna tilted her head, wondering at his folly. Buildings were easy to fix, easy to replace. He'd gone for the kill only hours ago, but this... this felt weak.

Then a scream broke through the already deafening sounds of destruction.

Brenna turned. Collette cowered behind her Black-Stars. Roots shot toward her, faster than Brenna would have expected.

She reacted.

Her hands flung forward, palms reaching toward the traitor as her eyes met his. His body jerked. His plants stopped, froze, and then wilted as he lost the connection. The green energy within him spiraled to his center.

The pain on his face grew; his breath came quick and shallow. Brenna's lips twisted into snarling victory as she yanked.

He screamed. Screamed and screamed as his power—his life—arched and pooled in her palms. It surged down her arms, feeding the hunger within. He seemed to shrivel. The light within him went out.

He collapsed to the ground, the rattling of the chains drowning the sound of his last breaths.

Silence fell.

Chapter Forty-Eight

Southern Mountains

The ache within hadn't faded by the time they got back on the road. Anthony had found Juliana sitting away from everyone else, her gaze distant, silent tears running down her cheeks.

When he'd mentioned healing Elaine, she'd scrambled to her feet, rubbed her face dry with the back of her hands, and told him she couldn't.

He didn't question it. She'd brought him back from the dead; of course she'd still be drained.

Ichi didn't understand her refusal. His flare of frustration led to a heated conversation, during which Anthony had stepped between Ichi and Juliana and told the man that, if he wanted to help Elaine, he needed to get them all in the truck so they could get somewhere safe.

The tension had only built from there.

Daisy drove. Taz had given her pointers during his stints behind the wheel, a fact Daisy had shared with Anthony through a fresh wave of tears.

Anthony had pulled her close and held her tight, like he had every time she'd gotten hurt protecting Taz from bullies in Abredea. The three of them had been inseparable for so long. The absence of Taz's laughter in the air created a crushing silence.

Anthony sat by the window, Jane between the two of them. He glanced over. Daisy stared straight ahead, her whole body stiff. Her power made this harder than it was for him. She was pouring every ounce of free concentration into keeping her emotions in check.

Jane had volunteered to ride up front with the two of them. Her mental wards were some of the strongest in the group; useful in case Daisy's power slipped through her own shields.

Juliana was in the back, sleeping. At least, he hoped she was asleep. She needed the rest.

He wanted to be beside her, hold her hand, rub her neck as she drifted to sleep. But it was clear she wanted space. And, as much as he would benefit from being close to her, it wouldn't be fair to take that comfort when she needed time alone.

Besides, his guilt cut into him so sharply, he wasn't sure he knew how to talk to her about it. This was so different from what had happened to May. This was something either of them could have stopped, something that could have been entirely avoided had they made a few different choices.

Anthony shook his head, his jaw tight. At some point they'd need to talk. He'd need to explain how much this wasn't her fault.

It was his.

Hours passed and the sun eventually broke the darkness to their left. Light peeked over the barren rolling hills. Ahead, monstrous mountains rose into the sky. They were taller than anything Anthony had seen before. Where the mountains outside of Abredea were green, these were rocky and brown. Instead of forest and rivers, dry fields of golden grass sloped up, turning to foothills that then faded into jagged, rocky terrain as they drew closer to the mountains.

What they'd do when they reached the end of the road, Anthony didn't know. They'd been told to go south, and they had. In about an hour, they'd likely be as far south as the truck would allow. If they had to go on foot, would they traverse the mountains in the hopes of finding a path through? Or an abandoned village they could repurpose? Or were they leaving Pangaea?

It had all been discussed, every option they could think of. Anthony was of the mind that finding a place to settle would be best. Jason wanted to hunt down whatever help Carthik had promised the Haven kids. He'd sent them south for a reason; there must be something *here*.

Yet, as Anthony dozed off and on, the scenery didn't change. Everything was dry, dead, cold. He missed the trees.

Jane grunted and broke Anthony from his thoughts. He followed her pointed finger.

Hawk swooped down from the sky, darting in front of the windshield as Daisy pulled the truck to the edge of the gravel trail they'd been following.

Anthony tossed Hawk's pants out the window, and a moment later the man was panting beside him, his eyes wide with fear.

"Black-Stars, behind us."

Anthony's blood went cold. The wolf within him growled; the rumble vibrated through his body. Furious heat flared.

"How close?" Anthony asked, jerking the door open and stepping out to join Hawk.

The other man shook his head. "Close. Maybe an hour. They're coming up fast. A few bikes and two trucks."

Jane met Anthony's eye, then turned and slid through the wall connecting the cab to the bed of the truck. A few seconds passed before there was a commotion of voices.

Jason jumped from the back, followed closely by Samaira, Cho, Ichi, and Juliana.

"What's the plan?" Jason demanded, striding toward Anthony and Hawk with his hands clenched into fists.

"Can we outrun them?" Ichi asked Hawk.

The man shook his head. "They're faster than us, by a lot. I'm guessing an hour before they catch up, maybe a little longer if we're moving."

"Plan quickly," Samaira shot out. She looked at Ichi, then Juliana.

Jules flinched. She met Anthony's gaze, and he tried for a comforting smile.

"We need to go," Ichi said. He gestured to the mountains ahead of them. "We can lose them in the mountains."

Juliana shook her head. "I don't know that we can. We have no idea if this road continues, or if we will hit a dead end when we get past the hills. We could be leading ourselves into a trap or leading the Black-Stars to..."

She glanced at Cho.

The younger man nodded. "Carthik didn't say what was waiting."

"We have to do *something*." Hawk crossed his arms over his bare chest. His gaze darted around, anxiety in every tight movement.

Anthony inhaled, his hands feeling unnatural at his sides. He longed to interlace his fingers with Juliana's, but she stood across the small circle from him, avoiding his eye.

"This is a bad spot for it." Anthony glanced around, they were entirely exposed here, no high ground and nowhere to hide.

"We need to move." Juliana sighed, her brows drawn together in her thinking frown. "Get as far as we can, and then give the little ones a chance to make it."

Silence permeated the group for a few long seconds.

"What does that mean?" Ichi turned to stare at her.

Juliana clenched her jaw, and Anthony prepared to step between them again. "It means we fight."

Samaira let out a pained sound, crossing her arms and clutching her elbows.

Jason's gaze flicked to Cho for a moment before a grin crossed his face. "Finally." He turned to his twin. "Time to get some revenge."

Samaira looked startled for a brief moment, then nodded, determination chasing relief across her features.

"We don't have many fighters," Ichi said with a sigh. "Those of us without active powers have limited abilities to help."

"We have weapons." Cho met his brother's gaze and held it. "If we can give the children time to get ahead, get somewhere safe or—"

"We've tried that before," Ichi interrupted, his expression twisted with fear and frustration.

Anthony clenched his hands, recalling Cho's horrific description of the raid on Haven.

"This is different, Ichi," Jason said. "Besides," the smile slid from his face, "what choice do we have?"

Another second passed.

Anthony shook his head. "We don't 'ave time for this; we've gotta go."

Juliana nodded, turned from the group, and went to the driver's side of the cab. Within a minute, the rest of them had climbed back aboard. The front was cramped with Jason, Cho, Daisy, and Anthony snug beside Juliana. Hawk had left his pants again, choosing to fly above them and help Juliana locate a good route.

The gravel road deteriorated just as Juliana predicted. The truck was built for Black-Star troops. It was sturdy, but the tires weren't designed for the rocky terrain. The trail was uneven, sloping up at times, then dipping down into deep rocky crevices between the rolling hills.

After only a few more miles, they were forced to stop. The sound of transports reached their ears as they hurried to turn the truck sideways, wedging it between the natural rock walls and giving themselves some cover.

The mountains towered ahead of them. Their road petered out into a smaller, dry riverbed. It wound up into the mountains, disappearing into the towering stone.

Anthony pointed the trail out to Daisy as the children clambered out of the truck. "Through there. Yeh'll find a place that's hidden from the sky as well as the ground. So none of the flyin' things see yeh."

"Helos," Juliana filled in. Her cheeks went pink when he glanced at her. She met his gaze for half a second, then looked away. She fiddled with the plasma gun in her hands, checking the cartridge and shoving an extra plasma block into her pants pocket.

"Find a place," Anthony continued, his stomach churning at the thought of sending Daisy away. "Hunker down, try to cover yourselves with brush or somethin'. Stay outta sight. When the fightin's done, we'll find yeh."

Daisy's expression was mutinous.

She looked from him to Juliana with tears in her eyes. "Why are you staying?" she demanded. "You don't have an active power."

Juliana closed her eyes, her lips trembling as she turned to her friend. "I'm sorry, Daisy. The children need someone like you with them. Someone safe."

Daisy's lips twisted as a few of the tears fell. She shook her head. "I hate this."

Juliana nodded. "I do too. I'm... I'm sorry."

Anthony inhaled; the tears of his friends sent a salty smell into the air.

Daisy shook her head, her jaw tight. "I know it's not your fault. We only have so many guns. And you're right, the children need someone with them."

It had been a tense drive. Shouting from the numerous children who wanted to stay and fight had culminated in Ichi pronouncing his verdict, his tone and demeanor effectively halting the arguments. It was Anthony's first glimpse at the leader Cho had described when talking about his brother.

Jason had snorted from the front seat, earning a nudge from Cho.

Ichi was staying to fight. Jane as well, which Tommy had reacted to by going invisible for a full minute. Luna and Nova were joining them. Abilene stood a few paces away preparing her weapon with Samaira doing the same beside her. Jason and Cho spoke in hushed voices, inches from each other, Jason's hands on Cho's shoulders.

There were others who wanted to stay and may have been helpful. Kim, with her electricity. Sky, who might have pulled plants from the ground to slow the Black-Stars. But this wasn't their time to fight. They were too young.

Daisy reached out, pulling Juliana into a tight hug. She did the same to Anthony, releasing him as the sound of buzzing filled the air.

Her eyes went wide as she gawked up into the distance.

Anthony turned, heart already hammering in his chest, and winced. Three helos zoomed toward them, pinpricks at the moment, but approaching fast.

"Go," Juliana called, her voice high and tense. She stepped away from Daisy and gestured with her free arm. "Go, everyone, now."

There was hesitation. Tommy clung to Jane's hand as the girl tried to pry him off without hurting him. Elaine stood vacant as Ichi pushed her fraying braids out of her face and kissed her cheek.

Juliana climbed onto one of the truck's thick tires. "Listen," she shouted. "We don't have time for this. You have to go. You have to go now and give us a chance to get them off our tail. Please."

Anthony nodded, clapping his hands together and calling out as well. "Yeh heard her, get movin'. Get as far as yeh can, and we'll join yeh when we've made them think twice about comin' after us. Go."

Jason and Cho joined them, herding the younger children ahead. Daisy took hold of Sky and Kim's hands and began a hurried pace toward the narrow opening in the rocky cliffs.

The others followed. The walking turned to running, short legs pumping quickly as the *whump whump whump* of the helos became audible.

Anthony held out his hand, and Juliana took it as she jumped down from the tire. He gave her a grin; a shadow of the smile he'd worn the first time he'd taken her into the forest.

She'd returned it that day. A bit of derision in her gaze, but a smile on her lips. This time she pursed her lips together, pain etched into her expression. "Anthony, I have to tell you... I couldn't—"

Her words were cut short by Jason's shout. "Shooters, position yourselves toward the back so you have some cover. Let's get four of you behind the truck." He turned to Luna and Nova. "You two, stay with me and Samaira, here and here." He pointed to the rocky hills on either side of the gravely gulch. "I plan on taking those helos down just like last time, but it'd be good to have someone stopping the pieces from shredding us to bits."

Nova went a little green, but Luna nodded, her eyes narrowed into a fierce gaze.

Juliana turned back to Anthony as the others moved into position. "I have to–"

Anthony leaned in. "I know, but we'll 'ave the time when we're done with all this, I promise."

Juliana's mouth opened, and she sucked in the smallest of breaths. Anthony stepped forward and gently pushed his forehead to hers. She stifled a sob.

He turned and darted behind the truck, pulling his shirt over his head, and kicking off his jeans. A few seconds later he returned on four paws. The sounds of the Black-Stars, heightened by his wolf's ears, raised the hair on his back.

Juliana stood at the edge of the truck, gun in hand, gaze fixed on the road they'd come up. Anthony went to her, nuzzled her hip, and then continued on.

He leapt, powerful hind legs launching him to the top of a set of crumbling boulders. He sank down, eyes watching for the approaching Black-Stars. They had the mountain to their backs, surprise on their side, and the little ones were safe.

Now was the time May had talked about. The time to fight for the people he loved.

She hadn't done it. She hadn't told him the truth.

Juliana trembled. She stood alone, Daisy gone with the children, Anthony on the rocks, Taz dead.

Taz dead.

Juliana inhaled, her stomach tight, and poured effort into shoring up her mental wards. The wall within her was strong, it would keep her power at bay. It would stop her from hurting anyone else she cared about.

"We have to survive this."

Juliana turned her head. Jane stood beside her, worry and anger intense in her eyes. She looked at Juliana, holding her gaze. "We have to."

Juliana nodded.

Chapter Forty-Nine

Southern Mountains

The metal of the plasma gun felt odd in Cho's hands. The texture of it against his skin sent a ripple of anxiety through his already worry-clenched stomach.

Rumbling engines of the Black-Star vehicles echoed through the hills around them, the rocks and mountains eating the sound.

"Hey."

Cho turned, warmth easing his nerves. Jason leaned against the truck door, aiming for casual and missing it entirely with the intensity of his gaze.

Cho sighed. He took a moment to lock down the tendrils of power reaching for Jason.

They didn't have much time.

"I'm not leaving this fight," Cho said as Jason opened his mouth.

The man hesitated for a second, closed his mouth, and jutted his jaw to the side. "I know. I wouldn't ask you to. I just wanted to..." Jason reached out, and Cho took his hand.

They stayed that way for a moment, fingers intertwined, hearts pounding with fear and anticipation. Then Cho stepped forward, and Jason pulled him close.

"I trust you," Jason murmured against Cho's scraggly hair. "If it gets bad—"

"I'm not leaving, Jason." Cho leaned back to look up into Jason's dark eyes. "But I trust you too. If it gets bad, we all run, together."

Jason nodded, his jaw tight. The two separated. Jason squeezed Cho's hand and then he was gone. He jogged around the bottleneck space they'd chosen to make their stand, and a moment later he was above them, standing at the top of the dry grassy mound with a view of the terrain and approaching Black-Stars. Luna stood beside him, her hands in tight fists, the wind whipping at her hair and dress.

Cho swallowed. He shook his head to clear it, tightened his grip on the weapon dangling at his side, and turned to face the road.

They'd angled the truck and wedged it to block the rough gravel road. With any luck the Black-Stars would be slowed to walking. If they came through the small gap between the crumbling rocks and the truck, it would be a tight fit and, hopefully, they could be stopped.

Juliana came up beside him a few seconds later. Cho caught a fragment of the overwhelming grief and guilt within her before she cast him a glance and slammed her shields into place.

"Are you all right?" he asked.

"Thought you had a grip on not feeling other people's emotions," she muttered through gritted teeth.

Cho raised and lowered a shoulder. "I don't need my power to read the guilt on your face, Juliana. I miss him too, but this wasn't your fault."

"That's the thing, Cho," she said in a low voice. "It was. And I can't fix it." She shifted, stepping away from him, and crouched at the edge of the truck with her gaze trained on the road ahead.

He frowned, trying to pin down the meaning behind her words.

Not far from them, Anthony let out a long howl. A shot rang out, Samaira shouted, and Cho returned his focus to the matter at hand.

Chapter Fifty

Southern Mountains

Samaira cracked her neck and glanced down at Abilene from her position atop the hill across from Jase. The woman was crouched with her back to a truck tire, a plasma gun clenched in her hands. She looked up, caught Samaira's eye, and gave a weak smile.

A month ago she'd been a promising Blue-Star, rising up through the ranks of medical researchers with a promising future as a high caste citizen of Pangaea ahead of her. Now she was crouched in the dirt, holding a gun, prepared to give her life for a group of raggedy kids with powers.

Samaira's heart lurched.

Her fingertips burned. The heat from her power shifted within, flowing through her veins, and causing an ache to build in her arms.

Claire was with the little ones.

She'd offered to stay. She was nearly as old as Luna and Nova and was arguably more powerful than the twins when it came to combat. But Samaira had insisted she go. The girl wasn't like her power; she wasn't cold. Taking a life would hurt her more than some of the others.

Still, it would have helped to have her close.

Samaira glanced at Nova. She knelt in the dry grass, her braids a frizzled mess, dress as dirty as the ground beneath her. Their eyes met and Nova tilted her head. Samaira offered up as near a comforting smile as she could.

It was difficult. Part of her mind was busy keeping the cage holding her power intact.

The fury within her, at the helos growing ever closer, the transports rumbling toward them less than a mile away, fed the fire. These Black-Stars had chased them across the country. They'd tortured and murdered children. They'd never let them rest. Never let them sleep.

The fire within burned so bright it had been too long since Samaira had gotten a full night of sleep.

Jason watched her from across the crevice. His dark gaze, identical to hers and their mother's, had kept finding her since Taz had died. She couldn't get a read on him. Not like she used to.

Instead, she felt a chasm between them. Their connection had been fractured, and she knew he was still angry with her. Even his earlier comment about revenge, which had seemed so like the old Jason, had been tinged with something else.

Samaira's power flared. She gritted her teeth, a grunt escaping as the muzzle of her plasma gun dipped to the ground.

"Samaira?" Nova murmured.

Samaira shook her head, clenching her jaw so tight it felt like her teeth would crack. Now was not the time.

Ahead of them, the first of the Black-Stars had rounded the final bend.

Two motorcycles roared toward them, a massive transport not far behind. This truck was larger than the one they'd stolen. Larger than they'd anticipated when they'd set this trap.

The Black-Stars might try to ram the feeble barricade.

Nova whimpered.

A helo soared overhead, the chopping sound it made drove another rush of rage through Samaira.

Time seemed to slow. The seconds before action ticked by, each stretching far longer than they should have.

Below them, Anthony howled, someone shot off a plasma bolt, and time sped up again.

"Take the driver!" Samaira called to the people below.

She raised her gun, fell to one knee, and took aim at the helo circling back toward them. It fired sporadically, projectiles slamming into the dirt and throwing debris.

Samaira fired back.

Chaos reigned around her as she aimed and squeezed the trigger. Fear and worry clenched her heart. Someone screamed. Another person shouted. There was a crash. More plasma bolts flashed in the trench below. The stench of smoke filled the air.

Jason let out a vicious screech. Samaira turned as her brother brought flames to his hands, pulled them together, and sent a swirling vortex of fire into the heart of the helo.

It exploded.

Nova screamed, throwing up her hands as shrapnel rained down on them all. Across from them, Luna did the same.

Bits of metal still fell, sharp chunks crashing to the ground with loud slams. But the twins held most of it at bay.

"Send it toward them!" a voice called from below.

Samaira glanced down. Juliana stood behind the hood of the truck, a gash across her arm, and a smoking plasma gun in her hands.

"Luna, Nova," Juliana called up again, catching the twins' attention as they struggled to hold up the massive amount of debris. "Rain it down on them, aim for the soldiers and the engines."

It took time, precious seconds as the twins concentrated. Samaira fired over and over. The transports had finally halted. Black-Stars poured from them in numbers that sent a chill through Samaira's overheated chest.

Luna and Nova dropped the debris.

Over the din of agonized screams and shouts of pain, Jason's voice reached Samaira's ears.

"Get rid of that gun and *help*!"

She caught his eye, fire burning in his palms as he threw flame after flame at the Black-Stars below them.

A plasma bolt grazed his shoulder, and he snarled. The man who'd shot him went down, a burst of fire slamming into his chest before Anthony in wolf form leapt on him and tore out his throat.

Nova screamed again.

Samaira followed the girl's gaze to two more helos headed their direction. Her skin burned; the pain of keeping her power in check was becoming too much.

Below them, the Black-Star transport crushed by helo debris had been pushed out of the way. The second transport sped forward so fast that Black-Stars had to leap aside to avoid being flattened.

Samaira spun, tossing her weapon aside and shouted to the fighters below, "*Get back!*"

Juliana heard her. Blue eyes met black for a split second before the woman jumped into action. She sprinted along the side of the truck, grabbing arms and shoving people out of the way.

She'd barely cleared it when the Black-Star truck T-boned their little transport. The roar of metal and fire and splintering wood drowned the sounds of the helo for a few brief seconds.

Then the aircraft reached them.

One of the helos circled above, close enough for Samaira to make out the pilot's hateful expression before—

"*No!*" Samaira shouted as a blast of plasma flew from the helo, slamming into the cliff Jason and Luna stood atop.

The hill exploded. Jason and Luna flew through the air before hitting the ground hard and rolling down into the gravel road. Rock and dirt thundered down on top of them. The Black-Stars in the trench were pummeled by the cascade of debris as well. A number of them retreated around the bend, arms above their heads to avoid being knocked unconscious.

Nova was screaming. Screaming and not stopping. Samaira's ears rang.

She backed up a few feet, and then took a running jump off the hill. Samaira rolled as she landed on top of the Black-Star's truck. Fear and fury spiraled within her. She hopped to the ground, kicked a Black-Star in the gut as he tried to stand, and scrambled toward her brother.

Jason lay face down at the side of the road. Blood dripped from the base of his neck.

Samaira let out a furious grunt of denial and grabbed his shoulders. She flipped him.

He was breathing.

Her relief was fleeting as she realized they were on the wrong side of the truck wreckage.

"Where's Luna?" Nova's terrified voice sounded from above, and Samaira looked up to see her floating down from their hill. "Where is she?" the girl demanded, tears bright on her cheeks.

Samaira glanced around, her chest heaving. The oxygen within wasn't enough to cool the flames of her power. Clouds of dust obscured her vision.

"There." She pointed. A few yards away, Luna lay half-buried under rocks and dirt. With a lingering worried look at her brother, Samaira ran to the girl and began digging her out.

"I've got it." Nova landed beside her and turned her palms toward her twin. The rubble on Luna began to shake, then it rose and fell to Luna's side. "Get Jason."

Samaira would have put a hand on Nova's shoulder, but there was too much heat beneath her skin. Instead, she gave a firm nod and hurried back to her brother.

"Wake up, Jase," she breathed.

He didn't move.

The thumping of the helo sounded above. Samaira blinked back tears as she looked up. It bore down, guns trained on them.

Something shrieked through the sky, from the direction of the mountains. A small projectile slammed into the metal hull of the craft. A split second passed.

The helo exploded.

Samaira turned, covering Jason's body with hers as twisted metal and flames rained down on them. Less of it hit than she expected. Pain trickled across her back, but the brunt of the debris had somehow missed them.

"Got it," came a limp voice.

Samaira raised her head in time to see Nova sway and then collapse beside her twin.

"*Nacra,*" Samaira muttered.

Three unconscious people, a second wave of Black-Stars audible down the road, and a pile of twisted truck metal between her and the others.

Bodies littered the ground around them, the remains of the first wave of soldiers. The debris from the helo had fallen almost exclusively on those nearby, shredding them to pieces.

A shape raced toward her from a gap in the trucks. Short, furry, black.

She exhaled her relief as Anthony sprinted past on all fours, his wolf's jaws bloody, teeth bared as he took up a guard position in front of them, facing the approaching enemy.

Juliana and Abilene were close behind him.

"How bad?" Abilene called before they reached Jason.

"He's hurt," Samaira responded. "I don't know. Nova overexerted her powers and Luna..."

Abilene darted past Samaira and straight to the girls.

Juliana knelt beside Jason. She closed her eyes and inhaled, her hands moving slowly over his body. Blue light seeped from her palms. Tendrils of it danced around the bloody splotches on Jason's clothes.

"Wake up, Jase," Samaira repeated, the strain in her voice clear against the din around them.

"His leg is broken, and he has two cracked ribs," Juliana murmured. "That's the worst of it, at least. There are a handful of other wounds, but nothing he can't recover from."

"He has to wake up, Juliana." Samaira's throat caught.

"I know," Juliana whispered through clenched teeth. She closed her hands into fists, her fingers trembling. "I can... I can get him on his feet, but I can't heal it all."

Samaira nodded vigorously. "Anything. Can I help?"

Juliana shook her head. "Keep them off me, but besides that, no." Her power emerged again, stemming from her fingers this time as she placed them on Jason's chest.

"Luna?" Samaira asked, turning to Abilene.

The woman glanced up, her face taut. "She's in bad shape. Still unconscious and I'm not sure exactly what's wrong. I think she hit her head when she fell. There isn't much other external damage."

Abilene grunted as she rose, Luna cradled in her arms like a small child. "I'm getting her back to the others, then I'll come for Nova. Hold them off as long as you can."

Samaira nodded.

She picked up the gun Abilene had dropped and fired a few shots over Anthony at the Black-Stars poking their heads around the bend in the road. Plasma slammed into the rocky wall of the crevice. The Black-Stars returned fire, their shots leaving divots in the road. Samaira took one down before the other scurried back.

"Come on, Jase," Samaira snarled.

Juliana glanced up, her eyes wide as the light went out of her hands. "That's as much as I can do."

Samaira knelt. "Wake up."

Jason's eyes fluttered, and he let out a groan.

"Wake up, Jase," she shouted this time, loud enough to get a jerking reaction as his eyes popped open and he blinked up at her.

"I'm up. Frost."

"We have to move," Samaira said. She and Juliana hauled him to his feet.

He cried out in pain, and Samaira shifted to take more of his weight.

"I think," he bit out through gritted teeth, "my leg is broken."

"I'm sorry," Juliana said from his other side, where she was helping to support him. "I got your ribs back together, the leg was too much."

"Frost," he said again.

"Juliana, you got him?" Samaira swallowed, her throat thick with dust. She couldn't leave Nova.

"Yeah."

Samaira ducked out from under Jason's arm as he let out a yelp. She ran back to Nova and hefted the girl across her back. She sucked in a breath and exhaled, urging the heat in her hands to retreat in order to avoid burning Nova's skin.

Anthony howled. Samaira spun, dread plunging into her stomach.

The wolf sprinted toward them, a third Black-Star troop transport, flanked by half a dozen bikes, roared around the bend behind him.

"*Go!*" Samaira shouted. She raced forward, catching up to Jason and Juliana.

They were twenty yards away from cover when Cho burst out. He caught sight of Jason and blanched with fear.

"Get back," Samaira called. "Cho—"

He ignored her and ran to Jason and Juliana. He shoved his shoulder under Jason's dangling arm and helped haul him toward the opening between mangled trucks. Abilene returned a split second later, hurrying to help Samaira carry Nova through.

Samaira handed her the girl.

Abilene hesitated as Anthony sprinted by on all fours. "Samaira?"

Samaira gritted her teeth. "Get everyone back. Far as you can."

Abilene shook her head, eyes going wide. "No. You don't have to do this."

Samaira's gaze flicked to her brother, being helped through the gap with more curses of pain, to the Black-Stars behind them, to the dull orange glow beginning to show beneath her skin. "Yes, I do."

"Nacra," Abilene spat. "What if you... Sam..."

"Get them back. And tell Jase... tell him I'm sorry."

Samaira turned back without another word. People called after her. Jason's voice grew louder in the mix of confused shouts as she strode toward the oncoming killers.

She wasn't sorry for Abilene, for the stolen kisses in the dark, the comfort she'd provided in that wretched place, the warmth of her gaze when she thought Samaira wasn't looking.

She was sorry she hadn't explained. Hadn't told Jase about the crumbling cage inside her that was barely holding her power together. Hadn't fixed things with him before this moment. Hadn't realized he was in love too.

Angry tears burned in the corners of her eyes. A plasma bolt hit the ground a few feet to her right.

She glanced at the scorched dirt, then toward the man who'd fired on her. He brought his bike to a screeching halt, dust flying up from the back tire as it skidded along the gravel.

Jason's voice echoed off the rocks behind her. He was screaming, cursing, and shouting at Anthony to let him go.

Samaira met the gaze of the Black-Star before her. She raised her hands.

She let go.

The cage within her did not *open*. It exploded. Heat scorched every nerve in her body, every inch of skin felt as though it was being burned from within. All around her, the world turned red. Heat in hues of orange and yellow splintered and warped the air.

The first Black-Star to meet the flames didn't have time to scream.

The ones behind him did.

Their terrified voices shouted to retreat, get back, take cover... all things it was too late for.

Samaira's heat grew. Her power was hungry, angry. She focused every fiber of her being into keeping the flame burning forward, away from the smoldering trucks behind her. Away from her family.

Her skin blistered.

The Black-Stars continued to die.

Eventually, pain overcame power. She opened her mouth, her scream drowned out by the roaring of the flames surrounding her.

The energy dwindled. The inferno within died down to a mere ember.

Samaira's eyes drifted shut. The world went dark and cold.

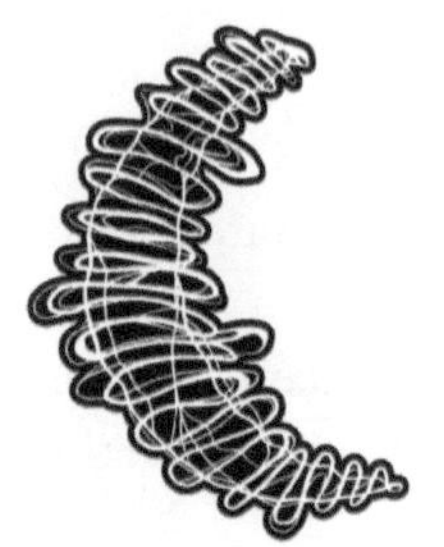

Chapter Fifty-One

Southern Mountains

Samaira was gone. She'd been right behind Juliana and Jason. Just a few yards from cover, from the relative safety of their barricade.

Jason launched off of Juliana's arm the second he realized his sister wasn't with them. He whirled, causing Cho to stumble, and yelped in pain as he hurried toward the trucks.

"No." Abilene blocked his path.

Jason snarled. "Get out of my way."

Juliana hefted her weapon back into both hands, darting between the trucks to glance through an opening of shattered glass. Samaira walked toward the Black-Stars.

"What is she doing?" Juliana demanded, turning to Abilene.

The woman bent to set Nova down. Anthony darted in, back in human form with a ragged pair of pants hastily pulled up. He took the girl and carried her to where her sister lay.

"She's stopping them," Abilene said. Her voice broke.

Juliana's blood went cold.

Jason's eyes widened, and he shoved Abilene to the side. A plasma shot went off in the distance. Anthony rose from where he'd placed Nova and leapt at Jason as the injured man tried to get through the gap.

"Stop," Anthony urged through gritted teeth. "Jason, yeh can't go out there. There are too many."

Jason didn't hear him. Even with the broken leg, he struggled against Anthony as though he was the enemy.

Anthony's strong arms held fast, tightened around Jason's, pinning them to his side.

"Jason," Cho said softly.

Jane leaned against a rocky cliff wall, guarding Luna and Nova's unconscious bodies and clutching her side, tears streaming down her cheeks as she looked on.

Juliana took half a step forward. Her heart broke at the desperation clear through Jason's fury.

"No," Jason shouted. "Get the *frost* off me!"

A roar took the breath from all of them.

Anthony's grip loosened. Jason limped to the gap and gasped.

The rest of them hurried to see, catching glimpses through the debris with varying degrees of horror.

Juliana put a hand over her mouth.

Samaira was the center of a flaming vortex. The Black-Stars scrambled for escape, but there was none. The flame thrower thrust her hands forward and columns of fire erupted from her.

Mere seconds ticked by as men and machinery were incinerated beyond recognition. It felt longer.

The fire grew smaller, the shades of blue returning to red, and then there was nothing.

Samaira fell, her body smoking.

Cho and Abilene were the first through the gap. Jason was frozen, his face twisted with horror.

"Help them?" Juliana murmured as Anthony glanced her way. He nodded and darted off after them.

A thwumping sound drew her gaze. The third helo had done a full circle over them. She raised her gun, aiming for one of the weapons strapped to its side.

It was out of range before she lined up the shot.

"Is it leaving?" Jane asked breathlessly.

Juliana turned. The girl sucked in strained gulps of air, one hand on her weapon, the other holding her side where a plasma bolt had burned away a chunk of her shirt.

"Jane."

"I'm fine," she spat.

Juliana ignored her, hurrying over to at least inspect the injury. She didn't dare heal anything else. Not with how much she'd put into Jason's ribs. The fear of...

"It's not too bad," she murmured as her blue power dissipated. "I can't—we'll be able to patch you up when we get somewhere safe."

Jane scoffed, but there was relief in her eyes.

"You know what I mean," Juliana said with a weak grin.

"She's alive!" Came a shout from beyond the trucks.

Jason let out a sob, sinking to the ground with his wounded leg stretched out in front of him. His hands went to his face, covering the tears as his entire body shook.

Juliana caught a glimpse of Cho, Abilene, and Anthony dragging Samaira back to them, Abilene's jacket draped over the woman's torso.

Relief bit into her as well. Dull pain called to her from the small cuts and bruises she'd sustained from various debris and near-misses from plasma bolts, but she barely felt it. They were alive.

They'd survived the attack.

The helo's thump, thump, thump, faded into the distance. They'd need to do a sweep, a double check for Black-Stars from the convoy that had chased them down, but Juliana doubted anything survived Samaira's fury.

Scuffling sounds echoed through the gap, and Juliana rushed forward to help pull Samaira's unconscious form through. They laid her beside Jason, draping another jacket across her legs. Her clothes had burned off. Every inch of her skin was red and blistered.

Juliana winced at the pain Samaira had endured and was silently grateful she wasn't awake to feel it now.

"Do you both heal quickly?" Juliana murmured to Jason.

He nodded, his jaw tight as he stared at his sister.

"Good," she exhaled.

"Jules."

Juliana froze. Anthony's tone sent a shot of renewed fear through her.

She turned slowly, along with the others as they all followed his gaze.

Ichi stood at the far end of the little section of road where they'd staged their stand. He faced away from them, his back tight, hands outstretched, fear locked in each word.

"Let her go; this is over."

Standing with her back to the rocks was a Black-Star. The woman's eyes were wide, terror drained the color from her face. One arm was locked around Elaine's shoulders, the other clenched a plasma pistol, the muzzle pressed against Elaine's mid-section.

Juliana sucked in a breath. Behind her, Cho let out a sound like a wounded animal.

Anthony took two steps forward; Jason struggled to get up behind him. Juliana put up her hand to stop them.

The Black-Stars spoke. "What... what *are* you people? What did you do to my team?" She glanced up, her gaze darting in the direction the helo had fled.

Juliana slowly set her weapon on the ground. "You don't—"

"Stop," the woman shouted, her gun pressing harder into Elaine's side.

Juliana halted.

Ichi cast a glance her way. He shook his head.

Juliana gritted her teeth, helplessness striking a familiar chord in her chest.

"We're just trying to live," Ichi said. His voice was low, but in the hushed aftermath of the battle, it carried the few yards back to the rest of them. "We don't want to hurt anyone—"

The Black-Star let out a derisive laugh. "Tell that to the frosted firebug. You killed my men. All of them."

Juliana swallowed.

Ichi's hands, out and empty before him, trembled. "Please. Don't hurt her."

"You're gonna kill me." The Black-Star's voice shook. Her dark eyes darted around the group.

Juliana wondered what she saw. A pair of twin girls bleeding from various wounds, unconscious on the ground? A man barely able to stand on his broken leg? A handful of children fighting for their lives?

Or did she see them all the way Juliana saw herself? Dangerous. Deadly. Unable to stop the disastrous effects of their power.

"We aren't," Ichi said. He glanced back and Juliana nodded along.

"We don't want to hurt anyone," she added in a small voice.

The Black-Star shook her head. "I don't... I don't believe you."

She glanced down at Elaine. Ichi's lover was shorter than the Black-Star by several inches. Her gaze was distant, a soft smile on her lips as though she didn't have a care in the world at that moment.

"Please," Ichi's voice cracked. "I'm begging you to let her go. You let her go, we let you go. No one needs to get hurt."

The pain in Ichi's voice broke Elaine's reverie.

"Ichi?" Elaine blinked into lucidity. She glanced back, freezing as the gun was shoved into her side again.

"Don't move," the Black-Star snapped, panic in her voice.

"Ichi, what's happening?" Tears grew in Elaine's dark eyes. They streamed down her cheeks as the Black-Star tightened her grip.

"I'll ask you one more time," Ichi said through clenched teeth.

Juliana inched forward. There was no way for her to get around behind the Black-Star. Ichi's tone had shifted; the fear melted into anger.

"Let. Her. Go."

The Black-Star's hand shook. She cast her gaze around the group again.

Ichi took another step, and the Black-Star froze. Her limbs appeared stuck; eyes wide as blood began to seep from them like tears.

"Let her *go*," Ichi repeated. He lifted his hand.

The Black-Star choked out half an unintelligible word. Blood vessels popped under the skin of her face, and blood flowed from her nose and ears. She gasped. Collapsed.

And as she fell, the crackle of a plasma shot filled the air.

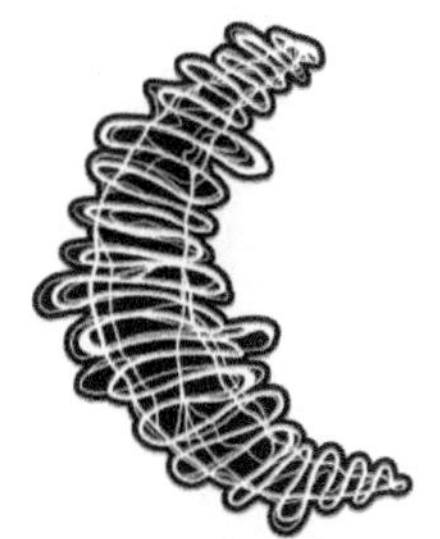

Chapter Fifty-Two

Southern Mountains

Elaine's body crumpled to the ground. The sound was startlingly quiet. The echo of the gunshot muddled the stillness.

Juliana was moving before the Black-Star finished twitching on the ground. Ichi reached Elaine before her, the sound coming out of him enough to halt Juliana in her tracks and send heartbreak through her core.

Cho got to Ichi first. "No, no, no," he murmured, tears streaming down his cheeks as he stared at Elaine.

"Is she..." Jane stopped a few paces away, one hand still at her side where blood oozed slowly from her wound. Her face was pale, fear and pain etched in the lines that aged her well past her fourteen years.

Juliana put a hand over her mouth, trying to stop the tears before they fell.

"No." Ichi turned, Elaine half-cradled in his arms as his eyes met Juliana's. Blood dripped from his right nostril and eye. "She's not dead."

A pit seemed to open in her stomach. She hurried forward, like she was supposed to, and knelt at Elaine's side.

Ichi was wrong. Wrong or desperate or lying, maybe all three.

Elaine was dead. A scorching hole had blasted through her side and out her stomach. It had been quick.

"Ichi," Juliana breathed, fear pumping through every vein in her body at his expression. "I can't. She's gone."

"No." Ichi rested Elaine's head on the ground and stood before her and Juliana. "No, you brought him back," he pointed furiously at Anthony, "you can do it again."

Juliana's lips trembled as she shook her head. "I can't."

"You *won't*," he spat.

"Ichi." Cho put a hand on his brother's shoulder, but Ichi knocked him away.

"I can't bring her back, Ichi." Juliana sucked in a breath.

Uneven footsteps crunched across the gravel. Anthony and Jason hobbled over; Jason's arm looped around Anthony's shoulder.

"Why?" Ichi demanded. "Because she's not as important to you? Because you don't love her?"

"Ichi." Jason's voice was soft, tearful as he and Anthony came to a halt beside Jane. "That's not fair."

Juliana's heart beat at an impossible rate. She reached out, her power seeping through Elaine as she searched for any flicker of life. A spark, small and dying, remained in Elaine's head and heart.

Juliana swallowed.

"I don't give a *frost* about fair!" Ichi shouted. "She can save her." He wheeled on Juliana, pointing a shaking finger at Elaine. "You can save her. You're the only one who can do this. So please—"

The anger in his voice cracked, despair and grief and pain splitting through.

"Please..." he said again, his voice barely a whisper.

Juliana's power flared and swirled. It danced within, ready to heal, wanting to fix the bloody mess before her.

She looked at the group around her. The other faces seemed to fade away. Anthony's furrowed brow, confusion and concern lining his features, was all she saw. He gave her the smallest of nods. A motion of comfort, reassurance.

It did nothing to reassure her now. The fear of someone dying like Taz...

But she had to try.

For Ichi, for Cho and the others, for Elaine... she had to try. If this took too much, it would be from her. She'd be paying it back.

"Back up," Juliana whispered.

"What?" Cho knelt. "Juliana, if this is going to hurt you—"

She met his gaze, and he fell silent. There was desperation in her look.

"Keep everyone back."

He nodded.

"Jules," Anthony's voice nearly stopped her.

She didn't respond. Couldn't.

Instead, she sat on her knees and shifted her hands to Elaine's forehead and chest. She sucked in a shaky breath.

Footsteps reassured her that the others were backing up. Before her, Cho took Ichi's arm and pulled him several yards away.

Sweat beaded on Juliana's temples, sliding past her moon-white gemstones and mixing with the tears at the edge of her jaw. The guilt of Taz's death gnawed at her insides. The weight of it pressed into her chest so hard she couldn't breathe.

The pain of the secret, the lie of omission, was somehow greater. Like she betrayed him by not telling their friends the truth. Like she was killing him all over again.

The light of her power sparked within. She dredged it forth, blue tendrils dancing in the air, pressing into Elaine and lighting her midnight skin with a bluish glow. Juliana's vision took on its odd, Alter-seeing characteristic. Ahead of her, Ichi's silver glow and Cho's saffron light were bright against the reddish rocks that surrounded them.

Eliane's golden light was but a speck in the darkness that had taken her.

Juliana bit her lip, exhaled, and poured her power into Elaine. The darkness shrank at the first touch. It melted away like ice under fire, pouring from her body and seeping into the rocky soil below.

The wound healed first, flesh and sinew stitching themselves together under Juliana's watchful eye. Weariness sank in before the gaping hole was gone. Juliana's hands trembled against Elaine's skin.

The light within Elaine flickered. A candle-like flame, facing down a windy night alone.

"Hold on," Juliana breathed.

The golden flame within Elaine blew out.

A familiar hook latched into her chest, just behind her ribs. Terror broke her concentration.

"No," she whispered, trying to pull her power back. It resisted.

Hunger built within the blue light.

"Get back," she tried to shout, but it came out barely a murmur. "Please..."

Her right hand rose. Ahead of her, Ichi's eyes went wide. The silver outline against his almond-colored skin diminished. It pooled at his core, a thin line stretching out, sliding through the air toward Juliana's hand like a magnet pulling metal.

"No." Juliana let out half a sob.

She jerked her hand, but it didn't budge. With every ounce of strength she had, she pulled at her own arm. Her nails sliced through her skin, but it made no difference.

Wind ripped through the rolling hills. Above, the sky darkened with thick clouds.

Ichi stared. He didn't look at the silver strand, didn't seem to see it, but he looked at her as his power contacted her palm.

He gasped. Pain carved lines into his face. He doubled over, barely able to breathe.

Juliana bit through her lip. Tears flowed free, regret and pain and terror clenching her heart.

This couldn't happen again.

Juliana gritted her teeth. No. Not *couldn't*.

This *wouldn't* happen again.

"I won't let it," she breathed.

She hadn't let Wolfe influence her. Hadn't let Steel kill Anthony. Hadn't let Daisy's father hurt her. Hadn't let the medicine for Jimmy be lost.

So many things she'd refused to let happen. Refused to give in to.

This was another. Another moment she would *not* allow.

Juliana closed her eyes and focused the pull. She shifted her power, aiming its hunger toward herself instead of Ichi. The blue light hesitated. She snarled, yanking her hand down.

The movement worked. She broke contact with Ichi. His silver strand slammed back into his body, and the man flew backward.

Juliana barely noticed. Pain pulled at every nerve. Thunder clapped above and she faced the sky, opening her eyes to take in the clouds one last time.

She gasped.

A dark grey storm swirled above her. It was speckled with blue light. Her light.

The clouds shifted as she stared. They spiraled like a tornado, the point fixed on her and Elaine as the wind roared hard enough to whip up the rocks on the road.

Juliana stared, terror and awe gripping her as the storm sank closer to earth than any she'd ever seen. Her power sparked, calling for its matching light. It buzzed through her body, and thrilled every nerve with a pain that was so sharp it was almost a relief.

There was a split second of hesitation. A brief pause as the clouds hovered above her. And then, as had happened with her hand, Juliana's body arched of its own accord.

The cyclone slammed into her chest. Sank *through* her. Without knowing how she did it, her power guided the clouds through her hands. Energy slammed into Elaine. Her body spasmed and a golden light spread across every inch of her skin.

Juliana's palms burned. The storm emptied itself into her. The clouds had been so dark that once the sky was clear again, the sunlight was blinding.

The power lingered inside Juliana, too strong, too intense. It needed out. There was no conscious thought as she pushed it, eased it through Elaine and into the soil below.

Everything blurred. Juliana's ears rang. She stared at her shaking hands, unable to see them. Unable to feel.

The ground roiled and churned beneath her. She took a shallow, faltering breath, and then collapsed across Elaine's body. Everything went dark.

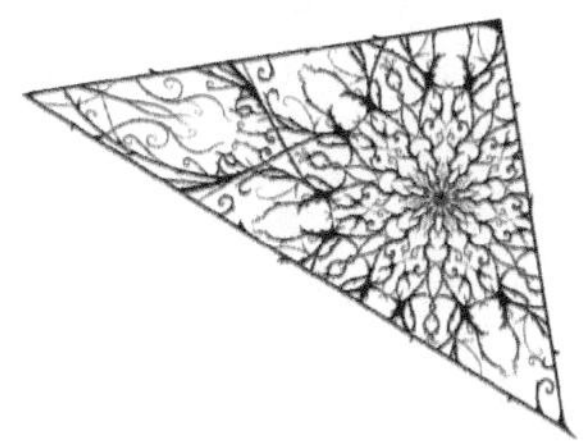

Chapter Fifty-Three

The Ruins of Dolor

Flames had consumed most of Dolor. The wreckage of glass and concrete, failure and ruin, clinked underfoot as Wolfe picked her way through the remains of her office.

There was little left.

"Ms. Wolfe," Keith murmured from behind her. He was bandaged, a burn along his arm healing under white gauze. If his mind didn't hold half the data that had been destroyed, she'd have killed him then and there.

"Yes, Keith." Wolfe stooped, picking up a fragment of a token that had sat on her desk. She tucked it into the little front pocket of her bag.

"Steel is gone, ma'am. He didn't join the squad sent after Brenna. He... we believe he is with Lectius now."

Wolfe nodded absently, her gaze absorbed by the marble-like warping of the glass window that had allowed her to overlook the experiments. "And the squad? Was Brenna able to collect the girl?"

"I'm—no, ma'am. The Black-Stars sent after the subject have been..." He hesitated, finally drawing Wolfe's attention. Her grey eyes met his. "Only one helo returned. It seems the serum we administered to 1129 worked better than anticipated. She destroyed them."

"Hmm."

"Fortunately, it appears the effort ended her life. The pilot saw her collapse as he fled. Apparently, she burned like her victims."

Wolfe waved a hand. She couldn't care less about the fate of the Black-Stars who were unable to complete their mission. No, this news about the serum had her mind spinning.

Lectius's assistant had access to the information she wanted; it wouldn't take much to sway the girl. Keith contained the secrets of the serum. Between the two of them she had no need for Steel, Collette, or the council.

No, it appeared that doing things within the bounds of Pangaea's grip didn't lead to the results she wanted. It was time to go her own way. It was time to achieve her own goals for once, instead of constantly working toward someone else's.

"Collect what you can," Wolfe said, bending to pick through a pile of glass and plucking out her earpiece. "We must be gone before the Council's guard arrives."

Keith gave a curt nod and disappeared down the crumbling hall.

Wolfe found a few other fragments of Dolor and tucked them neatly in her bag. Her mind was preoccupied with plans. They'd need to gain access to a few of the camps. It would take time to find White-Stars with power, but it wasn't impossible. Simply another complication.

A shadow appeared at the side of the door.

"Come in," Wolfe called softly without turning.

Hesitant footsteps crunched the glass stuck to the carpet.

"I tried, Ms. Wolfe." Brenna's voice shook as it had when she'd taken her first life. When her true power had finally emerged.

Wolfe straightened and turned, a maternal smile settling on her lips. "I know, darling."

"Did I..." Brenna took a rattling breath and stumbled toward her. The woman was filthy, a coating of dust and sweat staining her clothes and skin. "Did I do well?"

Wolfe hitched the bag across her shoulder and crossed to her ward. She put a hand on Brenna's shoulder. "You did well."

Tears glistened in Brenna's eyes as relief flushed her cheeks.

"Now," Wolfe continued, "prepare yourself. We are changing venues. There is much to do."

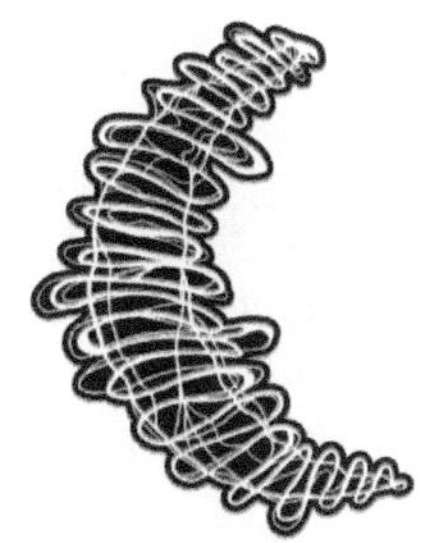

Chapter Fifty-Four

Location Unknown

Juliana woke with fog clouding her mind. Awareness came through a long tunnel; light was piercing, sending spikes of pain through her head.

When she reached full consciousness and was able to open her eyes, she was greeted by a stranger's face. A heavy woman with amber tones in her dark skin sat a few paces away from the bed.

Wariness tried to pierce through Juliana's foggy state, but she had no energy for it. No energy for anything but vague curiosity.

The room in which Juliana lay was as strange as the woman. A cavernous place, stone and rock walls, an opening at the far end, and something like a window—but completely open with no pane of glass—to her right.

Everything had a reddish tinge. The air was thick with oddly comforting scents. The fog began to clear.

Juliana's memories returned before she spoke, before she asked where she was, or what was going on. As they did, fear clenched in her gut.

She glanced at the woman, who waited patiently with her hands folded in her lap. Her clothes, a collection of multi-colored skirts and a russet vest covering an ivory shirt, were well cared for. Her hair, tied back in a thick braid, was neat.

Juliana meant to ask who she was, where they were, anything other than the question that sprang from her lips. "Did I ki—" She stopped herself as the woman raised an eyebrow. Juliana swallowed, sucked in a breath, and asked, "Is Ichi all right?"

The woman's shallow nod brought a rush of relief to Juliana. It was quickly followed by panic.

"And the others? Where is Anthony? Samaira? Daisy and the children? Did Elaine..." Her stumbling speech came to a halt as the woman raised a calloused hand.

"Your friends are fine. Both sets of twins have healed from most of their wounds. Ichi and Elaine are recovering well. Your gift brought back a part of her they thought was lost."

Juliana swallowed again; her tongue and throat were dry. "Daisy? The children?"

The woman nodded. "They are well. Safe."

"What happened?"

At this, a soft smile crossed the woman's lips. "You showed a level of power I never thought I'd see. You brought Elaine back to life, among other things."

Juliana frowned; a buzz of anxiety shot through her. But she let the woman continue without interruption.

"We were on our way down from the mountains when you healed Elaine. It was... it was a sight I'll never forget."

"What do you mean?" Juliana murmured, unease heavy in her chest.

With a deeper smile the woman rose from her chair and crossed to the bed. She held a small rectangle of glass.

The woman handed Juliana the tablet and then pressed the upper left corner. An image flashed onto the screen. A vivid forest, lush and green. The person operating the camera moved through it slowly, panning to the left and right to capture tender young saplings among the larger towering trees, violet and blue flowers, and vines of ivy.

"Why—"

"Watch," the woman interrupted Juliana's question.

Juliana focused on the screen. The forest looked similar to the one Anthony had introduced her to. Something was wrong, though. Juliana frowned, trying to place the problem. Then the image focused on the ground.

The dirt around each tree was churned up. Like the plants had erupted from the earth rather than grown over years.

Juliana shook her head as the video faded and handed the tablet back to the woman. "I don't understand."

"What you just saw is at the base of these mountains. It is where you were when you brought Elaine back to life."

The room seemed to shrink, or maybe it was Juliana's lungs. Either way, there was not enough air for her next breath. Her lips parted, disbelief mixed with terror, and she shook her head.

"That's not possible."

"A great many things are not possible, until they are." The woman's voice was soft, smooth, yet her words stirred irritation in Juliana.

The heat of it broke through her fear, and she scowled. "And what does *that* mean?"

"It means I'd have said this was not possible a week ago. But since then, many things have changed."

"A week..."

The woman gave a solemn nod. "You've been in and out of consciousness for a while, my dear."

It was 'my dear' that made Juliana ask the next question. The phrase was so like the way May had spoken; it rattled the grief weighing down her heart. "Who are you? What is this place?"

"My name is Harmony." The woman's smile grew. "And this, Juliana, is the Resistance."

To Be Continued...

Acknowledgements

Reader, thank you so much for coming with me on the second chapter of this journey. You make the work it takes to tell these stories worth it. If you enjoyed the story, please leave a review wherever you can. If you want to read more of my works head over to chlyn.com.

Where to start...

Mom. Your time and effort put into this story has made it what it is. I can't express how much I appreciate you. I love you, mama.

I must thank my husband, not just because I'm married to the man, but because of the endless sea of support he's constantly offering. Thank you, love, for the time, the reassurance, the backrubs, and the input.

Tracey, where would I be without you?? Way behind on my goals, that's where. Getting to write with you, do signings with you, and accomplish our dreams side by side is a gift beyond anything I could ask for.

The rest of the Llama Ladies!! I love y'all so much. I value our writer group more than you know.

I have to thank the Y again, because as with the last Abredea book, their phenomenal childcare helped me get this thing written. You all bring me such a peace of mind; I can't thank you enough.

Dana, we've been friends going on twenty years. I'm so grateful to have you in my life. Thank you for always reading my stories.

Beta readers: Dana, Thea, and Iris, thank you so much for your notes, your comments, and your angry messages. They made my day each and every time. You are all incredibly valued and so important to me.

The other readers and writers in this amazing community we're building, thank you.